The Calligrapher's Daughter

# The Calligrapher's Daughter

A NOVEL

## Eugenia Kim

Henry Holt and Company
New York

Henry Holt and Company, LLC
*Publishers since 1866*
175 Fifth Avenue
New York, New York 10010
www.henryholt.com

Henry Holt® and ⊞® are registered trademarks of Henry Holt and Company, LLC.

The poem "A Dream," which is quoted on pages 185 and 223, is from *Among the Flowering Reeds: Classic Korean Poems in Chinese*, translated by Kim Jong-Gil, White Pine Press (Whitepine.org), 2003.

Distributed in Canada by H. B. Fenn and Company Ltd.

Library of Congress Cataloging-in-Publication Data

Kim, Eugenia.
   The calligrapher's daughter : a novel / Eugenia Kim. — 1st ed.
      p. cm.
   ISBN-13: 978-0-8050-8912-7
   ISBN-10: 0-8050-8912-8
   1. Korea—Fiction.   I. Title.
   PS3611.I453C35 2009
   813'.6—dc22

                        2008046306

Henry Holt books are available for special promotions and premiums.
For details contact: Director, Special Markets.

First Edition 2009

Designed by Meryl Sussman Levavi
Painted illustrations by Alice Hahn Hyegyung Kim

Printed in the United States of America

10   9   8   7   6   5   4   3   2   1

*For my mother and father,*
*whose lives inspired this novel,*
*and for my family*

The Calligrapher's Daughter

PART I

# Gaeseong

# The Daughter of the Woman from Nah-jin

## SUMMER–AUTUMN 1915

I LEARNED I HAD NO NAME ON THE SAME DAY I LEARNED FEAR. UNTIL that day, I had answered to Baby, Daughter or Child, so for the first five years of my life hadn't known I ought to have a name. Nor did I know that those years had seen more than fifty thousand of my Korean countrymen arrested and hundreds more murdered. My father, frowning as he did when he spoke of the Japanese, said we were merely fodder for a gluttonous assimilation.

The servants called me *Ahsee*, Miss, and outside of the family I was politely referred to as my mother's daughter. To address an adult by name was considered unspeakably rude. Instead, one was called by one's family relational position, or profession. My father was the literati-scholar-artist, the calligrapher Han, much respected, and my mother was the scholar's wife. And because my mother wasn't native to Gaeseong, she was also properly called "the woman from Nah-jin," a wintry town on the far northeast border near Manchuria. Thus, if a church lady said, "That one, the daughter of the woman from Nah-jin," I knew I was in trouble again.

I wasn't a perfect daughter. Our estate overflowed with places to crawl, creatures to catch and mysteries to explore, and the clean outside air, whether icy, steamy or sublime, made me restive and itching with curiosity. Mother tried to discipline me, to mold my raw traits into behavior befitting *yangban*, aristocrats. An only child, I was expected to uphold a long tradition of upper-class propriety. There were many rules—all seemingly created to still my feet, busy my hands and quiet my tongue. Only much later did I understand that the sweeping change of those years demanded the stringent practice of our rituals and traditions; to venerate their meaning, yes, but also to preserve their existence simply by practicing them.

I couldn't consistently abide by the rules, though, and often found myself wandering into the forbidden rooms of my father. Too many fascinating things happened on his side of the house to wait for permission to go there! But punishment had been swift the time Myunghee, my nanny, had caught me eavesdropping outside his sitting room. She'd switched the back of my thighs with a stout branch and shut me in my room. I cried until I was exhausted from crying, and my mother came and put cool hands on my messy cheeks and cold towels on my burning legs. I now know that she'd sat in the next room listening to me cry, as she worked a hand spindle, ruining the thread with her tears. Many years later, my mother told me that the cruelty of that whipping had revealed Myunghee's true character, and she wished she had dismissed her then, given all that came to pass later.

I didn't often cry that dramatically. Even at the age of five, I worked especially hard to be stoic when Myunghee pinched my inner arms where the bruises wouldn't be easily discovered. It was as if we were in constant battle over some unnamed thing, and the only ammunition I had was to pretend that the hurts she inflicted didn't matter. Hired when I was born, Myunghee was supposed to be both nanny and companion. Her round face had skin as pale and smooth as rice flour, her eyes were languid with what was mistaken for calm, and her narrow mouth was as sharp as the words it uttered. When we were apart from the other servants or out of sight of my mother, Myunghee shooed me away, telling me to find my own amusement. So I spied on her as she meandered through our house. She studied her moon face reflected in shiny spoons, counted silver chopsticks, fondled porcelain bowls and caressed fine fabrics taken from linen chests. At first I thought she was cleaning, but my mother and I cleaned and dusted with Kira, the water girl. Perhaps she meant to launder the linens, but Kira did the laundry and was also teaching me how to wash clothes. Maybe the bowls needed polishing, but Cook was very clear about her responsibilities and would never have asked for help. As I spied on Myunghee, I wondered about her strangeness and resented that she refused to play with me.

My mother's visit had brought me great relief, but my stinging thighs sparked a long-smoldering defiance and I swore to remain alert for the chance to visit my father's side of the house again.

And so on this day, when six elders and their wives came to visit, I found my chance after the guests had settled in—the women in Mother's sitting room and the men with Father. I crept down Father's hallway, nearing the big folding screen displayed outside his door, and heard murmurings about resisting the Japanese. The folding screen's panels were wide enough for me to slide into a triangle behind an accordion bend. The dark hiding place cooled the guilty disobedience that was making me hot and sweaty, a completely unacceptable state for a proper young lady. I breathed deeply of the dust and dark to calm myself, and cradled my body, trying to squeeze it smaller. Pipe smoke filtered through the door, papers shuffled, and I wondered which voice in the men's dialogue belonged to whom. The papers must have been my father's collection of the *Daehan Maeil News* I knew he'd saved over the past several months. This sole uncensored newspaper, distributed nationwide for almost a full year, had recently been shut down. The men discussed the forced closure of the newspaper, Japan's successes in China and unceasing new ordinances that promoted and legalized racial discrimination. Naturally I understood none of this, but the men's talk was animated, tense and punctuated repeatedly with unfamiliar words.

I slipped from behind the screen, tiptoed down the hall and, once safely on our side of the house, ran to Mother's room, eager to ask what some of those words meant: *Europe, war, torture, conscript, dissident* and *bleakfuture.*

The men's wives sat around the open windows and door of my mother's sitting room, fanning themselves, patting their hair and fussing about the humidity. I spun to retreat, realizing too late that Mother would be in the kitchen supervising refreshments. A woman with painted curved eyebrows and an arrow-sharp chin called "*Yah!*" and beckoned me closer.

"You see?" Her skinny hand pecked the air like an indignantly squawking hen. The others turned to look, and I bowed, embarrassed by their attention, sure that my cheeks were as pink as my skirt. Garden dirt clung to my hem, but I managed to refrain from brushing it off and folded my hands dutifully, keeping every part of me still.

Another woman said, "She's pretty enough." I felt their eyes studying me. My hair was braided as usual into two thick plaits that hung below my shoulders. Still plump with childhood, I had gentle cheekbones, round rabbit eyes wide apart, a flat bridge above an agreeable nose, and what I hoped was an intelligent brow, topped with short hairs sprouting from a center part. Unnerved by their stares, involuntarily I grasped a braid and twisted it.

"Still, it's unusual for such a prominent scholar," said the arched-eyebrow woman, "don't you think?"

"Unusual?"

"Well, yes. Granted, she's a girl," and she turned her head theatrically to hold every eye in the room, "but isn't it odd for a man whose lifelong pursuit is art, literature and scholarship—the study of words!—that such a man would neglect naming his own daughter?"

The ladies chimed in with *yah* and *geulsae* and similar sounds of agreement, and the woman waved me away.

I left for the kitchen, frowning, and though I don't like to admit it, pouting as well. Cook and Kira were helping my mother prepare platters of fancy rice cakes, decoratively sliced plums and cups of cool water. Before reaching the door I heard my mother say, "Where is that Myunghee?" I stopped to eavesdrop, surprised at her obvious irritation. She regularly cautioned me to never speak crossly to or about the servants. Myunghee was notorious for disappearing when work called, and now had pushed my mother—who hardly ever raised her voice—into impatience. Remembering my tender thighs, I gloated a little.

"Is that you?" Mother said.

"It's me, *Umma-nim*." I remembered my quest. "They say I don't have—"

"See if you can find your nanny. No, wait. Ask the gardener if he found more plums. Hurry."

Beyond the courtyard, skinny Byungjo peered into a fruit tree with a bamboo pole in hand and a half basket of plums at his feet. He said he'd take the fruit to the kitchen, so my task was done. I roamed around to the front yard, and not seeing Myunghee or anyone else nearby, I crawled into a little natural arbor I'd found beneath the lilac bushes near the front gate.

Though I wasn't sure what not being named meant, it was obviously something bad enough to make those snake-mouthed women find fault with me and, alarmingly, with my father. Since I had heard the year of my birth, 1910, mentioned many times by the men, I wondered if my lack of name was linked to their urgent discussion. I wanted even more to know those words, but my mother was the only one I could ask. I hugged my knees and drew stick figures of the elders' wives in the dirt. I pretended they were nameless too, an easy game since I called them each Respected Aunt and knew none of their given names.

The lilac's clotted perfume suffused the enclosed arbor, and my eyes grew heavy. I nodded sleepily and it seemed the vines shivered, scattering purple petals like a shaking wet dog.

The gate slammed open to Japanese shouts, and uniformed men crashed through the yard. Sunlight refracted from their scabbards and danced on the walls, trees, shrubs, the earth. Father's manservant, Joong, came out the front door with his arms opened as if to gather the six men in a giant embrace. "Master, the police!" he cried. A policeman punched Joong in the neck. He fell, gasping. I heard my father say, "You have no right—" and then rough indecipherable commands. Blows, scuffle, an animalistic cry. Women screamed. Something splintered. My hands unknowingly covered my ears, every muscle in my body clenched with terror.

Two policemen came from the house with sabers bared. They shoved three stumbling elders, who held their hands high and heads bent. The remaining police pushed the other men as they staggered across the yard, my father trying to support a friend who groaned as his arm hung crazily from his gashed shoulder. All the men were forced through the gate, which banged twice against the lintel, and then they were gone. A stark silence filled the yard, then came a high-pitched wail like that of a professional mourner, and then my mother's cry, "Daughter! My child!"

Through the shroud of vines I saw her run down the side porch followed by another woman, their eyes hunting the corners. They seemed small, like straw-stuffed dolls on a wooden stage. Joong struggled to stand and the woman rushed to help him. He gestured that he hadn't seen me. My mother opened shutters, kneeled into crawlspaces and called for me.

I wanted to leap into her strong arms but couldn't move. "Ummanim," escaped from my throat, then I felt my tears and cried aloud. She dashed to the lilacs and tore at the curtain of vines. I fell into my mother's hard embrace, freed from the honeyed, cloying flowers, scared to be patted and squeezed all over by her searching hands. She held me tight and rocked me in the garden dirt until we both could breathe without sobbing.

DURING THE NEXT four days our minister came and went. I was too afraid to leave the women's quarters and keenly felt my mother's absence while she greeted Reverend Ahn in my father's empty rooms. Watchful for her return, I saw that she gave the minister thickly folded papers each time he left. The fourth afternoon, they stood in the open courtyard with heads bowed, and he prayed. I could only hear when his voice swelled with impassioned pleas for the men who stood tall and the country they stood up for.

My father came home that night, filthy and limping, his face a monster's mask, swollen purple and yellow, his eyes black slits. A week passed before I glimpsed his face again and saw it recognizable.

I silently noted the absence of Myunghee, whose name was never again mentioned. Her few possessions were burned, and her room adjacent to mine was washed with caustic soap by Kira and cured with sage smoke. It eventually became a closet for broken shutters and torn mats. Byungjo repaired the main gate with dense oak boards and thick iron hardware, fortified with an interior drop bar. I thought we'd be safe then forever, but I was just a child.

Months later on a still, hot evening, the house normalized with Father healed, I sat in the sewing room with my mother to practice stitching. Focusing on straight seams to make an underskirt helped to pacify my restlessness. Insects thudded against the windows and added their chorus to the crickets singing in the courtyard. A welcome breeze cooled the still room, and the lamp sputtered and smoked. My eyes smarted and I looked up, blinking, to the open window. A thin curved moon hung high in the night sky, reminding me of the woman's painted arched eyebrows and that day, and a sliver of fear as sharp as my needle made me stop sewing. "Umma-nim, will they come back?"

Mother's face showed surprise, which swiftly changed to reassurance. "No, little one, that business is finished. Don't worry, they won't come back."

I pushed my needle in and pulled the thread taut.

"Not too tight. A little smaller. Good, that's right."

"Was that war, what they did? Is that what it means to say 'Europe,' 'torture' and 'bleakfuture?'" I couldn't remember the other words.

She frowned into her embroidery and explained the words to me. She added, "These are problems men have made, which other men like your father and the minister are trying to solve, or at least help change. If you behave properly and speak only to those you know, you need not worry about such things. You're safe with your family, and you know that God watches over children especially."

"Is that why—"

"And child," said Mother. "You must never again eavesdrop on your *abbuh-nim*, your father, or on anyone for that matter. Not only is it disobedient, it's disrespectful. And further, it's not wise for your young ears to hear things you cannot understand."

I nodded, mad that I'd stupidly exposed my secret. I sewed rebellious crooked stitches, outwardly contrite, inwardly vexed. Then, horrified by the thought that the police had come because God knew I'd been bad, I gently ripped out my seam and sewed it straight. When I knotted the end,

Mother checked and praised my work with such kindness that it freed me to say, "Did they come because of—because I wasn't being good?"

She put her sewing down, sighed and touched my cheek. "No, child. God doesn't punish the innocent. Your disobedience is harmful only to yourself." She held my arms and peered into my eyes. "You are my blood and my bones. It's as if your body is my body. Whatever is harmful to you is also to me, and also to your family. You must always think first of your family, your father, and put your own thoughts and desires last. We live in hard times that we pray will get better. Hard times. You must be careful and obey your parents in all things. Agreed?"

"Yes, Umma-nim." I started on the opposite seam, feeling without consciously understanding how her words made it as easy to be as joined with her as the two skirt panels I sewed. The room shrank and cooled as the shadows outside the lamp's glowing circle darkened with the late hour. I considered what my mother had said about the hard times and her explanation of a bleak future under the Japanese emperor. "Umma-nim, is that why Abbuh-nim hasn't named me?"

"What? Nonsense! Where did you get such an idea?"

I related what the painted-eyebrow woman had said that day.

"Why do they think children can't hear?" She stabbed her needle into the taut embroidery. "Yah—" She put her sewing down and smiled. "If they only knew how well you hear, even through walls!" She sewed until her needle grew restful, as if calmed by the serene beauty of the blue iris that blossomed from its tail of thread. "Ignore them. Some women gossip because— Never mind. You were born so soon after— Well, what's most important is that you are your father's daughter. You are yangban and privileged, a blessed child to have such a noble and talented father. You should respect him always. He thinks of his country and family first, always of others first, and his is the highest example to follow. We're fortunate that he survi—that he's modern enough to afford us many freedoms, and you should only be grateful."

I bowed my head obediently. I'd heard similar versions of this speech many times, usually at bedtime when my ears were sleepy and compliant.

"You take it for granted, but it's your father who allows us to come and go as we please. It wasn't so long ago that such a thing was considered scandalous for women of our class."

Having always had this freedom, I wasn't sure why I should be grateful, but I also knew not to ask more questions.

"Besides," she said. "Who knows? One day he might consider sending you to school. At last there are rumors of public schools! We'll see, very soon I hope. With education, what name you carry won't matter at all."

I didn't understand about "public school" but was pleased to know it would counteract the negativity attributed to my namelessness by the beak-tongued woman. I also heard something new in my mother's voice, and had I known more, I might have recognized it as hunger. My mother had been educated by her mother in both Korean and Chinese writing and reading, and like most yangban women, had studied the classic *Instructions for Women* and the sixteenth-century *Four Books for Women*. She was also teaching me to read and write, but the education she spoke of reached far beyond the morality literature, guidelines for female behavior and the classics she had studied.

"You've seen Missionary Gordon at church," said Mother. "She's old enough to have been married years ago, but she has the respect of the congregation and is free to go about unescorted, thinking her own thoughts, because of her education." My mother also told me about a school in Seoul for grown-up women, Ewha College, which the Japanese had allowed to be reopened the previous year. "Things are changing so much that these schools can teach all women, not just yangban daughters, about the higher way of living and our duty not only to our family but to our country."

Not fully comprehending what she said about the scary American missionary lady or the special place for women, I clearly heard my mother's admiration and yearning, and as I sewed my tidy stitches and knotted the end of the seam, those feelings grew to be mine.

At bedtime Mother sat beside me, the dim lamp making visible only the soft curve of her cheek, one ear and the shoulder of her white blouse. She told me again that I must honor the long legacy of my father's lineage and respect the ancestors buried on the mountain behind our estate. After prayers, she related the usual bedtime story of how these ancestors had rested peacefully for 550 years, assured that the Confucian canon governed the family with such constancy that only the seasons changed for the generations who had lived and died in this house. When my mother told this old story, her silvery clarity sounded like a brook in summer, its stream singing steadily onward, with pebbles, sand and small bits of nature's debris splashing rhythmically as it rushed through the ages. From this nightly recitation delivered in beloved cadence came my earliest education about the Way.

My ancestors' fathers had passed talent and privilege on to their sons, who continued to win acclaim for scholarship and artistry, and achieved high marks in the supreme literary grade of the civil service examinations, which opened the door to royal appointments or provincial officialdom. At times, for a generation or two, unfavorable political winds brought exile to the Han men, and twice, execution along with their wives and children, but time, landowner's wealth, and wisdom borne of scholarship helped maintain stability until royal approbation was restored. Fathers arranged favorable marriages, eldest sons prayed to be spared the ultimate sin of dying without male progeny, wives prayed for sons to confirm their worthiness, and daughters, like me, learned the threefold laws of a woman's life: obey one's father, obey one's husband, obey one's sons.

We were Methodists now and didn't worship our ancestors as gods. But the commandments that decreed the one true God also said to honor thy father and mother. So it was right, Mother said, to follow the old ways and esteem our predecessors who had paved the paths upon which we walked.

According to our family's history, in the Korean year 3699, a shower of stars marked the propitious location of a burial ground on a southeast foothill of Mount Janam, which then determined the location of the house and the spread of the estate grounds. Over the years, as I lay in bed listening to my mother's vivid storytelling, I elaborated on that moment in my imagination until I could see the night sky drenched with the fire of a thousand falling stars, one bursting high above our mountain to plunge its mystical power in the heart of our land. And perhaps this was the beginning of my difficulties—that I cherished the holiness of stars before I knew to love the Jesus my mother believed in.

We visited the burial ground on our mountainside several times a year: on equinoxes, solstices and Christian holy days. From a clearing near the cemetery grove, I could see parts of our estate, and to the distant southwest, the ancient South Gate, now surrounded by roads and a few modern buildings. Climbing farther past the cemetery to a ridge that pointed north, in the winter through the naked trees I could see the valley bowl crowded with the old city, and far on the southern slope of Mount Songak, a huge rectangular field geometrically dotted with foundation scars—the enduring footprint of Manwoldae Palace, center of the former Goryeo Dynasty.

Our tile-capped mortar walls had once enclosed several sprawling structures, but now only the main house remained. Composed of three wings laid out as three sides of a square, plus an audience pavilion and utility houses, it numbered thirty rooms altogether. The main gate faced west toward China, representing Korea's welcoming gateway toward the home of Confucian doctrine. Set back fifty paces from the front gate, the central north-south wing of the house contained a broad entryway and reception area flanked by two small rooms; the one to the south was my bedroom, followed by the storeroom that had been Myunghee's room. The northern west-east arm of the house comprised the men's side, beginning with Father's sitting room in the corner, then his study, a closet, his bedroom, washroom and two other rooms. Beyond his outer courtyard to the north, a separate structure held an audience room for large gatherings. The men servants' quarters and work and storage sheds stood east of Father's outer courtyard. Mother's sitting room took the southwest corner, then to the east, her sewing room, weaving room, bedroom, our washroom, another storeroom, a pantry and the kitchen. A kitchen garden lay a few steps beyond. Our outer courtyard had the women servants' quarters to the east, and to the south, workrooms and sheds for urns, straw and a crumbling disused palanquin. There were four latrines beyond all these structures, segregated by gender and class.

Except for the kitchen, most of the spaces ranged from two to ten paces wide. The house sat on a tall foundation of brick, stone and cement, which contained flues that heated the floors in the winter and held coolness in the summer. Elevated porches surrounded both sides of the house, and an inside hallway lined the inner porch. Made of wood and mortar with paper windows and doors, the main buildings had tile roofs, and some of the sheds had thatch. Byungjo's expert care kept the grounds neatly cultivated and made the gardens flourish year-round, an aesthetic we enjoyed and systematically exclaimed over each time we visited the grave-yard.

The walkway to the cemetery had been carefully planned to unite the heart, mind and body in proper Confucian contemplation. It began in the inner courtyard and curved through an arc of fruit trees. It circled veg-etable and flower gardens, a still lotus pond surrounded by willows, and a bamboo forest so dense it had crumbled the walls it straddled. The path inclined sharply through a tall fir wood and met a brittle passageway hewn between granite boulders. Weighty slabs formed steps on the mountainous trail where the way clawed too steeply for men's feet, then the path leveled beside a trickling crystalline brook. And, at last, a shady circle of pines and lush grass welcomed us—the tired family who had climbed an hour to reach the sacred grove.

My eyes closed to Mother's lulling refrain of our written history. "The cemetery has seen many feasts and gatherings—sad, solemn and joyous— and the ink that deepens the letters on its stone markers must never be allowed to fade. But more often than not, the tranquil glade is vacant of human life, and it is then that God whispers the ancestors awake from their burial mounds to watch over the lives in the house below." I heard these words fade as I entered the land of dreams and saw the shadow shapes of my ancestors witnessing the change that clamored at our gate. And then I sat beside them, enveloped in the smoky breath of their ancient wisdom, and I saw how the wind blew their sighs of sorrow, the rain scat-tered their tears, and snow spread their icy dismay as Western thought, Japan and Bleak Future crossed our unwilling, hermit's threshold.

In September our church used a deacon's ordination as an excuse to quietly celebrate Jungyang-jeol, the banned autumn festival of art and nature. Japan's efforts to assimilate Korea included decrees against many cultural traditions, and though these rules were rarely enforced, it was best not to flaunt our celebration. Parishioners nibbled rice cakes and sipped cold barley tea in the church's backyard. I stayed near the women and played in lively patterns of color and light speckling the shade cast by maples tipped in yellow and red. My hands reached to catch sunshine poking between the leaves, and my feet traced the maze of shadows that I pretended would lead to a cave of glories and awe. The American woman missionary, Miss Gordon, walked among us, greeting one congregant and exchanging polite words with another. And then she was in front of me, bending her long limbs and stooping to meet my eyes. "What pretty and colorful clothes. And what pretty little girl."

I blushed, bowed and looked for signals on how to properly behave with the towering ghost-eyed woman, but my mother was across the lawn talking to the minister's wife.

"Now then, the name of yours is being what?" Miss Gordon said in her funny accent and mixed-up syntax. Flustered by the presence of such an important foreigner, and reminded about my namelessness, I covered my lips with my fingers to hold nervousness inside.

Mrs. Hwang, the chatty wife of the newly appointed deacon, over-heard and quickly intervened. "She's the yangban calligrapher's daughter. And her mother is the woman from Nah-jin."

"Forgive me, my Korean is such still an embarrassment," said Miss Gordon. "Did you say Najin?"

We nodded.

"Well, Najin, that's a very pretty name," and Miss Gordon rose and patted the top of my head. So it was thus, with the missionary's dry baptism and Mrs. Hwang's glibness, that my mother's wintry hometown became my name.

As time passed, I clearly understood that Father's decisions could never be questioned, especially about a subject that only I seemed to care about. Like so many unspoken questions which, unanswered, eventually submerge into the deepest recesses of memory, the state of not knowing became normal, like a forgotten scar, and over time my curiosity about having no formally given name seemed to die; or at least I forgot the intensity of wanting to know. Like the locust that sleeps for seventeen years then bores out of the earth whirring, leaving behind an empty hole, I would wonder on certain occasions in the years to come why he hadn't named me something other than Najin, which had no meaning. I came to believe the reason was somehow related to that terrifying day, the thick smell of lilacs, those new words that had introduced me to apprehension.

# A Child's Shepherd

SPRING 1917–AUTUMN 1918

AFTER WORSHIP SERVICE, HAEJUNG, THE SCHOLAR HAN'S WIFE, SAT contentedly in a front pew on the women's side, waiting while her husband greeted his contemporaries and caught up on news. Midday light filled the apse and illuminated her fine, radiant skin as if giving truth to her name, which meant "noble grace." A center part in her shining hair began at a peak that defined the heart shape of her cheeks and chin, and ended in a neat bun secured with a simple jade pin. Her nose might have been considered too distinct for classic beauty, but her features were pleasingly balanced. Her greatest physical virtue lay in her bearing. Though small-boned and short, her posture gave her length, and she held her head neither too high nor too low, executing every movement with a subtlety that conveyed elegance and strength. She bowed her head for prayer but was interrupted by Deacon Hwang's wife sliding into the pew, eyes gleaming and hands aflutter with news of the new public school, two *li* south of the church. "Even though all the teachers are Japanese," said the chubby-faced Mrs. Hwang, "we'll send our second son there."

Haejung's hidden annoyance with Mrs. Hwang's bustling presence subsided. "Really? Do they only teach Japanese subjects?"

"They say they'll teach them *Hangeul,* Korean, even if they cover Japanese grammar first. We think any learning is better than none. Our oldest was lucky to have some classical education before—well, you know."

Haejung nodded. She wouldn't have to say much; the deacon's wife enjoyed talking more than listening.

"My husband tried to teach our boy, but he can't help being too soft on his son! And now he's already twelve and although he's quite smart, he likes to get in trouble and bother his father so much that my husband complains to me to control him somehow, always laughing inside, though, I can tell. I worry about those teachers, they can be very strict, and why must they wear swords? He's such a happy and free spirit! My husband says our son needs to be disciplined before he's completely lost. He's joking of course. He'll see how it is with Number Two before we think about sending Number One to high school. Yes indeed! They say they'll have a new upper school in a year or so, and if he does well enough maybe he'll follow his father's footsteps for college in Pyeongyang. And, well, don't worry—you'll have a chance for your daughter too! I hear they'll open a girls' school very soon, perhaps even next month."

"A girls' school—"

"—isn't far behind! There's some change in the government, I don't know. That kind of talk is— You know what I mean. And think when the time comes how you and I can compare the girls' and boys' schools! Oh, there he is looking for me. I must run, but I thought you'd like to hear the news!"

"Yes, thank you—"

"Goodbye, goodbye, and I'll be sure to tell you as soon as I hear anything more!" She sidled down the pew and hurried to the door, where the deacon and her two sons were showing impatient frowns.

"Goodbye," Haejung said faintly. Then silently, "Thank you, Heavenly

Father, for this possibility," and her lips grew firm with concentration as she tried to sort through the battle of obedience versus desire being waged within her. Typically, obedience, weighted by fidelity and virtue, gained the upper hand. She walked home holding her daughter's hand, following a few steps behind her husband. Absorbed in her thoughts, she wasn't aware of her husband's stiff back showing disapproval of Najin's aimless singing and intermittent skips and hops. Haejung barely smelled the sweet green of pear blossoms in the breeze that breathed fragrance on her neck, but the scent stroked the surface of her buried passions. A gentle exhale confirmed her surrender to desire on her daughter's behalf, and then she smelled the flowers fully and smiled. She considered how best to approach her husband. Certainly he'd have very pronounced ideas about the Japanese schools, but Mrs. Hwang's chatter had awakened memories of her own girlhood longing and unbecoming jealousy when her brothers had begun their lessons.

The first tutor had come to the house in Nah-jin twenty years ago when Haejung was seven, and at this moment she felt as if she were seven still, sitting outside her brothers' classroom window, fuming with envy. Her mother had already taught her to read, and she was versed in Korean vernacular with a respectable command of Chinese writing, which was used for Korean formal writings and official documents. Even though her books were then limited to tales of virtuous women and filial daughters, she'd been amazed to discover new vistas in internal worlds, vivid histories and a living past, and her excitement only grew over the endless possibilities that lay within books. And later, it stunned her to think that the Bible itself was a book—and oh! such a book! In addition to changing her family's life, it had shown her a quiet yet rich way to live peacefully within the natural confines of womanhood. The Confucian morality tales were filled with selfless and irreproachable noble women, but the courageous and persevering biblical women provided a higher purpose and a model of living she had admired; a model that was, with faith, easily internalized. She had longed to study the history of the Bible, the history of its writing, to see how these mere words had come to mean so much to so many. Without question, her duty to her husband and family prevented such study, and besides, in her day there were only dreams of formal schooling for females. Unlike now.

Haejung couldn't avoid supplanting her desire for learning in her daughter, though she knew her husband's opposition to the Japanese schools and his staunch traditionalism made the probability slim. The intensity of her longing led to an irrational belief that the rapidly changing times might suggest to her husband the value of a daughter's education. On the walk home from church, she laid a plan to make him receptive to the idea.

For the next several days she worked with Cook to prepare especially pleasing meals, choosing costly dishes that were less likely to cause another bout of his chronic indigestion. She made up the expense by forgoing a linen purchase to sew him a needed summer suit of clothes, knowing she had the skill to refashion last summer's clothes so cleverly he wouldn't notice. Her daughter had been learning how to serve meals, but such delicate service wasn't natural to her. Broth spilled and peas rolled off the table, provoking irritable grunts and stern reprimands. Haejung decided to serve him herself.

She sent Joong, her husband's manservant, to buy the superior grade of rice wine and tobacco that he preferred yet denied himself in consideration of her. He enjoyed his evening wine and pipe too much to sacrifice it completely, but because he had accepted Jesus, he imbibed a lesser quality to acknowledge it as a Christian vice.

Haejung's father, former governor of the Hamgyeong Province and an esteemed Confucian scholar in the town of Nah-jin, had converted to Christianity when she was a child. At that time the religion was spreading rapidly, albeit cautiously, throughout Korea, partly because Christianity's emphasis on ritual, its high moral standards and doctrine of responsibility toward social justice were analogous to Confucianism, making it easy to adopt.

The governor raised his children to be devout believers, and when Haejung grew to a marriageable age, he sought a Christian husband for her. And so, the yangban scholar Han, in order to join with a family as auspicious as his own lineage, had willingly converted. He had even learned to pray with the same fervor as Reverend Ahn, and being an artist, sometimes his prayers were more poetic than the minister's. Nevertheless, Han carefully referred to all church business as "hers." Like the token of the lesser quality wine and tobacco, Haejung knew it was his way of maintaining a semblance of Confucian orthodoxy.

Luckily there were no catastrophes in the news that week, no unsettling property conscriptions, no acquaintances accosted by the police, and mercifully, Najin for once had obeyed and behaved like a young lady around her father. On Friday evening Haejung went to her husband's sitting room with sewing in hand. The slight shift in his features, as if the lamp had flared, showed his pleasure with her company, and she found his mood to be jovial. He smoked and read, and they talked off and on about the expanded train service, the increasingly reliable mail and this church member's new grandson, that one's sick wife. He said their farm had met the government's first quota, and that it might be time to increase timber production from their forestlands in Manchuria. He would write to his uncle who oversaw the vast property that had long been in his family. By nearly shutting down production more than a decade ago during the Russian occupation of Manchuria, and with bribes, his family had held on to the timber forests.

Haejung showed him a mild questioning look, and he responded, "No, we're fine, but there's the building fund at your church."

"Thank you," she said. Her quiet tone belied the warmth of feeling this news brought. She never needed to ask for anything from her generous and considerate husband. They were like-minded—except, perhaps, regarding their daughter. She prayed for the right words to raise the subject of schooling for Najin, and instantly knew God must have heard her, because her husband said, "Hansu's father is letting him go to that new school." Chang Hansu, the neighbor's son, was a few years older than Najin. The two sometimes played together in the gardens and by the pond.

Before she could say "How enterprising!" or something equally positive about the neighbor's decision, her husband said, "I can't understand how any educated man could send his son to those teachers. Think of the lies they'll learn!" His volume and intensity grew, and the more he said, the more she knew her cause was lost. "Think of the propaganda those saber-wearing quacks will spew. The pirate teachers—peasants and shopkeepers—coming here for free land and opportunities stolen from our countrymen. Think of their maps—colonist geography! Their books—

imperial revisionist history! And surely nothing classic will be taught. They mean to raise a nation of ignorant collaborator sheep. And what do we do? We turn our eyes aside, we forget our responsibility to the nation and send our sons to learn what to think—like sheep to this usurping shepherd, the emperor—pfah!"

She hid disappointment beneath her practiced composure and sewed. Disturbed by his analogy of the emperor as shepherd, she prayed to Jesus, the shepherd of men, to forgive his angry words. Keeping her body serene, she sighed internally. Of course it had been foolish to think he'd consider it. After his arrest he had even less tolerance of anything Japanese. She worried every time he went outside the gate that his bitterness and anger would be visible to the police. They had beaten and questioned him, but he hadn't been tortured—twisting things they did to limbs with ropes and boards, slow drownings—acts still shockingly practiced that she had read about in court narratives of olden days. To further submerge her disappointment, Haejung deliberately brought to mind all she could be grateful for: her smart and spirited daughter, a secure and smoothly run household, her husband's restored health, and also, that the day of his arrest had exposed the traitorous and thieving nanny who had stolen two gold brooches, a fistful of silver chopsticks and a bolt of cotton cloth before she ran off to inform on an innocuous afternoon party. God's ways were not always easy to understand. However, that day had taught them caution, and her husband's life and others' had been spared. Mr. Suh's wound healed cleanly and he claimed only minor stiffness in the shoulder—nothing that would impede his journey to the insurgent army rumored to be forming in the north.

With these thoughts, she could be respectfully deferential to her husband's reaction to the public school idea, and said goodnight calmly. When she put away her needle and threads in their proper places in her sewing room, she tucked her hopes aside—their proper place for now— and prayed, knowing with the patient and open trust of the faithful that another opportunity would arise.

THAT OPPORTUNITY CAME a year and a half later, and when she considered how it had once again surfaced in God's house, she felt renewed in her conviction about the power of prayer. While other women talked to each other in the aisles, Haejung in her front pew relished her usual semi-private moment. The musty wet-plaster smell of the church, its expansive interior space, the shiny rows of organ pipes and the biblical scenes portrayed in colorful windows filled her with peace. The Methodists had built a single-story sanctuary, complete with a squat bell tower, wide front stairs leading to arched and carved double doors, a high peaked ceiling from which hung six Gothic electric fixtures above modest pine pews, and at front a pulpit, altar and crucifix of polished oak. On this particular day, her body just beginning to round, solid with the security of three healthy months of pregnancy, she thanked Jesus for the comforting certainty that he embraced in heaven the tender souls of the four older siblings Najin never knew: one boy stillborn, another dead within hours of birth, a premature girl who died during delivery and another boy dead with fever before his hundredth day. She renewed her thanks for Najin's sturdiness, her husband's steady health and safety, and for those who risked everything to reclaim their country.

A glorious autumn day, she had allowed Najin to play outside with the few girls who attended the brief Sunday-school session preceding the service, reminding her not to run, shout, play in the dirt or get in anyone's way. Haejung believed that spending time with other children could help make her daughter less self-centered and willful. This problem had frequently been addressed in her after-worship time, and she now gave thanks to God, who had answered her with this most unexpected blessing of another child. She would soon believe that he had provided more than one answer, for Missionary Gordon approached from the vestry, an eager smile on her strangely pink face.

Miss Gordon, tall, with jarring blue eyes magnified in round gold-framed glasses, had pillowy cheeks, a sharp nose that ended in a small flat plateau, a halo of busy pale reddish brown curls which refused to be contained in a knotted hair bun, and freckles. Until Haejung had seen more Westerners with freckles, she thought the missionary suffered an unfortunate skin ailment. She stood and bowed and Miss Gordon bowed in return. The missionary's bows had become more natural since the last time she'd seen her.

"How do you do?" Miss Gordon indicated they should sit. "I've been wanting to talk to you and I'm sorry it's taken this long."

Haejung noticed that the missionary's Korean had improved too. "Yes, how do you do? The pleasure of seeing you has been missed for some time." Her gracious formality hid her curiosity, having never had a conversation of any length with Miss Gordon.

"I think the men are having an impromptu meeting. If I'm not interrupting and you have a moment..."

"Not at all. I'm at your service."

"You've seen the new building in the back?"

"The new mission offices? Or is it— Pardon me for asking, someone mentioned it might be living quarters for new missionaries."

Miss Gordon removed her gloves. "It was meant to be both, but we've decided to make it a school. You've heard about the new policies?"

Haejung's stomach leaped. She deliberately relaxed her shoulders and shook her head, no.

With an urgency that Haejung began to see was the missionary's characteristic manner, Miss Gordon explained how they'd decided to take advantage of education reforms instituted by the new, more liberal Governor-General Hasegawa, and were transforming the finished building into a private school—a Christian school just for girls! Unlike his more militant predecessor, Hasegawa didn't believe that churches were hotbeds of subversion and that all Christians were seditionists. He advocated a milder colonial policy, and nationals were now permitted to teach elementary grades one through four for children ages eight through eleven.

While she talked, Miss Gordon crossed and uncrossed her legs, rested her arm over the back of the pew and fussed with the gloves in her lap. She described the curriculum and the schedule of a typical school day. Hearing all this and influenced by the missionary's fidgeting, Haejung thought that her own ears might be wiggling, or that she might lean forward so much as to fall off the seat. She straightened her back and remained outwardly composed.

"—and a young woman who was in one of the first graduating classes at Ewha College has just been hired. She'll teach the first grade. That's where I've been, in Seoul, interviewing and helping our new teacher and her family move to Gaeseong. Her surname is Yee," Miss Gordon hurried on. "She's lovely, from a yangban family and a devout Christian. I'm told she was a wonderful student, highly ranked. And she plays piano beautifully." The missionary's eyeglasses twinkled in the church's electric lights, and rainbow reflections from the windows flashed across the lenses. "May I ask your daughter's age?"

That morning, anticipating her daughter's birthday, Haejung had calculated the ninth lunar month and seventeenth day to her Western calendar, an annual Christmas gift from the church that she'd hung in her sitting room. "Her birthday's next week. She's nine."

"That'd be second—well, that should work. The first class is only half full and the second doesn't have a teacher yet. We've combined the classes for the time being. I hope you won't think it's beneath her to attend the first grade even though she should be in second. In any case, the few times I've led Sunday school have clearly shown me how bright she is, and her inquisitive nature is obvious. I'm sure she'd take to it regardless."

Somewhat puzzled by this speech, Haejung thought Miss Gordon's preoccupation with age peculiar. What did a child's age matter as long as she could learn? Then she remembered that Americans didn't count a child's gestational year, and said worriedly, "I'm sorry for the confusion, but in Western years she'll be eight. Might that be too young?"

"Certainly not! It's precisely the age we're allowed to begin enrollment."

Haejung bowed to acknowledge this, but mostly to hide the renewed hope she felt must surely be emanating from her eyes.

Miss Gordon glanced toward the doorway where the scholar Han was saying goodbye to Reverend Ahn and Harlan Gordon, the mission director and her brother. "Will you think about it?" she said.

Haejung corrected her gently. "Thank you very much. It's kind of you to consider my worthless daughter. I'll mention it to her father and he'll decide."

"Your daughter is very charming. Such terrific energy she brings to our little Sunday school," said the missionary. "Good! School begins a week from Monday. Let us know in advance if possible. I do hope she'll join us." Miss Gordon shifted her gloves to free her right hand, and moved to shake Haejung's hand, an embarrassing thing the missionary had done before, but she then seemed to remember her manners and bowed nicely instead.

That evening, without fanfare, Haejung brought her husband his wine and lit his pipe. No need for fancy cooking and expensive tobacco. At that moment she definitively had an advantage. Her husband settled on his cushion with an open newspaper—a moderate paper that Governor-General Hasegawa had allowed to be reinstated—and smoke floated around his shoulders. His pointed features, sternly framed by a black goatee, squared jaw and a severe headband, nevertheless held a mild expression, and his stiff, angular posture was eased by fluid drapes of flowing clothes. He wore his hair in a topknot, a revered symbol of Korean manhood that he refused to cut, though the Japanese had technically outlawed such cultural distinctions.

Haejung had pointedly brought a tiny dark-blue cap to embroider. Made of fine sheer silk, such caps were part of a baby boy's One Hundredth Day ceremonial garb. She kept her voice gentle and her eyes down, for without such softening traits, Haejung's mother had often said, a woman's presence would be like a thorn and not a flower. She spoke slowly with long silences between every sentence. "*Yuhbo*, husband, Missionary Gordon approached me today. They've built a Christian girls' school behind the church. Korean teachers only. Your daughter has been given the courtesy of an invitation to attend. The teacher is one of the first graduates of Ewha Women's College. What an honor for your daughter!"

He turned a page and continued to read his paper.

She patiently embroidered a geometric pattern with gold thread around the cap's edge. "She mentioned that the girls' class is only half full. They need more students."

Pause, puffs of pipe, another page turned, sips of wine. "Nothing comes from nothing," he growled, quoting a proverb.

She waited, sewed and said, "Yuhbo, so much changes every day. Think of what we've seen in our short lives. They say from Pyeongyang to Busan all kinds of children attend the missionary schools, many from yangban families. The new teacher is yangban herself." She let this fact sit for a moment and added, "Yee family, originally from Seoul," so he would know the teacher was of noble lineage and not the offspring of a commoner claiming higher status, which was often the case after Japanese-influenced reform laws had equalized the classes.

Han puffed the dying ember in his pipe, laid it aside and turned the last page of the newspaper. Haejung could sense his irritation at her persistence, though politeness dictated refrain in his showing it. She pressed on. "They teach the requirements—Japanese grammar, geography and arithmetic—but also Chinese and some English. And the missionary says they'll teach our language, our history and the Bible!"

He continued to read, and she noticed his lips tightly pressed. She let a long silence fill the room until she saw his chin and then his neck relax. As if musing to herself, she said, "Who can say if her schooling will be valuable? At least it can't be harmful." The embroidered edging finished, she gently flipped the cap right side out, pressed it flat on the floor between them and brought the lamp near, making the light catch on the stepped geometric pattern she had embroidered. She fussed with the cap, pressing its corners, and said boldly, "All that I learned from my brothers has been useful to me, wouldn't you agree?"

He folded his paper and took up his tobacco box. She approached to fill and light his pipe and poured more wine, positioning her two hands attractively and letting the liquid slap into his cup appetizingly. He raised his eyes to her, showing a mixed expression of annoyance and acquiescence, and gave an almost-snort. "It won't do if she's unprepared for marriage."

Haejung, shouting triumphantly inside, bowed her head slightly and folded one leg gracefully over the other, waiting until she knew her tone would be calm. "She'll be as prepared as I was, if not more so."

He snorted fully but couldn't quite hide the smile that sweetened the corners of his mouth. "If it makes her coarse ways any rougher, it must cease," he said. Pause. "I'll speak to the magistrate."

His eyes met hers when she gathered her sewing things and rose. She was pleased, so pleased, and saw that this pleased him. He stroked his beard, and she knew he did so to mask his emotion. "How many days?" he asked.

"One hundred and twelve."

"You're well?"

He was, of course, remembering the four before their robust daughter had come—this month eight years ago—wailing and flailing into a world they'd just learned was no longer theirs and would likely never again be the same. She thought this had to be the reason he hadn't named his daughter, even after a hundred days, and now, almost a hundred months. Perhaps with so much loss behind and ahead—and the disappointment he'd tried to hide when he saw she'd borne a girl—he could find no meaningful name to mark her place on this earth. Still, Haejung couldn't fully understand his unwillingness to name their daughter and felt in every part of her body that it would be different this time. "Yes, praise God, very well."

"Amen. Goodnight," he said.

"Goodnight. Thank you."

She passed the folding screen and put her hand behind its edge to beckon the child who most certainly hid there. Najin appeared, shamefaced but with eyes that matched her mother's in excitement. Najin scampered behind until Haejung gestured "hush." When they reached the kitchen they clasped hands, smiling broadly at each other.

"Lucky blessed child! Thank God for your generous father!" The brilliance of realized hope filled Haejung's eyes with laughing tears. Though it wasn't their family's custom to give birthday presents, she said, "Your father has given you the best birthday gift a child could ever have." Najin hopped and spun, asking if she'd have books and paper and pencils and new clothes. And Cook, beaming at the stove, banged a wooden paddle on an iron pot in congratulations.

A few days later, Haejung's husband asked her to join him after supper. This request was his way of obliging her, and it gave her contentment. The evening's early coolness hushed summer's singing night insects, leaving only occasional owls' hoots and frogs' croaks to break the companionable silence in his sitting room. She listened to the night and wistfully recalled the hourly clang of the ancient iron bell in the South Gate, whose clarion toll had for centuries pealed across the valley. She thought the Japanese had proscribed this useful tradition in order to sell more Seikosha timepieces, and after the family was late for church twice, she had indeed purchased a small windup clock. A high wind swept through the pines and bamboo, sounding like waves on a distant shore, and a draft refreshed the room and made the lamp flicker.

"Yuhbo," said her husband. "I saw Magistrate Watanabe," meaning he had officially registered Najin for private school.

Her eyes, raised from her sewing, showed her thanks.

He said irritably, "Yah, much more than I expected—almost as much as the tuition! That bastard will undoubtedly keep it himself."

She questioned him with a look.

"He said private school is for the privileged, that obviously this family had enough privilege to take advantage of it, and with my background it would be a simple matter to revoke this privilege and any such privileges in the future. Greedy son of a pig."

Fearing that their daughter's registration might have exposed her husband to the Thought Police, she asked, "Is this trouble?"

"Perhaps not. I believe this may ultimately benefit us. Now I know he's willing to be paid—a weakness that may prove useful one day."

She nodded and, remembering the nanny, worried that it could also prove to be their downfall. She would trust God. This thought reassured her, and with that reassurance she felt his living presence within her. "Amen," she said aloud.

He raised an eyebrow. "Speaking of that, I also visited the mission director." He harrumphed and drank his wine. "He said to me, 'Praise the Lord for your progressive example, Brother Han, and may others see the same light!' Yah, all that church talk and what else could I say but 'Amen!'"

Her eyes crinkled, and as she stood and bowed goodnight, she said with a heavy American accent, "Amen!" leaving him with an uncharacteristic mirthful grin.

Over the next few days she made two new *hanbok*—dark skirts and white blouses with fresh paper collars—and her daughter hemmed and embroidered a large muslin square to carry lunches and homework to and from school. Haejung was gratified when Najin asked to serve the evening pipe and wine the night before school began, and even more pleased when her daughter took the initiative to comb her hair anew, scrub her face and hands, and after seeing how much she'd splashed herself, change into her best blouse, tying the bow with perfection.

In her husband's sitting room, Haejung looked on approvingly as her daughter used both hands with closed fingers to carefully offer his cup. Holding one hand within the other, Najin decorously lit a strand of straw at the flame of the oil lamp to fire his pipe. She stood before her father, hands at her sides, her head bent and turned slightly, and with her back straight, folded her legs gracefully to the floor, bowing formally and saying thanks in the flowery language of the high court that he loved. Haejung saw a glimmer of satisfaction on his sharp but even features.

Long after Najin fell asleep, the servants retired in their quarters and the house secured for nighttime, Haejung prepared for bed. As she unraveled and combed her hair, her jade hairpin slipped from her fingers and bounced on the lacquer table, leaving two small scratches just so—the Chinese character for human. She smiled, reminded of evenings sewing with Najin, and how she'd scratched a needle on stiff fabric to teach her daughter Chinese characters. She snuffed the lamp, slid between her quilts and breathed deeply, happily, for behind her closed eyes she envisioned the blackboard of her daughter's new classroom written with the joyous code of learning.

# Autumn Walk

ALTHOUGH I KNEW THE ROUTE, MOTHER INSISTED ON ACCOMPANYING me to school the first day. I was, after all, the first girl from either side of the family to attend a real school. Cook had made breakfast special by drizzling honey on my rice porridge, and Kira and Byungjo had waved goodbye from the gate. At the bottom of our hill, we walked on the rutted main street beside the whitewashed wall that circled the wealthy neighborhood where Japanese officials and businessmen now lived with their families. The early fall morning filled my lungs with an invigorating crispness that called me to run or skip in my new rubber shoes, but Mother was instructing me on proper school behavior. I dutifully harnessed my footsteps to match hers. A new linen blouse chafed my elbows, and the heavy silk of my dark blue skirt swung deliciously against my shins, like the church bell ringing its Sunday welcome.

"You mustn't speak unless your teacher asks you something. Then lift your chin and speak clearly, but not loudly, and truthfully. If you don't know the answer, you should say so. There's no shame in not having the answer. Besides, with the lessons you've had at home, you'll know more than most girls your age. Remember to give your teacher the utmost respect. Call her *Sunsaeng-nim.*"

"Yes, Umma-nim." I repeated the instructions in my head in cheerful singsong.

"Treat your classmates courteously, especially if they know less than you, and most especially if they are peasant children. Some students' families won't eat for days to pay the tuition. They may be poor and have strange habits or mean ways, but you are yangban and more is expected of you. Never forget that you'll be treated as well as you treat others."

"How many students are there?" I trailed my hand along the iron bars that fenced the back lot of the Japanese police station, my fingers bouncing happily across the cold metal.

"Najin-ah! Look how dirty you're getting! Keep your hands closed."

I did so, smiling. Even her scolding couldn't dampen my excitement.

"The school is small, four grades, but they aren't all full. Since you're just of age, you might be among the youngest. Maybe you'll find an older girl who can be an *unnee,* an elder sister to you. You're a very lucky girl. I dreamed of going to school, but it wasn't considered proper."

"But then how did your brothers teach you?"

She gave me a look and recited under her breath, "What one says isn't only heard by mice in the night, but by birds in the day." In the silence that followed, I tried to walk modestly, ladylike, invisible. "I didn't say anything last week about finding you hiding outside of Father's room, and I don't think I need to speak of it again."

I nodded apologetically and resolved to stop eavesdropping. I wouldn't have time! Mother's lips were set, but her eyes—wide apart and curved upward at the outer edges as if always smiling—were soft.

"Najin-ah, be cautious with the things you overhear. The days are unpredictable— Well, you must promise to always ask me about anything you don't understand. It's wrong to be secretive, and there's no need to worry about things that confuse you or seem strange. Asking questions is sometimes the best way to learn. And be careful with what you say to others, as these are difficult times. Will you remember this?"

I promised, and tried to think humble so I would appear humble. After a contrite while, I cautiously asked, "Umma-nim, can you please tell me how you were educated?"

I sensed her smiling. "In those days, a girl of our class never set foot outside her family's gate until her wedding day, and then she'd go by palanquin to her husband's family's house."

"That's awful!"

"Daughter, you must learn to control your emotions. Such expressiveness isn't becoming for a young lady." My mother sighed. "Decorum, quietude, acceptance. Keep these things in your mind always."

"Yes, Umma-nim." Unfairness rumbled in my belly—I couldn't help it!—but I squelched it by silently chanting the triple mantra of her admonition.

"And it wasn't awful at all. My mother taught me all there was to know to become a woman, and anything I needed, and much that I merely wanted, was brought to me. Your grandfather's house was the largest in the province, and I had the entire enclosure to roam. You've heard Cook talk about how our gardens were famous for beauty and variety. I kept quite busy, especially as I grew older and took care of my brothers."

We reached a field stippled with hilly brush between our neighborhood and downtown. Habitually, on this route to and from church, neither of us spoke when we passed the checkpoint, where two silhouettes of policemen were now framed in the guardhouse's cloudy window. Once the checkpoint was well behind us, Mother continued. "Still, like you, I was curious about the world outside, so your grandfather gave my brothers permission to pass their lessons on to me, as long as it didn't interfere with their examinations or disrupt the household. When they told me what they'd learned, I drank from their lessons like a thirsty fish! Eventually, since your grandfather was the kindest of men, I was allowed to sit outside their studio when the tutors came." Her voice grew lighter, as if lifted by an inner breeze. "This is also how we learned about Jesus. A teacher brought news of foreigners and gave your grandfather a Bible. Then, after we became Christians, everything changed."

"Is that when you were allowed to go out?" I'd heard this part of the story before.

"Not only did I go out, but your grandmother also, the two of us, like commoners! We walked to church, you see, and actually sat in the same building as the men, since that's how the foreigners did things. People were shocked at first, but your grandfather was the governor and highly regarded, and soon, others did the same."

Whenever she talked about her family, her changed voice made me want to take her hand.

"Now that I think about it, I was older than you are now, but that first walk to church must have been like today is for you, except we veiled our faces with our coats. Thankfully it wasn't a hot summer day. In fact," she said, looking skyward at the treetops' changing colors, "it might have been this time of year. I can't remember. What I do remember is keeping an eye out for my mother's feet in front of me, and the dust from the road on our skirts and coats when we came home."

"Were you afraid?"

"Don't be afraid of new things, Najin-ah."

"I'm not!" I said before remembering my mantra. "Excuse me. I'm excited, Umma-nim, not afraid. It must be strange to walk with your coat over your head."

"That was for modesty. Something you should try to have a bit more of."

I knew to bow my head and close my lips. Straightening my shoulders, I focused on my mother's footsteps, imagining a veil of modesty covering me from head to toe.

We neared the market where the cool air held odors of decomposing scraps and trash. Anticipation had heightened my senses, making colors and smells more intense, shapes sharper, details bright and bold. A few star maple leaves, deeply red and yellow, scuttled along the ruts eroded in the dirt roadside. Passing narrow alleyways, I glimpsed heaps of rubbish, a dog rooting, a cluster of empty chicken cages, a man spitting tobacco between brown-stained teeth. The sounds of the market distracted me—cries of bartering, a rooster crowing, an underwhir of chatter and clamor.

"I was excited, like you," said Mother. "And yes, with excitement there's often fear. But I had little to fear since my brothers watched me as closely

as a tiger her cubs. Also, I knew by then that I would be married soon."
She smiled, her eyes crescents. "So I had many other fears to consider for
the future."

In the market square she pointed out a bakery and a small restaurant. "If
you do well with your lessons, I'll give you a few *jeon*. The owners of those
two shops are church members. You could buy treats there occasionally."

My mouth watered at the prospect of taffy, or kelp chips dusted with
sugar. We wove through the crowded market. Vendors shouted out the
merits of their wares, or "Best price! Best price!" while customers haggled.
Farmers and peddlers spread their goods on a swept parcel of ground:
piles of straw sandals and rubber shoes in muted hues, open bags of rice
and grains, stacked heads of cabbage, strings of pepper and ropes of garlic, green-flowering bunches of beets, radishes and carrots. One of my
favorite chores was to accompany my mother to the fish market and pro-
duce sellers to help carry tofu, cucumbers, salted cod, and to other shops
for cotton to spin, needles, medicinal herbs, dishes and pots.

"Umma-nim, who will help make all that gimchi?" I was stricken with
the realization that for the first time in my life I'd be apart from her nearly
all day, and it was gimchi-making season.

"Don't worry. After your studies, you can help me as always, especially
with your sewing. You're doing well with embroidery and you mustn't get
behind. Perhaps you'll learn new stitches at school." She slowed to inspect
a display of fresh-picked greens of many varieties, and I smelled apples
before I saw the bent-over peddler trudge past, his A-frame basket loaded
with the crisp fruit. When my mother sliced apples, they looked like
lotuses in bloom, each piece cupped in a starburst of peel, and even
though Cook said my skill in wielding the bamboo parer was impressive
for my age, my apple petals were still uneven.

"Like peeling apples into flowers," I said. "I have lots to practice."

"That way of thinking will help you become a good wife and mother
someday."

I warmed with this praise.

"A turtle can't move if he doesn't stick his neck out," quoted Mother.
We walked through the west end of the market, past a shimmering curve
of violet-hued silk in a dry-goods stall hung between bolts of golden brocades. A breeze from the public garden ballooned our skirts and swirled

dirt around our ankles. I pressed my hands on the indigo silk of my skirt. "Be patient," said Mother, continuing her lesson, "not prideful, and think of others first. Najin-ah, remember that your weaknesses are willfulness and self-centeredness."

I couldn't avoid the petulant swell to my lips.

"It's simply a fact. Understanding your weaknesses will improve your character. It's nothing to be ashamed of—merely something that needs improvement. You must always put others before yourself. Remember: think ahead about others first." She led me to a bench beside an enormous bush of second-blooming yellow roses. "Let's rest a moment."

Anxious that we'd stopped walking, I kicked my free-hanging legs rhythmically until she touched my knees. The rising sun deepened the morning's long shadows and dew evaporated from the roses, emitting sweet perfume. My mother breathed in, her eyes closed, a faint smile spreading peace through her features. "Najin-ah, you're going to be a *nuna.*"

A boy would call his elder sister Nuna. I smiled wide at this unexpected news, exposing many teeth, then quickly covered my mouth and said through my fingers, "You're having a baby? A boy!"

"Yes, in the second month next year. Our prayers for a son have been answered. Born in the year of the sheep in the earth phase—a good match for you. Soon you'll see my stomach growing and you'll be able to feel him kick, like you kicked before you were born."

A perfectly curled rose petal, vivid yellow in the sun, floated onto the wooden bench within inches of my wrist. Although bursting with delight and questions—what would Father name him, and how did Mother know it was a boy?—I heeded my manners and kept quiet.

"I'm healthy and strong—a good omen. I thank God for this baby, and that on this day, your birthday, you begin your education." We all celebrated our birthdays on *Sollal,* the first of each year, so her acknowledgment of today, the actual day, felt like a special blessing. She bowed her head, and the bun at the back of her neck reflected blue highlights in the sun. "We receive the bounty of your blessings, merciful Father, and are grateful. Amen."

I touched the rose petal lightly and it rocked like a miniature cradle. My feet began kicking again, flashes of white toes back and forth.

She stood. "Let's go, it's almost time."

To show something of my happiness, I held her hand tightly all the way through the neighborhoods and up the hill.

We approached the school, a long building of orange-brown brick with evenly spaced metal-framed glass windows. "I won't go farther," said Mother. "See if you can walk at least part of the way home with someone. Be well-mannered and respect your teacher."

I turned, panic rising, my braids lashing my shoulders.

She stooped to look calmly into my eyes. "Perhaps I'll send someone to get you later." Her fingers lingered on my shoulder. "The neighbor's boy, Hansu. He won't mind."

I gripped my lunch tied in the square of cloth I'd sewn and decorated with my own ivy pattern. "Thank you, Umma-nim, but I will walk home myself." I turned to enter the school's varnished double doors and felt the departure of warmth when my mother's hand dropped from my shoulder.

# Secret Flags

## WINTER, EARLY 1919

I WOKE TO AN UNFAMILIAR RASP—THE FRONT DOOR SLIDING OPEN and shut. Since my room was next to the vestibule, I sleepily wondered why I'd never really heard the door before. How easily something so common could go unnoticed! In other seasons, humming insects, nocturnal creatures crying, breezes swishing through trees, or leaves scratching the courtyard masked the sound of the door. But heavy new snow had wrapped the night in deep stillness. I heard my father giving instructions to someone outside and opened my eyes.

Easing out of bed, I saw that no lamp burned in my mother's room down the hall, meaning it was unusually late. Moonrise marked the beginning of a woman's private time, and long after I went to bed, she stayed up to sew, read, or write letters. I cracked my shutter open. Two silhouettes, outlined crisply against the snow like shadow puppets, headed toward the gate. I dimly heard a rattle of iron and wood when the bar was lifted and the latch released, then the sounds in reverse when Byungjo closed the gate. He went into the cold gatehouse where he'd await Father's return. My face chilled, I crept into my quilts, sleepless with curiosity. What seemed like hours later, I woke to sounds of my father's snow-crunching footsteps, then his shoes shuffling off in the entryway as he quietly, and surprisingly, hummed the Doxology.

Once alerted, I heard my father over the next several weeks go out in darkness with increasing frequency. It was especially peculiar because in winter, except for church, he rarely left the estate. And since my mother hadn't attended church lately—too noticeably pregnant to be seen in public—he hardly went out at all. I longed for answers, but I'd learned well how to suppress my inquisitiveness, particularly on matters related to him. With my father, I was like that raspy sliding door—always around but noticed only when something was awry, such as when I dropped a cup, spoke before thinking or skipped on the flagstones.

LATER THAT WINTER in February, the moon a strand of blue in a cold starlit sky, I sprawled on the bedroom floor with my favorite activity: filling thick pads of cheap paper with vocabulary in Japanese, Korean and Chinese, and an occasional English word in crooked letters. The courtyard rang with dripping thaw, loudly punctuated by sheets of ice crashing from rooftops onto the flagstones—a noisy harbinger of an early spring. My mother stopped at my door and I immediately sat in a more ladylike position, but she only said to come quietly to help with something.

In her sitting room, ghostly twin trails rose from two lamps and disappeared in the smoke-stained ceiling beams. Fabric and blankets tumbled from a linen chest, its woven grass lining lifted sideways to expose a false bottom. In this hiding place, bright scraps of cloth in familiar shapes lay in neat piles. I picked up red and blue half circles with yin and yang curves and fitted them together. "*Taegeukgi*, the flag."

"So you haven't forgotten. And you know it's forbidden. A secret, agreed? You hem. We have fifteen more to finish in less than a week."

"So many!" I whispered. "What for?" Sitting on the floor, I inspected her invisible stitches on the corner trigrams—heaven, earth, fire and water—and bent to her instructions to join the completed flag rectangles back-to-back.

"You're old enough to know about certain things," she said. "You're not to speak of it at school or even at home, to anyone. It's impossible to tell who's friendly to whom." She clipped a thread between her teeth and deftly tucked the edge of a cut form onto the background.

I thought of the Japanese merchants I saw at the market on my way to school, and the shouting men performing calisthenics every morning in the police station yard, but I'd rarely said more than a few words to a Japanese person and couldn't imagine anyone I knew being friends with the people my father called "heathens."

"What about my teacher?" I asked.

"Not even her, though I'm certain she's a patriot. We prevent trouble by keeping this secret in this room." She sighed. "Why must you always ask questions? Obedience."

"Yes, Umma-nim." I disliked the fussy exactness of sewing, but the warm floor and my mother's humming made the task almost pleasant. I assumed she withheld an explanation about the flags because of my questioning and tried to be patient, but my curiosity about their number and secrecy only grew. I worked to match the precision and speed of my mother's handiwork with little success. "So slow! How can we make that many? Abbuh-nim's right. I'm too clumsy"—one of my father's standard criticisms.

"Your work is beautiful when you attend to it. Don't worry, I've already made forty. It's been months."

"I've never seen you—"

"When you're asleep."

"Oh." A surging inquisitiveness, which I often felt at school, made me both circumspect and eager. What *did* she do in those hours that burned her oil lamp dry? What else didn't I know about the world of my mother? I knew I'd get in trouble, but out it came like water from a broken gourd. "Where does Abbuh-nim go at night?"

"It's not for you to question your elders!"

Questions burst through the limp walls of my propriety. "Why is everyone whispering so much? Why do we need so many flags? I hear him go out, but where?"

"Hush! Even the stones in the road can hear you. A child of mine would never talk back to her mother!"

I poked at my flag through frustrated tears. In the long quiet that followed, I managed to placate the spirits of curiosity by concentrating on evenly spaced, barely visible stitches.

Mother said, "Here's another one. You're working quickly." Our eyes met briefly, mine grateful and apologetic, hers forgiving and kind. "He goes to church at night."

A dozen more questions struggled to break through the newly installed guard at my voicebox, and one slipped through. "Is the minister a patriot-friend?"

Mother abruptly shouted for Kira, then louder for Joong, and I jumped. When no one answered, she gestured me closer. Lifting her sewing close to her face, like a cowl, she spoke very softly. "If I explain, perhaps you'll understand the danger and respect it properly. You're smart enough, and your curiosity and recklessness could jeopardize us all. I tell you this because I have faith you'll understand how everyone's safety depends on your ability to keep it secret."

Relieved I wouldn't be punished and subdued by her solemnity, I faced her directly and sat tall. "Thank you, Umma-nim."

"Did they tell you at school about His Imperial Majesty Gojong *Gwangmuje*?"

. I rarely heard my mother use high court language, and it took a moment to understand whom she meant. Then I nodded, for Teacher Yee had told us last week that Emperor Gojong had died in the middle of January. Dethroned and prohibited from returning to the main palace, he still commanded respect because, though he ultimately failed, at least he had tried to fight Japan's political assault, and his consort, the beautiful and outspoken Queen Min, had been murdered long ago. After her murder, he and his ministers had changed his status from king to emperor in a futile attempt to match the level of his sovereignty with that of Japan, but they lost the kingdom anyway. Japanese officials had entered the palace with troops, and Emperor Gojong was forced to abdicate to his second son, Sunjong, the only surviving offspring of the martyred queen. From the blackboard, I'd copied the new word *abdicate,* along with others Teacher Yee explained but didn't write on the board: *sovereignty, protectorate, coerce, annexation, propaganda.* Teacher Yee said that the Japanese had responded to public pressure by designating March 4 as the national day of mourning for Emperor Gojong.

Then she told us the noble and thrilling story she'd heard: that the emperor had committed suicide to protest the forced marriage of his son to Japanese royalty, Princess Masako of Nashimoto, which was Japan's way of saying we were the same country, the same peoples, when obviously it was their attempt to dilute the sovereignty—that new word—of the Korean royal line. Much later, I heard the other more plausible story of Emperor Gojong's death. Japan wanted him to sign a document asserting his satisfaction with Japan's union with Korea, which Japanese envoys would present at the Paris Peace Conference. But Emperor Gojong decided to send his own secret emissary to Paris to protest Japan's annexation, and when the emissary was discovered and killed, the emperor was also killed. Even if I had known this, for a young girl with a colorful imagination, Teacher Yee's story of honorable, romantic sacrifice was far more captivating.

To keep this dramatic story swirling in my head and not out of my mouth, I tucked a hem edge with a needle, pressed it tightly between my fingers and said distractedly, "Sunsaeng-nim said there'd be a big parade in Keizo for his national day of mourning."

"In Seoul," said Mother, to remind me that Japanese language was not allowed at home.

I wanted to ask not only if the emperor had committed honor suicide, but also if his son, the new emperor, was really a simpleton. Girls at school said he was an idiot, but I knew that term was mean. Mother had a relative still at court, a cousin who had married the last prime minister loyal to Emperor Gojong. When this prime minister refused to affix his seal to the Protectorate Treaty of 1905—which proclaimed Japan to be the protector of Korea and thus opened wide the gates for official Japanese takeover—he was removed bodily from the palace. Not long afterward, he and their only son, a four-year-old child, were killed. His widow, whom I called *Imo,* Maternal Aunt, still attended royal functions and would certainly know something about the young emperor. Because of Mother's warnings about my responsibility as a child of yangban, I'd known not to talk about Imo to my schoolmates. And I followed the same inner counsel and said nothing now.

Mother spoke as softly as the susurrus of thread being pulled through fabric. "Yes, there's a big funeral planned, and they're freely giving travel papers to anyone going to Seoul. What I'm going to tell you must remain between your ears." She looked at me meaningfully and I nodded. "Your father is helping to coordinate a nationwide protest. Instead of a parade of mourning, there'll be an enormous demonstration for independence. Every patriot knows about it. A wondrous event! At the same hour in every city and village across the country, a declaration of independence will be read." Her voice held an intensity, an excitement I had never heard before. "All the churches are involved. Ministers lead the movement in towns and villages throughout Korea. Think of what it means!"

I didn't really grasp what it meant, but her passion and the fact of everybody doing the same thing in a single moment intrigued me. Remembering my teacher's advice to go to the root of a problem to solve it, I said, "I think I understand, but how did it happen?"

"What a good question," she said. At that proud moment, I doubly appreciated my wise teacher and generous mother. "Our leaders were inspired by a speech given by America's President Wilson, called Fourteen Points. Your father says that President Wilson wants to help small nations who are dominated by stronger nations. And also, America supports self-determination, our right as a people to choose to be an independent and free country."

I kept to my sewing, questions bubbling in my throat. I didn't clearly understand what Mother meant by self-determination, but was pleased that she spoke to me almost as if I were grown. Was the American president stronger than the Taisho Emperor? How would he help?

Mother smoothed a finished flag in her lap. "Think of it! If all the ministers are involved, many countrymen will participate. We have much to be grateful for in our patriot leaders. Some are in Europe right now trying to make other nations see how unjust the treaties were. Did you also learn about this?"

I tried to merge Teacher Yee's lessons with this information. I recalled that my mother had once taught me about a European trip taken by Emperor Gojong's men, who, having failed in their mission to garner support for Korea, had all committed suicide. She'd spelled the strange-sounding place, *The Hague,* and I remembered how she quickly scratched the letterforms with a needle on a starched sleeve, and as quickly rubbed them away. But that Hague business had occurred long before I was born. I frowned.

"I suppose not." She sighed.

"Do you mean the foreign treaties that gave Korea to the Japanese without asking the emperor?" At least I could prove that I'd indeed paid attention to the lessons spoken over needlework in the evening hours with my mother.

"Yes," she said with a rewarding smile. "And not just the emperor but all the Korean people, who should determine for themselves what nation they are."

So that's what *self-determination* meant. Thinking about how hard it was to always behave properly, I wondered if people could also have personal self-determination—if they could decide for themselves what kind of person they were. In my quest to be demure, hadn't I finally learned to cover my mouth when I laughed? I supposed if one was determined enough, it could happen. I liked the word and decided I would strive to become self-determined.

"Let's see what you've done."

I pinched the corners and displayed the three flags I'd hemmed.

"When I give these to your father to hide, I'll point out your fine work. You've listened well and worked well. Remember that to speak of this and of your father's comings and goings is to put your family in the greatest of danger. Your father could be arrested again, or worse." She took my hand and pressed it on her pregnant stomach. "I'm counting on you to be secretive for the sake of your sibling."

"My brother," I said firmly. I'd informally measured the growth of my mother's middle when we bathed together, imagining I could see the baby swimming beneath the skin. "See how he lies?" she'd say as she poured gourdfuls of heated rinse water and the soapsuds trailed in rivulets around her mounded belly. "That means he's a boy." But my mother had known about the baby's sex much earlier, as early as when she first told

me about her pregnancy, and I wondered again how she could have
known.

I helped put away the fabric scraps in the false bottom of the linen
chest, repacked the spilled towels and bowed goodnight. In bed I listened
for the click and latch of the outer gate, thinking so intently about all I'd
learned that I fell hard into sleep and missed hearing my father tiredly
climb the porch stairs to head toward his side of the house.

PATCHES OF ICE-CRUSTED snow melted quickly in the increased hours of
sunlight during those promising days, and hardy crocus poked striped
shafts through frozen clods of earth. Early shoots, leaf buds and eager
insects thrived in a current of warm afternoons, before returning to dor-
mancy on the last waves of wintry nights. Several days before the funeral
parade in Seoul, we fixed dozens of meals for the men's foot journey.
Father had unearthed the finished flags from a secret pantry beneath the
floor of his study. Some smelled of tobacco, some of chilies and others of
dried persimmons, according to where they'd been stored. Still in my
school skirt but with a "home clothes" muslin blouse, I rolled the flags
tightly, amazed at their number and proud to see that only close inspec-
tion revealed which hems I'd sewn.

In the outside kitchen—a porchlike extension of the main kitchen—
my mother walked to and fro awkwardly, her billowing skirt barely mask-
ing her pregnancy, her hands agile as she added the flags to tidy muslin
packages of rice balls and strips of dried fish. Standing beside me at a narrow worktable, Cook and Kira formed rice into balls and rolled them in
crushed sesame or red bean powder. They chided each other good-
naturedly on the finer points of their work. Cook explained in exasperat-
ing detail how to guarantee the perfect consistency of rice for molding
into balls, while Kira insisted that the source of the water was the most
important factor. My mother diplomatically praised and admired their
combined results. Immersed in this activity with busy hands all around, I
thought there couldn't be a happier moment.

After sunset, our neighbor's son, Hansu, called greetings outside the
kitchen door and appeared with two empty sacks slung over a shoulder,
looking very grown up framed in the small doorway.

"*Oppa*, Elder Brother!" I could barely wait for him to remove his shoes before grabbing his hand to show off the fifty packets neatly piled on the worktable. The men from church who were going to Seoul planned to stagger their departures in small groups beginning at dawn.

Hansu, sixteen and recently betrothed, had been acting stuffy in recent years—too mature to pay me any mind—but my enthusiasm in packing his sacks brought out his boyish laughter. He tugged a pigtail. "Will you miss me, little one?"

"You haven't been around one bit this entire winter, so there's no one for me to miss!" I tossed my head and my long braids slapped his forearm.

"What! Such disrespect! Here I am, on the verge of a great adventure and not even one sad tear to see me off?" Hansu tied the ends of a filled burlap sack and hefted it to test its weight.

"I'll be sad only if you promise that when you come back, you'll help me again." I missed the afternoons our paths converged when we both walked home—he from Japanese upper school and me from the mission school. I practiced Chinese characters and Japanese language with him, and he learned the English alphabet from me. He had graduated months ago, and I had rarely seen him since then.

"Haven't you heard? I've got a fiancée!"

"I did hear." I fingered the rough knot of the bag. "You'll still be my honorary brother, won't you?"

Hansu carried the sacks to the back porch. "From what I've observed," he said, lowering his voice as if it were bad luck to talk about a baby before being born, "you're going to have your own brother soon enough."

"Even Abbuh-nim says it's a boy," I whispered back. The previous evening, when Mother had false contractions, Father visited her to ensure all was well. I glimpsed their profiles outlined in lamplight, their heads bent with noses nearly touching. He spoke as if in prayer, and I leaned closer to hear. "This child shall surely be my heir, for none other than a son could be born on the eve of our independence." I had never before heard him speak so emotionally and with such tenderness. It made me think of him in a new way, a way I couldn't quite describe that seemed to relieve a degree of my general state of fear around him.

"I have to see your father now," said Hansu. "Will you tell him I'm here?"

Going down the dim hallway to the front of the house, I privately admired Hansu's prominent cheekbones and the wiry peaks and valleys of his Western-shorn hair. "You'll remember everything about your adventure and tell me all about Seoul?"

"Shh! Not a word—you know it's a secret." He pinched my ear and smiled. "Of course. You're the only sister I'll ever have. Now show me in, will you?"

I held his hand until we neared Father's sitting room, then cleared my throat to announce us and bowed in the doorway. "Abbuh-nim, the son of our neighbor is here."

My mother sat across from my father, sewing a clean collar onto a laundered shirt. The room felt snug and overly warm, the air tinged with smoke and lamp oil. Mother indicated that I should fill and light Father's pipe and sit beside her.

Hansu bowed from the waist. "Good evening, sir. I received the gifts of your kitchen, and now if you'll allow me a great honor, may I receive your blessing?"

"Enter, my boy. Sit for a moment." Father's long sleeve brushed his lap as he gestured Hansu to the pillows beside his reading table. He asked about Hansu's family's health and reviewed the logistics for the journey. He noted that places to sleep would be plentiful; the travelers merely had to ask at any village church to be referred to a welcoming household or a dry shed. In a growing silence, I noticed in Hansu's bunched trousers that his calves contracted at regular intervals, as if he were already marching on what I imagined were the wide paved avenues of the capital city. The punk-punk sound of Mother's needle into the starched collar was like a steady drumbeat of victory.

"Yah," said Father with a regretful sigh. "If only it was a different day . . ."

Mother shifted her legs, and I wondered if her brows were knit with discomfort from the baby or the knowledge that her pregnancy was the reason that Father would not participate in the demonstration in Seoul. Or perhaps he remained in Gaeseong because of his arrest record. I wished I could ask.

Hansu cleared his throat. "Sir, since I probably won't be here when the baby comes, please excuse my early congratulations. My family offers their blessings and prayers for a healthy baby boy."

Father made his face stern, but his pursed lips held visible satisfaction. Mother's eyes twinkled at Hansu and I smiled outright.

"Well then," said Father, and everyone bowed heads for his prayer and blessing. My mother and I stood to escort our guest out. Surprisingly, Father also stood and bowed. Hansu's eyes opened wide at this honor from an elder, and he bowed low, backing out the door.

I heard the next day from Kira that Hansu had distributed the packages throughout the night, then left with two other men at first light.

# The Secret of Water

LOUNGING ON MY BEDROOM FLOOR IN THE LONG LIGHT OF YELLOW sunset, I lazily copied sentences. Kira stuck her head in. "Quick, Ahsee! Your mother calls—her time has come!"

I flew to my mother's room. A wrinkled woman with slits for eyes and a downturned mouth pointed her finger and barked. "No children! I'm a midwife, not a nursemaid."

"She's old enough," said Mother. "Her hands are strong. She can help and learn, and maybe she'll be more prepared when she becomes a woman than I was." My eyes widened at her forceful words and cross tone toward the lower-class woman. Scowling, the midwife tossed me a rag to tie around my hair.

The floor had been cleared of its mats. Cloths were piled neatly next to three containers of water and a large empty pan. Kira whispered to me importantly that it was her job to keep one bucket filled with hot, another with cold, and the urn with lukewarm water to bathe the new baby. My mother's table and chest had been moved to the hallway to make more room, but with the four of us moving about, the space was crowded and stuffy. I sat beside a bed pallet made of old quilts where my mother, in a cotton slip and old blouse, alternately rested and squatted, breathing sharply with tight lips when contractions came. Between those fearful episodes, she explained what would happen, but nothing she said could truly prepare me for the coming ferocity of birth. The midwife timed the spasms and instructed me to keep Mother's neck and brow cool with wrung cloths.

Mother squinted, her face white and sweating, and suppressed the cries that claimed her throat. Despite her earlier assurances, I was certain she was dying, and scared tears ran down my cheeks. I gripped her arm, wanting to keep her in this life. When the pain passed, my mother exhaled and relaxed. "Don't be frightened, Najin-ah." Her eyes were ardent, bright and peaceful. "This is a woman's natural act—a great gift from God—and though hard for the body, it's nothing to fear." After the next contraction, my mother said it was the same as when I was born, and look at the goodness that had come from such pain. I wanted to, but couldn't smile. I brushed aside the sodden hair clinging to her cheeks and burning forehead. The corners of the room seemed to approach; grasping shadows that clawed at the bubble of safety created by my mother's rhythmic breathing.

The labor pains intensified, and she clenched her teeth with such severity that saliva wet her chin. The midwife thrust a twisted cloth into my mother's mouth. Between her bouts of rapid breathing, I saw her face contort to a fierceness I'd never seen before. Petrified, I wanted to scream, and the same spirit that had entered my mother's body sealed my throat. It seemed obvious that screaming would help, but my mother was in a trance, her eyes pinpoints, her neck and shoulders sinewy and glistening, lips blue and stretched taut around teeth clamped on the wad of cloth. Then she groaned—a low and long animal sound, curiously soft, that seemed to emanate not from her mouth but from deep within her body—and her belly rippled like the spiraling wake of a rock tossed in a pond. She gasped for breath, and veins I'd never known existed pulsed like snakes on her temples. She curled her back and pressed downward, her face fiery red. I cried out in fear. The midwife stooped low in front of my mother and caught the baby's bloody wet head. He was ugly and alarming, but all my fear left when I saw his flattened human ear. "Umma-nim, look!" I shouted.

"Hush," she said through her teeth, and pushed again. Thus did I witness my mother's strength and the miracle of her body birthing my *dongsaeng*, my younger sibling, a wet and wailing mess.

"A boy!" cried the midwife, her stern features lightened with pleasure. She cut and tied the cord and swept the baby aside to clean and check him, encouraging Mother to continue pushing to deliver the afterbirth. An overwhelming stench and a surprising mess of blood and tissue made me afraid again, and I turned from the baby to my mother. I was unaware how tightly I clutched her arm until she said gently, "Let go now, and help me bathe." I was so happy she had returned to me that I burst into tears. My fingerprints remained white on her arm for the entire time it took to wash and help her to a bed freshly made by Kira. It was odd to see Kira treating my mother like a child, but her soothing clucks and instructions to lift an arm, turn the hips a little, and the sound of her rough hands coddling the quilts around my mother's body helped restore us all.

The midwife laid the infant against Mother's breast. "Huh!" said the old woman. "He's a smart one, eh? Look how hungrily he suckles!" They cooed over the perfectly formed infant while Kira and I soaked stained linens and washed the floor. The midwife gave me dried anise leaves and shavings of angelica root for Cook to make a tea that would promote milk production, relieve cramping and revive the uterus. As I left for the kitchen, I heard the midwife whisper admiringly to Kira that she had never before witnessed such refinement during a birth.

By the time I returned, dignity had been fully restored in my mother's room. I checked the corners, and no spirits were lingering. Mother showed me how quickly the baby took to each breast, and then her own breath and body quieted, and her eyes closed.

"Let her rest, now," the midwife said kindly. "You did very well," she added, as if I had done anything at all. I bowed gratefully and thought that she was a most amazing woman to come and work the arduous hours of birthing, to help bring order, and life, out of chaos and pain. She wrapped the baby in white silk bunting and took him to my father.

I sat outside the door partially hidden by the linen chest when Father came, holding his son in upturned hands as if he held a sacred relic. Mother woke when he crouched beside her, and the smile they shared seemed so filled with light it made me breathless. In the dim room, Father's features were as smoothly washed with wonder as Mother's. He spoke with a voice as gentle as the sunset filtering through the high windows. "On the hundredth day, I will name him Ilsun, first son of Korea."

I knew it was wrong of me to think that, as the baby's elder, I was then first daughter of Korea, and I remained a motionless shadow. But I admit that I was smiling inside.

THE NEXT MORNING, the house still felt strange. I tiptoed into Mother's room and, relieved, saw her sleeping peacefully. Wanting to be close to her, to be reassured after the previous day's ordeal, I knelt by the bed and touched a finger to her forehead. A shiver coursed up my arm, and with it, a dream of tall palms bursting from an oasis of shimmering water. The dream desert's clean light flooded my eyes, and the image nestled in my breast. I gasped with its sharpness, and my mother's eyes opened, smiling at me, confirming the vision, and my heart swelled with this surprising bond between us. Cook entered with herb broth and a basket of towels and chased me away. Like hearing the last echo of a wonderfully read story, I wanted to keep the vision in my head as long as I could and went to my room to lie on the bare floor. Yes, two palm trees, like those in Bible pictures, two long straight legs reaching to heaven, and water that I knew was absolutely clear, as cool and sparkling as the stars in the night sky, water of a purity that only a dream could hold. I ached to ask my mother what it meant.

She would stay in bed for five days cosseted by blankets and servants—postpregnancy being the only time in her life when she would allow herself to rest. As the day wore on, I felt lost without Mother on her feet. I didn't feel like reading or helping Kira or Cook, which I knew I should be doing. I wandered through the courtyard and saw my father sitting on his inner porch. I approached to see the prize he caressed in his lap. He gazed at his son with such steadfastness that I wondered if he could see anything else. I was nearly upon him before he noticed me, startled. "Yah!" He turned and held the baby close. "Have you washed your hands?"

"They're clean, see?"

"Don't talk back! Have you no respect?" His rebuke and the deepening furrow between his eyes confused me.

"Abbuh-nim—"

"Where are your manners? Where is graciousness? What kind of things will my son learn from an inept peasant of a sister!"

I knew that I should bow, offer an apology and go away, but somehow my body wouldn't bend.

"Look at your hands. It won't help to wash—dark as a peasant's! What will he learn?"

I had the terrible sacrilegious thought that it was I who had seen the baby born—I who *was* the firstborn—and that made me special, more special . . . I couldn't finish the thought and forced my feet to retreat, remembering at the last minute not to run in my father's presence. I turned at the edge of the courtyard to see him tighten the baby's bunting and go inside.

Dried stalks of tiger lilies whipped my arms as I ran toward the pond in the far corner of the estate. I stopped, panting from running and holding in my angry tears. I had only wanted to see him! The toes of my gray rubber shoes touched the edge of the pond, its surface spotted with lacy green mire. I remembered the tiny white elbow I'd seen in the bundle Father held. I wiped my eyes and face with my fingers and looked at my hands and wrists—ruddy brown, carelessly tanned. Remembering what he'd said, I rubbed my forehead as if to erase my skin color, and tried to retract my hands into too-short sleeves.

I walked by the pond late into the morning and listened to the rhythmic whir of dragonflies' wings, catching glimpses of their fleet black bodies reflected in clear circles left by melting ice on the algae-coated surface of the pond. Sometimes I saw my face mirrored as well, but I drew back to avoid the reminder of my features. Even if I swore to always carry an umbrella to shade me from the sun's baking rays, my skin would never be as fair as that pure pale newborn's. With a long stick, I stirred circles in the water, and the algae shapes swirled as inchoately as my feelings. I was thrilled to have a sibling, especially the boy both my parents had long prayed for, but I also feared that things would be different, like how my father had turned toward the house. I trailed through the willows, their bare wispy arms softly brushing my shoulders, and I remembered how my mother said she was counting on me to be a good nuna to my brother. It calmed me to think that fulfilling my responsibilities as older sister might favorably shape the changes the baby brought to our lives. I headed back toward the house, hoping he'd grow out of infancy soon, so I could prove how good a nuna I could be.

LATER THAT WEEK, after school, I sat on my knees next to Mother's bed, admiring the contented baby's appetite.

"Let me show you something," she said. "You should know this so you can understand your father better, and now your dongsaeng, and be properly respectful to them." Mother lifted the blanket and her nightskirt, and with clinical description explained the origins of the blood staining the cloth between her legs, the soft, loose flesh of her still-expanded belly, the seepage of milk from dark, flowering nipples. Having washed together with my mother countless times and having witnessed the birth, I merely raised my own skirt to examine my child's body with comparative interest as she described the biological process of life so recent that her body still trembled in remembrance of its violence and mystery.

"This is the great gift that God has given to women," she said, "and women alone." She smoothed her skirt and blanket over her legs. "Following the glory of Jesus's example, we suffer with the greatest gifts we receive. This is something that a man will never understand in the way a woman will. Certainly a man's seed is essential, but the creation of life is within us. For them it is outside. They are our fathers, husbands and our sons, and it's your duty to honor and respect them, but this they will always be standing outside of."

She patted my hand beside hers on the bed. "Do you remember how the palm trees sprouted from the lake in the dream?" A shiver ran up my back and became needle pricks down my arms. I looked at her fully, and my eyes rounded and fused with the warm blackness of her pupils. "Yes, my daughter, that was a dream of your brother. I knew when you touched me that you had seen the same vision. I dreamed of those palm trees many times when he was inside me. The first time was the night before your first day of school. That day was a double blessing for us."

I remembered that the trees seemed like long legs, so it made immediate sense that they would symbolize males. "That's how you knew he was a boy."

"Yes, and for you too. In my fourth month with you, I dreamt of catching a small white fish between my hands as I waded in a lovely stream, so cool, so fresh, so clean. Such a beautiful little fish, it made me laugh in my dream and I woke up laughing! That was you." She took my hand, and I felt as close and safe as if snuggled underneath her quilt beside her. I was made full and whole in her love, and she didn't let go of my hand for a long time.

"Dongsaeng was the trees?" I asked, and she nodded. "But why is there water in both dreams?"

"Men need water to live, but they cannot move as it does. Women are like the water that flows, feeds and travels over and under man's two feet stuck solidly in the earth. We are liquid. It is from us that he emerges, drinks and grows. And so," said Mother, brushing aside my hair sprouting wildly from restless braids and bronze combs, "when your father seems gruff, I want you to remember this. Women are especially blessed in a way that men can never grasp. Keep God's love in your heart and remember this always."

"Yes, Umma-nim." I clasped my hands tightly together in my lap, to prevent the secret of water from leaking between my fingers.

# Ten Thousand Years!

## March 1, 1919

Through an underground web of letters and couriers, news reached the men of the church that the nationwide demonstration for independence would be moved to the Saturday three days before Emperor Gojong's funeral. Japanese troops had been mobilizing in Seoul to control the large expected crowds, and staging the protest on March 1— *Sam-il*—instead of March 4, would catch them off guard. I was excited to hear this news. Since mission schools were closed on Saturdays, it increased the likelihood that Father would allow me to witness Gaeseong's demonstration. The day dawned dry, temperate and full of conviction. Branches tipped with flower buds and bursting leaves shone in the crisp morning sun. The tender pinks and baby greens of new growth attracted masses of birds, whose happy chirps and trilling made the trees ring with song. Outside the city, newly tilled soil filled mountain breezes with rich earthy smells, and sometimes the stench of fertilizer wafted through the streets.

My father and many others gathered at the church at two o'clock to hear the Declaration of Independence read by Reverend Ahn. Mother was on her feet and managing the household as always, but Father denied her desire to join him, deeming it unseemly for her to attend a political gathering, regardless of how many women they knew who would be there. Joong would accompany him and would run home at the proper time to alert the family to unfurl flags in celebration of freedom. How confident we were, and how naive.

That afternoon in a patch of glaring light in the southern courtyard, Kira and I wrung diapers and spread them on hedges to dry. The water was winter-cold on my hands, but the bright day warmed them as fast as flame. We heard a strange roaring sound and looked at each other as it grew louder. Nearing, the roar clearly became a crowd of people singing and chanting, most likely approaching the paved boulevard a few blocks south. I ran to Mother. "They're coming down the main road! Can we go, please? Can we watch?"

It took only a moment for her to decide. "Quickly! Get the flags. Call the servants!" Mother tied the baby onto her back and hurried down the street with Cook, Kira, Byungjo and me behind her unrolling our flags. We turned the corner and saw Joong sprinting toward us, all the spaces between his teeth visible in his big smile. He bowed to Mother and directed us to the next street. A parade passed through the intersection— a throng twenty times the size of a full church congregation. Men, women, boys and girls raised their arms in unison and shouted, "*Man-se!* Ten thousand years! Long live Korea's independence!" We waved our flags, our arms raised high like flagpoles, and hurried to greet the crowd. Cook and Kira lifted their skirts to dash up the street. Soon we saw Father in the midst of the marchers, his old-fashioned sleeves flapping with each salute of *Man-se!* his face youthful and joyous as he kept chorus with the others. Mother untied the baby and lifted him high above her head, and Father saw them and waved vigorously.

"Please, can I follow?" I asked. I felt flushed with everything looking lively and bustling and full of energy—the mass of people with their forward pulsing march, the froth of white sleeves and skirts brilliant in the sunlight, like a tidal wave whose force would sweep aside all ills. "Look, there's Sooyung from church, and look! His sister too! May I, please?"

"No, what would your father think? Come now—*Man-se!*" The baby cried at the thunder of the crowd every time Mother hoisted him in unison with each *Man-se!* and the servants shouted and raised their arms. We marched alongside until the street narrowed, then watched the marchers turn the corner a few blocks ahead, waves of song and rallying cries fading, then swelling through cross alleys, then diminishing to echo in the wind. Road dust swirled in a sudden surprising silence. Mother wiped the baby's face with bunting. "I'll remember this momentous day for you, little son, so you'll know what wonders you saw."

"Where are they going?" I waved my flag at the empty street.

"Father will tell us about it when he returns. Oh! It's a historic day for Korea!"

I was too eager for Father's return to sit and study in my stuffy room. I asked Cook how I could help prepare the celebration meal, and she sent me to gather fiddlehead ferns by the north wall.

In the cool shade of tall pines, shafts of sun warmed the patch of neck between my braids, my hair absorbing the heat like a woolen scarf. I tied the front of my skirt to prevent it from dragging on the ground and stooped to pinch tender shoots, collecting them neatly in a basket, and carefully harvesting every other fern to reserve a crop for the following year. The ferns smelled dark and loamy. I roamed beyond the woods to the meadow by the brook where we did laundry in the summer, and found wild leeks and new dandelion greens. I plucked them and savored their green sharp smell on my fingertips, my cheeks sucking in as I anticipated the tangy salad Cook would make.

When I returned to the house, the fruit trees in the courtyard cast long clawlike shadows at my feet. "Look what I found!" The basket thudded on the kitchen table.

"Where have you been?" said Cook, her tone unnaturally sharp. "Your mother's looking for you. Quick! Wash hands and go."

"Is Father back yet?"

"Go on!"

I dipped my hands in the washbowl and rushed to the women's quarters, dripping water, my worried steps shaking the walls.

"Najin-ah!" Mother called from her room. I helped untie the baby from her back, and he started to cry. Mother pointed to a pile of clothes, brown and yellow with road dirt. "Take the baby and give those to Kira to wash right away. She's to lay them out in Joong's room to dry. Ask Cook to bring more hot water and clean rags to Father's room."

"What happened?"

"Do as I say!" She went out the porch to the courtyard, and I was alarmed to see her cut through the garden to reach Father's rooms, where the lamps burned brightly.

I cuddled Dongsaeng, humming until he quieted. I bent and held him on my back with one hand, and clumsily wound the binding cloth around my torso, tying it tightly until he felt snug against my spine. I gathered the dirty clothes and saw dark stains on the collar. Unbunching what I recognized was my father's shirt, I smelled earth and metal before I saw that the garment was soaked with blood. I hugged the clothes and ran to the kitchen.

"Is Father all right?" I showed Cook the bloodied shirt. "What happened?"

"What did your mother say?" Cook stoked coals beneath a cauldron of steaming water.

"Nothing!" I almost stamped my foot, impatient for information, and afraid. I remembered my mother's instructions and took a breath. "She said to bring hot water and clean rags."

Cook shoved a block of wood into the stove and fetched a large ceramic bowl. Moving with speed, she rolled her sleeves down her wiry arms. "And what else?" She kicked a stool over to a cabinet, climbed up and grabbed a handful of folded cloths from a high shelf.

"That Kira should wash these clothes. There's blood—"

"I see that. Do as your mother says. Kira's out back."

"But is Father—"

Cook carefully ladled boiling water into the crock. "Your father is hurt. Just above his eye, thank God. It's messy but not deep. Joong went for the surgeon, who's in with him now." The spry woman tucked the rags beneath her arm and cradled the steaming crock in a towel. "Maybe you can help Kira wash those clothes."

I hurried outside. When she saw Father's shirt Kira said, *"Aigu!"* and clucked her tongue. Frightened childish tears wet my cheeks.

"Now then, Ahsee. You'll wake the baby. See how nicely he's sleeping? He must like riding on your back the best. Don't worry. We can get the blood out. Look, I'll show you how."

I wiped my nose and followed Kira, who plunked a tub on the washing platform near the drain ditch. The youthful water girl energetically filled the tub with a bucket from the cisterns. She crouched beside the tub, threw in a handful of salt and splashed cold water on the bloody clothes. "Ahsee, sit here." She patted a dry spot beside her on the planks. "I'll tell you what I saw and heard."

I squatted next to her, rocking from one foot to the other to keep the baby asleep. While Kira swished water through the clothes and patiently rubbed the stain with a worn bar of ashy soap, she spoke. She'd been filling the cisterns on Father's side of the house when he came through the gate. "He walked normally, but he was holding this very sleeve against his head. I could see something was wrong and I said, 'Master, how can I help?' He told me to get Madam and Joong, and some towels. I did that, and when I brought the towels in, he was sitting on the porch saying he didn't want to bloody the mats. He sent Joong for the doctor, and Madam tried to clean his wound. A lot of blood came from his head still." Kira wrung the shirt and changed buckets.

"I saw tears in your mother's eyes," she said with a kindly look to me. "But her hands were steady and calm. She said Cook should boil water and I should get fresh water and some clean clothes for the master. When I got back, I heard him talking. I waited a little apart before I went in. See how it's almost gone?" She plunged the shirt in a second bucket and soaped it again. "Your father said that when they got to the police station no one knew what to do. They decided to go back to the church, but some of the young men disagreed. Then your mother saw me and said to put the clothes down and take the baby, but he was sleeping so peacefully, she changed her mind and told me to go."

Kira tipped the washtub and poured bloodied water into the ditch.

"Cook said to bring them drinking water and take the soiled rags and wash them right away. This time the master was in his sitting room. I waited a little before I went in, so I heard him telling more." She looked sideways at me. "Except I don't think your mother would want you to hear."

"You must!" I stood to shift the baby higher on my back. "I promise I won't say anything."

"Come closer." Kira lowered her voice. "Somebody named Kim was shot, and your father tried to help another man who got stabbed in the shoulder clean through. Then he said something about a soldier and a spear. The master stopped talking then—maybe they heard me. When I went in, he was sitting calmly in clean trousers. Madam had tied a towel around his head and was washing his back. She pointed to the bloodied towels I should take, and as I left, the doctor came.

"So you see, the master is perfectly alive and talking as usual. And now the doctor is taking care of him, and soon I'm sure he'll be wanting to see you and the little master too." Kira laid her heavy hand on my shoulder. Icy from the wash, her palm delivered a chill through my light cotton jacket that cooled my rapid heartbeats.

"Oh, Kira."

The baby fussed. Kira said to take him to Cook and perhaps Madam would feed him soon.

"I forgot to tell you that Mother said to dry the clothes in Joong's room. Are they his now? It's still a good shirt."

Kira shrugged.

"She wants to hide them?"

"Some things I don't want to know. Never mind. Now you know how to take out bloodstains, and next time I'll show you how to make soap." The gold edging on her front tooth flashed, and I thought I'd never seen such a generous smile.

I found Mother saying goodbye to Dr. Mun. The doctor's dark Western suit passed like a night spirit through the gate. The baby started to cry, fully awake and hungry. Back in our rooms, Mother breastfed him, her brow deeply creased.

I folded the binding cloth and sat quietly in front of her, waiting until the questions stopped spinning in my head and I could speak calmly. "Umma-nim, may I ask if Abbuh-nim is badly hurt?"

The baby's soft feeding noises, his miniature chubby hand resting on Mother's breast, the creamy smell of milk and the twilit room worked to smooth her lines of worry, her cheeks blushed pink from breastfeeding. Her voice, a low singsong, kept rhythm with the baby's sucking. "Your father's doing fine. Resting now. No need to worry."

"May I ask what happened?"

Mother nodded, her eyes half shut and bright from lactation. "After we saw them on the road, your father and the crowd marched all the way to the police station. Everyone had sworn a pledge of nonviolence and understood it was to be a peaceful demonstration." She stroked the baby's head, gazing at him, and said, "'Be not afraid!' was the motto for nonviolence that everyone swore to."

I hugged my knees and waited while she shifted the baby. "But what happened at the police station?"

"There was confusion. Some said they should return to the church to wait for news from Seoul. Others said they should wait there and hear the Declaration read once more. But armed policemen came out with a firehose, and a truck drove up behind the marchers. Your father thinks it was a traitor's work since they were organized and well prepared. An officer said to disperse or be arrested, and they turned the hose on with such force that people were thrown against each other. Those who tried to run were met with blows from the soldiers. This made some of the young men angry and they threw stones and dirt. Just dirt and pebbles from the road!"

Mother straightened her back and the baby made little noises, waving his hands to find a nipple. I squeezed his foot. "But still, it was wrong, and dangerous," she continued. "Your father said someone fired a shot then. The soldiers drew sabers and people screamed. They shot into the crowd. Everyone panicked and the soldiers charged. They beat people with clubs and bayonets. Animals! Many were hurt and arrested. Saegong's father was shot. Poor man! You know him, the baritone soloist." She bowed her head, praying he would be spared and his family protected. "Your father stopped to help another badly wounded man, and that's when he was hurt."

"Is it bad?" I twisted the ties on my blouse, the ends wrinkled and increasingly damp. I felt suddenly and irrationally responsible. I did not love my father enough, did not respect him or honor him enough, was not well behaved enough.

"No, his hat protected him somewhat. He was brave and foolish, but now I'm afraid they—" Mother hugged the baby and hid her eyes, but I saw tear tracks and was struck with new fear that he would be arrested again.

"Don't worry," she said. "He's home. He'll be fine. The surgeon cleaned his wound with iodine and sewed it together as easily as a torn sleeve. The bleeding's stopped and he says there's little pain. He'll have to sleep sitting up for a few days. I must remember to ask Joong to bring more pillows." She closed her blouse and held the baby out by his armpits. "Here, learn how to burp your brother. Hold him close, that's right. Support his head and rub his back."

I brushed my nose against my brother's feathery hair, inhaled his delicious scent and rubbed a little circle on the small of his back as my mother instructed. He released a loud gassy burst and we laughed.

"A good one! Watch me change his diaper, then you'll know everything about taking care of your brother."

"Except I haven't any milk." I cupped the baby's head as I returned him.

She demonstrated her diapering method, her hands skillful, automatic. "It's simple to learn how to clean and dress a baby. Even to have a baby is a simple earthly thing. Understanding the physical world is nothing. Your father said the man he tried to help was stabbed in the shoulder through to his back. His ribs were caved in on one side as if he'd been kicked or trampled. Two other men helped your father carry the wounded man into a courtyard. They dropped him once because soldiers were beating everyone in sight. He saw a woman being hit with the butt of a rifle. Her skull was crushed, but the soldier didn't stop. Aigu! What of her family? What will become of her children?" Mother kissed the baby's forehead, murmuring a prayer for the woman, the dead and wounded. I remembered the smell of my father's shirt, and the heavy perfume of lilacs.

"A Chinese man came out of the house and said he'd hide him and call their doctor. Those are good Christian people, even if they're Buddhist." This impressed me as an odd and curious thing to say. She swaddled the baby. "Najin-ah, alongside such goodness are those who know only evil. It's something you'll need to understand sooner than I'd hoped. I'm sure you'll want to know how such evil can exist, as do I." She spoke tightly with an anger I'd rarely seen. I crushed a diaper, both wanting and not wanting to hear more. Mostly, though, I badly wanted everything to be like before. "We can't know God's will," she said, "it's not for us to ask. But how can it not be when it's we who suffer?"

"Is it the Devil? Are the ancestors angry?"

Her eyes refocused toward me and her voice quieted. "Yes, certainly the work of Satan in all his evilness, but we can fully trust that Jesus will keep you and your brother safe. You needn't worry. You need only pray with all your heart and behave well. Be respectful and thoughtful of others, especially those less fortunate than us. Take care of your brother and father. Pray for our leaders. Pray for Korea."

"Yes, Umma-nim."

"You must give thanks that Father made it home. The Chinese man also wanted to hide your father, but that wouldn't be right. Your father stayed off the main road and saw nothing else. He said the streets were full of wailing."

Mother cuddled the baby and spontaneously returned his smile. "But here's a happy little boy. Your father can't wait to see you."

"Umma-nim, may I see him too?"

"A little later."

"I picked *gosari*. He might like that tonight."

"I'll be sure to tell him you picked it just for him. Now see to your studies. I'll bring your father his food, then you and I can have a late supper."

I bowed and reluctantly left. Instead of studying in my lonely room, I took my writing pad to the kitchen, pretending to do homework while I watched to ensure that Cook dressed and sautéed the greens I'd picked for Father to perfection.

NIGHT FELL. AFTER the day's violence the dark seemed thick and ominous, the moon and stars buried in baleful clouds. Brittle winds from the mountains gusted through the house, shaking the windows and leaving behind a hostile chill. I was snuggled deeply in winter quilts when thunder woke me. Not thunder—pounding, metal on wood. Japanese shouts. Distant doors and shutters slammed and I heard quick footfalls outside.

Father called in Japanese, "One moment! Just a moment!" Then softly, "Byungjo, the gate!" Men banged on the sturdy wooden door, and the iron latch and hinges shook. "Yes, yes!" Father crossed the front yard, his shoes flapping.

Mother slipped into my room, the baby in one hand, the other pressed against her lips for silence. I couldn't see her eyes. The room felt cold with fear.

The gate slapped open and men shouted Father's name. "You must—"

A scuffle, curses, then I heard my father gasp and moan. More curses, grunts, and the gate clanged shut. From the neighbor's came muffled commands, a woman's scream cut short and sounds of breaking wood. Faintly—shouts, screams and slams from other homes. Then silence.

I clutched my blanket and the baby whimpered. Mother opened her nightdress. The sound of his feeding and a far sighing wind in the bamboo left a strained quietude. Mother began to pray. I bowed my head to focus on her hushed sounds, the whispered words, the baby suckling, and nothing more.

"The Lord is my shepherd," began Mother, and I joined her.

It confused me to say, "Thou preparest a table before me in the presence of mine enemies." How could anyone feast with one's enemies about? But I understood who the enemy was.

Mother said, "Go back to sleep. I think I must go out. If I'm gone too long, Cook will show you how to feed the baby rice water with honey."

"But I should go with you! Cook can—" I wanted to wrap my arms around her waist and scream that it wasn't safe.

"Not another word. I need you rested to watch your brother. Cook has her own worries." Mother put her finger on my lips. "This is the best way you can help your father." She dressed and took the baby to Cook.

Bundled in my blankets, I stayed sitting up and breathed in the last waft of milky scent as I listened to her pad down the hall and cross the yard to the servants' quarters. I buried my eyes in the darkness of my bedding and prayed, chanted, "Keep her safe. Keep her safe."

I woke to a still house, remembered, and thought it too quiet. There'd be no church on this Sunday. After washing and dressing quickly, I went to the kitchen where Kira rocked the whimpering baby while Cook boiled down rice water to feed him.

"Where's Mother?" I asked, scared when I saw Cook's face unnaturally red, eyes swollen and wrinkles deeply drawn. For the first time she struck me as being an old woman, but when she faced me, she looked nearly herself again.

"Joong is out with her. She'll be fine. Are your hands clean?"

I nodded.

Kira made room for me on a low bench beside the hearth. "Your mother said to show you how to feed the baby when there's no wet nurse."

I wanted to shout at them. How could they act like everything was normal? "Where did she go? Is— Was Abbuh-nim— Is he—dead?"

"Such crazy ideas!" Cook grasped my shoulders and turned me toward Kira and the baby. "Feed him first, then you can have breakfast." She turned to the stove and stirred honey into her bubbling reduction. "Not dead," she said. "They arrested him last night. Your mother went to find out why, and where. He's done nothing bad, and she's sure to get him released soon. Aigu! This morning the night-soil man said many were taken like that. He heard women crying in the houses. What a time we live in!" She wiped her face with her apron. "You're to stay close to home today. No wandering off. Your mother will want you to take care of your dongsaeng."

I untied him from Kira's back. He began to wail and I held him close. My arms felt heavier than the infant's weight. I watched the two women busy themselves in the kitchen and looked at my hands; their veins seemed filled with mud.

"Hold him thus." Kira repositioned the baby in my lap. He instinctively turned toward my heartbeat and flailed his arms at my chest, his mouth opening and closing like a fish.

"Take this and knot it, see?" Kira dipped a twisted cloth into the soupy mix Cook had set before us. "It should be neither hot nor cold. You shouldn't really feel it."

I felt nothing of the moisture Kira dripped on my inner wrist and realized I didn't feel anything at all—not the roundness of the baby in my arms, his fists floundering at my unformed breasts, the temperature in the kitchen, my own weight on the bench. I took Kira's words to mean that I wasn't supposed to feel anything, and was relieved.

The baby quieted, rhythmically sucking the knot I repeatedly dipped for him. Kira left to replenish the cisterns from the stream while Cook prepared a breakfast of porridge and sautéed greens. I began to feel the kitchen's heat and hoped that this warm day might make my father suffer prison a little less.

I played aimlessly with the baby strapped to my back all morning, wandering through the courtyard and gardens, dawdling by the locked front gate, jealous that besides my brother's need for Mother's milk, he was unaware of our missing parents. I fed him twice more with the cloth and rice-water solution before Mother returned with Joong.

Mother kept her cloak fastened despite the warmth. Reassured that she acted calm, I saw that she also looked drawn, and fragile. Cook immediately set about preparing food for her. Mother held the baby a moment then gave him back to me. "Wait for me in my room," she said. "Ask Kira to bring bathwater. I have a few more things to take care of before I can feed him."

Mother spent some time in Father's sitting room. I heard her call for Joong, who hurried across the yard swallowing and wiping his mouth.

Between arranging flat pillows beside my mother's eating table and bouncing and tickling the baby to distract him from hunger, I paced the room. From the window I saw Joong again crossing the yard, stuffing letters into his vest. Mother finally came in and removed her cloak, revealing the front of her blouse and skirt stained dark with wetness.

"Is that blood?" I almost screamed.

"Heavens, no! It's milk your poor little brother didn't get to drink. Help me undress and bathe, so I can feed that hungry boy, will you?" She touched my cheek and let me gaze at her calm, tired eyes. "Your father's alive, in jail, although no one can say how he is. I haven't seen him, but the deacon and our friends are working to get him, the minister and others released."

My hands shook with relief as I helped my mother disrobe. I bathed her elegant neck and narrow shoulders, and with each stroke of the washcloth, I felt I was reclaiming a small amount of our lives from before. Mother said she'd keep the baby and rest, that I should thank God that Father was alive, and pray hard for his quick, safe release.

In my room I knelt on the floor, clasped my hands and squeezed my eyes shut. I tried to do as Mother said, but my head was filled with confusion and angry questions, my body anxious with fears that prayerful words couldn't assuage. The mat felt rough against my ankles, and I wondered if my father's prison cell had flooring. Was he alone or with others? I hoped his stomach wasn't bothering him as it did when he was upset with me. I promised God that I'd be respectful to my father forever and would always be ladylike, someone who'd never be a bother to him again. I'd never forget he needed elegance and beauty around him, and I'd do all I could to provide that. I would eliminate my gangly manners and unruly ways, if only he would come home safely. The more promises I made, the more I felt alone and incompetent. I knew it was bad to think that God didn't really care about my family or me, but it seemed an easy truth.

The remainder of the day passed with unusual quiet. Joong came and went once more with letters, and Mother kept to her room with the baby, praying. I sat for awhile inside my open doorway and listened. My mother's murmured prayers seeped down the hall and reached my hungry ears, the unintelligible sounds giving me more assurance than any prayer I could voice. When the hallway grew silent, I tried to study for an arithmetic test and eventually fell asleep on papers carelessly scrawled with long division—homework from a time when homework mattered.

Seven days passed, the house somber with the relentless strain of not knowing and waiting. A quick look out the gate showed dozens of posters fluttering from tree trunks and fence posts. They pronounced a curfew and listed names of agitators. I almost stuck my entire head out to see more, until I saw two soldiers come out of the near alley dragging something across the street. I withdrew and quickly, quietly latched the gate, my chest pounding with what I'd seen.

Mother and I sewed and prayed together for many hours, which simultaneously irritated me, gave me calm and left me sleepy. Sewing was an endless chore. Skirts, pants and tops were deconstructed before laundering so the fabric would fold perfectly flat and we could beat out the wrinkles with two smooth sticks. Stitch after stitch, threading one needle after another, I grew resentful of the necessity for Confucian perfection in dress. With Mother's help, I had begun studying the *Four Books for*

*Women.* Though written in Korean, the vernacular was archaic and difficult, and many proper nouns were in Chinese characters. Schoolwork in Japanese and Korean had taken precedence over home studies, which left me weak in Chinese writing. I had recently read that a virtuous woman ensured that every member of the household was impeccably and properly clothed according to class and family position. As my neck cramped over the exacting work, my head was abuzz with resentment. Who cared about impeccable shirts and virtuous dress when my father was in prison?

Among unnamed errands that made my mother venture daily beyond the gate with Joong, she took as much food as she could carry to the prison. When she returned, her face was always gray, her eyes dark, their expression hidden. There was no way to know if the rice was actually delivered to any of the prisoners. The unusually temperate days and the sweet smells of spring were an affront to our vigil. Playing with Dongsaeng was a distracting, guilty relief. On Monday Mother said the authorities had announced that all businesses must reopen, and children were required to return to school. She refused to let me go. She herself did not visit the market, and we ate dried fish left over from winter storage. I wasn't allowed to leave the estate, and I assumed that Mother was too afraid to have me outside our walls. In the meantime, we waited for news about Father.

On the seventeenth night after his arrest, I woke to scratching sounds at the front gate. My eyes snapped wide to the fading black of predawn, and I heard my father's muted voice, "Yuhbo—"

Mother rushed by my door, calling for the menservants.

"Wait—" I yanked off my covers.

"Watch the baby!"

The gate creaked open and Mother cried out. Father said things I couldn't discern. I heard Byungjo's and Joong's voices, then receding shuffles. In my mother's room, I tucked myself in beside my sleeping baby brother, telling him not to worry, Father was home now. God did watch over him after all. All was well, at least for now. "You're safe with me, Little Brother," I said. "I'll never leave you. I'll take care of you always." I said a silent prayer of thanks, whispering that I wouldn't forget the promises I'd made.

In the morning they remained cloistered in Father's rooms. Cook delivered the baby to Mother for feeding, but I wasn't allowed to go in. I broke several rules of protocol by eating breakfast in the kitchen with Kira and Cook, who told me they'd heard that nearly all the town's men who weren't already in jail had since been arrested. Several were missing entirely. Cook said, "It's a lucky thing your family knows how to make influence." She turned her body, but I saw her make a counting-money gesture to Kira.

I was kept from my father for two weeks, until his most pronounced bruises healed. When allowed to see him at last, I was warned not to show in my face anything that might indicate his changed appearance, including his head, shaved of its topknot. My mother's instructions on this point were so firm that I barely dared to look at him at all, and it took several days of surreptitious peeks to understand that he'd been severely beaten—far more than the last time. His face wasn't as monstrously swollen as then; his cheeks were gaunt and lax. It was worse. With stooped shoulders and eyes that looked vacantly at me, his presence was wraith-like. His stitched head wound seemed like a careless, forgotten brush-stroke. Visible through bandages wrapped like a leper's, his thumbs were enormous and black. The first few times I saw him, his empty stare reminded me of what I had seen outside our gate soon after that joyous and then terrifying day. The two soldiers had dragged from the alley a dead body—bloated, stiff, the color of dirt. Only when I saw the clothes did I know it was a woman. Her gruesome remains, the foul stink, the flies, the utter absence of life in her body, I would never forget.

Although he breathed, ate and slept, even smoked, my father seemed like that the first few times I was allowed to see him. Only when my baby brother was laid in his lap did I see a glimmer of my father, and only then was I not afraid of him.

I finally did go back to the classroom several weeks after the command to return to school. I discovered that none of Korea's children had complied with the command, nor had the businesses reopened for some time, and I realized it was defiance that had closed the shops and kept me home.

Over time, we learned that the national demonstration had prompted unprecedented brutality from the military and police. Months later I heard whispered reports at church about massacre and carnage: all the men in one village burned alive in a chapel, women and girls humiliated, slashed and shot, countless beheadings, people beaten unconscious and revived to be beaten again. Half of the men from our neighborhood who had gone to Seoul were dead. The remainder were imprisoned, flogged and tortured to reveal the names of the movement's leaders.

Our neighbor, Hansu's father, had also been arrested, beaten and eventually released. When he recovered, he and Hansu's mother traveled to Seoul at great risk and found their son still alive, although wounded, and sentenced to West Gate Prison for eighteen months. They returned to raise money for bribes that could reduce his term or at least improve his conditions. I took all the jeon I'd received for good schoolwork, and a chipped jade comb my mother had given me long ago, and slipped them through the neighbor's front gate wrapped in a piece of paper marked only with his name.

# One Hundred Days

MAY 31, 1919

UNCEASING GRIM NEWS OF THE FAILED MOVEMENT BLANKETED THE city. A solemn household and intermittent rains during three days of preparations for the baby's One Hundredth Day naming ceremony chastened my anticipation of the occasion. Earlier, I'd heard my parents discussing the propriety of hosting such a party at all, but Father said, "It's in such times as these that we must rely on our traditions and continue to observe them."

"I worry that we appear to feast when others have suffered much more than we," said Mother.

"We aren't feasting, Yuhbo," he said after a characteristic long pause.

"We're flaunting our way. They cannot suppress forty-five centuries of a people in one season of violence."

I had felt renewed purpose then in my search for the tokens that were needed to forecast the baby's future. When Mother had enlisted me to gather the items, she said our paths were carved by God, not fate or folklore, but this was tradition and harmless. After the naming, the gathered objects would be spread on a table in front of the baby, concealed by a cloth. The cloth would be lifted, and the item the baby chose would foretell his professional destiny. If he grasped the brush in his chubby fist, he would be a scholar. The abacus meant businessman; the brick, a mason; the pen, a clerk; the nail, a carpenter; the coin, a man of wealth; and if he chose the skein of thread, he'd be guaranteed a long life. Mother had added to the list of items a wooden crucifix for pastor, and Father would place on the table a small gift that the Daewongun, Emperor Gojong's father, had given to my grandfather: a polished bronze signet to commemorate his scholarship, painting and calligraphy. This token was what Father himself had chosen on his own One Hundredth Day.

I cleaned the objects, found a suitable length of pale green silk to cover them, and wondered what I would have reached for if Han girls were allowed a One Hundredth Day celebration. Before I delivered the items to Mother, I arranged them on my study desk and tried to spontaneously pick one with my eyes closed. But no manner of turning the table or shuffling the objects blindly in an attempt to fool myself gave authenticity to my choice of the pencil I'd added to symbolize teaching, and I gave up with a sigh.

When the sun reached its zenith on the day of the celebration, it melted a haze of cloud and fog. Soon, warm breezes from the south dried the rain-soaked flagstones in the courtyards. Streaks of water evaporated and puddles swirled with wind. The guests arrived. I helped arrange tables and mats, and carried platters from the kitchen. The elders gathered in the rarely used audience room for the naming ceremony, and to witness the forecasting.

I squeezed between the women in the courtyard, who hovered around the younger men on the porch, who in turn jostled for position around the wide-open doors and windows to watch. Seated inside, knee to knee, were men who were fathers, brothers, uncles and grandfathers of victims of Sam-il—the failed March First movement. Many of the older men were dressed in the straw sandals of mourning, their pristine white hanbok a somber backdrop to the food tables stacked with delicacies. Oranges, apples, plums and buns stuffed with sweet bean paste or dates towered in neat columns among platters piled with rice cakes that had been rolled in green, red or beige pulverized peas and powdered grain. Displays of pure white rice cakes the guests would take home were positioned like guards by the doorways and gate. It may have been sinful, but I felt proud when I heard the murmured exclamations over the lavish party food; the men impressed with the cost, the women impressed with the artistry.

Plump as a dumpling, my baby brother sat propped on pillows in silken finery behind a broad lacquer table. His transparent blue peaked silk cap, edged with a gold geometric pattern, bobbed beside vertical piles of pastries, and his rainbow-striped sleeves brushed precariously against carefully arranged fruit. People smiled and slapped their fans open and shut, seeing hope in the boy's puffy cheeks, and as wine was poured, more laughter was heard.

Father asked for a prayer from Reverend Ahn, who appeared weakened from his time in jail. But when he asked God to bless this new son of our beloved nation, his voice rang clear and true, and with sound and word he delivered a message of pride, strength and perseverance to all who could hear. Old men and women wept. Young men straightened their shoulders, their eyes fierce. Then Father stood with Dongsaeng in his arms and ceremoniously uttered his first son's name: *Ilsun*. People clapped and called out approvingly. Mother positioned Dongsaeng—as was proper, I would always call him *Dongsaeng*, Younger Sibling—in front of the forecasting table. Father swept aside the cloth covering the objects, and a corner of the silk flicked a nearby plate of sorghum balls, tossing one directly into Dongsaeng's lap. Everyone laughed as the baby raised it to his mouth, so no one but I noticed the fleeting change in Mother's expression. Did she think the sweet was Dongsaeng's choice? What did it mean?

Sunlight sparkled on the surface of the king's signet, and the baby picked it up. Shouts and clapping filled the room. Startled by the noise, Dongsaeng cried. Father grabbed him and swung him high, nodding and smiling to the cheers of the men calling, "Yah—just like his father and his father's father. The emperor's loyal artists, the king's favored calligraphers!"

# Books, New and Old

## Autumn 1920

Although it galled Han that something as simple as his daughter's walk to school could threaten his family, he warned Najin to give the police station wide berth. During his walks to town, he noted the increased number of Japanese "businessmen"—who, ridiculously, all wore black trench coats and gray fedoras—meaning the ranks of Thought Police in Gaeseong had multiplied. New spirals of barbed wire, glittering in the sun, topped the fortified concrete walls of the police station, behind which he heard trucks rumbling and the unison shouts of troops exercising.

In the marketplace, posters seeking certain men fluttered in the fall wind. He strode to the bookseller, his outer vest flapping, his head wrapped with a headband and topped with a horsehair hat despite their odd appearance on his shorn hair. A gnarled street sweeper crossed his path, causing him to wonder how such a man of low birth could feed himself since the price of rice had doubled. It made him consider his younger brother's choice with less rancor.

Han's only brother, Chungduk, had married the sole child of a logging family in Manchuria; wealthy landowners, yes, but commoners all the same. Chungduk had taken the position of eldest son in that family and declared that his wife's family was as honorable as the Hans, who owned similar Manchurian forestlands. He claimed his status exactly matched that of the Han uncle who managed those lands. Chungduk added, scornfully, that at least someone in the family would be making real money.

Years before, after their father had died, just as Chungduk began his studies in Seoul with an old tutor from the closed Confucian Academy, it fell to Han to find his younger brother a wife. Han assumed that Chungduk would be married shortly after his studies, and hoped that a few seasons at home together would redefine their boyhood camaraderie on a scholarly level. He couldn't have guessed how much change would occur in the three years of Chungduk's absence, including dissolution of the yangban class, rise of a new intelligentsia spurred by multifarious newspapers and patriotic clubs, and Chungduk's decision to attend the Methodist college. As soon as Han had adjusted to his head-of-household responsibilities, his new wife and her Christian religion, his mother died. At that time Han understood the Japanese at court coveted his paintings, but he believed that only the highest ministers, or the king himself, had authorized the commissions for his work. He continued to study the old texts, painting and writing calligraphy in classic style, refusing to see that the outside world encroached like wind and rain lapping at sandstone, eroding the once-solid ground that generations of Han men had stood upon to guide their lives.

Han ambled across the market square, passing a row of shops that included a photographer's studio. He recalled the day Chungduk returned from Seoul, waving a photograph of a young woman. Han had greeted his brother warmly, taken aback by Chungduk's height and strong features shed of adolescent ambiguity. But the familiar dimple appeared on

Chungduk's right cheek when he flashed the same broad smile, his eyes as mischievous as ever.

"*Hyung-nim,* Elder Brother," Chungduk had said, flapping the photo. "I've decided to spare you the headache of finding me a wife. Wait until you meet her. She's completely perfect!" He mentioned the woman's family name and described their business in Manchuria.

Shock and disappointment had erased the joy of seeing Chungduk. "You couldn't wait for me to find you a suitable wife. Instead you choose to dishonor this family by lowering yourself!"

And now, even as he felt a breeze penetrating his Western-barbered hair, Han refused to regret his decision. He could acknowledge, however, that it had been conceived in anger, particularly since his brother had said, "Better a commoner who can feed his family than a yangban with no position, dwindling funds and no future. Tell me what your old-fashioned education is doing for you now!"

"How dare you speak to me thus!" he'd said to this rebellious stranger in Chungduk's body.

"Hyung-nim, it's 1907! I have the right to choose my own wife."

Enraged that tradition would be sacrificed so quickly for so little, Han had spoken the last words he would utter to Chungduk. He had stood and turned aside. "No brother of mine would ever consider such a thing." But now, as he climbed the few steps to the bookstore, Han saw that his heart believed otherwise, for his mind's eye was full of the laughing dimpled boy he'd taught to swim in the back pond. Perhaps their ancestors or fate—or God—would intervene.

In the bookstore, Mr. Pahk removed his spectacles and greeted him cordially. Han breathed in the comfortable mustiness of aging paper and ink. The dust held the light as if it were filtered through old trees in a forest glen. "Have a seat," said the bookseller. He produced a stool from behind a narrow counter and slid aside piles of magazines and newspapers. He shook his head, his thick lips gloomy. "I'm afraid more are gone." He made a striking-match gesture.

Han's stomach turned acidic. He said nothing for a time, then swallowed. "Yah, I wondered when they'd find your mother lode."

"They warned me that I must carry only authorized periodicals and books." Pahk wiped his glasses on his sleeve and rewound them around his fleshy ears. "I know I was lucky for too long." His eyes appeared enlarged through the lenses as he peered at Han. "Now it's up to you."

The two men stroked their beards. Han shuffled through the newspapers and magazines on the counter, then sat upright to examine a slim bound journal printed in Korean. "What's this?"

"Hmpf. 'New cultural policy,' they say. A 'literary' magazine delivered from Seoul this morning. Propaganda written in Korean to fool us." Pahk spat.

Han quickly scanned the bylines. "I've heard of this man. He's an intellectual, and him, too." He shuffled through the pages. "These are all patriots! Have you read any of this?"

Pahk snatched a copy from the counter and pored through it. "I didn't believe the rumors, but it's true. And there's the government stamp. New cultural policy! So that explains all those Korean Christian newspapers from Seoul."

"Rumors?"

The bookseller leaned forward, his eyes on the front door. "They say Admiral Makoto is a moderate. They say that his replacement of Governor-General Hasegawa signals a new era—one that is culturally directed. It's their reaction to international pressure about March First. There's even talk of a women's journal, but I'll believe that when I see it!" He cackled, making a crude gesture about women.

Han reached inside his pouch, but Pahk waggled his ears and waved him away. "First issue, free to you!"

Someone entered the store. "Yes," said Han loudly, switching to Japanese. "Fine, then. I'll check back next week to see if you've got those translations." He pivoted away from the arriving customer and exited, taking note of the man's black cuffed trousers and shined leather shoes. He avoided his urge to examine the man further. There was little he could do at the moment if the bookseller was in trouble.

He walked slowly through the busy market street, arms clasped behind his back, the journal tucked comfortably beneath his vest, the sun warm on his shoulders. In the afternoon, he read the new journal in his study. His restful reading was disrupted by an impolite call, "Abbuh-nim!" and his daughter entered abruptly. Always this child managed to find ways to irritate him!

"I hope your message is lighter than your footsteps. Heavy as iron!"

Najin bowed and said, chastened, "Excuse me, Abbuh-nim." She sat to his nod and waited to be acknowledged.

He tried to ignore her rustles and breathiness, and attempted to finish reading his paragraph, an impossibility. "What is it?"

"Yee Sunsaeng-nim said they have new Japanese maps and teaching guides, and I must return all of my books, even the old ones from first term."

Though the news interested him, he wondered why she bothered him with it. "Show me the new lessons." What further lies would they teach now? Those heathens with their mere hundreds of years of existence knew nothing of history and culture.

"There aren't any books yet. We copy from the blackboard."

He frowned impatiently.

"Abbuh-nim, it's the books they want us to return. Must I?"

"Bring them."

She dipped and rushed to her room.

"Yeh-yah!"

Her footsteps slowed to a more ladylike pace. She returned and presented three booklets: a Korean children's primer, an annotated chart of world history and a pocket volume titled in Chinese, *A Complete Guide to English Conversation with Tone Symbols.*

"Who gave this to you?" He thumbed through the phrase guide for tourists.

"Sunsaeng-nim. One day after school." Her voice lowered. "She said I needn't sign for that one."

"They account for all your books?"

She nodded, her eyes down, her kneecaps bobbing.

"Sit." He examined the mass-produced phrasebook, its brittle pages already yellowed, the blue rubbery cover cracked and curled. "A gift?"

"Yes, I believe so. May I please keep it?"

"Do others have the same?"

"No, Abbuh-nim."

Her tone made him glance at her. It was good she was afraid of him, he thought. He'd talk to her mother about those unsightly scratches on her ankles. She was more rambunctious than Chungduk! He examined the other books. The historical timeline, printed in Japanese and wretchedly falsified, elicited a childhood memory: the exact timbre of his recitation of the ancient periods at age three before his surprised father, his proud tutor crouched outside the doorway. He asked Najin, "Have you memorized this?"

She recited the true dynastic chronology rather than the one printed in the book: "Gojoseon, Gija Joseon, Wiman—"

His chest knocked with sudden patriotism and a sliver of pleasure at her education, but he said, "Quiet! Do you want to get us all arrested?"

She crossed her hands and folded into herself.

"How is it you refuse to control your tongue! Best to be at school all day or your brother would learn your habits." There, at last she was still!

He considered the Chinese-English phrasebook. One day, they'd be a free nation again. The Shanghai provisional government worked to gain international support, particularly from America, but what did other countries care about Korea? He put the books before her. "Well then. You must return the two you've signed for and ask Yee Sunsaeng if she requires the third. In the meantime, keep it out of sight, as if it never existed. Should anyone come close to finding that book, it must first find the fire in the stove. Understand?"

Keeping his face stern as their eyes met, he was surprised by the pleasure he felt at her obvious gratitude. Her high regard of books satisfied him. Times were changing him despite himself! He dismissed her and fingered through his library, selecting anything that might be considered nationalistic or subversive. Mindful of Pahk's misfortune, he dusted his collection of *sijo* and other poetry, classical essays and history books. He wrapped them in expensive writing paper, thinking it a shame since it was precisely such days as these that demanded a basic Confucian convention: religious study of the mores of the past for insight into matters of the present.

He called his manservant and devised a plan to create a deeper hiding place for his books. He'd have Joong dig a pit below the wooden floor of the secret pantry, line it with camphor wood, then bury a chest of books. Joong was to do this work without speaking of it and without the aid of the gardener. Han considered the importance of Joong's silence in this task and counted five *won* into Joong's hand, the first time he'd ever given him money. Joong bowed deeply as the money disappeared, then he helped pack books.

HAN RARELY TOOK his meals outside the house unless an occasion required a supper, such as a visiting dignitary, a marriage or death. News about the independence movement's clandestine activities passed quietly from lip to ear when men greeted each other at church. As autumn advanced and the sun set long before the hour of curfew, it became obvious that such casual conveyance was too risky for anything other than a few words. The rash of new parishioners were clearly police spies and collaborators. Among the church elders, a chain of information passage evolved as the men began inviting each other to suppers.

One such evening, Han visited Deacon Hwang. The two men had finished eating and pushed aside their tables, Han silently regretting that Hwang's lay position prevented the serving of wine or tobacco. A portly graying man who wore Western clothes, Hwang, a yangban of lower status, had gained notoriety as a result of an education from the missionaries in Pyeongyang. Unfortunately, a terrible stammer undermined his desire to become a minister. He liked to say that his affliction was his calling to be a more humble man.

"Yuhbo!" called Hwang, adjusting his knees. Mrs. Hwang entered with a skittish young woman who presented yellow melon slices and sweet rice tea. Under Mrs. Hwang's critical eye and unceasing instructions, the young woman bowed nervously, served the fruit, cleared the dishes and slid the door closed.

The melon's ripe scent reached Han, giving him a sense of contentment that almost made up for the lack of wine. He nodded toward the door. "How's the daughter-in-law coming along?"

Hwang shrugged. "F-f-fine! Fine. Very shy. My eldest is probably more pleased than his mother, ha!"

Han grimaced at this remark, thinking that Hwang's efforts to overcome his verbal weakness left little opportunity to edit the appropriateness of what he said.

"At first," said Hwang, "she scorched my shirt trying to d-d-dry it by the fire, but now she's doing better. A mediocre cook, sadly. My wife will improve her soon enough. I'm told she's not crying herself to sleep anymore. Rises early and doesn't talk much."

"A blessing."

"Yes." The deacon cleared his throat and lowered his voice. "Reverend Ahn told me something he heard from the mission director. Overseas, it seems they're finally getting reports about the March First bloodbaths. There's political outcry, especially from the Russians and Americans."

"Ya-ah." Han put his cup back on the table; overly sweet and burnt-tasting.

"As a result, Admiral Makoto's every move is bound to be monitored. It's said the Japanese relied too heavily on the outdated B-B-British model of military colonization. They now think it more politically apt to focus on education and social reforms." Hwang bit into a melon slice and juice dripped down his chin. He wiped it with his fingers and flicked it aside, sprinkling the mat. He slurped another bite and smacked his lips. "What do you think of this, Brother Han?"

Han turned his head to hide his annoyance at Hwang's use of familiar address. He attacked the messy melon with his handkerchief ready. "I can easily imagine the title of this reform proposal, 'Educate the Natives.' Education? It's brainwashing!"

"An important distinction, to be sure. Time will reveal their intent."

Although this platitude was what Han expected from Hwang, its passivity aggravated him. He shifted to accommodate a growing stitch in his side. Mrs. Hwang's kitchen had yielded greasy dishes, heavily overspiced. The food had compacted to a clod in his gut, which he felt starting to rebel. "I've heard about new cultural reforms like these."

"You have? F-f-from whom?"

Han ignored the question and chose not to mention the new journal. Hwang would see a copy soon enough. "What can we expect? More schools so they can lie to our sons?"

"As a matter of fact, they're planning new universities, and reform for that women's college in Seoul, Ewha, to—"

"So they mean to further undermine our core principles!"

"Brother Han, women are b-b-bound to be given more latitude regardless. You know how many mothers were slaughtered and jailed in the name of their country. That c-c-country girl, Yu Gwansun, look at how her martyrdom is inflaming the people!" The story of the young Ewha student's recent death, after more than a year of torture in Seoul's prison, had reached the streets, spurred by Ewha president Lulu Frey's demand for the girl's body. Despite the atrocities she suffered, Yu Gwan-sun reportedly cried out for freedom and independence each day she was dragged from her cell to the torture chamber.

Han's ears burned, thinking of her ordeal and her remarkable bravery, and what *he* had withstood, and how easily they had broken him. "They shouldn't have marched—"

"Did they not shout as loudly as we did? Did they not die as tragically as men? Do they not desire independence as passionately as we do? Isn't your own daughter pursuing an education?"

"That's not your concern. Did your wife and your daughter-in-law appear on the streets that day?"

"Forgive me, B-B-Brother Han. This isn't the discussion we should be having."

Han settled onto his cushion and surreptitiously slipped a hand beneath his vest to press on the growing pain in his belly. He wished he had his pipe.

Deacon Hwang took the last melon slice. "There's news that bodes well. It actually might be advantageous for our sons."

"What could they possibly offer that would benefit us?"

"Advanced study abroad."

"They've already coerced thousands of our youth to attend university in Tokyo. Our sons are forgetting what it means to be Korean! Now they'll take the women too?"

"Not just Tokyo. Any worthy student, man or woman, can study in America, Germany, or France, perhaps. They also plan to expand Soongsil Academy and Union Seminary in Pyeongyang."

"Bribes. Means to control us!"

"Brother Han, I sympathize completely. I'm not arguing, just conveying what I hear."

Han quelled a rising desire that Ilsun might study in America. But what was he thinking? What of classical education? Would he even be able to find a tutor when Ilsun was ready? He changed the subject. "What news from Shanghai? Will a response be organized?"

"T-t-too many were arrested and shot." Hwang drank his tea and gazed steadily at Han, who kept his face impassive.

Han wondered, not for the first time, how the deacon had escaped beatings or arrest, and if others wondered the same thing about his relatively short prison term. However, he had scars to prove his loyalty. Indeed, spies were everywhere—but again, what was he thinking? Hwang was an old friend, a familiar face long before the annexation, and a trustee of the church! This was yet another evil of the occupation: that a man would suspect treason in his own circle.

"I'm weary and impatient," he said as an apology.

Hwang demurred, "On a long journey, even one's eyelids grow heavy."

"Thank you for dinner." Han clapped his thighs and stood slowly, feeling a recurring stab in his lower back and knees. He cursed those bastard guards who were to blame for his stiffness.

"There's one other thing, Brother Han." Hwang examined the melon platter as if more fruit would appear. "They say the expenses in Shanghai are exorbitant."

"I'll send Joong by tomorrow." He had already donated thousands to Syngman Rhee's provisional government and wondered now if he was merely throwing money into the sea. Another independence movement faction and a provisional government in Hawaii were also calling for his support.

"You've always been very generous," said Hwang, ushering him to the door.

Han grunted to pass off the perfunctory remark. He bowed goodbye and walked into the setting sunlight, an hour well before curfew, yet his eyes stayed keen on the darkening profiles of passersby, watchful for policemen.

# The Curious Power of Words

AUTUMN 1920

THE MORNING AFTER I TALKED TO FATHER ABOUT THE BOOKS, I RAN to school, hoping to catch Teacher Yee before the other students arrived. In the field by the checkpoint, patches of fog faded in sunlight streaming like bright fans from high clouds. From the humidity coating my cheeks, I could sense the coming heat. I rejoiced just to be running before the temperature rose. The woman who owned the bakery stood outside of her shop beside a tray of small cakes. "Hello, Auntie!" I flew by, breathing deeply to fill my lungs with the warm sugary smell of freshly baked goods.

"Aigu! You won't catch a husband running like that! That's not a girl. That's a wild animal, no doubt about it." Her words were lost in my footfalls. *She wouldn't yell to a boy,* I thought. *She'd say something about such*

*sturdy legs, what a perfect day for running, how clever to be in such a hurry!*
Up the hill, I reached the turn just in time to see my teacher's skirt slip
behind the school's front door. I walked the remainder of the way, so I
wouldn't be out of breath when I arrived.

I'd decided that, not counting my mother, Yee Sunsaeng-nim was the
most beautiful and smartest woman in the entire world. She became my
hero on my very first day of school, when my name was called and all the
girls tittered and whispered over its oddness. She rapped on the desk and
made it clear that such meanness would not be tolerated, and that my
name had a lovely and pure sound. Now in my second year with Yee
Sunsaeng-nim, I still looked forward to the special smile like the one she'd
given me that day, with which she continued to recognize me as I did well
with my lessons. When she paced sedately between the students' desks,
nodding rhythmically to arithmetic recitations, I admired her graceful
long torso, the way her slim hips made her skirt swish like a muffled bell
about her ankles. When she passed my desk, she left a sweetness of spring
air in the stuffy classroom.

However, after the summer monsoon break, two frown lines had
made permanent inroads in her silken forehead. Teacher Yee's perfect features usually exuded warmth and serenity, even when girls hadn't finished their homework. My neighbor Hansu used to tell me how his
teacher yelled and regularly beat their shins and forearms with a stick.
Until this term, Yee Sunsaeng-nim had been a model of studied calm, but
yesterday she'd snapped at one of the brighter students for a simple pronunciation error. All the girls whispered during lunch break about her
strange irritability and wondered what hidden malady she suffered. "She's
not coughing up blood!" one girl said. I told them they were acting as stupid as headless chickens with their pointless gossip, and it was no wonder
that Yee Sunsaeng-nim looked exhausted. Everyone snubbed me for the
rest of the day, even my best friend, Jaeyun.

Below the sign CHUNGHEE SCHOOL FOR GIRLS, I composed myself,
straightening into the posture of an intelligent young lady. I listened for
my teacher's daily classroom preparations—maps snapping on rollers,
papers riffling, chalk tapping and squeaking—but not a sound came from
the classroom. I cracked the door, peeked in, then quickly shut it. Yee
Sunsaeng-nim was sitting stiffly at her desk, her shoulders rigid, her face

covered by both hands. The morning shadows made her appear as translucent and still as a block of salt.

I tiptoed outside and thought a moment. Then I banged against the two front doors, ran down the hall slapping my feet, dropped my book bundle and kicked the classroom door open. "Good morning, Sunsaeng-nim!"

She now stood at the blackboard, as if posting the day's schedule, and said, "A sloth of bears! A gaggle of geese! Not one young girl." She smiled, saying, "Have you come early to clap erasers?" and I was relieved to see her returned to normal.

Cleaning blackboard erasers was still my favorite classroom chore, although at my heady age of ten, I'd outgrown it. I'd knock them against the brick building, banging out new Chinese characters we'd learned. By the time the erasers were clean of chalk dust, my favorite words were also clapped away. *Imagination. Teacher. Independence. Goddess.* The wind ciphered my dust words and scattered them above the heads of the townspeople, through the tops of tallest pines, along craggy mountain ridges, high into rain clouds to drizzle on the vast waters of the Yellow Sea. I imagined the dark-tanned faces of fishermen turned up to greet the rain, unaware of my special baptism by words. Yesterday I'd tried to feminize the word *scholar.*

"Sunsaeng-nim, I'm returning the books I've had at home." I unwrapped my bundle and removed the books.

"Yes, and now the principal says that all the books, no matter what kind, must be reviewed. I'm afraid they'll be destroyed." She turned her head, but I saw tears.

"Please don't worry. I've promised to hide it well."

"What?"

"The Chinese-English phrasebook you gave me."

"Yes, perhaps that's right. Everything else is ruined." Her shoulders slumped and she hid her face in her hands.

Something was terribly wrong. Fear and concern made me bold, and I touched her wrist. "Are you ill, Sunsaeng-nim?"

She grasped my hand, her face contorted in a way that reminded me of my mother giving birth. "Illness! If only it were that simple!" She twisted my fingers painfully.

"Excuse me, Sunsaeng-nim. Should I get help? Do you want the principal?"

"No! No—oh, I'm sorry, Najin." She touched my shoulder. "Come sit for a moment before the others arrive."

My fingertips thrummed with released blood, and I thought to offer her a hand massage, anything to help relieve her of her demons. "My mother taught me how to relax the hands. May I show you?" We sat on the front students' bench and I opened my palms.

"No, thank you." She held my hands gently in her lap. "Such a thoughtful young woman you are. Yes, you should hide the phrasebook. And should the Japanese ever come to your door, you should hide yourself as well as you can." Her skin turned waxen and her eyes seemed to tunnel inward. "Even if it's the police. Especially if it's the police. Monsters! You must hide, do you hear me?" Her voice sounded trapped in her throat; her breath smelled of ash. She twisted our hands together. I was surprised at my own feelings of being more worried about her than afraid of her strangeness. My mother's lessons had finally sunk in, I thought, but it was easy to think first of my beautiful teacher, whom I deeply loved. I examined her fingers as if they were wounded birds, and massaged the thickest part of her palms as my mother had taught me.

She turned her hands and held mine still. "Thank you. You have a healing touch for such a young girl. Perhaps you'll be a nurse someday."

Warmth from the compliment spread to my neck and ears, and I wanted to give her something back. "Is anything wrong?" I asked shyly.

"I'm going to tell you a secret. You mustn't tell any of the other girls. You're my best student and I have only the highest hopes for you."

I flushed again and lowered my eyes.

"Times are only going to get worse and I may not always be your teacher." I looked at her in alarm. "Not now, but one day, yes," she said. "It doesn't matter who your teacher is. You must never stop learning and asking questions. A woman's life is hard. Without a husband it's nearly impossible. But nowadays, with education, a single woman such as myself can at least be of some help to her family." Her voice broke, her cheeks rivulets of ignored tears. I sat bound by the intensity of my teacher's heightened emotion and inexplicable revelations.

"My brother and my betrothed—both—died this summer. The last time I saw my fiancé was more than a year ago, the day before the demonstration. I learned only recently that he died, and for all that time I knew nothing about him. His father wrote to say he'd been badly beaten during the madness in Seoul, and he became like an idiot and lived on, unable to care for himself, more helpless than a deformed newborn, until mercifully he died. My brother also went to Seoul and was taken to Gyeongseong Prison. He died of pneumonia there. They came for my father two weeks ago, and no one can tell us where he is or even if he's alive."

I could think of nothing to say and almost wanted to cover my ears. I wondered about Hansu in prison. Had he been beaten? Was he still alive? I felt crowded on the bench with Yee Sunsaeng-nim, the sides of our skirts touching. What was I supposed to say? I couldn't think of a single lesson from my mother that would apply. But oh! My poor teacher!

"If only that was the worst of it." She slumped and turned away, a hand covering her eyes. "I'm glad my fiancé is dead! The shame!"

Not understanding what she was saying, I was both frightened and thrilled by her rawness. My heartbeats seemed to inch us closer together on the school bench. I wanted to say, How awful! How sad! but the words wouldn't come out.

"It doesn't matter," she said. "I can never marry now. One day you'll understand. Once a woman's virtue is stolen, everything is ended for her. If my mother didn't need me, I would, I would—if only I could!" She gazed blindly toward the window, silent tears wetting her sleeves. She shuddered and pulled a handkerchief from her waistband, wiped her eyes and blew her nose loudly, oblivious of the crude sound. "So you must study hard, learn a good profession and at all costs avoid the police." She stood and looked at me, appearing almost wholly Yee Sunsaeng-nim again. "Can you promise me you'll do that?"

I nodded, though I was full of questions. Was having a dead fiancé shameful? What had she been looking for outside the window that might have helped her? My curiosity loosened my tongue at last. "I'm sorry for your brother and future husband, and . . . my neighbors' only son is in prison too. They say he'll be home soon. But when your father returns, won't he find you another husband?"

"I—I've said too much. I haven't talked to any— I only wanted to impress upon you the importance of your education. I was much like you when I was a girl, always in trouble for talking back to grownups." Our eyes met. I thought the wetness in her dark irises made them only purer. "Try to take advantage of your willful independence. I know your mother worries about these traits, but you can learn to manage them and advance yourself. You must remember not to deaden your natural instincts, but instead hold them living inside of you like a sword sheathed in your intelligence. Think of what Shakespeare says: 'How noble in reason; how infinite in capacity!' You're smart and capable, very empathetic for a girl so young, and with our lives in turmoil, you'll need all your talents developed to their fullest in order to sur—" Her word caught on a sob, and she stopped long enough to calm her breathing. "Yes, in order to succeed."

I was among the advanced students and had just been introduced to Shakespeare, but her reference to him now made him seem like a scholar-god. "Yes, Sunsaeng-nim. You're sounding like my mother," I said, hoping she would smile.

"The first bell will ring soon." She rose, pressed her hands against her temples and smoothed her hair. She seemed smaller, her skin drawn tightly across her cheekbones. "Why don't you take the books down to the principal's office? There's a crate by his desk for them."

I was reluctant to let go of the private adult moment we'd had, aware that it had made me more special than all of the other girls, and contrary to what I might have expected on any other day, this made me feel bad. I ambled slowly down the hall, shuffling the two books front and back. Confused and feeling helpless, I wondered why her personal tragedy sounded more like a warning than the terribly sad news it was.

WHEN SCHOOL LET out, my classmates gathered as usual to walk down the hill together. They yelled at me to hurry up, but I waved them on, pretending I'd forgotten something. It had been a long day. During class, Sungsaeng-nim had acted mostly normally, sometimes a little sterner than usual, but I was all jumbled inside and needed time to think. I leaned out of sight on the side of the building, the brick hard against my shoulder blades. The coarse surface caught hairs from my braid, which tugged at my scalp. The image of Sunsaeng-nim at her desk, head buried in hands, surfaced. I tried to separate my confusion into subsections—like tackling a complicated sentence, my desire to help my teacher foremost. With eyes shut, a prayer came to my lips. "Father God, please bring Sunsaeng-nim's father home and make everything the same as before." But it was more than that. "Father God, please find Sunsaeng-nim a new fiancé and make her father safe. Her mother too." I tried again, feeling increasingly lonely. "Father God, please help Sunsaeng-nim to be happy." Too short, and my eyes had been open that time. "Father God," I began, with hands clasped tightly to my chest, "I promise to be more ladylike and less willful and independent. I promise to study hard and learn all that I can, if you let Sunsaeng-nim marry again and bring her father home. Amen. And make her brother an angel. And let her know that somehow. Amen."

As I walked home, the lengthening shadows seemed darker, their origins unknown. I wondered if it was cheating to make the same promise to God for Yee Sunsaeng-nim as I had for my father. Although Mother would say it wasn't Christian to honor esteemed elders with prayer in the Confucian manner, I decided I'd also say a prayer on my teacher's behalf to Shakespeare. It was all I had to offer.

The smoke of burned trash clung to the alleyways. I dragged my feet, the stones in my path no longer begging to be kicked, fallen brown leaves fluttering aimlessly about my ankles. I didn't notice the vendors packing their goods and rolling up mats, nor did I smell the enticing steam of *jajang* sauce from the noodle man. But the sideways glance from a policeman patrolling with his partner quickened my step, and then I ran until my family's gate came into view.

I heard a commotion behind the neighbors' wall. Perhaps the Changs had returned! Was Hansu released? Maybe that meant Teacher Yee's father would also be home soon. I remembered my prayers and straightened my shoulders, primly hurrying home. Byungjo opened the gate holding a hand hoe and wearing his beaten straw hat. The gardener was a mere head taller than me and looked much older than his thirty-six years. His wrinkled skin, darkly tanned from spending most of his working hours outdoors, hung from his narrow bones like forgotten rags. I asked if he'd seen the neighbors.

He shrugged. "I see nothing, but your mother had me open their shutters and untangle their courtyard this morning." He walked away, muttering about stubborn overgrowth and the disgraceful state of the Changs' garden.

I kicked off my shoes at the front door. "Umma-nim!" My feet slid on the shiny wood.

In my mother's room, Kira was washing the floor. "Not here. The neighbors are back, and your mother went to bring them food."

"Is Hansu home too?"

"I don't know. She said you could go over there after you wash your face and hands." Kira wrung her floor rag and brushed sweat from her forehead with the back of her wrist. She smiled at me, her gold-lined tooth glinting. "You look clean to me, but she'll want you to do as she says."

I splashed so much water on my sleeves that I had to change my blouse before letting myself in through the gate adjoining our properties, which had been left ajar. I was glad to hear laughter. I hadn't been to the neighbors' for a long time, and their house looked shrunken, the gardens raw from Byungjo's work.

"Umma-nim?" Following sounds to the kitchen's back door, I found my mother and Hansu's mother mixing eggs with meal, chopped scallions and squash for pancakes. Dongsaeng sat on the porch just outside the opposite doorway, playing with gourds. From the steaming pot on the stove I smelled bone marrow soup. The Changs' kitchen was half as small as ours with only one stove and no hearth. Most of its few shelves were dusty and bare.

"Yah, here's the thoughtful neighbor girl!" Hansu's mother wiped her palms on her apron and grasped my hands. A tiny woman with gray streaks in her hair, she had the same straight brows and scoop-shaped eyes as her son. "I told your mother about the mysterious gift we received before we left for Seoul, and just as we guessed, she said the comb was yours. You've made your mother proud."

I blushed as she patted my shoulder. Mother smiled, saying, "You'll spoil her." Dongsaeng flapped his arms, and I lifted him and kissed his pudgy hands.

"How is Hansu's father?" I asked politely.

"He's very well; sitting with our son as if he were still a little baby. And yes," she said, seeing the question on my lips, "he is well. Weakened, and grown in ways we prayed that God might have spared him . . ." She turned to the stove and wiped her eyes with her apron. "We're making healthy soup. Go and see him! In the front room."

Hansu's father, a gaunt and lanky man, had a long face topped with thick hair that stood straight up, reminding me of carrot greens. He seemed to be dozing, sitting against pillows that obscured my view of a makeshift bed. I bowed and said softly, "It's the neighbors' daughter."

"Najin!" said Hansu. His feet stirred beneath the quilt.

"Don't get up, son," said Hansu's father. "Come in, young lady, and visit a while. I've things to do." He patted my shoulder as he left.

Hansu, pale and shockingly thin, beckoned me to sit on his father's vacated cushion. Something was wrong with his other hand, which rested outside the blanket. The last three fingers were crooked and bent, zig-zagged at wrong angles. I looked at him in pity and gasped at a shiny red scar tracing his hairline down to his ear.

"Just a little cut," he said.

"Your hand—"

"Still works." He wiggled the fingers. "I'm used to them already. But mother's had to give up her dream of me playing the *gayageum*," he joked, referring to the stringed instrument women entertainers played.

I settled next to him and soberly held his good hand. "I missed you, Oppa." It made me feel warm and content to call him Elder Brother.

"It's good to be home."

"Are you— Was it bad?"

His eyes narrowed. "It's past. But I met many patriots! Men from Pyeongyang and Seoul. I wouldn't have survived without them."

"How was— Do you mind me asking?"

"It was hard, little one. Nothing you need to hear about. But God was with me, and for that reason I was meant to be there. I'm certain of that."

"But you're so good! Why would he want to punish you?"

"No, it wasn't God's punishment." He closed his eyes, and I saw a new frown line cut deep in his brow, which reminded me of Sunsaeng-nim. "It was the Japanese who arrested us, but it's far more complex than that. One of the good things that happened was I now have an opportunity to go to college in Pyeongyang. A man I met—a famous intellectual, known throughout Pyeongyang!—he offered to sponsor me, even if I decide not to study theology."

I remembered on our walks home from school, Hansu's resignation when he spoke of what his future held: the unwanted possibility of a clerical job with his father or the slim chance of an academic scholarship to Yonsei University. Without position, contacts or cash, and with less than stellar grades, the latter option was more of a dream than a hope.

I patted his arm to show him my genuine happiness, and he smiled. "You would have laughed to see how we managed to communicate."

"What do you mean?"

"Talking wasn't allowed, so we wrote in the dust with our fingers. It was months before I heard my mentor speak a single word." His smile faded. As curious as I was about his experiences, I wanted him to not remember bad things.

"Will you still marry?" I said, thinking of my teacher.

"That also is a blessing. She still waits and agrees that more education is a good idea. Otherwise I'd be stuck like my father, working half-pay to fill out papers for the government." I hadn't realized that Hansu's father worked for the Japanese. It must have been helpful when Hansu's father was arrested. I'd seen him trudge the sidewalks at sunup and sundown, to and from some place of business that I'd never thought about before. It would be rude to ask more about his job. Self-censorship won over my curiosity and kept me silent. I twisted a corner of his blanket, thinking how strange it felt to be tongue-tied with Hansu.

"How's school? What's your favorite subject?"

"I love words the best!"

"Ah! There's a new subject in school, is there? Words?"

"Father studies words!"

"I'm teasing, silly girl."

I punched his shoulder playfully. "I like reading and writing. We just learned about Shakespeare and I learned something new I can teach you."

"Teach me."

"Listen." I took a breath and said carefully in English, "Whe-la eesu bus-u stop-u tow-tow-nuh?"

"Wonderful! What does it mean?"

"Where can I catch the bus going downtown?"

His smiled warmed the room. He had me repeat it and then tried it himself. "There are buses in Seoul, and trams, trucks, automobiles, rickshaws, dozens of carts, hundreds of shops. So many things you would have loved to see."

"Maybe one day," I said, my eyes down.

"You would've loved our parade of patriots! So many men—and nearly as many women—shouting and marching together. I'll never forget that. A sea of people, and I was swimming among them." He closed his eyes, his lips peaceful.

"We had marchers too. Not as many as yours, I'm sure. We saw Father marching."

"You have much to be proud of. Another great patriot."

I had never before considered my father as someone to be proud of. I remembered my fear on the night of his arrest, then felt shame. Although he'd been beaten, he was home after sixteen days, while Hansu and others, like Teacher Yee's poor family, had suffered much more. "But others fared worse. You've been gone a long time . . ."

"You mustn't think like that. Your father is an important scholar, well known in Gaeseong. They couldn't keep him locked up the way they could a marginal student who was merely one of hundreds, could they?"

"But you're not a marginal student!"

"Maybe not marginal, but still one of many. I'm blessed to be back in my own home, my parents strong, my betrothed still willing, my purpose renewed, my dongsaeng, little sister, beside me." He clasped my hand.

He seemed older and wiser, and I knew exactly what it meant to feel blessed—to have him as my honorary oppa. I gripped his hand. He was someone I could tell anything to, and it wasn't long before I opened my mouth, then frowned, then acted as if nothing had happened.

"What is it? You've grown—very pretty, I might add . . ."

"Don't say that!" I blushed. "My nose is huge."

"Yah, you're right about that. Big as a stubborn boar's." He laughed, and I slapped his arm. "I know you too well," he said. "You're thinking about something you're afraid to ask. Ask away! I've nothing to hide."

"I heard something today I don't understand, but it's a secret."

The outer edges of his eyes curled with familiar mischievousness. "Can you go outside the secret part and tell me generally?"

"Well . . . if a woman is to be married but her future husband suddenly dies, can she not get married at all?"

"Is this your way of telling me you're betrothed, little one?"

"Me? Never! Oh, you're teasing again."

"I'm sorry. How does the future husband die?"

"Um, an accident, or illness, or maybe in prison, like you were. Does that matter?"

He studied me gravely. "None of the causes you name matter. Especially the last. Maybe the woman says she won't marry again because she is suffering a broken heart."

"Is that the same as broken virtue?"

His eyebrows flew up.

"What's wrong?" I saw his neck then his ears turn to flame. "Please excuse me! Did I say something rude?"

"Not quite the same, Najin." He averted his eyes. "These are quite grown-up questions for a—um—young lady. These are subjects a girl might discuss with her mother."

"Oh!" Understanding by his response what I'd asked, I blushed just as deeply as he. "Oh!" I covered my mouth.

"Never mind. I'm your oppa, right? No secrets between us."

I was so humiliated that I said an abrupt goodbye, stammering that I had homework and I hoped he felt better soon. I ran from the room, trying to keep the image of his indulgent smile foremost, anything to mask my embarrassment at broaching such an unbelievably crude subject—with a man!

It was only a little later in my room that I began to suspect the appalling thing that had happened to Yee Sungsaeng-nim. I was distressed at the horror of it and frustrated by my ignorance and that I had no one to ask.

I USUALLY WALKED to and from school with Mun Jaeyun, with whom I shared a desk. She was the only child of the doctor who had stitched up my father's forehead on March First. Their house was halfway to school, and when I called at the gate, my friend would come running. We held hands and chatted about other girls and the allegiances and rivalries that seemed to come and go with every classroom period. We also talked about Yee Sunsaeng-nim, who seemed fine during the several weeks after our private conversation—even cheerful sometimes—despite her pallid complexion. But one morning in early October when we entered our classroom, we saw Principal Shin sitting at Sunsaeng-nim's desk, leafing through the day's lessons. I dropped my copybook and Jaeyun jostled into me. Frowning at the commotion, the principal told us to sit until all the other girls arrived. The ten-minute wait was an eternity. I held Jaeyun's sweaty hand under the desk, my own palm bloodless and cold. Everything seemed enlarged: the intake of breaths as one then another girl came in and saw Principal Shin in the teacher's chair, a bench scuffing, the sweet-sour smell of men's hair oil that now filled the front of the room, the chalk screeching as he wrote the day's schedule on the blackboard. I thought I heard my heart beating. All the girls had long been seated, and if he didn't say something soon, I felt I'd explode.

Principal Shin closed the door, faced the classroom and clasped his hands behind him. "Attention, girls," he said in a voice as soft as water. He cleared his throat and found his usual authoritative tone, "Attention, girls! I have bad news. Yee Sunsaeng-nim has died." Some girls cried out. Jaeyun put her head on the desk and her shoulders shook with sobs. I struck the desktop once with my fists as tears fell unnoticed on my books. In a corner of my mind, I thought how odd it was that we all knew something terrible had happened, and yet it still felt like a blow when Principal Shin finally said the words. I wanted to raise my hand to ask Yee Sunsaeng-nim about this curious power of words, and then I felt the loss, and buried my head in my hands.

"It's a very sudden . . . a sudden illness that . . . moreover, a tragedy for us all. You must pray for her soul. Let us pray." Amid weeping and sniffling, Principal Shin bowed his head. "Heavenly Father, give us comfort as we learn of this sudden loss of our honored teacher. Please help the young ones to understand this—so sudden, and that Sunsaeng-nim rests peacefully in heaven, well, and that Sunsaeng-nim . . . And, moreover, with your great mercy, these students will only remember her with the greatest kindness, as we all do, and help us to study hard to honor our teacher's memory, and—" He cleared his throat and ended hastily.

The remainder of the day passed somehow. My head pounded and I couldn't stop crying. I blew my nose and remembered Yee Sunsaeng-nim loudly blowing her nose on the morning of our talk, and I cried again. By midday, a cold hardness settled inside me, and I felt empty and exhausted. Principal Shin tried to motivate us by saying that Yee Sunsaeng-nim would want us all to continue as before. "Think of how you can prove to everyone what a fine teacher she was! Moreover," he said, "your new teacher—yes, a new teacher will come soon—must see how well she taught you." He plowed through our lessons, visibly agitated by our unceasing tears, but not once did he lose his temper.

By the end of that long school day, I was sad and confused, yet also strangely alert. Jaeyun and I walked wordlessly to her house and clasped hands tightly before parting at her gate. I hugged my book bundle to my chest and headed home, the familiar roadway feeling as foreign and insignificant as the classroom was without Yee Sunsaeng-nim. What had really happened to her? I thought about the conversation we'd shared, and ached for her and what she must have endured. I didn't want to believe my heart, which told me she had ended her suffering herself. God didn't let victims of suicide enter heaven. I remembered the special sermon once given at church to condemn this method of preserving pride, made popular by tales of family betrayal and dishonorable love. I worried that her ghost would never rest, that she'd mourn her tragedies forever in the shadows of the classroom.

But I also believed that my teacher's spirit was now free, and that God would never turn away someone as good as Yee Sunsaeng-nim. I remembered what my mother had said about self-determination, and that I had understood it to mean I could decide things for myself. I raised my eyes to the treetops, to the swelling gray clouds and pure blue sky beyond. I would do as I had promised my teacher. I would be strong and become educated. And I would choose to believe what felt most true, that Yee Sunsaeng-nim was at peace, and that she would always be my teacher, looking down from heaven.

THAT NIGHT, THROUGH my bedroom window, the full moon cast faint silvery shadows until storm clouds hid its unmoving features. In bed, I smelled the tangy smoke of goldenrod and marigold flowers my mother burned in her brazier to chase mosquitoes from our quarters. When I told her about Sunsaeng-nim's death, she had cried out, then filled the afternoon with deep sighs and prayer. I said nothing about secrets or suicide. Mother told me that Sunsaeng-nim, a devout Christian, was in heaven. She read to me "in my Father's house are many mansions . . ." and the beautiful words made me cry. The tears also came from my confusion at feeling both comforted and guilty, because my mother's assurances were misinformed. I longed to speak with her honestly. Praying with her had given me solace, but now alone in bed, these feelings troubled me. And I understood fully that my beloved teacher was not here and would never be again, and I grieved.

Wind rattled the shutters and the roof tiles hummed with rain. I wiped my face and rolled off the bedding onto the cool floor. As I closed my eyes, I saw images of my teacher drowned in a river, her body broken at the bottom of a ravine, her belly slashed with a dagger in the way I'd heard the Japanese committed *seppuku* to save honor. I saw her in a dark forest in the rain picking poisonous roots to boil into a deathly broth, her hair wet tendrils dripping tears down her agonized face. Was this her ghost come to haunt me? I shut my eyes tighter to pray, but only a promise to study hard came to mind. I repeated that promise again and again to the rhythm of the rain, until at last the graceful curve of Sunsaeng-nim's body moved across my vision and I saw her walking by the blackboard, in her hand a piece of chalk dancing like a spring blossom in a breeze, bowing gracefully to the tempo of the morning's recitations.

# The Royal Seal

## SPRING 1924

THE SCHOLAR-ARTIST HAN DECIDED THAT NAJIN SHOULD BE married. That would be his response to yesterday's letter of inquiry from an old acquaintance as to the availability of his daughter. On this fine morning, he would write his consent. Temperate breezes brought scents of apple and plum blossom through the fully opened door leading to the outer porch and garden. Cardinals and sparrows called and sang early mating songs, inspiring him to flowery salutations, while a mockingbird mother squawked irritably at a squirrel too close to her nest. As Han glimpsed the swoops of her tail, it seemed to write in the air the symbol for many sons—her prayer for a nest full of boys. All of nature was aligned with his purpose on this day! At his writing table, he sat comfortably on a soft mat of double woven grass, and tied his sleeves above his wrists. He wrote elegantly on sheaves of whitest paper, using Chinese to reflect the formal solemnity of his response, and quick brushstrokes to hint urgency.

He thought that at age fourteen Najin was woman enough. She'd graduate from the girls' school when the term ended in three months, and what better time than soon after that? A providential harvest moon wedding! And since such a decision was beyond his wife's role, it mattered little that she would be opposed. The Kabo Reforms said women couldn't be married until sixteen, men until twenty, but this unenforceable law was generally ignored.

Han considered it his personal responsibility to challenge Japan's attempts to suppress Korea's mores and ethics. Hadn't he refused to name his own daughter for that very reason? After the death of so many infants in his attempts for an heir, it was difficult to deny the irony that the first to survive was female, and one with health that was as stubbornly strong as her obstreperous personality. Now there was Ilsun. Japan's laws were meant to eradicate the ancient moral right of male ascendancy, and he refused to support the implication that a female child could come into this world with the same rights as men. He believed that the highest standard of resistance was existential. He would campaign against colonialism with the example of his own life choices. At first he had little desire to find a name for a girl-child whose birth a few weeks after the Treaty of Annexation foreshadowed Korea's decline. And then as she grew, the Japanese occupation also grew entrenched. The more his traditions fell by the wayside of modernization, which he blamed entirely on the Japanese, the more he saw that his daughter thrived in the change, and she came to represent to him Korea's failures. He would resist the failure that surrounded him by refusing to name it—by refusing to name her.

Han wrote his letter and thought little of this resolve that had evolved over time—time that was its own kind of god, one that allowed procrastination, justification, forgetfulness—means to excuse one's own failings. He dipped his brush in ink, his thoughts centered on his moral obligation to his ancestry. As his father and his father's father would have wished, it was also his desire that his daughter be attached to an appropriately scholarly family. But damage had been done. He'd need a family liberal enough to accept a missionary-educated girl, yet traditional enough to subdue his daughter's ambitions for more. His prediction that the imperial educational initiatives were thinly veiled plans to educate Korean youth into becoming Japanese sympathizers had come true. *They can build a thousand public schools,* Han thought, *they can ban our native tongue, our flag, the teaching of our long independent history, but they cannot abrogate our traditions.*

To prevent his wife's involvement in the engagement, he'd eschew the services of a matchmaker to spy on the boy's family. Besides, he knew them well enough. Han remembered the boy's father from their days studying together at the Confucian Academy, preparing for the civil examinations, until the reforms had eliminated the exams, which were the only opportunity he'd had to gain a ministerial post and follow his ancestors' tradition of officialdom. Instead, he was left to wait for royal recognition through occasional commissions for artwork or calligraphy. Yes, he had gained renown, but the method had been slow and undignified.

The prospective groom's father, Chae, slightly younger than Han, was a lesser scholar from Yuncheon, one hundred li east in the mountains, a day-and-a-half journey. They were both painters in the Chusa tradition, and Han remembered that Chae was as much of a stickler for form and propriety as he was. Plus, he'd heard that Chae, a leader in his village, had been jailed and tortured for his participation in the March First movement. Upon learning this, Han had renewed the acquaintance and regularly corresponded with Chae as part of his resistance activities. In yesterday's letter, Chae had casually mentioned that his eldest son had turned twelve, and he would be honored if Han might consider a union between the two families.

So be it. His daughter's graduation come July would satisfy his wife's wish that the girl was schooled. If his wife needed help with domestic duties in lieu of his daughter's hands, she could find a decent girl who'd be grateful to work. In fact, since they were squeezing more taxes from everyone, there were plenty of girls from good families who'd embrace such an opportunity. *Aiu!* How irritating to think of women's concerns! But among those concerns was Ilsun's development. His son was exhibiting many of the rambunctious traits of his daughter—the prime reason to have her married off. It annoyed him that he was forced to pay attention to the children at all, but somehow he kept being drawn into their affairs. He was torn between his Confucian duty to ignore his young son lest he spoil him, and the fact that Ilsun was, after all, quite a plucky boy!

Although Ilsun's tutor, Khang, was quite old and not at all famed, he was a *chinsa,* a certified poet-scholar in the old tradition, and a vestige of the crumbling Confucian University in southern Gaeseong. Han had enjoyed a few evenings discussing poetry, history and philosophy with him, confirming that Khang was sufficiently versed to take on Ilsun's classical education.

Every now and then, during his habitual morning walk through his estate and to town, Han stopped in his son's study to listen to Ilsun's lessons. He appreciated the detailed attention Khang Chinsa gave to the T'ang Dynasty classics, and the chinsa's firm reproaches for Ilsun's mistakes. Hearing his son's five-year-old timbre reciting passages with exquisite clarity brought pride that wet Han's eyes. But his hardest struggle against pride was when he regarded Ilsun's calligraphy. For one so young, the boy showed remarkable communion with the brush. He had a natural instinct for pressure and stroke, as if his little boy's arm possessed an ancient sage's wisdom of the correct life force needed to express harmony between letterform and its meaning.

Yes, Han expected greatness from Ilsun. He refused to lament that Korea might never again be the kind of genteel nation that recognized classical scholarship and artistry. In one mere decade he'd witnessed a dependable and flourishing way of life, which had remained unchanged for centuries, fray like the tail of a kite caught in the razor winds of imperial breath. Winds of such violence could just as easily blow the other way.

Using a sophisticated code of metaphor and nuance that had developed among the yangban resistance, Han ended his sincere response to Chae's marriage proposal with a poem that reported on the growing presence of Japanese spies and the workings of key individuals in Gaeseong's independence movement:

> *Abundant growth in eastern fields shall triple both labor*
> *and yield.*
> *In fallow soil the farmers toil, while westbound crane and*
> *steadfast mule*
> *Cry songs, sow seeds, and evening's sun sets five hundred*
> *beams upon them.*

With this, Han conveyed that the number of Japanese police had multiplied, and revolutionaries with the code names Crane and Mule had traveled west to Shanghai with five hundred won for Rhee's provisional government. By "songs" and "seeds," Han alerted Chae to watch for articles published by the men in the national Christian weekly. He felt confident that the unrefined Japanese censors would see nothing hidden in a dreadful sijo about farming! He considered the large sum he'd given to "Crane" for Shanghai. He would have to reduce such contributions, though they never ceased asking for more. Taxes took anything extra from the farm, and it had been months since his last painting commission, a simple calligraphic scroll. Once he saw that a known collaborator in the palace had stamped the commission, he never fulfilled the order. With no income from calligraphy or painting, every donation he made to Shanghai now came directly from the family savings. This was the other reason Chae's proposal for his daughter's hand was timely; Han could no longer afford private secondary school for her or, God forbid, fees for Ewha Women's College.

He called for Joong, who hurried across the courtyard, shoes flapping. His servant crouched in the doorway to receive instructions. Joong, narrow-framed with a chest like a spoon, was yet unmarried at thirty-one. High cheekbones accented the crescents of his eyes and a boned ridge along his brow. His family had been serfs and slaves to generations of Hans. Slavery was abolished by the reforms, but Joong's mother, uncles, brothers and their wives still tended Han farmlands in a village sixty li north. As part of his household position, Joong received Han's worn clothing, except for the garments that distinguished the scholar's status, and had garnered a bonus of beautiful clothes when Han's younger brother had married and moved to Manchuria. As head of his family, his father having died years ago, Joong had responsibly taken the spare clothing to his uncle and brothers on his annual visit home.

Han folded and sealed the letter and gave Joong coins for the post, cursing as he silently admitted that for the price of a few jeon, he could rely on the letter arriving in Chae's hands within days, rather than having to send his servant to Yuncheon. The postal service had escalated in reach and efficiency after the Japanese crisscrossed the country with train tracks. The image had once inspired him to create an unusually stark painting: a resplendent phoenix struggling to fly in iron chains. It was urgent that Ilsun receive classical training. The last time Han had visited Deacon Hwang, there were men of all ages sitting together, not just chronological peers. What would be next? Women and babies joining in men's talk?

Han sighed. His consent in the mail, he would soon tell his wife. For now, he perused his winnowed shelves and settled on a slim volume of poems on the renewal of spring. When his wife appeared with Cook to ask if he wished to eat in his study, Han felt refreshed from his reading.

"In my sitting room," he said, choosing that formal setting as preferable for her to receive his decision. His wife took the tray from Cook and followed him, and after he sat, she arranged it so comfortably and with such pleasing grace that he was loath to ruin the simple moment of domestic harmony with upset. He said nothing, and she left.

He ate slowly, selecting morsels of rice, spring greens, winter radish gimchi, mashed soybean flavored with pork belly, and egg pancakes with wild leeks as carefully as he'd choose the words to tell her. Perfectly balanced in the ancient fivefold way, the food, washed down with sips of bone broth, sank warmly to his stomach. He quietly gave thanks for his wife's cooking skill, which with every meal provided variety and nutrition, and kept his sensitive digestion in balance.

After he'd eaten and Cook removed the dishes, he reached for his tobacco box and called for his wife. She sat before him, poured wine and folded her hands together on her lap. Her skin shone with the kitchen's heat, and though he surmised her mind was always busy with household planning or the children's concerns, she appeared calm and untroubled, the moon curves of her face still as smooth and pale as when he first saw her on their wedding day. He had been twenty; she, seventeen. Except for her well-defined nose, she had classic beauty, her eyes like two clean strokes of ink, her brow smooth and rounded.

The serene lines of his sparsely furnished room gleamed in slants of afternoon light. Birds chattered happily outside. He could hear their wings beating against budding tender leaves. He sucked dryly on his pipe. "Yuhbo, your daughter will soon receive a chest of fabric for her trousseau." The groom's family typically sent these early gifts—the first exchange toward the coming bond. Ignoring his wife's sudden sharp intake of breath and her surprised eyes directly on his, Han tapped and filled his pipe, and as she lit it, he noted that her fingers trembled. "From the yangban son of Chae Julpyang in Yuncheon. We studied together and I know his is an honorable family."

"But she has school until—"

"After her graduation. A harvest moon wedding. It's settled."

Her cheeks flamed. "Without once consulting your wife?"

His eyes narrowed and his mouth tensed in dismay. Never before had she raised her voice to him. "It is my right."

She straightened and glared openly. "Our only daughter. She's far too young!"

"The boy is twelve. It's a respectable gap. They'll have enough years before children."

"And you would refuse me the courtesy to decide for myself if this boy-husband is appropriate for her?"

"The decision is made! The letter of agreement was sent this very morning."

"This morning? She's still a child and not yours alone!"

Why would his wife persist in creating such outright discomfort between them? Having never seen it before, he hadn't expected her anger. "Your own mother married at this age."

"Yes," she said, her mouth bitter. "And lost three babies because of her youth."

"The girl is strong—"

"And intelligent and educated and deserving of better consideration than this!"

He smelled bile on his breath. "How dare you talk to me thus! You've roused the entire house with your anger!"

"Your action provoked it, your old-fashioned ideas! Are they even Christians?"

He tapped his pipe so hard it broke. He threw it across the room and it narrowly missed striking her cheek before shattering against the wall.

She paid no attention to the tobacco embers smoldering by her knee. Her voice was low and tight. "No one marries at this age anymore. And for good reason! What of a Christian marriage? What of your own Christian vows? I can't allow her to go, too young, still so much to learn, my hopes, her education—" She faltered as tears captured her breath, but she did not lower her eyes.

"She's had education enough. And see what it's done! She's less worthy as a bride. Her mind is full of the outside and her actions are as bold as a peasant's. Before she becomes completely useless she must marry! What does it matter if they're Christian or not? We owe everything to the generational traditions of my family. What is more venerable—a Christian visitation of a mere few centuries or thousands of peaceful years of orthodox living?" His nose flared; his breath flew hot in his lungs. "Woman—you make me argue with you—I won't have it!"

She bowed stiffly, her face white.

"It's decided!" He waved her away.

She rose, her blouse stained with disregarded tears as if she'd been caught in a rainstorm. She said at the doorway, so softly he barely heard her, "We shall see."

He wanted to fly at her and smash her stubborn will. Instead, he stomped furiously on the ember scorching the mat. "The house could've burned down! I won't have it!" His cries rang hollowly in the courtyard.

He paced, every step sending pain to his back. The church's Western influence was obviously at the root of her disrespect for him. When other men complained about their bickering wives, he had easily, proudly, kept his mouth shut. Now that he understood their grousing, it irked him all the more.

From the other side of the house he heard Najin cry, "No!" then her shouts, rough with tears. His mouth hardened and he yelled for Joong to get his coat, before remembering that he'd sent him out on the very task that had caused this unacceptable uproar. Tying on his hat, he shoved his feet into shoes and strode out the gate.

The downhill slope propelled him toward the market, and the high afternoon's brilliant freshness soothed his pounding temples. His lunch jostled loudly in his stomach, but his nose soon cleared to the faint scent of plum blossoms swaying high above the slab walls bordering the roadway. *They may have chased me from my home today,* he thought. *They may cry day into night, but they can do nothing to counter my decision.* He headed purposefully to the marketplace to engage in civil conversation with the bookseller.

IN THE FOLLOWING days Najin was not to be seen, though he heard her coming and going to school and her occasional donkey laughter or reprimands to his son. His wife appeared only as necessary and spoke perfunctorily, her shoulders stiff and her expression closed. Han quelled his wish to call her to his bed, aware that it was his body's base need to control her. He felt sure her higher sense of duty and obedience would soon prevail.

Indeed, as the rainy season came and went, his wife's arms seemed less rigid in her ministrations toward him. He could relax in her presence, and soon he breathed in quiet relief that she had accepted his decision. Sometimes in the gardens and on the outskirts of his awareness, he heard his children playing as before. He assumed a few more weeks would restore everyone to complacency.

One Sunday in May, as the family walked to church, Han felt a cool but nervous detachment from his wife and daughter walking behind him, and for once he was glad to suffer Ilsun's continuous nonsensical chatter as he ran about his knees: "Abbuh-nim, after church can we go to the bakery and get cakes? Abbuh-nim, look at how funny I can dance. Watch me kick this rock. See how far? Abbuh-nim, see how fast I can run circles around you!" Irritating as it was, it was better than the icicles at his back.

As a result of an injunction that cited modernization, the partitions dividing the church by gender had been removed last year. Everyone knew that the collaborators in the congregation wanted to watch both sides of the aisles. Han could now see his family across the aisle and a little ahead of him: Najin's unruly braids, his wife's small taps on Ilsun's head to quiet him, her perfectly tucked hair bun, her neck curve when she bowed for prayer. He recalled his wife's accusations about the wedding vows they'd made in this very church. He was certain that accepting God and Jesus as his Lord and Savior didn't conflict with his Confucian beliefs. Furthermore, four hundred years *before* the Bethlehem star heralded Jesus's birth, the Christian story and the practice of universal love had been expounded by the philosopher Mo Zi.

The sermon ended and everyone stood for a hymn and benediction. He glimpsed the dark suits of yet more new congregants and despaired. Not long after last autumn's terrible earthquake in Tokyo, Gaeseong was flooded with Japanese citizens, many of whom superstitiously believed that Koreans had both contributed to the devastation and taken advantage of it. Police reacted quickly and impartially to many street clashes—eruptions of pent-up resentments and imagined slights. The more the Japanese came and stayed, the more they usurped, compounding the difficulty in fighting complacency. He wished his wife could join him in seeing his daughter's marriage as a deterrent to stasis, an act of defiance against Japanese-instigated modernism.

Outside, Han bowed to Reverend Ahn, greeted others, had a few private words with Deacon Hwang, then walked home, his family a few steps behind. The rains had left a thin veil of moist air on a rapidly warming day. He remembered from his childhood the deep, cool dampness of the tall pines of the family's forests in Manchuria where they summered annually. Thinking of childhood and Manchuria naturally led his thoughts to Chungduk. A wedding celebration would present an opportunity to reconcile with his brother. His step quickened and he thought he'd take some time in the afternoon to consider this possibility. How would he find him?

Once home, his wife and daughter went to their rooms with Ilsun. It struck him as odd that they hadn't headed immediately to the kitchen as they normally would this hour on a Sunday. A bit later he heard the side gate open and saw his wife and daughter carrying a bundle to the Changs. Han settled into his study, his desk neatly spread with brushes, a carved inkstone, a celadon-glazed turtle with a small *o* for a mouth—his grandfather's water dropper—and sheaves of paper. He composed a letter to the future groom's father, whose last correspondence had welcomed the match and lauded the virtues of the bride. Chae had also mentioned in code his dissatisfaction with both the Shanghai and Hawaii provisional governments, and conveyed news that Kim Il-sung's guerrilla army had ransacked a Japanese copper-mining operation in the north. Han had whispered this news to Deacon Hwang.

He was surprised to see his son following Cook when she brought the midday meal, Ilsun asking to eat with him. He consented, and she left to bring Ilsun's table. He washed his son's hands with his at the basin, cautioning him against splashing. When Cook returned, she acted so jittery he was tempted to ask for his wife's whereabouts, but it wouldn't do for Ilsun to see his father begging information from a servant. It wasn't a market day and many shops were closed on Sundays—a testament to how much Christianity had made inroads into their daily lives. Well, the soup was hot and Ilsun's table manners required supervision. This mystery would unfold soon enough. He told Ilsun to pray and they ate.

When he heard his wife call "I'm home!" from the foyer, he took note of the long shadows cast by the fruit trees—an hour past the conclusion of his meal with Ilsun. He put his book aside and waited.

She entered and without a word handed him a letter. He felt his neck tighten even before looking at it. He refused to ask where she'd been, angered that she hadn't offered this information, which was obviously wanting. She sat composed in front of him and seemed subdued, although still distant. He deferred his attention to the letter.

He flushed when his fingers fell upon a torn royal seal. "You've read this!" he said before seeing that it was addressed to her. "Ah, your cousin writes. But why does she use such formalities?" Naturally, his wife and her cousin in Seoul wrote each other occasionally, but never had his wife received a document with an official seal. She remained silent and bowed. He opened the letter. The covering once seemed to have held something thicker than the single sheet it contained. It was dated two weeks before. Pressure mounted in his temples as he began to understand the depth of her betrayal.

> Dearest Cousin,
>
> How delightful to hear from you, and how wise of you to commend your daughter for Court. I, too, can never forget our days together long ago, for which I am eternally grateful. I will enjoy very much teaching her the highest of manners. Much has changed, but she will still benefit from the training, especially if she is as rounded in the arts as you say, and educated too. Many of the girls have some outside education now. In fact, there is an upper school nearby and I will see if she can be enrolled. Times change! But our memories are forever the same, and I cherish them as much as I do your letters.
>
> Enclosed herein is the official decree requesting her indefinite service to Her Imperial Majesty and the required traveling documents, all signed and stamped, tariffs paid. Of course she

cannot travel alone. I will send my handmaid and her husband to chaperone her journey, although it is no more than half a day. Arrange to meet them, Pang Longhee and Khang Kyungmee, by the ticket stand at the Gaeseong station at an hour past noon on Sunday, May 6. Perhaps I will be able to meet her train when it arrives in Seoul. If not, she will be well taken care of. Do not worry.

I am looking forward to her being with me in this lonely house, and I will be certain to keep you apprised of her progress, which, since she is her mother's daughter, is sure to bring respectful praise to her family's honorable name.

Fondly yours.

The letter shook in Han's fingers as he returned it to her. She raised both hands to receive it, and the graceful female gesture unleashed his rage. He dropped the letter and struck her fully on the cheek. She grunted and fell sideways to the floor. Blood trickled from her nose. She clutched the letter and struggled to sit up. Her hair came undone. He struck her again and she fell. He stood to deliver a blow to the back of her head but glimpsed his shadow on the wall, his arm raised high over the lump of her fallen body. He saw that he was no better than the prison guards who had hung him by his thumbs and beaten him senseless. With a cry, he fell to his knees. She shrank from him until she saw him sobbing. She held his head in her lap and laid her cheek to his, mixing blood and tears, crying out how sorry she was—not for sending Najin away—but for having to defy him.

# The Last Palace

SPRING 1924–SPRING 1926

I CRIED MOST OF THE WAY TO SEOUL, MUCH TO THE DISTRESS OF THE handmaid and her husband, who were sent by Imo, my aunt, to chaperone me. I was upset to be leaving home, anxious about what lay ahead and fearful of my father's reaction to my mother's deceit. Mother told me he wouldn't call me home, since the invitation had come from the palace. It showed how carefully she had planned my escape from marriage, and how deeply she had betrayed my father. My tears were for her sacrifice of her principles of duty and honor to Father because of me. I was overwhelmed with new understanding of her love, only to be saddened at having to part from her.

If I hadn't been so emotional, the train ride would have been wonderful.

Speed and noise, coal smoke, the massive quantity of steel that made trains possible, the passing countryside, soft armchairs in first class, people of all sorts in all manner of dress, the very act of traveling—in my misery I missed the excitement of all these things. I marveled at it in memory after I grew accustomed to sleeping in my little room down the hall from Imo.

Her house was traditional and tidy, with an inner square surrounded by twelve rooms, and a smaller courtyard that was flanked by the servants' quarters. Many homes lined her street, so foot traffic beyond her walls was steady. In addition to my travel chaperones—the handmaid Kyungmee and her husband, Pang, who was gardener and guard—Imo had a cook, a water girl and a housemaid. My bedding was fine, rather plush in fact, but the unfamiliar light patterns, the room's strange angles and noise from the street made it difficult to fall asleep. At first I mourned and wept a little, missing my mother's nighttime voice, but after that pain eased, I could fall asleep by forming the street-cast shadows into mystical words, and by trying to glean the secret messages whispered among the foreign noises.

With no men in the house to cook and sew for, Imo was eager to lavish her time on me. I didn't know what was planned beyond the vague directive of "court training," and only hoped to attend upper school. After a day of rest and a few days of sightseeing, Imo took me to her sewing room and showed me a chest full of beautiful fabrics. "You'll need new hanbok," she said, tossing bolts of linen and sheer silks on muslin she'd spread on the floor.

"For what?"

"Yah, you need to wait and listen to everything spoken to you before you start asking questions." She said this kindly, but I was embarrassed.

"Excuse me, Imo—"

"You see? Like a monsoon wind! Everything inside comes wildly out of your mouth. When sightseeing you didn't talk much, but I doubt you're aware of your many exclamations and sighs. Monsoon wind!"

I bowed my head silently, my ears feeling as if they were screaming red.

"Much better!" She patted my knee and smiled. "Well, you do sit perfectly and I've watched you walk. Your mother shaped your posture well. That's to your advantage." I kept my mouth shut and peeked at her face. Her wave-curved eyes showed warmth, but her closed-lip smile had a pronounced artifice. The smile tightened her jaw, accentuating her cheekbones and incrementally raising her carefully drawn eyebrows. I wondered if I would learn that smile.

Imo was a little taller than my mother and not fat, but pillowlike, soft and round in all possible ways: her nearly white skin and hands, full lips, tiny rounded nose, curved elbows and even her earlobes. She looked pliable and receptive, as if you could toss anything at her and it would make a dent, then settle in, but her austere elegance permitted only respect. She wore a scent that brought to mind lilies and oranges, and her artful use of cosmetics required close examination to see the painted lines and feathery powder. The few marks of age on her face only appeared when she frowned. Because she was a widow, she wore her hair in a simple bun, and this, too, was soft and round. Every gesture seemed practiced to perfection. With my pointy elbows, gawky legs, bony hips, wiry hair and scratchy voice, I was like an explosion of needles compared to her. She was right—thanks to my mother, my spine was straight—but I was of an age when all the other bones and muscles didn't quite know when and how to behave. Apparently, my tongue was in that same league.

"You'll learn feminine rituals and protocol. You will meet Princess Deokhye. When I told the empress who your family is, she thought the princess might enjoy meeting you, or at least she could study with you, and even if that doesn't flower into something more, you'll come with me now and then to visit the empress, so you'll need suitable clothes. Close your mouth," said Imo casually. She unfolded and refolded different bundles of fabric. Thrilled at the prospect of new dresses made of such gorgeous fabrics, I sat on my knees, trying to hold my body still.

"Princess Deokhye, the poor thing, is twelve. She's the Gwangmu Emperor's last child. Oh, how he doted on her! He had many children, and many died young. Only four are left, including the Yunghui Emperor. Princess Deokhye's mother, Madame Bongnyeong, whom you'll also meet, was the Gwangmu Emperor's third concubine. The women live in Nakson Hall—the Mansion of Joy and Goodness—in Changdeok Palace;

the princess in the third house, the most colorful." She studied me for a moment and said, "I will tell you a secret. She's been betrothed to the nephew of the lord steward for some years now, but unlike your engagement, it's a necessary arrangement to protect the bloodline. Yes, I know about your betrothal. I see a thousand questions written on your face. You have much to learn before I'll venture taking you to the palace."

Her casual way of being critical made it easy to accept, and I froze my features and waited, hoping she'd say more about the royal family. I knew that the former emperor Gojong's reign was titled Gwangmu, and that he had remarried after Queen Min's death, but I hadn't known he'd also had concubines. Jaeyun's eyes would open wide if she heard all this, and especially that I would meet the princess! This last thought gave me shivers of nervousness. The princess might be my junior, but she would be accustomed to manners I didn't even know about. I pledged to work hard and learn from Imo. She said nothing more and rummaged among the fabrics, and I kept silent too.

She called Kyungmee, and after undressing to my slip I was measured, prodded and exclaimed over. Accompanied by many tsks of dismay, *bony* was the most-used adjective during this ordeal. Imo chose five different pieces for skirts and two sheer neutrals for a half-dozen blouses, for this season, she said, with more to come for fall and winter, a wealth that exceeded my mother's and father's wardrobes combined. In addition to a stipend from her dead husband's family, Imo's riches came from land in the south managed by a younger brother, her only sibling. Her widowhood allowed her to spend impetuously, but I knew my mother would frown at this excess. "Imo-nim—"

"Yes, child." On the floor she smoothed lengths of rose-pink silk with an interwoven butterfly pattern and laid the measuring string against it, while Kyungmee wiped the scissors and snapped them open and shut.

"They're so beautiful, and so many, I'm embarrassed— Is it— Will I really need all these clothes?"

A quick smile passed through Kyungmee's neutral features before she bent to cut the silk, and I guessed I'd said the right thing. Imo handed me my clothes. "Not really. You probably only need three." She had the practiced smile from before, but this time her lips matched the softness in her eyes. "But look how much fabric I have just sitting in this chest. Why not indulge a little? I've hardly made new clothes since—in a very long time. It'll be a pleasure."

I knew that Imo's husband and son had been killed by the Japanese almost fifteen years ago, though I didn't know the whole story. Her genuine enthusiasm and her response had made it possible for me to not appear greedy. I bowed low, as graciously as I could, and used the honorific idiom. "This person gives deepest thanks, Imo-nim." She was so pleased she clapped her hands.

Imo's instruction took fifty days. She was a firm perfectionist and tried to inspire me by saying that when the present empress was betrothed, she had completed her far more stringent training in an impressive twenty days. I relearned how to sit, bow, eat and talk with an exacting precision that made me long to be home running in the gardens with Ilsun. I memorized the royal genealogy of several generations, including birth, ceremonial and posthumous names, style of address and reign title—a feat, since such titles typically filled an entire page. I also memorized the pavilions and halls of Changdeok Palace, which, with the famous Biwon Garden, comprised a square half-kilometer in the middle of the city.

Despite her strictness, Imo treated me more like a little sister than a student, and we laughed often, demurely of course. Her humor and attention helped alleviate my homesickness. She switched from being playful and finding enjoyment in all that we did to being frustrated and blunt when poise and precision leaked from my body and brain. I stabbed at a morsel of fish with my chopsticks, and she cried, "Rude! Rude!" She glimpsed a tiny part of my tongue when I put rice between my lips. "Disgusting! Dishonorable! Bow your head, you must bend to it!" My foot wasn't in the proper angle in the second stage of sitting down. "Decorum! Decorum!" My artificial smile was too artificial . . .

Copying her mannered style, and with her reprimands and reminders, I eventually achieved enough inner silence to present a correct face and posture, and I grew comfortable with the distinct inflection of court language. At home I had read the vernacular translations of the *Four Books for Women,* but Imo required me to read the original Chinese texts. I also slogged through *Instructions for the Inner Quarters, Notable Women, Concise Accounts of Basic Regulations for Women* and *Mirror of Sagacity,* among others. Reading these archaic roots of a thousand rituals was slow, but I persisted, for this study in itself helped prove my virtue, dutifulness and grace, and thus my filial obedience to my family, my father and hence to the emperor. While none of this was entirely new to me, the training was vigorous with seemingly more at stake. I often thought about my father's devotion to tradition. Certain that my leaving home had enraged him, I hoped this training would one day help to prove my own devotion.

On sunny days we went sightseeing, walking long distances to see ancient Buddhist holy sites and parks, or what remained of the four other palaces in Seoul. Sometimes the crowds were so thick that strangers— both nationals and Japanese—jostled against us, and I clung to Imo like a little girl. Downtown, we walked in the angular shadows of new government buildings and scaffolded steel skeletons. The broad paved boulevards and our occasional rides on the tram recalled my neighbor Hansu's boyish exclamations about the wonders of the city, but its telephone poles and ugly wires caging the streets, malodorous alleys, clumsy rigid buildings and unceasing noise made me yearn for mountain paths and unfettered skies. In Gaeseong, the Korean language was most often heard on the streets. Here, there were equal numbers of people speaking Japanese and Korean.

On a cloudy day in early June, we went to the north market, an entertainment activity for Imo who always wanted to buy me things, which made me uncomfortable and shy. On the way home we passed Gyeongbuk-gung, the former main palace, whose grounds were now dominated by a large white building with columns, the Japanese government seat. I sensed Imo's mood growing pensive. The gray day darkened and it began to drizzle. Saving my questions for later, I held on to Imo beneath her umbrella and we trudged home, stepping over streaming muddy gutters and past the concrete facades stained with rain.

It rained steadily into the evening, splashing loudly on the porches. In Imo's sitting room, Kyungmee served sweet rice tea, sliced pears and the fancy miniature rice cakes that Imo had bought at the market. She seemed subdued still, like an unfluffed cushion, and corrected me perfunctorily, "Two hands, that's right. Fingers closed when you hold your cup."

I asked to speak and she nodded. "Imo-nim, if I may ask, is Gyeongbuk Palace where Queen Min died?"

"You mean Her Imperial Majesty Empress Myeongsong. Yes."

This was the posthumous name and title of the former queen, the second consort of King Gojong before he changed his status to emperor. I sipped and carefully returned my cup to its precise position on my little table. "Imo-nim, at my school, classmates told different stories about her, and even my teacher couldn't say what was true. Did you know her? May I ask how she died?"

Imo sighed. I apologized and asked if she was too tired to talk. If I hadn't been so young and piqued to hear the dramatic stories from court, I might have considered that remembering this past would be painful for my aunt.

"No, you should know what happened. I was about your age and still living at home when she died, so I never met her. They say she was unusually strong-willed and intelligent, very involved in politics. Some say she was ambitious and cared only about power. As a matter of fact, when the Gwangmu Emperor acceded to the throne, most of the ministerial appointments were given to her clan."

I admired how Imo handled her chopsticks to pick up pear slices, and while waiting for her to finish chewing I recited in my head the high court positions: minister of the left, minister of the right, minister of the state council, minister of justice, minister of war, minister of rites, minister of personnel, minister of public works . . . I was confused if this was the cabinet before or after the 1895 Kabo Reforms, but suddenly recognized the reform year as being the same as the queen's death, and wondered if the two were related.

Imo told me to finish eating. One was supposed to eat everything served, hence portions were small. She continued, "After Japan won the war with China, the queen spoke strongly against foreign influence in court. This was also immediately after the Donghak Revolution, the peasant uprising, and it was a complicated time. You probably don't know that many officials were actually grateful for the Japanese. Japan was seen as a generous friend who would help guide us into the modern age. Hundreds of newspapers came out, and suddenly anybody who could read, or anyone who could listen to someone else read, had an opinion about how things should be. There was a widespread popular movement toward 'civilization and enlightenment.' Since it meant following the Japanese example, it raised opposition from traditionalists, like your father. But it was fashionable and trendy to strive for modern ideas and Western goods." She sipped her rice tea. I wondered what kinds of "civilized and enlightened" products of that time might have attracted Imo.

"So you see," she said, "Japanese advisers were already involved in court. The queen was like a rock they had to kick from the road to pass through." She moved her tray aside, checked mine and called Kyungmee, who removed them. Imo told me to get my sewing from across the room and asked Kyungmee to light the brazier and bring a shawl.

"In early October 1895, in the evening, a eunuch alerted the queen and her ladies that the new Japanese envoy, Miura Goro, had entered the palace with soldiers and was heading her way. To conceal herself, the queen dressed in simple clothes and sat among the ladies-in-waiting. The soldiers couldn't know which of the ladies was the queen, so they slashed to death the women closest to them. Some say she tried to save her ladies-in-waiting by identifying herself, but who knows? They killed all the witnesses, desecrated her and burned her body in the garden."

I couldn't swallow. *Desecrated* rang in my ears. I felt terrible for wanting to hear the story as if it were gossip. I remembered Teacher Yee and what she'd suffered. My eyes filled with the horror of it, and the shame. "Yes, child," said Imo quietly. "When the news came out, everyone was shocked and there were many protests." I felt pangs of sadness for my teacher and the queen's tragic end, and was glad to have sewing to hold my attention until the intensity of the feelings eased. Imo asked me to get her a deck of cards from across the room, which allowed me to pull a handkerchief from my skirtband and surreptitiously blot my eyes and nose. Her example showed me how women could help each other preserve decorum, and I hoped that one day I would be as deft as she in this regard.

Imo shuffled cards and played solitaire, while coals smoldered in the iron brazier. I embroidered a floral edging on several meters of heavy blue silk that would be a gift to the princess. The rain fell and fell.

"They tried to suppress the news for as long as possible, and held the king at the palace, as if under house arrest. A few months later he managed to escape, hidden in a palanquin. He fled to the Russian legation where he stayed for almost a year. As you can imagine, this was an extremely difficult time for the royal family, for the whole country. The Japanese had taken control of Gyeongbuk Palace entirely. The king had no alternative but to move into Deoksu Palace—back then it was called Gyeongun Palace. He tried to consolidate power and strengthen the monarchy during that time. He made Korea an empire and initiated many laws that changed the old ways. But he had no army, no palace guard, and the Japanese had maneuvered Korean ministers favorable to their cause into his cabinet. The government was in chaos, and the people were angry because the queen had been murdered and nothing was being done. They had a trial in Tokyo for the assassin, Miura, but everyone knew it was a sham." She stopped speaking for a while. Her cards clacked against each other, the silk in my lap rustled and the wooden embroidery frame creaked. The sound of rainfall on the roof tiles gently thinned.

Captivated by this tragic story, and remembering that Imo said she would've been about my age when the queen was murdered, I felt very close to my aunt. I sewed and waited for her to continue.

"Yah, I won." She displayed all forty-eight cards face up and perfectly arranged.

"Lucky!" I said.

She admired the cards and swept them together to shuffle. Her features and posture remained unchanged, but her words sounded deliberately casual. "Yes, lucky. I was married in 1900 because it was supposed to be a lucky year. Indeed, good luck came soon. I bore a son, and soon after that, my husband was appointed prime minister."

My needle went in and out, in and out, and now, knowing where her story was heading, I felt sorry and incompetent. I tried fruitlessly to think what my mother would do or say in the coming moment.

"Lady Om, Emperor Gojong's third consort, knew my husband's family was completely loyal to the emperor, and since we were both young mothers, I became her companion. My son played and studied with Lady Om's son, Prince Yi Un, who was just a little older. By then, the crown prince—the present Emperor Sunjong—was married, and his wife, Lady Yun, also asked for my companionship. So I was blessed to have the affection of these sage personages. It was around that time that the crown prince's coffee was poisoned, and he and the tasting eunuch nearly died. After that, because it's easier to find blame than to uncover truth, many thought this illness had spoiled his intellect and made him weak—and yes, his body was weakened and he was rendered impotent—but he proved his piety to his father and his kingdom by fighting death, by remaining alive. Do you understand what I'm saying?"

She asked this with surprising severity, so I took time to think. Before meeting Imo, I had wondered about her widowhood. I'd read that in the old days, a yangban widow—unmarriageable, with a childless future, and a burden to the family—was considered supremely virtuous if, when her husband died, she committed suicide. I had questioned Yee Sunsaeng-nim's death as being an honor suicide, and understanding what she'd suffered, thought that in a way it was. It angered and saddened me anew that her unbearable shame caused her to kill herself, especially since she was blameless. Across the room the lamplight touched my aunt like moonlight reflecting on the surface of a well. She was deeply beautiful in that moment.

I knew that many people blamed Emperor Gojong and now his son, Emperor Sunjong, for Japan's dominance, and that several ministers and court officials had committed suicide after the Protectorate Treaty of 1905, and again after the annexation in 1910. That my schoolmates had spread rumors about Emperor Sunjong's idiocy showed the degree of disrespect with which he and the monarchy had come to be regarded. Even my father said that nowadays only traitors and collaborators received high appointments in court. Emperor Sunjong hadn't chosen to be wedged in the impossible situation between royal responsibility to his bloodline and accepting blame—and shame—for the annexation. I was too confused to clearly say what these thoughts meant, but concluded that casting blame was far easier than learning more and thinking deeper about the whole story, the whole person—like Imo and my beloved Teacher Yee—and to die because of it was horrendous, and wrong.

I put my sewing down and looked at my aunt. "Yes, Imo-nim, I understand." She nodded as gravely as I had spoken.

"So then," she said slowly, placing cards face down in a careful pyramid, "years later, Deoksu Palace was where Emperor Gojong died, as did Lady Om. Neither was sick, yet both died in their sleep." She collapsed her unfinished game and gathered the cards. "My husband the prime minister and our five-year-old son also died there."

I felt terrible for my imo-nim but could think of nothing correct or helpful to say. All the words I knew seemed pointless. We sat quietly performing our activities, our backs straight and fingers steady. My needle worked the silk almost automatically, its thread a gossamer shadow in the lamplight. I realized that the high manners and the virtue of decorum permitted and encouraged this silence, and I was somewhat comforted in knowing that it was proper to leave so much unsaid. But it made me feel helpless, uncaring and young, and I felt a frustrated spark of rebellion nudging me toward anger, but I subdued it. After that evening, Imo never again mentioned her husband or son, or anything at all from those years, nor did I ask.

At last, Imo decided I was presentable and sent a note to First Marquis Yun, who was also the empress's father. An invitation soon came from the palace. Monsoon season had come and gone, washing the city of pollen and the yellow dust from spring's southwest winds. Bright colors burst from gardens and flowerboxes, and trees grew heavy with birds singing on supple young branches bright with new leaves. I rose at dawn, ate porridge and studied the usual three hours to keep pace with schoolwork. After I bathed, Imo tamed my hair with oil and braided it tightly, added augmenting hairpieces and wound it like a thick halo around my head. She patted powder on my cheeks and clipped white jade yin-yang shapes on my ears. We ate the midmorning meal, then she helped me dress and colored my lips. Wearing the rose-pink skirt with a sheer linen blouse, new socks and gloves, I sat in the entryway and waited for her to dress. The earrings pinched, giving me a headache and adding to my nervousness. I breathed deeply and folded my hands in my lap. The appearance of calm will generate calm, Imo had said.

We walked to Changdeok Palace, where Emperor Sunjong's Yunghui reign had begun after his father was forced to abdicate in 1907. We regarded him as our emperor, but Imo had taught me that we were to officially address him as His Imperial Highness the Grand Prince, and the empress similarly. That this was clearly a demotion of title was among the many things that remained unsaid during my time with Imo. At the main gate, our papers were checked and a phone call was made. I had never seen a telephone used before, nor had I been near so many Japanese guards. All I saw were pocket flaps, belts, buttons and leather boots. Two guards escorted us across the broad first plaza past a smaller but equally colorful and as heavily guarded gate, through which I could see the abandoned, expansive royal courtyard where all the cabinet ministers and court dignitaries had once stood, ceremoniously facing the audience hall further on, all its doors now shuttered. We walked sedately to avoid raising dust in the immaculately leveled courtyards, and passed the emperor's residence far to our left, where a fancy automobile sat in a semicircular driveway and more guards stood by the doors.

Another turn to the right and we saw the empress's residence of plain mortar and unpainted wood nestled serenely in trees, a scene which made me yearn for home. At the third house of this complex we were shown into a broad sitting room, where the princess was playing cat's cradle with a middle-aged lady-in-waiting. After bows, formalities and giving her the gift of the embroidered blue silk, I murmured, "Your Imperial Highness, this person gives sincere thanks for your kind invitation."

"What fun. How sweetly spoken! Please come and sit with me. How thin you are. Look at your wrists compared to mine!" Her tiny voice was measured and lyrical, and she grasped my hands. Surprised at such casual touching from royalty, I almost withdrew. Her wrists were rounded and soft like Imo's, and her skin's delicate whiteness recalled my father's description of me as being dark as a peasant. She wore a sheer white silk top and pale green skirt of exquisite quality, and her hair was styled in elaborately wrapped braids. She draped the cat's cradle cord around my fingers. "Do you know how to play?"

How graciously she had put me at ease! "Your Imperial Highness is too kind to allow this person to sit beside you." She looked smaller than me but acted with far more refinement than one would expect from a twelve-year-old.

"Yes, of course. Let's play. You start."

With Imo watching, I knotted patterns that would be easy for the princess to refigure. I was careful to position my hands to avoid touching hers. Her rice-cake cheeks and the simplicity in her straight-line eyes gave her an indolent air, as if an easy summer's day had begun its descent into dusk. I kept the game going until I sensed she was losing interest, then pretended to fumble and lost the figure.

"Oh no!" she cried with obvious pleasure. "We must try again." After a few turns, Imo bowed to the princess, gave me an approving look and left to spend the morning with Empress Yun. The princess and I played for hours. Naturally, I had played all sorts of games with Dongsaeng many times, but never for as long as I played with the princess. I greatly enjoyed the leisure and won and lost just the right amount to keep her amused. Her playthings, most foreign and still in unopened boxes, filled two cabinets that I longed to explore, but she was only interested in simple games. I found it easy to be both deferential and inventive with her toys. Kaleidoscopes became telescopes. Each turn of the glass showed another aspect of her magic kingdom, which we described to each other, back and forth, until she said it was perfect. We made her wind-up tin toys waddle and roll across the floor, then gave them all names and roles in her magic kingdom. Of the characters I made up, she wanted to know more about the *jajangmyeon* man—the vendor who ladled a sweet black-bean sauce over a steaming bowl of noodles—the sandal peddler, mermaid, missionary, and neighbor girls who walked arm in arm to school. She made her tin characters into changing guards, chamberlain, nephew of the lord steward—to whom I knew she was secretly betrothed—duke, ladies-in-waiting and eunuch. I was curious to know more about the chauffeurs and how it felt to ride in the Daimler or the Cadillac, wanted to hear more about the fourth and fifth wives, and what it was like to have a tasting servant, but didn't ask.

I was presented to Empress Yun in Nakson Hall late in the afternoon. Spare furnishings enhanced the harmony of the spacious rooms trimmed with intricate shell inlay and carved wood. I could tell that Imo was pleased with my bow and greeting. The empress was tall, with heightened hair that made her look even more imposing. She wore a deep pink-and-white hanbok with delicate gold borders. Her straight eyes had brows that pointed slightly downward to an elegant nose, making her gaze appear sharply intelligent. Her full bottom lip underlined an impression of resolve. She nodded to a folding screen spread behind her that was made of eight separate but related paintings of the Four Gentlemanly Plants— plum blossom, orchid, chrysanthemum and bamboo—with dramatic mountains and valley in the background, each section showing changes of season. On the fully opened screen they comprised a complete and stunning panorama of fore- and background subjects. "Do you see how skillfully the artist has used the writing as its own element in the composition?" she said, indicating how the expressive calligraphy of four poems, songs to the seasons, was strikingly positioned to enhance both images and poetry. "And see there—" She pointed to the signature, and I recognized my father's chop.

Of course I knew my father was a literati painter of some renown, and that our ancestors had a long history of royal patronage, but to see his work in the sitting room of the empress made me both understand his talent and respect him in a different, larger way. I bowed deeply. "This insignificant person is honored and indebted that Her Imperial Highness has generously allowed recognition of her father's art."

"She's quite charming," Empress Yun said to Imo. "There's another screen that's even more impressive in Huijongdang. Perhaps we'll arrange for you to see it one day." Huijongdang was the emperor's residence, so I knew I would never see it. It was enough to know that my father's art lived daily among the royal family. It made me quite breathless.

The empress received a message and smiled at me. "It seems the princess also finds your niece charming," she said to Imo. They discussed a schedule, and my aunt thoughtfully requested that allowances be made for me to attend upper school.

It was decided that I'd go to school six days of the week and attend to Princess Deokhye in the afternoons until an hour before sunset. Then Pang would come to escort me, or I'd walk home with Imo if she were there. The palace had electric lighting generated by an on-site powerhouse built in 1886, which allowed us to study and play late into the day and long after sunset, even in the winter. Because of the electric lights, and because my school was closer to the palace than to Imo's house, during the week I began spending nights in a room vacated by a lady-in-waiting at Sugang Hall, the princess's house. In the beginning I was so self-conscious to be an overnight guest that I could barely sleep, but it wasn't too long before the princess's retinue referred to the room I slept in as mine. This was a relaxation in protocol that was just another wave in the ebbing tide of royal glory.

I MET THE emperor on Chuseok, the Harvest Moon Festival, that year. It was also the Japanese holiday Shubun no hi, Autumn Equinox Day, so this most important Korean holiday continued to be celebrated under a different name. It brought the court together for the first time since I'd been there. I woke sad that morning, missing Dongsaeng and my mother on the holiday, but the colorful preparations for high ceremony soon chased my homesickness away.

At the palace, we watched Japanese military officers and guards on horses lead a procession of palanquins carrying the royal family and dignitaries down the road to Jongmyo Shrine, which held the memorial tablets of Joseon Dynasty kings and queens. The day was crisp and clear, making the traditional dress of the royalty and ministers brilliant with jeweltones and sheen. Then came rows of men in dark uniforms festooned with ribbons, gold bullion fringe and sashes. A few of these ministers and court officials were Japanese; the others probably were—as my father would disgustedly say—collaborators. We were among the guests following on foot with a rear guard, after which a number of invited spectators joined the parade. The streets were closed to traffic and the route lined with guards, behind which ordinary people thronged to watch the rituals. Since I had never seen a Confucian ceremony, I hadn't expected the religious solemnity throughout the morning—from the ceremonial march, to the bows, prayers and offerings to the ancestors. Imo told me later that the order of worship had been drastically shortened, and she didn't mention the obvious, that it had also been altered to include references to Japanese imperial ancestors.

We went back to the palace to line up in the courtyard and wait our turn to bow to the emperor and empress—Imo with her group of the empress's courtiers, and me with the princess's retinue. My feet ached from stiff cotton dress shoes, but the pain was forgotten once I reached the steps of Sungjong-jun, the airy hall where, in the olden days, administrative matters were dealt with. That the throne room wasn't being used for this ceremony joined the things that no one mentioned.

A musty damp smell seemed trapped by the tall colorful ceiling, and the walls painted with decorative patterns and peacock murals were faded and peeling. Dignitaries and ministers and their wives sat on floor cushions in order of rank around the perimeter. The emperor sat in a chair on a raised platform made of red lacquer and mother-of-pearl. He had changed his clothes to a Western-style military dress uniform studded with medals and festooned with gold braid, and as I neared I thought irreverently that he looked stiff and awkward sitting on a gold-leafed chair placed in the center of a cinnabar-colored riser. The chair didn't belong on a platform designed to be directly sat on. To the right of the platform the empress also sat stiffly on a chair, and on the other side, the chamberlain sat on a floor mat at a table, announcing the name of each person as he or she stepped forward and bowed. Several officials clustered nearby, some with obvious roles, such as the secretariat who recorded every word the emperor uttered, and others, Japanese men—wearing white gloves and what I later learned were tuxedoes—who stood near the walls and behind the platform looking stern.

"Han Najin," cried the chamberlain. I approached and carefully bowed. He announced I was the daughter of the calligrapher Han, the Gaeseong scholar and literati-artist from the Gwangmu reign. I dared to steal glances at the emperor's face as I approached, and was reminded of what I had once overheard two ladies-in-waiting say, that his eyes were as empty as a broken pail. They didn't look empty to me, but melancholy and simple, like Princess Deokhye's, and with a sweetness that comes from such simplicity. He had the same pale soft cheeks as his half-sister. I found his presence neither commanding nor particularly regal except in posture and dress.

The empress said with just enough volume for me to discern it, "Your Imperial Highness knows the young lady's father's scrolls."

What an honor that she would mention this! I stayed in position and kept my head bowed.

"We remember it. An excellent screen." His high voice had richness to it, as if his words floated on a river of seed oil. "It was greatly favored and is now on display at Seokjo-jung." This structure at Deoksu Palace was an enormous and hideous Greek revival that an Englishman had started to build. The Japanese had recently finished its construction and made it into a public art museum. Years later I would remember this conversation with the emperor, when I learned that the best Korean art in that museum had been shipped to Tokyo, and could only conclude that my father's screens were among that conscription.

I bowed again to the emperor's recognition, although I wasn't sure if my father would be pleased or find fault with public display of his work. A pause ensued. The emperor's features were placid, and it seemed he might be waiting for me to speak. I sneaked a look at the empress, who nodded imperceptibly. "Thank you," I said, using the elaborate idiom reserved exclusively for the emperor, "for Your Imperial Highness's kindness to this person's worthless family."

"Ah, now we remember that our little sister favors your company. We are glad for your companionship to her." He smiled beneath his mustache, and I was awed.

"Your Imperial Highness has blessed this person's family with his generous kindness and affection. May the bounty of heaven on Chuseok bring good health, prosperity and long life to Your Highnesses." I rose and retreated, bowing, trembling with excitement, and grateful that Imo had taught me so well.

AND SO NEARLY two years passed. I wrote home frequently and received as many letters from Mother, who reminded me always to be considerate of my aunt, respectful to the royalty, kind to the servants, and to read my Bible and study hard. As the seasons changed, she described which bushes had blossomed, when the maple tree turned red then brown, and how much snow filled the courtyards. She kept me updated on Dongsaeng's progress with his tutor, and when Ilsun came of age and was required to attend public school, that Father had enrolled him in the missionaries' lower school for boys. She mentioned how proud my father was of Dongsaeng's calligraphy, and told me consistent good news about Father's health. I didn't expect that she would say more, but wondered how angry he was with me, and if he was still angry with her.

During my stay with Imo I saw the emperor more than a dozen times, on holy days and festivals, and he always remembered me and was consistently kind. Because of Imo's companionship with the empress, I saw Empress Yun more often, and she was most attentive and affectionate. In those years I finished upper school and helped Princess Deokhye with homework from her tutors, particularly the sciences that she found boring, but which fascinated me. Someone was always nearby, even when she slept, which made the hours we spent together, playing, studying or sewing, formal. Only rarely did we find a chance to speak intimately.

One such opportunity came late in April 1926 on a sultry afternoon. Princess Deokhye and her retinue, including Madame Bongnyeong, her mother, were going to the large pond in Biwon Garden to see the cherry blossoms. We had visited the garden weekly to enjoy the various stages of bloom, and the flowers were now in final decline, a stage considered by many to be the finest. Servants had gone ahead to prepare the south pavilion with mats, pillows and refreshments. Two Japanese guards accompanied us: one in front near the princess being carried piggyback by a maid, and the other trailing me at the rear. The princess wasn't allowed to leave Sugang Hall without protection, and these two guards were often in our company. In a basket I carried bamboo propellers to toss and paper to make flowers. We all walked slowly in single file enjoying the petals, windblown like snowflakes and coating the path with pink. I smelled the cherry blossoms' delicate perfume and idly twirled a propeller in my hand. A broken flagstone made me trip, my hands flailing. I caught my balance, but somehow the propeller flew from my fingers and hit the face of the guard behind me. "Ow!" He stopped and covered his right eye.

"I'm so sorry!" I said, alarmed that I'd struck a Japanese guard. He grimaced, and my manners automatically surfaced. "Sir, are you hurt?"

"It's nothing." He picked up the propeller and gave it to me, and I studied his face for damage. Tears streamed from his reddened eye. He smiled. "You've made me cry."

"I'm sorry!" Startled, I turned back to the path. The ladies ahead were around a corner and out of sight. My glimpse of him registered a teasing, youthful smile and handsomely hollowed cheeks. I stopped to look at him again, to be sure I'd understood him correctly. Had it been a painful or furious grimace? His expressive eyebrows, one up and one down, clearly showed a mix of pain and joviality. "Don't rub it! You'll make it worse." It must've been because he reminded me of Hansu that I spoke to him with such familiarity—and then gave him my handkerchief.

He blotted his eye, then stiffened, his hand midair, caught between using my handkerchief again and returning it. "My apologies. I shouldn't have used it."

First teasing, then politeness! His tears continued and he winced rapidly, so I knew I'd scratched his eye. "No, it's completely my fault. Please keep it." A vision of Imo's alarmed-and-dismayed expression at this enormously inappropriate exchange dropped like a curtain between us, and I turned and hurried up the path, certain he could see my neck aflame. When I reached the line, I heard the lady ahead talking to me midsentence about the loveliness of the garden, not knowing I had just reappeared. I clutched the guilty propeller, thinking only of the guard with the tearing eye—and with my good linen handkerchief—following behind. My head spun.

The princess sat beside a wide window in the pavilion cantilevered over the largest pond in the gardens. Newly flowered azaleas and green-budding trees colored the surrounding terraces. In the pavilion's corners lay swept piles of fallen petals, which an occasional breeze fluffed, then let settle, as if they breathed their last of spring. The maids served water, southern strawberries and apricots, while Madame Bongnyeong read from a Japanese novel. I half listened to the story of love, fate and social pressure—a typical romance. The walled-in pond was brimful with flat and standing lily and lotus leaves. Dark pond water glistened artfully between the floating leaves, and dragonflies skimmed the surface with singing wings. We folded paper flowers that would decorate the towers of ceremonial food for the princess's fourteenth birthday the following month, then most of the group walked farther around the pond and north beyond a gateway to the big pavilion that was once a library and classroom for princes. I breathed a bit easier seeing the red-eyed guard follow them.

We sent the propellers whirring out the window and into the pond until my basket was empty. A eunuch wielded a long-handled net to fish the bamboo toys out, amusing us by reaching far and pretending to almost fall in. Princess Deokhye fell silent, and I sat back to unravel the confusing incident with the guard.

"Are you not well, Your Highness? Is it the heat?" said Madame Bongnyeong.

"No, Madame, I'm fine. Is it too hot for you? Are you comfortable?"

Both the empress and Princess Deokhye were overly polite and solicitous to Madame Bongnyeong. Custom dictated that a wise woman would maintain harmony in the household by treating a lower concubine—typically a commoner who had once attracted the favors of the king—with respect, and to fully educate the woman's offspring, even though the sons were barred from the civil service examinations and thus any future official rank. Daughters of concubines, therefore, fared better than sons, since being fully educated they could achieve higher status through marriage.

"No need to worry about me. I'll manage." Madame Bongnyeong's responses typically called attention to herself in this way, an indication of her lack of refinement.

To distract the princess and to try to chase the sadness from her eyes, I invited her to lean out the side window with me to feel the sun on our cheeks and to let the petals fall on our hair. We watched the servant scooping propellers around the blossoms and sat companionably listening to his splashes and the buzzing insects. I murmured, "I have something to tell you later." She would be amused by the propeller-and-guard story, and I could omit the handkerchief part.

She smiled and mouthed "wait," then turned to Madame Bongnyeong. "Madame, I'd be delighted if you'd please read another chapter to us."

She seemed happy to oblige. After a page, the princess gestured with mischievous eyes to turn toward the window, and she looked at me expectantly, our faces inches from each other.

With Madame Bongnyeong's droning covering our whispers, I couldn't help myself and told Princess Deokhye the whole scandalous story, which she loved. It helped me to see the incident for what it was—a little accident, meaningless—yet I couldn't seem to erase the guard's charming smile from behind my eyes.

Involved in the novel, Madame Bongnyeong turned another page. Princess Deokhye whispered, "You think he's handsome!"

"No! I—"

"Oh, don't worry. I've noticed him too, mostly because he's young and not as stern as all the others. They only send us the educated boys. Of course, I wasn't ever going to say so. Can you imagine? So I'm happy you agree!"

"The princess is too kind—"

"Silly. You're my friend."

"This person is honored."

She sighed and glanced at Madame Bongnyeong. "No, Hyung-nim, I'm grateful. I didn't know how lonely I was until you came."

Surprised and flattered that she used the intimate and respectful word for friend, I bowed my head. "Your Highness."

Madame Bongnyeong finished the chapter and said, "Shall I continue?"

"Yes, if you'd be kind enough to indulge us. Your reading is very soothing." The princess picked up a paper flower and gazed at the gardens. "Now I will tell you a secret." I leaned closer and she smiled smugly. "Do you know the lord steward? He's the tall one with glasses and the pointed nose. Skinny, like you. He has elegant manners, and maybe if he took off his glasses, he could be very handsome for an old man."

"I've seen him from far away." Knowing what she would soon reveal, I said, "He looks regal. I think he has strong features—quite good-looking and distinguished."

She leaned closer. "I'm secretly engaged to his nephew."

I acted appropriately surprised. "Since when? Have you ever met your betrothed?"

"Of course not. His family doesn't even live in Seoul. Since I was seven and he was four."

"So early!"

"Yes." She unfolded and refolded the paper flower. "Do you know about my fourth brother, Prince Uimin?"

"The one who went to study at Tokyo University?"

She nodded. "Lady Yun told me that because he was the heir apparent, they made him go to school in Japan. When my family learned he had become engaged to a Japanese princess, they betrothed me right away. They wanted to be sure I'd marry someone appropriate." By *appropriate* I knew she meant Korean.

"I'm sorry," I said. I thought I understood her bouts of melancholy. For such a young and always-watched girl, her family's complicated circumstances undoubtedly made life hard to bear. In light of this and my foolish propeller story, I said, "I'm ashamed I told you about the guard."

"No, don't be. It's partly why I'm telling you this. She was very nice— my brother's wife, Princess Masako of Nashimoto—very good to me, kind and beautifully poised. We call her Princess Bangja."

"When did you meet her?"

"A year after they married, they came home to visit." Princess Deokhye tore a corner of the crimson paper flower and shredded it. A breeze floated the pieces until they landed on the lotus leaves. "Maybe they shouldn't have come, because their son got sick and died here. Only nine months old—too sad!" She scattered the last tiny pieces on the pond, where they melted like drops of blood.

"How sad!" I echoed sympathetically.

"He would've been heir. I heard gossip from mean people that it was just as well—better than having a half-Japanese heir. But the emperor mourned as much as the parents."

As it had been with Imo, I felt helpless and could think of nothing to say. I handed her another paper flower and leaned a little closer to her. We sat quietly, watching cherry blossom petals fluttering to the pond, and listened to Madame Bongnyeong's steady reading. The other group climbed noisily down the path toward our pavilion. Princess Deokhye touched my hand and said, "Princess Bangja couldn't have been more refined and affectionate to me, even in her grief. And some of the guards—like yours—"

"He's not mine!"

"He is if I say so!"

I mock-frowned, and she laughed behind her hand.

"He always speaks courteously, not like some of the others who show nothing on their faces but that stupid smug superiority."

"Here they come. I understand what you're saying," I said quickly. "They're not all the same, yes?"

She nodded.

"Your Highness is most gracious in her concern by sharing her feelings about Princess Bangja. This person is undeserving of your affection and kindness."

"You are my friend." She smiled and held my hand a moment, then turned and said to Madame Bongnyeong, "Thank you for the exquisite reading. We enjoyed it immensely." She raised her voice to the returning ladies and servants. "Aigu, but what a wonderful reading you missed! Madame, next time you must favor us again and reread those chapters." Madame Bongnyeong bowed, and it was time to go.

The princess climbed on the back of her strong maid, the ladies-in-waiting gathered the baskets of flowers and empty food containers, and the eunuch and servants cleared the pavilion of mats, pillows, dishes and cups, leaving it as serene as before we came. I walked close behind the princess and thus avoided the rear guard, whose red eye, I noticed, had calmed somewhat. I wondered what would become of my handkerchief, which was most likely tucked into his breast pocket. The image of my hand-stitched linen lying close to his heart made me flush with pleasure and shame.

I SPENT THAT night, a Saturday, in Sugang Hall. On most Sundays, Imo and I attended the Methodist church southeast of the palace, near Ewha, but the princess's requests to keep her company on Saturday nights took precedence. I worried what my mother would say upon learning how infrequently I went to church, but Imo said I'd be fine as long as I kept up with Bible reading and prayers. By then I was reading the boring Acts, skimming, and my prayers had grown rote and hasty. I also regularly invoked Heaven and Ancestors with the princess, but not for a second did I think I was any less Christian than before.

Sunday morning, as usual, I woke at dawn to the sound of guards marching on the palace grounds. I snuggled in the blankets for a few minutes, warmed by thoughts of yesterday's declarations of friendship from Princess Deokhye. As I washed and dressed, I ashamedly wondered if I'd see the young guard today before going home to Imo.

Keening cries swelled in the dawning morning, and I wondered how roosters could have entered the palace. Then I heard commotion and Princess Deokhye cry out. I quickly tied my blouse and hurried toward her rooms. Her eunuch was prostrate and several maids were crowded around her door. Exaggerated cries of mourning came from the ladies who surrounded her so thickly that I couldn't see her. The breakfast tray and bowls were scattered on the floor and steam spiraled from spilled porridge. Fear struck and I shouted "No!" Then came tears of relief to see the princess sit up, and fear again when I saw her face contorted in pain. The strong maid pulled me into the room and pushed me to the princess. Sinking to the floor beside her, I instinctively opened my arms, and she clung to me, her body shaking with sobs.

"The emperor—my brother—is dead!"

I remembered Queen Min and felt cold. The princess cried and I held her close.

"They—they—tell her!" she cried.

One of the ladies said, "They found him dead early this morning. The doctor said he died in his sleep."

Someone else said softly through tears, "ChoongHo was also found dead this morning, laid out in bed still in her clothes." A woman wailed the quivering song of mourning. ChoongHo was the emperor's tasting servant. I remembered Imo's stories about Gyeongbuk Palace, and the eunuch and then–Crown Prince Sunjong, who both had nearly died in the coffee-poisoning plot.

I held the princess and rocked her. "Oh, my poor dear sister." The pulsing laments filled the room, seeped into our souls and poured out the windows, sending our grief to the heavens. The cries were met by others coming from Nakson Hall, and I said, "You must go to the empress." And by uttering this last word, knowing that Crown Prince Uimin lived in Tokyo, I truly understood that the emperor, and thus, the empire, had died.

This enormity and grief for the princess weakened my legs, but I helped her stand and, with the others following, walked toward the passageway that connected Sugang Hall to the empress's house. Four guards stood in the passage entrance, shoulders stiff, feet spread, hands on their sabers. "For your protection and that of the grand princess, you must remain here," said the guard with a stripe on his sleeve.

Outrage erased my fear. "It's Her Highness! Sister to the grand prince and princess, she must—"

"It is forbidden!" The guards seemed to expand with severity. I saw the red-eyed guard behind the two in front. He looked straight ahead with the same iron face as the others. I stared at him until I felt my eyes had struck him as sharply as that silly toy had the day before, a lifetime before, but he remained impassive, hateful and impassive.

"Come, Your Highness," said a lady-in-waiting. "Best that we rest."

We returned to her sitting room where we remained until night fell. The women lamented loudly, a sound that sometimes helped release into tears the grief held within our bodies, and also sometimes seemed pointless and irritating. I wanted to shout, "Let her mourn in peace! Let her pray for her brother, her family, and let her voice her fears." She did not have Jesus in her vocabulary, but she could appeal to Heaven to reward the soul of the emperor, and for the merciful future of her vanquished family.

The servants had more mobility than we did, and so desperate were we for news that we relied on them to pass messages through the kitchen. At lunch came word that my aunt, who'd come from church to walk me home, was with the empress. When we asked for fresh water, we learned that the minister of rites and certain Japanese officials had visited the empress to speak of funeral preparations. At dinner the death of the tasting maid was confirmed, and at bedtime snack came news that the emperor's cause of death was ascribed to apoplexy. I remembered the spider-knobbed hands of Dr. Hakugi when in the past he'd examined the princess, who often had headaches. I could envision his spindly face and wiry mouth attesting to the emperor's cerebral hemorrhage, apoplexy, with the professional confidence of a longtime falsifier.

I stayed with Princess Deokhye that night, sitting by her bedside with the strong maid, the eunuch posted outside her door. I dozed until the princess woke with sad tears or nightmares. I felt my mother's spirit and her dream of water, of women's resilience, with me, and regardless of propriety or prohibition, I softly sang hymns to help the princess fall asleep again, to bring something pure and good to the room. There was no way to know if news of the emperor's death had yet reached outside the palace.

We were detained at Sugang Hall for nine days. I sent word to Imo and the empress through the servants that we were unharmed, and received similar reassurances from Imo. On the tenth day, Imo was released and allowed to stop in at the princess's house for a short while before taking me to her house. She told us what she knew about the days ahead. My imo looked determined and strong, if somewhat tired, and I was relieved to have her near. I hadn't realized my degree of fear until I felt the safety of her presence, the comfort of her flower and citrus smell. Then I felt guilty because Princess Deokhye could not share this relief.

By then, news of the emperor's death had reached the city and had quickly spread throughout the country. While spontaneous demonstrations of outrage and sadness, and cries for independence clogged the town squares and city plazas, rumors about the cause of his death and about his mental health continued to propagate. To mollify the people, a formal state funeral was slated for several weeks later, June 10, which would bestow the proper Confucian burial rites to the last emperor of Korea. In the meantime, Imo would send me home to Gaeseong for my safety, while she would continue to do what little she could to support the few survivors of the once-great Yi royal family.

Imo said it was time to leave the palace. Although I had been waiting for this moment all the past nine days, it felt too abrupt. I thought it was similar to the fate that had shadowed the palace and the royal family for decades. The Yunghui emperor's unnatural death had always been feared, and imminent, and yet its occurrence felt sudden and unexpected. I said my goodbyes to the staff and bowed low to the princess, saying all the formalities of honorable thanks and farewell in the special language reserved for royalty. My eyes were wet, but my voice was as steady and sure as the training I had received. I did not look up as I left the room, though I knew I would never again see the princess. I heard her tearful voice saying goodbye, and, softly, "You are my friend."

Imo and I walked across the courtyards that had become as familiar to me as my father's front yard. We passed beneath the top-heavy south gate where our papers were checked and checked again, and went home on roads empty except for policemen or mounted soldiers who guarded every turn.

Several months later, long after the failed second national demonstration on June 10, the emperor's funeral day, we heard through the underground that seven thousand additional troops had been dispatched specifically to suppress the uprising the Japanese had anticipated for this last emperor's funeral. Bamboo rakes, sticks, pitchforks and raised fists were no match for swords, guns and military precision. Not long after the funeral, the princess and the royal family and some of their staff were taken to Tokyo. Rumor had it that the strong maid carried the princess on her back as they left Changdeok Palace, which was soon emptied of all but peeling gilt and ghosts of a glorious dynasty that had lasted five hundred years.

PART II

# Higher Education

# Riding the Bicycle

SPRING 1926–SUMMER 1928

TRAVELING HOME ON THE TRAIN, I LOOKED OUT THE WINDOW AND noticed that my line of sight now reached above the center bar, proving how much I'd grown in the two years since leaving Gaeseong. I recalled that sad yet exciting journey, which seemed so long ago, and smiled inwardly, remembering how Imo had called me Monsoon Wind. The train lumbered to the outskirts of the capital. Having grown accustomed to swept courtyards and pruned gardens, I saw squalor all around me, even in the first-class compartment. On the other side of the car a middle-aged Japanese couple in Western clothes ate lunch in their armchairs, the man's newspaper strewn on the floor, the woman's painted lips shiny with oily fish. They whispered to each other and sent occasional curious glances my way.

I sat erect, my hands calmly folded as if to straighten with my posture the riot of wires barring my view of the sky. I stole peeks at the woman's skin-colored stockings and high-heeled shoes buckled tidily across the arch, and at the light fabric of the woman's peach-colored dress clinging to her curves.

The train shuddered as it turned on an overlook of the Han River, and engine smoke blew through the compartment. I coughed and covered my nose with a handkerchief. In its folds I smelled the jasmine incense that Imo had constantly burned in her brazier to mask the sewer odors from the street. My eyes blurred with tears. No one knew what fate awaited Imo. Forbidden to leave the city and fearful of her unknown future, she had quickly arranged for my traveling permits and ticket home, spoiling me once again with her generous insistence on the best ticket. When we parted on the station platform, I wept to express my gratitude and love, for words were inadequate. She held my hands tightly and murmured uncharacteristic praise, calling me Beloved Daughter. Neither of us said when we might meet again.

The Japanese man shut the window with a loud snap. "I'll open it again when the fumes aren't blowing in." I lowered my head in courtesy. He bent, then twisted to arrest his bow to me, and returned to his seat frowning. He told his wife to gather the scattered newspaper and wrap the fish bones. Conscious of his stare, I kept my eyes averted.

"Going to Gaeseong?" He crossed a leg, his foot in the outer rim of my vision.

I nodded, noticing a darned patch on the back of his sock.

"Might I ask why?"

Startled by the polite tone he used, I looked at him. His dark eyes crinkled with warmth.

"My home is there, sir."

"Why, she speaks perfectly!" the woman said, and they both smiled at me. "How did you learn to speak so well?" She folded the trash in a neat package and wiped her mouth and hands on a train towel. She opened her pocketbook and applied lipstick—a crude display of vanity, I thought.

My Japanese had grown refined at the palace, but I wouldn't say so. "In public school, sir." I'd completed the required two years of upper school and was just then missing the graduation ceremony. I had hoped to apply to Ewha Professional School, but that hope faded with the same smoke that now put Seoul behind me. The school's original name had been Ewha Women's College, but as with many other places and positions in Korea, its status had been demoted by the Japanese, who attempted to limit Korean women to vocational training, or believed we weren't capable or worthy of academic achievement. Ewha was built by the American missionaries in 1886 as Korea's first girls' school, and over the years had grown in size and stature as Korea's only women's college. It maintained its prestige despite its loss of academic labeling, and though most of the school's administrators were Japanese, nearly all the teachers were Korean. I longed to attend.

"There, you see?" said the woman. "Not a farm girl. I told you her clothes are too richly made."

I lowered my eyes, annoyed at being the subject of their guessing game. My blouse and skirt were traditional white, plain, but the linen was finely combed, the stitching tight and invisible, my collar newly sewn in that morning. I thought of the colorful silks and brocades that Imo had insisted I take home, packed in a large old suitcase of hers now on the baggage rack at the end of the car, sure I'd never wear such showy clothes again.

"You see," said the woman, her voice light and friendly. "You look the same age as his students, yet here you are during examinations traveling alone in first class. And most of his students have the most horrid Japanese. We've wondered if Korean girls are capable of speaking properly at all! So you've piqued our curiosity."

The woman's rudeness made it possible to ask my own questions. "Pardon me, sir, but are you a teacher?"

"At one time, yes," he said. "Literature and history."

His wife broke in, "Most recently, dean of admissions at Ewha!"

"How prestigious!" I said to flatter and supplement the woman's crows of pride. "I've wanted to attend—"

"And why not?" The woman clutched her husband's arm. "Give her your card, won't you? Such a pretty thing and well spoken! Think how it would be if all the girls were as civilized as she."

I had often seen this attitude from my schoolteachers and was practiced at hiding my reactions.

"Have you a certificate from secondary school?" The man dug in his chest pocket.

"I graduated this year while visiting my aunt in Seoul. I—I took the Ewha entrance examinations last month." Imo had urged me to take the exams, saying, "Sown soybeans, reaped soybeans!" She'd given me a box of lead pencils for the occasion as well as the examination fees, which Father had neglected—or refused—to send.

"Good! And did you do well?"

"Yes, sir." Modesty required silence about my first-place score.

The man watched me carefully. "Very well. I'll look it up." He handed me a fountain pen and two little cards. "Give me your name and that of your upper school, then apply as soon as you can. We're considering applications now."

I'd seen such pens used, but had never handled one. I opened it, heavy and cold with gold trim, and formally wrote my name in Chinese characters on one of his cards. I relished the pen's easy flow of ink, and by the third syllable of my name, had mastered its ability to replicate the departure of brush from paper in a delicate swash, despite the bumpiness of the train. I returned the pen and extended the wet card between my fingertips. The man wiped the pen and scrubbed his palms with his handkerchief. "Han Najin," he said professorially. "Beautifully done, but why don't you write in Japanese?"

My cheeks flushed. They would be narrow enough to diminish the most ancient and elegant of letterforms in all of Asia, but Japan had perennial—and lately, escalating—problems with China. I remembered the proverb "The lower stream runs as clear as the upper stream," and swallowed. Besides, it seemed this man—who thoroughly wiped his pen after I had touched it—had no official capacity to do me harm, and could be quite helpful should I ever find the opportunity to apply to Ewha. "My apologies, sir! I have much to learn."

"Yes. I see you've had some of the old training. Well, well." He exchanged a look with his wife and tucked the card into a book, which he commenced to read. His wife fussed with her baggage and called the porter to dispose of the trash.

His card read, PROFESSOR TOSHIRO SHINOHARA, DEAN OF ADMIS-
SIONS, EWHA PROFESSIONAL SCHOOL. I placed it carefully in my string
pouch and removed a length of thread and an unfinished swatch of
embroidery. By the time the train reached Gaeseong, I'd completed the
square—plum blossoms against a dark branch—and gave it to Mrs. Shinohara. "Thank you for your generous offer to personally apply." I bowed
to them both. I doubted if Mrs. Shinohara would recognize the royal
flower of the Yi family and felt a strange bittersweet justice in giving the
square to her.

She said, "Such beautiful handiwork! You must apply for the degree in
domestic arts." She bobbed rapidly in the Japanese way. "Don't forget to
write the dean of admissions! Goodbye! Goodbye!" Mr. Shinohara nodded curtly, and I struggled through the compartment door with the heavy
suitcase.

I searched the platform, my chest pounding in anticipation of seeing
my mother, but no familiar face appeared. Fumes making me nauseous, I
dragged the suitcase toward the station and waited as the depot gradually
emptied of travelers. A man in tattered clothes lay beside the entrance to
the station, begging for a coin, his filthy legs stretched out before him, his
brown teeth broken, his stink staining the pavement. I'd never seen such
misery and lack of pride and felt ashamed for him, for seeing him, for his
sad existence. As the sun sank behind the buildings, I left my suitcase with
the stationmaster and walked home, guessing that Mother hadn't yet
received Imo's letter about my homecoming, or the postal watchdogs had
censored it into oblivion.

Vendors in the marketplace shouted last-minute bargains, long shadows mimicking their hurried packing of unsold goods. I walked the
beaten earth of the road and passed the noodle shop and bakery that had
tempted me with treats after school. A lifetime ago! The market seemed
dingy and small, the road home short. I climbed the hill and saw the
happy curved roof of my home gate. Tears stinging, I began to run, all my
court training lost to emotion.

I reached the gate just as Byungjo came to latch it at sunset. His tanned
face lit up when he saw me. "Ahsee! The master's daughter! She's home!" I
stopped a moment to take in his familiar wrinkles, my smile as wide as
his, then I flew to the house where I heard Kira repeating Byungjo's cries

and Dongsaeng's excited little boy voice from afar, and at last I fell into my mother's open arms.

IN THE COMFORTING evening light of my bedroom, with Mother off to instruct Joong about my luggage, I washed my neck and face and smoothed my hair. It was time to see Father. I could only guess how angered he'd been at my departure. I regretted each day that my mother had taken the brunt of his fury, and she refused to tell me its extent. I regretted his loss of face with the Chae family. I wondered if their son, now fourteen, had married. If Father only realized how much things had changed!

"He's waiting," said Mother from the hall.

With trepidation, I went to his sitting room. It seemed dark and close. I bowed low to the floor, my movement slow and controlled, the bend of my neck graceful. "Honored Father, this person is returned home."

"So I heard."

I sneaked a look. The lines by his mouth were deeper and new white hairs edged his beard, still short. He'd kept his hair shorn. His eyes were cast to a book at his side.

"I apologize, Father, for the shame I brought with my departure."

A noncommittal sound came from his throat. I smelled his tobacco flaring and heard slow puffs. "What did you learn in Seoul?"

"I hope to please you in the coming days with all that I have learned."

In a lengthening quiet, I added, "I was honored to see Father's screens in the palace." Long pause. "Imo-nim sends greetings and blessings for good health."

Another long pause, then he spoke. "So it's true what they say about his death."

I looked at him, startled by this mild questioning as if from one peer to another. He fiddled with his pipe. "Everyone believes it," I said as humbly as I could. "Dr. Hakugi was most influential."

"They said apoplexy."

"Abbuh-nim, if I may." He nodded, and I continued. "His Majesty was healthy and thin. The maid who served his food is also dead—they say she died of fever. But the servants who found her said she was dressed in her day clothes and had obviously been arranged to appear as if she slept."

Father nodded and spat bits of tobacco. "How is your imo?"

"She remains at home, awaiting exile or something worse—"

"No, they won't bother with a widow. After things settle, she'll have her house and be fine."

I bowed, grateful for this assurance. I heard him adjust his legs then empty his pipe. The silence grew, and I thought I hadn't heard such silences as this in all my days in Seoul.

"You've grown."

"Thank you, Abbuh-nim."

"You may go."

"Thank you, Abbuh-nim. Goodnight."

Walking slowly to my room, I let go the breath I hadn't known I was holding. My nose filled with the pinesap smell of floor polish, and I felt unnamed sadness.

WHEN THE COCK crowed at sunrise, the clean scent of my bedding reminded me I was home. Pale green sunlight swept across the familiar crisscrossed beams on the ceiling. I smiled at the nooks where I had once imagined stockpiling new words and Chinese characters. I quickly dressed, happy to hear waxwings' shrill whistles in the garden rather than the measured commands of guards on sunrise march. In the kitchen, I presented Cook with a dozen linen hand towels embroidered with images of Seoul's city gates.

"Your mother will be proud to see how you've mastered your needle!" said Cook, grasping my hands.

"Where's Mother's rice?" I said, inspecting the four trays Cook had prepared for the family. My mother's worn brass bowl held millet with barley.

"Rice is dear," said Cook.

I switched my bowl of white rice with Mother's and delivered two trays to Father and Dongsaeng, then took ours to the women's side of the house. Seated in front of a folding mirror, Mother brushed her long hair, now shot with silver. "So wonderful to have you home," she said. We shared a morning prayer, and she opened her rice bowl. "What's this?"

"What happened, Umma-nim? Cook says rice is dear."

"I was hoping to spare you at least one day." She sighed. "Your father was forced to let go of the farm. Oriental Land Company conscripted the property and sold it to a Japanese man. We received a pittance in the exchange."

With the steadily increasing censorship, my mother wouldn't have written this kind of news in her letters, nor was it her habit to send any bad news through the mail. I felt remorse for being angry when Father didn't send the examination fees for Ewha, and chastised myself for self-ishly hoping to attend Ewha at all. "When did this happen? What happened to the family?" Joong's family, whose loyalty and service to the Han clan went back several generations, had long farmed the property.

"Yah, slow down. Did you already forget everything Imo taught you?"

I blushed until I saw that my mother was gently teasing me. We smiled, and she said, "Imo was very proud of you." Instantly I was her little girl again and simply, purely happy to be with her.

"They tried to work the farm for another year," Mother continued, "but the new owner took all their harvest and left them nothing for winter. Some of the peasants stayed, some went to join the resistance, and Joong's family went north to your grandfather's in Nah-jin. Joong's youngest brother decided to find work with Uncle in Manchuria. Your father was quite generous with them and sent them off with all the grain and cloth that wasn't due for taxes. He told them to sell what they couldn't carry and take the things they'd need, and not worry about the repercussions. We were fined for the missing goods and tools, but Father said it was the least we could do."

That Mother imparted these kinds of details to me proved I had indeed grown up, and beneath my worry for Joong and our family's situation, it made me feel proud. I swore I'd be worthy of her acceptance of me as a young woman.

"It happened about a year ago," said Mother. "There were so many refugees here after Kanto, they had to give them land or businesses to work. So the laws changed again, and another land reform . . ." She was referring to the Great Kanto Earthquake, which had completely devastated Tokyo, killing thousands and causing hundreds of thousands to flee to Korea for the many new opportunities the government had carved out for earthquake victims. I'd seen Japanese in all jobs and styles of life in Seoul but thought it had always been that way in the capital since the annexation. I now realized it was probably as much of a new influx of Japanese citizens as my mother was describing, a condition that might have contributed to the empire's last breath.

"Much has changed." Mother's lips set and she put the rice bowl aside. "Save this for the men's porridge tomorrow."

In the kitchen I exchanged the rice for millet, then returned. "Joong must be missing his family."

"We thought he might join them, but it seems that he and Kira are betrothed." She beamed. "Their own choice. I don't know why I didn't see it, especially since now their happiness seems to fill the house! Your father is agreeable."

We talked quietly through breakfast. I described the last few weeks at the palace, without mentioning my fears for Imo. Nor did I mention that seeing Mother now made me realize how deeply I had missed her, how essentially I loved and needed her, how grateful I was that she'd sent me to Seoul. She relayed outrageous market prices and news of church families, without mentioning how much she'd missed me, how proud she was of me, how happy she was that I was home, and safe. I had learned to read the meanings behind the politeness of things not said, and for this I was also grateful. And finally, I didn't mention Dean Shinohara's card, which I'd tucked into the Chinese-English phrasebook still hidden in my room. Hearing about the farm prevented me from raising the subject.

Mother said Hansu's parents were well, pleased with his excellent marks from Soongsil Academy in Pyeongyang. With a sideways glance, she said that my old friend Jaeyun had enrolled in the nursing program at Ewha for the coming term. My face remained impassive, but my stomach turned with envy. She also said the public upper schools were now entirely Japanese, and Father planned to send Dongsaeng to a private school in Seoul, following his graduation in two years. I filed this information into the beginnings of a plan. My mother started to take the tray, but I told her I was home now and she could go back to her morning reading. We reviewed the household and gardening schedule, and I made her agree to let me do the heaviest work.

After unpacking my trunk, which Joong had delivered, I spent the morning with Dongsaeng. At seven years old, he'd grown up to my hanbok ties, his hair closely shaved in the required schoolboy cut. I marveled at all he showed me: his favorite rooster in the pen by the kitchen garden, the rock he fell on by the pond that caused the dragon-shaped scar on his knee, bamboo canes he saved for sword fights with schoolmates. I noticed a larger chicken coop and counted numerous hens. I also saw that the azalea, peony and iris gardens had been demolished in favor of cucumbers, squash, beans, peppers, potatoes and cabbage. Dongsaeng led me to his study to examine his schoolwork. "And see!" He handed me a crumpled sheet. "I wrote you a sijo."

> *The crying bird that flew away, took breath and light and*
> *laughs that day.*
> *No toys to share, my games are hung, my clapping songs*
> *are halfway sung.*
> *More suns, more moons, and yet I play. The bird, I know,*
> *for me she prays.*

These lines moved me to the same gratitude I'd felt with Mother, and I was astounded by their sensitivity from one so young. "Wonderful! How beautifully you write." I crouched by his desk. "I'm sorry you were sad. I'll keep the poem forever. Thank you, Dongsaeng."

He shrugged. "Who cares?"

I tweaked his ear. "Such talk! Are you studying for entrance exams?"

"Yes, it's easy. See?" He held up his last teacher's report showing high marks in all subjects. His round face gleamed, his chin puffed with pride.

"And Khang Chinsa-nim? Are you behaving with him?" Before I left for Seoul I'd unabashedly copied my mother's childhood example and listened outside Ilsun's study to hear Chinsa-nim's lessons whenever I could.

He made a sour face. "Old fart."

"Dongsaeng!" I rapped the back of his hand.

He slapped my hand from his, making me wonder where he'd picked up his sullen ways. "Never smiles! Never says anything good about me! I know Abbuh-nim thinks I'm smart. Why is Chinsa-nim so stingy?"

"It's his job. He does things the old way. You know, too many compliments will ruin your character. See how you're behaving now." I said it mockingly, but he avoided my eyes, his lips turned down, and he rubbed ink on his stone.

"I'll leave you to your homework." I decided that if he was good, I'd buy him a fountain pen as a graduation gift.

I started to tell him this, but he pouted. "I thought you'd come home and we'd do something fun."

"Mother needs help. It's my duty, and yours is to study hard."

"You're just like all the other grownups."

I smiled at his petulant acknowledgment of my new status and left for the stream to help Kira wash clothes.

Beyond the bamboo grove that bordered the backyard, a small mountain stream ran fast and deep after spring monsoons. By the time the sun rose hot with summer, the flow trickled more modestly but remained clear and cold. On the opposite bank of the narrow creekbed, bees and insects hummed, darting in and out of wild grasses and chickweed tangled in a rocky meadow that sloped up toward hilly woods. Balanced on her wide brown feet, Kira squatted over a flat stone half in and out of the stream, beating clothes with a laundry stick. I tied my skirts and rolled my sleeves to join in.

"You shouldn't. Your hands will lose their softness."

"Don't be silly. There's work to be done."

"Aigu! Such a shame. From princess to washerwoman in two days." Kira's sandy voice rang with teasing.

I soaked some clothes and scrubbed them against the stone. "Not princess at all. Just a student in a different kind of classroom."

"How scary to get swallowed by the iron demon and spat out. To think that you've done this twice! Very brave."

"Oh Kira, not at all. It's like a very fast cart ride, maybe not as bumpy. It is smelly, though. One day you'll see."

"Never! My own two feet or, when I'm old, on the back of my grandson. That'll do for me."

"And I hear news that certainly one day grandsons will be coming!" An uncharacteristic redness swept down Kira's tanned neck. I touched her wet hand. "I'm happy for you. A wedding date?"

"After Harvest Moon," mumbled Kira, blushing thoroughly.

"Blessings for the marriage. A good man. Works hard."

"Hardly works!" We laughed and talked, singing silly laundry songs as we pounded and washed. I climbed off the rock to fill two water buckets upstream, wading in delicious coolness. A splash cast a shadow, or perhaps it was glare from the noontime sun, and I saw a sinewy gray fish dart past me to slip between Kira's ankles. I remembered my mother's pregnancy dreams and wondered what sort of omen had at that moment passed between us.

Kira hefted a heavy basket of wrung clothes onto her head, and we walked downstream along the bank, our skirts still tied above our knees, picking careful steps between clumps of weeds and sharp stones. Kira said that the past two winters had dealt them only minor illnesses and none-too-severe snowstorms. As we neared the bamboo grove, something made me look ahead. I saw the dust-blue of a soldier's uniform disappear behind a rocky outcrop. I stopped. Kira bumped into me, and the buckets sloshed. I could see by Kira's eyes that I hadn't imagined it.

"It might be the same fellow I saw two weeks ago," she whispered. "See if his face is pockmarked."

"Who is he?"

"A kid. He yelled something. I think it was lewd." Kira spoke only enough Japanese to get by in the marketplace.

I tightened my grip on the buckets. Beads of sweat formed on Kira's forehead beneath the weighty basket. We walked forward slowly.

"Who is it? Excuse me, what do you want?" I called in Japanese. The path curved in front of us and we were footsteps away from seeing who was behind the rock twenty meters ahead. "We have no money. Just water and laundry."

He leaned against the rock, not such a young man, his trousers unbuttoned, stroking himself. His lips grim, he stared at our bare legs through black slits of eyes, his scarred cheeks bobbing in and out of deep shade.

"Bastard son of a pig!" said Kira. She pushed me. "Don't look, Ahsee!"

I saw his hand work faster and the two points of his canines as he laughed out loud. "Son of a pig!" I screamed in Japanese as Kira pushed me to run.

"I'll be waiting for you next time, whores!" he yelled.

We ran to our west gate, panting, the water splashing, and I turned in time to see his blue-gray back slipping into the far woods. Inside, Kira bolted the gate firmly and unloaded her basket, her fingers shaking. The sound of wind filled my ears, but no breeze struck my face, surprisingly wet with tears. My back to Kira, I dipped my fingers in the bucket, wiped my face and stood tall. "Nothing but scum!" My harsh tone surprised me.

Kira hunched down, her head between her knees. "Shame! Shame!"

I squatted beside her. The high sun darkened the gaps in the dense bamboo grove behind us. My heart pounded, and I stopped the words *heathen Japanese filthy pig* from tumbling off my tongue, shocked that I had such words at ready. I said tightly, "We won't send you to the stream again without Joong."

"You mustn't tell him! What will he think of me then!"

I considered what to do. Joong might indeed find fault with his bride if he knew she'd seen another man's sex.

"Can you draw from the town pump instead?"

Kira wiped her eyes and nose, shaking her head. "That water is foul!"

"Then we must tell Mother that we saw a soldier near the stream, nothing more. That's enough cause for Joong to accompany you. If nobody is going with you, wash clothes in the courtyard from now on. Never mind about wasting good water."

"It scares me to think how many hot summer days we bathed and swam there."

"Remember those as days of happiness. Freedom. They'll come again, Kira, I'm sure of it."

"Ahsee has come back a woman. Wise and strong."

"No," I said, untying my skirt. "Older, perhaps, but still not much of a woman." I thought of the soldier and shuddered. We walked back to the house, and Kira spread the clothes out to dry while I emptied the water buckets in the cistern, wishing it was bath day. I wondered if I should withhold the real story from Mother. Father would be appalled to hear of such a thing. How could I speak of it? I was unwilling to tell my mother of vileness so close by. There were no words to convey the filth I felt coated with, no words to explain how home had become so suddenly fragile.

The moon rose, and Father and Ilsun were ensconced in their rooms. I joined my mother in the weaving room and told her the story I'd prepared.

"There are more and more soldiers everywhere," said Mother at her loom. "Your father thinks they still fear a national rebellion after the emperor's death."

It made sense that this soldier was part of an increased and nervous military presence. "But Umma-nim, this man was alone. He looked at us the same way that Yee Sunsaeng-nim talked about the soldiers at her house."

Mother worked the shuttle without speaking for a while. "So, when did Yee Sunsaeng-nim tell you what had happened to her?"

I frowned at my stitches. In Seoul I had often thought of Sunsaeng-nim, and her frequent presence in my mind tarnished the promise of secrecy I'd sworn. "Forgive me, Umma-nim. She spoke to me about a month before she died. I caught her one morning crying at her desk. She blamed herself for saying anything to me at all, and I promised to never repeat what she'd said."

The loom clicked and whirred. "Najin-ah, I know you've become a woman, but you're still my child. You cannot have secrets from your parents. How can we know your heart if you keep it hidden from us?" Her hands worked steadily, but her voice quavered. "Tell me what you know and what it has to do with the soldier today."

"Umma-nim, I didn't know then that she'd been sexually molested. Imo-nim told me about Queen Min, and I realized it then. It's horrible that Sunsaeng-nim took her life for that reason—"

"You know so much, you should know this as well." Mother cast her shuttle firmly. "She was pregnant from it."

"Oh!"

"Yes, poor thing. She felt she had no recourse. I've prayed many hours for her, and I trust that God took her in his mercy, because there is no Japanese or Korean or Chinese in heaven. Only souls, free souls, like hers now and the unborn baby's."

I was relieved to hear my mother's conviction about my teacher's soul, but I also wanted to cry out, Why was she raped? Why do they hate us? If there is glory in martyrdom, where was it for my teacher whose pain was too great to continue living, only to be denied heaven? Why does God let them treat us like that? Why does he let men do what I saw today?

I squinted into my sewing by the wobbly light of the lamp, jabbing the seam. The room hummed with the rhythm of Mother's beater comb against the weft.

Presently she said, "Tell me about the soldier."

I told her the truth, and that I'd been reluctant to do so, both to protect her and because it required speaking crassly. After she was sure that neither of us had been touched, she said, "How frightening! Of course we should tell your father."

"Umma-nim, please excuse me, but here's why I was reluctant to tell him. It'll only make him more upset. He'll never let us go outdoors by ourselves again. Isn't it household business? If Joong were to find out, Kira is sure he'll reject her."

She thought a moment, weaving. "Yes, he's as old-fashioned as your father that way. Well, I can certainly tell Joong that you saw a soldier, and to go with her to the stream. My guess is that he'll be more than willing. It was he, after all, who noticed her first. As for your father, leave that to me."

"Thank you, Umma-nim. Thank you for listening to me." My throat opened and I breathed relief, my eyes blurring on my stitches. I'd been feeling the violation of that soldier more keenly than I'd realized.

"I can see how you've grown in more ways than physical," said Mother, shuttling quickly through the warp. "I pray for your safety and wisdom, and I see my prayers answered today." I wondered at how Kira had said the same. We worked until the oil sputtered in the lamp. Mother said a prayer in my room and tucked me in as if I were still her little girl.

I drifted in my smooth quilts, felt them pressing coolly on my neck, hands and thighs. I smelled the water-scent of my bedding, ran my fingers through my scalp and rubbed my feet together. A beguiling seed of pleasure at my base pressed for relief and I drew my knees close, wiggled my hips, pressed my muscles in, so, and again, as I'd discovered the last few months alone in my room in Seoul. My small breasts freed from the day's bindings itched with warmth that spread from below my belly, and when I pictured the soldier's hand pulling up and down, I closed my eyes and shuddered with lightness, only to collapse moments later in guilty tears of shame and self-loathing. I was no better than he. Never again would I seek this private pleasure.

ONE HOT SUMMER Sunday, as parishioners filed from the church, Missionary Gordon approached and walked the aisle beside me. "Are you Han Najin? How you've grown!" The Gordons had gone back to America for a while and had recently returned to Gaeseong. Even after many years of seeing her around the church and mission, Miss Gordon's glassy blue eyes unnerved me. I dipped my head.

"My brother told me you were in Seoul for a time." Her Korean, now fluent, still had strange lilts.

"Yes, Madam."

"Please call me Miss Gordon, won't you?"

I tried and apologized for stuttering over her name. She smiled. "Don't worry. Everybody has trouble with it. Did you like it there?"

"Yes." I was too shy to say anything else.

"You know, I recently went to Seoul myself." I nodded receptively, and she continued. "I visited Ewha. A marvelous place! Have you seen it?"

A mute nod.

"Well, you must study hard and make good marks for college."

"I—I've already graduated."

"Of course! Now I remember hearing from Harlan what a good student you were at the girls' school. A favorite as I recall. Why, you must be planning right now for Ewha."

I blushed with both modesty and discomfort over the familiarity of Miss Gordon's reference to Director Gordon. Her casual use of his first name truly made me squirm. "One day, I hope—" I lost my courage to say more. Near the front door, Reverend Ahn and my parents were bowing to each other. Mother turned and made a tiny gesture that clearly said *stop bothering the American lady and come outside at once!*

"Are you planning to go?" said Miss Gordon. "How wonderful. This fall?"

"No. I don't—it isn't—the fee—" Since my tongue refused to speak normally, I stopped. With my head bent I could only see Miss Gordon's freckled wrists and sturdy fat-heeled American shoes, but I sensed her smiling encouragement. I took a breath and made a huge, bold and very selfish leap. "First I must have a job."

"Is that so?" Miss Gordon tapped my shoulder and sat in the last pew. "Let's stop a moment and talk before going outside." I indicated to Mother to go on without me, and sat beside the missionary. I smelled a pleasant, powdery sweetness as Miss Gordon fanned herself with her hand.

"Now then. What would you like to study at Ewha?"

Having never forgotten the intensity of Dongsaeng's birth, I wanted to be an obstetrician but knew that the only medical training Ewha offered was nursing. That the practice of medicine was beneath my family's class was a problem I'd face if my wish became a possibility. At Imo's church, I'd met young men from Seoul National University who told me that its medical program was no longer taught in German, Japanese translations of medical textbooks having finally arrived. Change was coming, but not soon enough for me to become an obstetrician. I quickly calculated that the missionaries, who had started a great many schools, would be most interested in supporting anyone who pursued religion or teaching. Someone like Yee Sunsaeng-nim. "Childhood education," I said, almost as a question.

"Wonderful! I believe the tuition is around two hundred fifty."

"That much! I had no idea." This news—just punishment for my manipulative thinking—dashed my hope of missionary sponsorship.

"For the full two years. I don't know if you've heard—no, probably not since you've been away. My niece and nephew are coming to live with us next month."

"Excuse me," I said to explain my startled expression. "But I didn't know Director Gordon had children."

"Yes. You see, my sister-in-law died in childbirth years ago. Harlan guessed correctly that his work would be demanding, and knew he couldn't properly raise his youngsters here. The children were living with our parents in New York." She must have seen my face light up at the mention of the famous American city, for she added, "In Syracuse, New York State." Miss Gordon fanned herself rapidly, her hand like a hummingbird hovering over perfumed water cupped in a flower. "They're old enough now to join their father, and I'm afraid my parents are quite old enough for a break from child rearing." She chortled and I smiled back, uncomprehending. What grandparents wouldn't adore having their grandchildren around?

"Why, Harlan and I spoke about this very thing last night. God must have told me to greet you today!"

Thinking that I would have to learn to suppress my unseemly ambition, I listened politely, my hands folded, my eyes on my knees.

"We'll need extra help around the house, and of course we must hire you!"

"This person?" I blurted in surprise, mouth agape.

"I'm afraid it's not much. Housework, you know. Some babysitting, but it's a start. We certainly need more Korean Christian teachers for our flocks. What do you think?"

I rudely grabbed Miss Gordon's hand. "Yes, please, thank you!"

"Wonderful," said the missionary, squeezing my hand in return. "Then it's settled."

"I—I'll have to ask my father's permission."

"Of course, I should've thought of that. Here's a better idea. I'll have Harlan speak to your father, and you can start a week from Monday."

I concentrated on not exposing my teeth in my grateful smile.

DESPITE THE HONOR of having the school director himself request my services, Father said it was undignified for his daughter to work as a servant, even if it was for good pay, and refused permission. Then, the evening after Director Gordon's visit, I heard him say to Mother, "You ask me to contribute to such a frivolous pursuit as a ladies' journal?" I opened my window to hear more. "There's nothing left!" he said. Then, "What little there is from Manchuria goes to Shanghai. You dare question me on this?" Mother said something, and he quoted a proverb, "What kind of man would send out his women to work!" And a little later, "Then let her shame this family, but don't speak of it again!"

By the end of August, I had two jobs. The Gordons already employed a cook and an industrious housekeeper, so my responsibilities were simple: tidying the children's rooms and tending the garden. As a second job in the late afternoon, I tutored the children in Japanese language and grammar. If she happened to be around, Miss Gordon sometimes took part in those lessons as we sat around the dining room table, casually joining the children to recite "this is a yellow pencil," which provoked me to extreme discomfort. However, Harlan Jr. and Christine behaved better when their *gomo-nim*, father's-side aunt, was there. When we learned that all Ewha applicants were required to have some musical proficiency, Miss Gordon gave me lessons on the church's pump organ. Over time I felt easy enough in my patron's company to correct her Japanese and laugh with the family at her domestic ineptness, such as the time she baked Christine's birthday cake, which sank to the bottom of the pan, looked like a sponge and tasted like ash.

I rose hours before dawn to iron, shell peas, patch clothing—any housework I could do without waking my family. On clear summer nights, I weeded the kitchen garden by moonlight. On winter mornings, I swept snow off the porches. Then I'd walk across town to the Gordons' tall house behind my old primary school, which reminded me always of Teacher Yee.

TWO SUMMERS INTO my job, my savings for college were nearly met. On a humid evening I decided it was time to alert my mother, upon whom I relied to gain final permission from Father. If he said yes, I could enroll for the fall.

Beetles creaked in the underbrush and mosquitoes buzzed beyond the circling smoke of smoldering goldenrod. At her writing desk Mother displayed a letter from Imo.

I sat nearby, my back erect, my braid hanging straight and almost touching the floor. "How is she? How is the new house and her family?" After the royal family had been taken to Tokyo, Imo had purchased a traditional house of wood and mortar far from the palace, in the well-to-do Bukchon neighborhood, and had invited a struggling cousin's family from her husband's side to live with her.

"Things seem to be working out well. She's quite fond of her young nephew, and his parents are very helpful around the house. She asks if her favorite niece will register at Ewha this fall."

I smiled at this serendipitous opening. "Umma-nim, I've saved enough money. Director Gordon says I'll have a job teaching at the school when I've graduated. And when I'm in Seoul I think I can get tutoring jobs to help pay Dongsaeng's high school expenses. Miss Gordon says she'll give me the names of missionaries she knows there."

Mother clasped her knees. "If your room and board is too expensive, maybe you can live with Imo."

"Her new house is quite far from Ewha, Umma-nim. I'm told that dormitory housing or even a room in the school valley is quite cheap. Plus, if I'm nearby, I can more easily watch over Dongsaeng while he's at boarding school. He's still such a baby."

"I'll wait to finish my letter to Imo." I knew by the pleased smile delivered with this phrase that she would speak to Father, and that the consideration of Dongsaeng's well-being added a positive angle to the plan.

The summer drew to a close. I was diligently working and full of anticipation as plans for Ewha solidified, although Father had not yet approved. Each day, after I tended the garden and then practiced an hour on the organ, I crossed the churchyard and entered the back gate to the director's house. Both children had mirror-blue eyes and pudgy faces edged in white-blond curls. It was impossible not to think of them as the boiled potatoes they frequently ate. Harlan Jr., a slender and quiet twelve-year-old drawn to books, was a cooperative if sullen student. He disliked being cooped up for the two hours of tutoring, and I let him ride his bicycle prior to their lessons "to get the wiggles out," as they'd say in English. Christine said repeatedly that I was the prettiest Oriental girl she'd ever met. Since she was only seven years old, the inappropriate compliment was considered charming. She invited me to practice English with them. They were bright and gangly, these foreign jewels, and as the months progressed and their conversational Japanese improved, the Gordons kept me on less as a tutor than a companion.

During our lessons, the children corrected my pronunciation of memorized sentences from the Chinese-English phrasebook. I learned how to drop the last syllable from English words that ended on hard consonants: *book* instead of *book-uh*. Our sessions were merry, and I was proud of my conversational English. They laughed at my never-ending confusion with Rs and Ls in *frock, flock*, and the subtlety of Bs and Ps in *crab, clap, bright, plight*.

At last their lessons came to an end. I'd been accepted at Ewha, although Father refused to consider it. Harlan Jr. would soon leave Korea for a boarding school in upstate New York, already on the path to become a Far East missionary. After a hundred thank-yous and sad goodbyes, the Gordons gave me Harlan's bicycle, which they thought might be useful in Seoul. The children had taught me how to ride in the school lot, and though I'd seen no other woman on such an ignoble contraption, I delighted in its trundling speed. As I walked the bicycle home, the temptation to ride it overcame my concern about the propriety of cycling. Sure enough, catcalls and jeers followed me as I pedaled through the market, but the breeze blew coolly down my neck and I pedaled on, reveling in downhill coasts, dignity restored when I pushed the heavy machine uphill.

Word soon reached Father that I'd been seen riding the bicycle. His displeasure was distinct. From across the courtyard I heard him yell, "Will she never cease to shame us? Going around like a man in a skirt!" My mother responded with something I couldn't hear. "Good for nothing but shaming the family name," I heard him say. Mother again, then, "Send her to Ewha then. Better to have her out of this house!" This permission born out of anger wasn't ideal, but it would do.

The bicycle became Dongsaeng's, to be sent ahead to Seoul for his use during school. I rode it one last time around the yard while Mother laughed at the sight of my skirts and braid flying as freely as the ancient spirits that roamed our ancestral compound.

# *Nuna* Means "Elder Sister"

## AUTUMN 1928

I OBSESSED OVER SMALL THINGS—STROKES OF LETTERFORMS, CREASES in the sleeves of dark school dresses, the compact arrangement of my few possessions in my locker—my concern with minutiae analogous to my focus on learning. I shared a high-ceilinged room with twenty other girls in the Truth wing of the dormitory, which I thought was more ironically appropriate for me than the other two wings: Beauty and Goodness. I was glad to have had experience living away from home. In the beginning months, much sniffling was heard after lights out, and some simply couldn't adjust to living among the many different classes and personalities of students and teachers, and went home. Academically I did well at Ewha. I majored in early childhood education, minored in nursing and received special permission to take courses in English literature as a way to improve my language skills. Drawn to anatomy, I studied bones, muscles and organs as if by memorizing their function and interdependence, I would gain clarity to new feelings of ambiguity, along with an increasing sense of dissociation that filled the hours I wasn't studying.

The stately Ewha campus had spacious lawns, a soaring church and impressive Western-style granite buildings bordered by trees and shrubs. Paulownia, magnolia, dogwood and cherry blossom trees filled the air with flowers and scent in the spring, maples and beeches brought color in autumn, and dozens of varieties of pines and junipers kept winters green. Inside the buildings were many stairs and large classrooms with hard wooden seats. I walked the grounds and knew it was wonderful, that I should be ecstatic—here I was, fulfilling a dream! It's true that we all felt privileged, because we were Korean, and women, and thoroughly modern. Our skirts went up an inch a year, we wore baggy trousers cinched at the ankle, and many girls bobbed their hair. So much was exciting and new, like hot showers, and yet, though I tried to hide it even from myself, something was wrong with me and I couldn't say what.

I searched the Bible, looking for the calm it gave my mother. I rediscovered the inspiring beauty of the Psalms, found fascinating stories and marvelous history in the Old Testament, and lessons about the liberation of faith in the New Testament. But, much as my father might have, I saw the Book as a chronicle of a foreign people's faith and history rather than a map that would lead me to salvation. For a moment I considered that my growing alienation from the Bible meant I was becoming a political isolationist and conservative traditionalist, very much like my father. Then I attributed the religious estrangement to homesickness and academic overstimulation. But I loved learning and losing myself in studying, and while I naturally missed my family and the familiar spaces of home, I was proud and pleased to be an Ewha student. I embraced the lessons exemplified by my mother's Christian living, and then put the Bible aside when it became clear that I lacked spiritual passion that could sustain belief once I closed its pages. Keeping these agnostic sentiments hidden, I further discounted my worth when it grew obvious that I possessed not a single spark of the religious fervor exhibited by my classmates at daily chapel. I often found myself wishing I were in the library instead.

Obligation mustered me to Sunday worship, and I was conscious of envying the few Buddhist and atheist girls' freedom from church attendance, though those girls were shunned. I did love listening to the renowned Ewha choir. The women's seamless harmony often brought me to tears, which I attributed to the fierce beauty of the swelling music. But over the months, then years, I doubted that beauty could feel so full of pain and inexplicable longing.

I avoided joining friendship circles, averse to the meanness of gossip, but found diversion with a few friends. My classmates welcomed me when I accompanied them for an afternoon of hiking or swimming in the summer and ice skating or snowball fights in the winter. I declined most sightseeing excursions—too sad to be reminded of places I'd been with Imo, and people like the princess, her strong maid and even that Japanese guard, whose lives were far more restricted and controlled than mine would ever be, and whom I would never see again. It didn't matter. My reticence about those years and the refinement of my manners were mistaken for aloofness, and such invitations dwindled over time.

Happily, a renewed friendship with Jaeyun, who would soon graduate, offered occasional companionship at a restaurant or a walk in a park. It was Jaeyun who told me the story about Dean Shinohara. For hoarding an illegal personal library of Korean poetry and Chinese classics, he'd been relocated from Ewha to a rural boys' school. He wasn't fired, though, until his week's "vacation" in the country had come to a close and he was packing to return to Seoul. I deduced that when I'd met the Shinoharas on the train, they were unknowingly on their way to exile. Although he was a Japanese supremacist, the girls at Ewha considered him a quasi hero because it was his love of the classics and Korean poetry that had led to losing his plum job.

I visited my beloved aunt once a month and during school breaks. A gasoline train that ran between Ewha and downtown, where I would pick up Ilsun, shortened the long walk from one side of the city to the other. My dongsaeng grew so rapidly that every season I sacrificed precious study hours to make him a new school uniform. One icy winter day I waited thirty minutes outside of his dormitory before he finally rushed through the vestibule. Shaking with cold, I said, "We'll have to hurry now. Imo-nim is waiting."

"Give me my money." His voiced scratched with teenage change, and he made to grab my string purse.

"What are you doing?" I pushed him away.

"I need my allowance now!"

I retrieved a handful of won—savings from tutoring jobs that I portioned to Dongsaeng monthly. "Why? It's supposed to last you all month."

"Nuna, you said we had to hurry!" He snatched the cash and ran off.

Wrapping my coat tightly, I followed him to the doorway and leaned in. "That's only half," said a boy's deep voice. "You better get the rest by tomorrow." A door slammed. I stepped outside and headed toward Imo's without looking back. Dongsaeng joined me and soon caught his breath. I could sense his agitation beside me, but I refused to break the silence. Our shoes crunched on frosty dirt pathways.

"Cold," Dongsaeng said, his shoulders hunched, his hands buried in armpits.

"Where's your coat?"

"Don't know."

"What do you mean?"

"Lost it."

I clutched my collar around my neck, glad that I was too angry to give him my coat, something I would have typically done.

We walked half an hour more, Dongsaeng blowing on his fingers occasionally. "Hey, Nuna, I got first place in my history examination last week."

"Good."

The sun set in a gentle fade of brilliance. I'd read somewhere that fishermen predicted weather by the color of the evening skies, and wondered what they'd say about the dark high clouds glowing with silvery trim, the far sky deepening blue, the treetops frosted with ice. Perhaps snow. I remembered at home how I'd rouse Dongsaeng to wide-eyed wakefulness on mornings when the yard was transformed by magical new snowfall. I breathed the blue-cold smell of winter and sighed.

Dongsaeng looked at me hopefully. "I wonder what Imo-nim will have for dinner."

"Just be happy with whatever she serves and refuse seconds. Do you hear?" He shrugged. "Times are hard, Dongsaeng! I think she goes without in order to feed us."

"But I'm famished!"

"Why do you owe that boy money?"

"None of your business."

"Your business is my concern." Except for the sharpness of my tone, I realized I sounded like Mother. "Especially when it comes to money, especially when it's *my* money. You're lucky to have even a few jeon. If Father knew what I gave you, don't you think he'd want to know what you do with it?"

"Give me next month's, won't you?—or I'll get in trouble."

"Why do you owe that boy?"

"We had a bet, and I lost."

"You've been gambling, haven't you? Dice!"

"It's just games. Who cares? He cheats, and besides, that's not what it's for."

"Oh, Dongsaeng!" Frustrated and angry, I walked fast. He burst forward to keep up. "What will happen if you don't pay?"

"His gang will beat me up." He sounded too smug and my anger swelled.

"Why must you gamble? Why can't you just study hard?"

"Like you? Boring old you? At least I'm having fun!"

"Where did you learn to talk like that? Think about what your parents sacrificed so you could come to this school. Think of how hard Mother worked! And what would Father say?"

"Well he's not here, so I don't care. But you're so stingy it's as if he were right here! I thought you were supposed to help me."

I counted twenty terse crunching steps before speaking. I no longer felt the cold. Imo's house was not far ahead. "I'll help you, but you must tell me honestly why you need the money. There shouldn't be secrets between us. It's just the two of us here, and I'm your nuna."

"If I tell you, will you give it to me?"

"How much?"

"Ten won."

"That's as much as two weeks' pay! What have you done?"

"I didn't do anything! I just went along when they—"

How distasteful his whining sounded. What had happened to my sweet baby brother? I thought back and wondered if he'd always been this self-centered and inconsiderate. He typically talked back, but I had likened that to my own streak of childhood stubborn independence and thought he'd grow out of it as I had. With Imo's gate in sight, I stopped to look fully at my brother. He stared at his feet and kicked icy mud clods. I saw with surprise that he was now slightly taller than me. Under his cap his shorn head made his face seem rounder and whiter than usual. Pink dots of cold, or agitation, colored the flat of his cheeks. "Look at me," I said. I recognized in him the familiar fullness of my mother's lips, his chin dimpled with pouting. "Where did you go?"

The pout flattened to a smirk. "They took me to a teahouse."

"You're just a boy! How could they do such a mean thing?"

"It wasn't mean at all. I liked it! People were really nice to me. That's why— I borrowed from— She wanted me to buy— I went back— I mean, that's why I need the money."

Scarlet spread down my neck. I pulled him into an enclave beside a lone oak tree out of sight of Imo's gate. "You borrowed money to visit teahouse girls? And you sold your coat, didn't you?"

"Don't tell, okay?"

"At least you know it's wrong!"

"It's not wrong. It's fun! There's nothing else to do, and they're nice to me!"

"For money! They're only nice to you because they want your money. How can you be so stupid!"

"I'm not stupid!" His eyes met mine. In the graying evening, I could only see their blackness. "I'm lonely and bored."

Remorse overcame me as quickly as the anger had risen, and I took his hand. "I'm sorry. It's my fault. I should be a better nuna to you. I get caught up with studying and forget about friends and having fun. We could do things together on Sundays. When it's warmer we can tour the old temples."

"Can you give me the ten?"

"We'll see. Next Sunday let's go to the big Methodist church around the corner from you. You must promise me you won't go to those places again. Think of how angry Father would be if he knew."

"There's plenty of church at school already." He gave me a boyish smile. "Let's do something fun instead. There's a cinema. Have you seen any films?"

"After church, we can do something. Not too expensive, though. Agreed?"

He nodded.

"No more teahouses?"

He turned toward Imo's and mumbled something. A breeze rattled the dead leaves clinging to the oak, and he said, "I promise. Thanks, Nuna." Or at least that's what I thought he said.

# A Good Christian with Modern Thinking

## WINTER 1930–WINTER 1934

Sunday, December 28, 1930

Daughter,

When I think of how hard you have worked to achieve your dream, how diligently you pursued your education, my eyes overflow with joy, my heart cries with pride. To think that my only daughter has a degree in childhood education and nursing from the first women's college in Korea! You are among the pioneers for women in this new age, blessed with opportunities you have managed to take advantage of, even when faced with many obstacles. To also learn that you were among the top ten in your class has given me new reason to say that my cup runneth over. I am proud of you beyond measure.

As for the coming year, I think it is fine for you to stay in Seoul. Be grateful that your patrons are happy as long as you are teaching in a Christian school, even if, as you say, it is just first grade. Praise God there are schools at all! Miss Gordon says the Hoston School is well established and uses modern methods. Think of how many girls' minds you will influence! Do not take this work lightly. These days, it is a wonder that you can earn money at all. Remember the old proverb "A women's lack of talent is in itself a virtue." Can you imagine that your own mother once followed this kind of thinking?

It is good that you stay in touch with the Gordons. The little yellow-haired daughter asks me about you every Sunday. "Is Sunsaeng-nim coming home soon?" She speaks very prettily, and Director Gordon worries she will lose her English. He says he is losing his English as fast as his hair, but I think he is joking. I cannot tell with them.

Naturally, we will miss you on Sol-lal, but do not fret. With your degree, you have done more to honor your parents than you could by coming to pay respects. Besides, poor Imo should have somebody bowing to her on New Year's, and who better than you, her favorite? Just be sure to return the money she gives you without her knowing. Put it where she will find it later. I know you will think of this, but I worry.

The squawroot powder you sent is well received. I have had it as tea the past few weeks, and it helps relieve the troublesome women's fevers. How blessed I am to have such a knowledgeable daughter. The money and herbs for Kira and Joong were put to good use. Although only prayer can help ease her grief over the baby she lost, the medicine can heal her body. I have told her of your prayers, and she cried. She says thank you and that she wishes you had met her daughter. There is little else to be done except to leave the healing of her spirit to God's grace and mercy. They have said nothing, but I suspect the day will come when Joong will take his wife north to his family, and I fear that moment. What will Father do without him? Byungjo could never fill that position. I see that I am anticipating worries when there are plenty in the present to keep me occupied.

Congratulations on graduating with honors. I am so proud.

Mother

Sunday, March 11, 1931

Daughter,

I received the money fine. Rather than getting medicine for myself (it is warmer and I am better), I will save it for your dongsaeng who will need school money. I did trade two of your nicer hanbok for mulberry plants. You are good to sacrifice them toward my project. I have only been able to pay for the start-up supplies, but our first harvest later this spring should bring relief to our pockets. Your father still does not know that the sheds by our side of the house are devoted to silkworms. He will discover it eventually, but by then there may be enough of an income to ease any upset. He complains little, but I can see that he suffers from dyspepsia and is losing weight. Of course we will be grateful if you can learn about any other traditional medicines. He refuses to visit the acupuncturist after learning that this particular doctor does not exclusively treat our people.

Be sure to let us know when to meet Dongsaeng at the train station. No, you are not to blame for his falling marks last term. The absence of his letters led your father to suspect something. He has always been willful, even more than you in your youth! Time spent at home should help to even out his bumpy character. There are other worries about Dongsaeng's future and other reasons we needed him home. You understand this.

Do not impose yourself too much on Miss Gordon. She tells me how she looks for graduate schools for you in America. She whispers this to me after church, and I am embarrassed that people will think we have secrets. You should be thinking about how to repay her kindness rather than what more she could do for you. I know you do that, but think and pray on this more, for your mother's sake. If it were based on your merits alone, I know it would be inevitable, but she tells me there are new quotas limiting

Orientals in America and sponsorship is more difficult than ever. And I have only heard of one woman being sponsored by the missionaries, and that was a long time ago. This is not to diminish hope, but so you may consider how likely or unlikely this possibility is. It frightens me to think that an ocean may one day separate you from your family, but as you can see, I am anticipating worries I have yet to have. How can I live, torn between pride and worry if you go to America?

I meant to tell you they are quite strict about not allowing white clothes, which is one reason why your colorful hanbok fetched good prices. Is it the same there? Poor Cook came home from market the other day angry as a caged fox, her skirt splashed with blue paint. They said if she wore white again they would paint her skirt again. Father says it is meant to equalize the classes, but in reality it is more about how a bully sits on a beaten man just to show who is on top. We dyed our skirts with safflower and knotweed.

The silkworms are calling me, as is Father. He sends greetings and blessings. Work hard and think of others first.

Mother

Sunday, October 25, 1931

Daughter,

Your contribution to Dongsaeng's tuition arrived fine. Together with the earnings from the cocoons, it adds up to half a year's fees. He is doing well, making good marks and studying at night, much to Father's satisfaction. I do not want to overly worry you, but the forestland where your father's uncle lives has gone the way of the farm. We do not know what became of Uncle. Your father suffers, unable to eat or sleep because of it. He needs your faraway prayers to soothe his angry heart. I also pray daily for your father's dongsaeng, as we cannot know where he is or if his wife's family's similar concerns have also ended. We pray that God's mercy has spared him, and that one day he will come back to his home here, and then you would be able to know him. I remember his character as being opposite from your father's: as spirited as your father is solemn, as carefree as your father is devoted to duty. It was almost as if you could see his smile from the back.

I worry that the midwifery apprenticeship might interfere with your teaching. Lack of sleep can lead to mistakes, so be careful. We made the parsnip leaf into tea for your father, and he did have trouble reading the day after as you warned us. He claimed the sun was too bright. He has not shown any pain for several days. I am writing down how often we use it.

Your father is doing a little carpentry—the most beautiful pieces! It started when a leg on my study table broke and he decided to fix it rather than burn the old thing. How easily he whittled the curve of the leg to match the others exactly. It gave him enough satisfaction that he carved a decorative panel to replace that missing one in front. I had forgotten there was a hole there until it was filled. It makes me wonder what other broken things I no longer see because time has made them unseeable. The new panel is almost alive, the birds and branches beautifully shaped. The wood seems like clay in his hands. This pursuit occupies many fulfilling hours.

I am well if a little tired tonight, perhaps because the moon is obscured and the leaves colored little this season. It seems they went from green to brown in one moment, giving us no chance to notice and enjoy the changing season. Perhaps a harsh winter is ahead. Perhaps it is God's way of showing His sympathy to us. No money came from the forestlands for some time, so we worry only about family, and, of course, your father is concerned about the legacy he leaves for his son. But he gives him generations of yangban ancestry and auspicious grave sites (we had a smaller ceremony this year on the mountain). He has a talented and smart heir, and a clever and intelligent daughter. We are blessed a hundred times. What more is needed?

I write mainly to tell you to do well in your job, do not overdo it with your second job, stay warm this winter and worry not for us. God keeps us safe from harm and we have more than enough. Work hard so you can come home soon and find a good husband.

Mother

Dragon Festival, June 8, 1932

Daughter,

I received your letter and the money fine. We are blessed that times are not as hard here as you seem to be experiencing. Do not send any more of your earnings to us. We are fine. If you do not need it for yourself, buy food for your students, or paper and pencils. It is right that you say nothing to the Gordons. They are having as hard a time as anyone. Was this rainy season worse than last year, or is it my imagination? Four houses south of the market collapsed in floods last month. Thank God, no one drowned. I have never seen beggars in Gaeseong in my entire lifetime, and even the Gordons say it is unheard of, that Koreans have too much pride to beg, but there are beggars now. You know what your father says causes this shamefulness . . .

I saw Jaeyun's mother at the market last week. In one breath, she is pleased that Jaeyun studies at Tokyo University but also worries about the distance, as well as the slim chance her daughter will have a good career as a surgical nurse there, so far from home. Her talk about Jaeyun reminded me of you trying to advance yourself in a world too slow for your ambitions. I can understand her worries. Jaeyun gave up a decent nursing job with her father at the hospital. At least she pays her own fees. A thoughtful daughter, like you. It is good of you to write to her, to keep her home spirit high and true. I am afraid I boasted about you a little to Jaeyun's mother, but what mother would not be proud of her daughter becoming school principal in a year and a half? She did cluck her tongue when I described how far outside of Seoul you will be. And I have to admit that I silently clucked my tongue when I saw the price she paid for a sorry slab of pork. I guess she did not see there was hardly any meat on it. Forgive my pettiness, Lord.

It will be much colder in the mountains. Does your room have heat? Do you have enough winter clothes? Do not send us money. Keep it for moving and buying warm quilts.

Sadly, Kira remains barren. I wish we had the nourishment she needs to improve her chances, but there is less and less available in the market. She continues to work hard, and once I actually saw

Joong carrying her water buckets back from the stream for her. He turned pepper red when he saw me, and Kira covered her head with embarrassment. What could I do but smile? Nowadays, she usually draws water from the new pumps they installed down the street. The water is not pure, and the missionaries say we must boil it for drinking or cooking. Despite hard times or maybe because of them, Joong has pledged to remain with your father. An occasional bit of news from the family in Nah-jin keeps us assured that all is as well as can be. We fear they suffered winter harshly and can only trust God to feed and protect them. Cook is well, if a little more bent in her back from age. Write soon with your Yoju address, and be a strong leader, and kind.

Mother

Sunday, August 20, 1932

Daughter,

You were right to say that the mail is less reliable from your new post. I received your letter six weeks after you wrote it. At this rate, it will be autumn in the mountains when you receive this. In that case, think of the star maples in the backyard as you read this letter, their colorful brilliance and the cool shade they offer on the last few hot days.

Dongsaeng says thank you for the money. I was not aware you were sending to him. You are a good nuna. He has a hole in his pocket as big as his appetite. The lack of variety and lesser number of side dishes hit your brother the hardest. At least he is not so fat! That is a joke, like the missionaries do. Did he complain this much about food in Seoul?

It is good that you enjoy the mountain beauty and your new job. Never mind about how time-consuming it turned out to be. Hard work will keep you warm when the winter comes. You are clever to take the older girls on walks to show them edible plants. A wonderful practical knowledge that will come in handy if times get any worse, and many say they will worsen before they improve. I laughed when I read your description about nailing the broken window shutters. Now all the girls have learned that a principal's job is to fix everything! It reminded me of seeing you riding that bicycle. Dongsaeng takes good care of it still, pedaling to and from school, and sometimes running errands for Father.

Your father is fine, perhaps quieter than usual. He has put aside his brushes and paints. He says there is no one now who can correctly understand his work. He does not seem upset, but I notice that he is reading late into the night, or at least the light in his study burns long, and yet he rises as early as before. His appetite seems smaller also.

The neighbors' son, Hansu, is home from Pyeongyang and will be married next month. He says they will move to Gangdong, a small village in the northwest mountains, as the missionaries found him a teaching position there. My, how his future wife patiently waited for him! I cannot even remember how many years it was since his betrothal. Do not worry about a wedding present. I will have something by then. Speaking of which, I know you will close your ears and grimace, but you are twenty-two now. What do you think? As promised, you will meet the prospect Father might find for you before anyone agrees to anything, so do not worry about that part. There is someone at church who is eligible, and Hansu mentioned someone. You now have no excuses except, of course, your job. Let me know your thoughts on this. You are nearly an old maid, so think on it, will you? Do not worry, we will find a good Christian with modern thinking.

We are all well. Pray every day for better times and for your father's good health.

Mother

Sunday, July 16, 1933

Daughter,

That was too generous a gift for Dongsaeng's graduation. You spoil him! You must not have eaten all month in order to send him that much. Your father has yet to decide what to do about his upper school. My guess is he will remain here where we can keep an eye on him. Expenses and fees notwithstanding, he is coming of age, which brings a host of other concerns, and provincial registration.

Along with joy on his graduation, there is great sadness. Kira lost another baby, not even two months into term. We took her to the hospital this time, although she protested because of the cost. I feared she would lose too much blood without hospital care, and she needed rest and time to mourn, which she would not have at home. She would start up the very next day with toting buckets, and I think that might be one reason she has this trouble. There is sadness in the house, and we pray day and night for her renewed strength.

What you say about prayer worries me. Are you reading the Bible between church days? How can prayer not help the hardships of your poor little school? Prayer won't feed hungry children, I know, but it will fill their spirit with richness. Perhaps you do not pray with a pure heart and honest feeling. God knows if you try to take the easy road. Clear your mind and approach prayer with openness, willingness, faith and trust. Opening your heart will open your mind to unforeseen possibilities, the richness of faith.

You probably have not heard that Jaeyun is back in Seoul as a surgical nurse. Most of the hospital is Japanese, but she was able to find a position because of her Tokyo education. Her mother reports she makes good money, especially considering the Depression. Jaeyun's mother implied this was one of the benefits of studying in Japan, but who can say such a thing as fact? Forgive me, Lord, but her chitchat is annoying.

I heard from Imo, who is considering adopting one of her cousin's sons. She needs to keep the family line going, and I encouraged her. Write to her if you have time. She is better off than most. We have much to be grateful for with Imo.

Cook and Kira, before she took ill, have both been helping with the silkworms. Also on Wednesdays, Cook takes half our garden crops to sell at the market. Can you believe it? You should see her fuss with the display and bargain with customers. She is the toughest saleslady in the market, and I am thankful she is on my side! Who knew about this hidden talent? Conditions here are as you thought. No rice. They blame two seasons of drought, but one can guess otherwise.

Your father is proud of Dongsaeng's good grades, and I of your consideration of him. I worry about your Christian spirit and think maybe you need a husband and children in your life. Do not be like those modern girls who refuse to marry.

Mother

Sunday, February 25, 1934

Daughter,

I fear this letter may not reach you before you depart Yoju, so I will write briefly. Once we learned your post had ended, coincidentally, we heard about a certain bachelor from Pyeongyang. Chang Hansu has returned to Gaeseong under what I can guess is the same situation as yours, since he is looking for work. You will catch up on all that when you come home. More important, he brings news of a good prospect. The gentleman is the second son of a famous minister, someone Hansu met years ago in Seoul—of course you remember that time when he went to the capital. At first, Father was none too keen on this gentleman since his family is common. However, he is the grandson of a district governor, and his father, the first Christian in his province, is the first Presbyterian Korean minister in Pyeongyang. I believe his moral worth can counterbalance his lack of class distinction. I will try to learn more by the time you arrive.

Do not be alarmed to find your father greatly reduced in health and in his attention to these matters. His main concern is rightly toward Dongsaeng's education and training, and he has little patience for much else. This can be advantageous to you, since he will not be as concerned about the quality of your husband's name as he might have been ten years ago. You say you refuse to marry, but that is nonsense. You are already old now! Besides, your father's health would greatly improve were his daughter's welfare settled once and for all. Think about that and travel quickly to us. I pray for an uneventful and safe journey home.

Mother

# A Measure of Faith

## SPRING 1934

I CAME HOME FROM THE TRAIN STATION SO LATE IN THE EVENING THAT I could barely see the outlines of our gate. Tired from traveling, I quickly unpacked, breathing in the welcoming scents of home: the dusty wood in my room and Mother's sweetness on my cheek after an uncharacteristic hug. She had waited to have supper with me and was in the kitchen getting it ready. I went down the dim corridor on the women's side of the house, the smells of garlic, hot pepper and cooking oil growing stronger with each step. Dongsaeng's rooms were dark—he was away at boarding school across the valley—but a glow in Father's studio showed him still awake. A half moon cleared the trees and spread thin light in the yard. I stepped onto the veranda and smiled to see the gentle hollows worn into the courtyard slate where I had often swept and played. Father's silhouette behind his screen door shifted in the lamplight, and I heard him call for Joong, who would ready his bedding. I would attend to Father in the morning when Chang Hansu came to visit. I considered this impending visit with unease, suspecting Father's willingness to have me home would culminate in my being married off as soon as possible. The pleasurable comfort of being home was mixed with childish feelings of caution and rebellion, and I was surprised and disturbed by this reversion.

In the kitchen, Cook stirred a boiling pot with long chopsticks at the stove, her back now slightly hunched at the shoulders. "I told Mother not to disturb you," I said, clasping Cook's hands, warm with steam. Although her eyes were as fiery as always, she looked tiny, her wrinkles deeper.

"What could I do?" said Mother, slicing gimchi at the table. "As soon as she heard you had crossed the threshold, she was stoking the fire."

"Aigu! How did you grow so tall? And didn't anyone feed you?" Cook fished buckwheat noodles from the pot into a bamboo strainer. "Sadly, here we have only poor man's food."

"What you're cooking smells wonderful. Even the finest city restaurants with the best ingredients can't match your skill."

Cook's lips spread wide, showing a new gold tooth at the edge of her smile. It made me notice that her neck was bare of the fine hair chain she had always worn, from which had hung a gold cross. When I was little, Cook had often told me the story of the little cross, her eyes sparkling.

From a poor peasant family, at the age of nine she had joined my maternal grandmother's household in Nah-jin, originally taken in as a nanny for my mother, who had just been born. It was soon apparent that her skills were more suited to the kitchen than to child care, which required a patient, persistent personality, and one not so prone to outspokenness. She was trained in diet and food preparation to become a competent cook in Mother's future household. "You should see your grandfather's house," Cook used to say. "Sixty-six rooms and land the size of a village. Four kitchens and every winter a straw pantry twice bigger than this kitchen! Your grandmother treated me and all her servants with kindness and generosity, and I wondered how I came to be part of such goodness." Cook would finger the cross and wipe it with her apron. "Your grandmother taught me about God and Jesus, and then I understood where her goodness came from. She allowed me to be baptized when I was fifteen and gave me this cross, the first gift I ever received." She would show me tiny indentations on both sides. "See that? I couldn't believe it was real gold, so I bit it! Oh, she was generous! And your mother is exactly the same as her mother, so you are a doubly blessed child."

I silently vowed to replace the cross and wondered why my mother hadn't provided for the dental work. It seemed things were worse than I'd suspected. "I learned a lot doing midwifery, and have many new remedies to add," I told Cook, who had a memorized catalog of several hundred recipes to create a healthy, balanced diet according to the old way.

"Anything for peptic ulcer?" said Mother, as Cook shot me a pointed look.

So, Father had lost his gastric battle. "There're quite a few things. We can visit the pharmacist tomorrow."

"You should hear that man complain about business," said Mother.

"Isn't he still the best in town?" I wandered through the kitchen handling familiar pots, utensils, bowls and cups, noting empty pegs where sacks of meal and grain should've hung. True, it had been a long winter and our pantry would likely be replenished soon, but I could feel my ribs protruding. Children had come to class with nothing to eat since the day before when I'd fed them. We bartered books, pencils and paper for noodles and barley.

"He says his access to suppliers is limited ever since Manchuria," said Mother about the herbalist. Her pursed lips signaled me to wait for further discussion. Brightly, she complimented the earthy pepper blends in the gimchi.

"Kira's first crop of cabbage, not my handiwork," said Cook.

"True, she and Byungjo perform miracles in the garden," said Mother, "but it's you who mixes everything perfectly."

"Your recipe!" said Cook, blushing.

"Your touch!" We all laughed.

"Let's eat. I was waiting for you, Daughter." She arranged two sets of bowls on trays, and when Cook went outside to retrieve spiced anchovies from a cold-storage urn, Mother laid out another set. "Now she'll have to eat something tonight." She lowered her voice. "You see how she's shrunken. She pretends to have no appetite, thinking to save food."

My expression was so full of questions that Mother whispered, "It's not as bad as that. She just thinks so. Later—"

Cook returned, her fingers red with spice and fish oil, and placed the anchovies on young lettuce leaves. She sprinkled steamed bean sprouts with vinegar and soy sauce. Mother portioned the food into threes as Cook quickly chopped scallions and sprinkled sesame and pepper on the noodles, ignoring the third setting. With the trays apportioned, she cracked raw eggs into our noodle bowls. "I saved these for you from this morning," she said, beaming.

"Lovely!"

Mother said to Cook, "Pour the tea, won't you?" Using her body as a shield, Mother quickly switched her bowl with Cook's, while the old woman poured roasted barley tea.

In her sitting room, Mother and I settled in behind our table trays. She chuckled. "See how I have to trick her? She'll be mad when she sees the egg, but she can't let it go to waste now."

I gave Mother half the vegetables and egg in my bowl, and we ate, the thick noodles rolling deliciously on my tongue, fiery with gimchi and smoky with anchovies. She said things really weren't that bad. They'd met Dongsaeng's tuition for high school with cocoon income, my contributions and the amount received from Oriental Land for the forestlands. She told me that shortly after Japan annexed Manchuria, jewelry and silverware were given to Father, as well as the best of the jade, and were buried. "That was foresight on your father's part, because a few days later a Japanese tax official visited us." She frowned. "Well, *visit* isn't exactly the correct word. He demanded entry to inventory the household."

"He was here? Counting things? How dare they!"

"Anger is pointless, Najin-ah. Laws are made to match their desires, it seems. They've even started 'clean house' inspections, so they can come in at will." She blew into the barley tea, showing calmness, but I heard the tremor in her voice. She continued, "This man expressed interest in purchasing some paintings, but your father wouldn't hear of it." Father would remain firm in the Confucian sentiment that to sell a scroll would taint it with mercenary concerns, reducing its true artistry. "The worst of it was he threatened Dongsaeng's student status. 'A stroke of the pen one way or the other' were his words. It seemed for a moment that our intention to bring Dongsaeng home from Seoul specifically to protect him from conscription was in vain."

Tiny anchovy bones scratched deep in my throat. "But students are supposed to be exempt from labor conscription!"

"Yes, and thankfully, Dongsaeng is still underage. Your father took additional steps to prevent him from being drafted. He remembered meeting this man years ago when he had to register your school enrollment, and knows how to satisfy him with occasional gifts—a jade pin or a vase particularly admired during inventory." Mother looked rueful. "I'm sorry to tell you about this. I didn't want you to worry. You should know that your dowry will be simple. Cook traded some raw silk for a bolt of cotton for you. Use it for your dowry, which I'm sorry to say will only be what you can sew for your future children and husband in the time that you're home."

The words spoken, I could do nothing but hold myself very still. I wanted to insist that marriage would be a waste of my education, that I could be more helpful to the family by working. The light wobbled and the dark blush under Mother's eyes deepened. I noticed her lax cheeks and faint worry lines crossing her forehead. Outlined in moonlight, the room's spare furnishings and clean simplicity reflected the rare sense of peace and wholeness I felt in her presence. At that moment, I wanted only to please her. I hid a sigh. "So then, Chang Hansu's friend . . ."

Mother's worry lines disappeared. "A son of Minister Cho from Pyeongyang. Even your father is impressed with Reverend Cho's involvement on March First, at least enough to ignore his woeful bloodline." She added quietly, "Perhaps your father finally realizes the old ways are ending." This gave me pause, and I noted it to ponder later.

Mother said that the eldest Cho son was already an ordained minister, an encouraging sign that the second son—the one in question—would follow those footsteps. My stomach knotted, and not from a plentiful supper in a shrunken belly.

"And he's pursuing advanced theological education in America. Who knows?" she said, her eyes curved with warmth. "Isn't it natural if two people dream the same dream, their paths will flow together?"

Hearing *two people* and *together* made me speechless with dread.

"We'll learn more tomorrow from Hansu. Your future lies ahead of you in ways only God can say," she said, looking at me closely. "I fear you haven't been talking enough to God. You must trust in his plan. And get a good night's sleep."

"Yes, Umma-nim." We said goodnight and I returned the trays to the kitchen. Cook was gone, the stoves banked and tidied for the night. I washed the dishes with a crock of water thoughtfully left by Cook, still warm. Heaviness tugged at my thoughts as I dried and put the bowls away. On the shelf I found my childhood brass rice bowl, kept polished and shiny. I laid its coolness against my cheek, and as tears wet the brass surface, I rolled the cold metal on my skin, trying to replace the tightness in my chest at my impending loss of freedom with the joy of being home.

Sleepless in bed, I recalled what Mother said: that perhaps Father finally realized the days of bloodlines and class distinctions had ended. Had he really given up fighting? I realized how important it was that he be as much of a stickler for the old ways as he used to be. I'd previously regarded his stubborn adherence to tradition as a limitation, but the thought that he might have given up made me see otherwise—it wasn't stubbornness but strength of conviction. When I read in Mother's letter that he'd stopped painting because he believed a proper audience for his art no longer existed, it seemed a prideful conceit. I now began to see the magnitude of what he had lost as he put aside each part of all he had known. Whether by force of law or by social pressure, all the insidious change maneuvered by the occupation in each passing day was irrevocable. Could this laxity in my father's defense of tradition be indicative of the state of our country? I hoped not. With these thoughts, and because it was right to obey my father, I would acquiesce with all the grace I could muster to his choice of a husband for me, though this decision made me cry.

I searched the beams for words that might inspire a peaceful resolution to my warring sense of duty and hard-earned freedoms. Where once the simple memory of a pattern of stars would trace words for me, now nothing came. I thought I should pray, but when I tried, I remembered instead the vision shared with my mother after Dongsaeng's birth. Like water, flowing around, beneath and through rooted trees, we would always flow. I said a small prayer then, with thanks for my mother, for

Dongsaeng's safety, for my father's continued stubbornness, for a husband with kindness.

BY MIDMORNING THE clouds had dropped and a wet fog hid treetops and gardens. I ran fingertips fondly over the hammered hinges of the folding screen outside Father's sitting room, where he and I would wait for Hansu. Straightening, I went in. My father sat at his desk, his hands idly turning pages of a well-worn book. "Thank you for asking me to join you, Father. I'm relieved to see you're looking well." He looked drawn and hollow, his skin chalky.

His eyes caught mine, and I was surprised and touched to feel their warmth. He quoted slowly in Chinese, "The way home is a thousand li . . ."

My mind was far from classic poetry. I looked at him blankly, trying to remember the stanza and discern his meaning.

He frowned, a teacher prompting a young student, and continued, ". . . an autumn night is even longer."

I remembered the poem, and my eyes flooded with love and gratitude for his paternalistic formal welcome and his scholar's insight, as I finished it, "Ten times already I have been home, but the cock has not yet crowed."

He looked pleased, turned his eyes aside and mentioned the nineteenth-century poet Yi Yangyeon, in a tone that said *well done.*

Overcome by the intimacy of the moment, I sat quietly, feeling pride and a different kind of closeness than I had ever felt before with my father. He had never instructed me on classic poetry, yet rightly assumed that with the training from my mother and from Imo, I would know this poem. It was the closest he had ever come to acknowledging me as an intelligent and educated person, separate from our bond as father and daughter. Perhaps it was his way of recognizing my academic achievements, even if I'd ended my career selling pencils for millet. I thought about the poem itself, and my heart swelled again. His selection demonstrated that he had spent some time thinking of the world through my eyes, and what better way could love be expressed? The last line was perfectly appropriate to the hour of learning about one's prospective husband. It could also be inferred that it comprised a gentle apology, but the idea that a father would offer an apology to his daughter was too disrespectful, and the thought disappeared from my consciousness as quickly as it had surfaced.

We sat together in comfortable silence, and the cloudy light filtered through the shuttered window in muted hues. After a while I asked if I could open his shutters to freshen the room, and he nodded. Soon, we heard the side gate creak open and shut and Hansu being met by my mother at the front door. I stood aside as he greeted my father with bows and a proper exchange of conversation about the weather and everyone's health. Then Hansu and I bowed and he vigorously shook my hand. "It's wonderful to see you, Dongsaeng! I've counted thirteen years since we last met."

Although my eyes stayed low, they shone with pleasure. "It's also good to see you again, Oppapps."

"I've been hearing about your wonderful accomplishments in Seoul and Yoju."

I reddened with his enthusiastic praise and glanced at Father, who fondled his pipe, long empty of tobacco. "Someone's been making up stories," I said lightly.

"I heard that your school post ended for the same reasons mine did. May I ask what happened?" Hansu sat near Father, who indicated that I should sit and answer.

"Since it was a small private school and far from the city, it didn't seem to matter how many Korean teachers we had." The year I'd graduated from Ewha, a new ordinance decreed that all teaching be done in Japanese language, and required that Japanese nationals comprise half the staff in any school, private or public. "At least girls were learning to read and write, but by the end of the term, with scarce supplies and food even scarcer, everyone was fired, myself included. They closed many rural schools, and I heard that in the city all the teachers are Japanese now, and the principals too."

"It was the same in Pyeongyang, sir." Hansu correctly addressed Father. "The Depression must have hit Japan as hard as here. Hundreds are looking for jobs. My replacement used to work in a dry goods store in Kyoto—a sales clerk turned mathematics professor! At least he can add and subtract."

I hid my smile at his familiar teasing humor. I was curious to know what work he'd seek in Gaeseong, but conscious of Father's presence, I asked a question more appropriate for a woman. "How is your wife?"

"Very well. She looks forward to meeting you. Perhaps you'll join her singing in the church choir?"

"Not likely," said Father. "No offense to your wife, you understand, but it's time to think about a husband." It was just like Father to get to the point.

Mother entered with drinking water and dried plums. "Perhaps Hansu-oppa will say something about his friend," she said. I dutifully served the men and sat beside Mother, who handed me a laundered shirt to reconstruct.

"Before I tell you about my visit to Reverend Cho and his second son," began Hansu, "may I tell you what I know of him?"

"A close friend of Hahm Taeyong, isn't he?" said Father. "Whatever happened to Mr. Hahm?"

"Yes, sir. He's exiled in Shanghai." The men exchanged looks, and Father nodded for Hansu to continue. The moment revealed to me how much things had changed at home. Not only did Father treat a younger man as an equal in his sitting room, he directly sought information from him as well.

"Reverend Cho is the minister of West Gate Presbyterian Church and an influential community leader," said Hansu. He met my eyes to acknowledge the coincidence of the church's name to West Gate Prison in Seoul, where Hansu had met this man who became his mentor. "When I was at Soongsil Academy, he was my instructor in Chinese for two years. But before I studied with him, I had already heard about this second son." Hansu looked around at us. Father sucked on his dry pipe and sipped water, and Mother and I pretended to be absorbed by our sewing. Outside, a gentle rain trickled down the tile roof. His storytelling voice matched the soft rhythm of the rain.

"In prison, I learned it was Reverend Cho who led the movement in Pyeongyang. It was he who read the Declaration of Independence to a packed crowd at his church. That morning, he had sent this second son— who was ten at the time—on a special mission. The boy's mother sewed a secret pocket in the lining of his coat to hide several mimeographed copies of news about the two o'clock reading, as well as parts of the Declaration. They wouldn't suspect conspiracy from a boy running in the streets! This is how most of Pyeongyang learned where and when to gather that day. Even at such a young age, this boy showed his patriotism!"

Father grunted his approval and Mother smiled outright. My sewing grew increasingly crooked.

"While I was at the academy," Hansu continued, "I didn't meet Reverend Cho's family. He was far too busy for a nominal student such as myself." I frowned at his self-criticism, but his grin showed he'd been baiting me.

"Last year during the term break in Gangdong, I had an opportunity to visit Pyeongyang and called on Reverend Cho. That's when I finally met his son, who was by then a man. He's twenty-four now, a year older than my honorary sister, am I correct?" Mother nodded while I bent my head further into my sewing, wanting to be the needle sliding deep into the fabric. Hansu smiled broadly. "Their house was enormous! Two stories of brick—" That Father gave no reaction to this information was another indication of how much things had changed at home. In his day, no structure could be taller than the king's palace, something he frequently mentioned when he passed tall buildings. "But I think the family now lives in a smaller house," said Hansu. "This brick building was part of the church and had many rooms filled with boarders—refugees and other souls the minister had met in prison, or who'd come because of his reputation. I've never seen a church as large as his. It's the biggest American-built church in all of Korea, they say."

"It's known as Jerusalem of the East!" said Mother in a surprising outburst. It confirmed that she and Hansu had previously talked in detail about the Cho family, and that she was quite excited for my father and me to learn about the gentleman.

"His sermons are full of wisdom. Somehow he manages to infuse all who listen to him with pure patriotism and love of God. I always feel on fire for my country and full of hope for our future when I hear him preach." His earnestness made me smile—same old Hansu! I hardly knew what to do with the shirt placket I held, being unaccustomed to fine handiwork after years of grading papers, writing reports, chopping kindling and—now and then at odd hours in poor huts—helping a woman give birth.

"I knew many of those men from Seoul," Hansu continued. "It was wonderful to see them again."

Mother murmured "Amen," to acknowledge the reunion of former prisoners.

"But what an industrious place it was! Reverend Cho had purchased stitching machines from a nearby factory that had been taken over to make bombs or guns for those bastards' usual usurp— Uh, pardon me." He bowed his head apologetically toward Mother. "Anyway, his entire household was making socks."

My eyebrows rose.

"I know, strange work for a minister." Hansu lowered his voice. "But the income is used to pay ransom for political prisoners and to support Kim Il-sung's guerrillas, who I hear are growing hundreds of thousands strong in the far north."

"I see," said Father.

"But pardon me, what I wanted to tell you about is this: the minister took me on a tour of the house. A very noisy house!—sewing machines, people talking in the hallways at all hours, discussing books and arguing philosophy—like a schoolhouse for grown men." Hansu's thick hair shook and his cheeks dimpled. I smiled back, remembering his infectious animation all those times when we walked together to and from school.

Father put away his empty pipe and stroked his beard. The sky thickened and rain pelted the porch. Mother gestured to light a lamp, which I set between the men. Knowing Hansu would soon describe the eligible bachelor, I squeezed my knees together, clamped my teeth and forced my features to relax in order to hide any reaction my body might betray me with.

"We passed through the family's quarters, and in one tiny room I noticed a young man deeply absorbed in his studies, concentrating as if he were alone praying in the middle of an empty church. Even when his father coughed outside the open doorway, this young man didn't look up. This was the reverend's second son."

"Excuse me," I said. "May I ask what he was reading?"

"Curious you should ask, because I clearly remember it as being quite odd. He had in one hand the Bible and in the other a Chinese translation of Karl Marx."

I couldn't avoid showing Hansu the interest this statement had ignited in me. He smiled broadly. "Of course, when Reverend Cho finally got his son's attention, he was quite gracious. A very serious-minded fellow, I should think."

My parents remained expressionless. I remembered that Mother's letter had touted the Cho family's Christian and political worthiness, and guessed that most of Hansu's storytelling was for my benefit. My legs twitched as if they'd forgotten how to sit quietly and graciously receive a guest, as if they wanted to run outside and splash through puddles.

"Cho Jeongsu is his given name," said Hansu. "But he's taken an English name, Calvin, since he attended both the academy and Union Seminary. His name is said to have some Christian meaning, but there's no Calvin in the Bible that I can think of." Hansu produced an envelope from his vest with a flourish. "Anyhow, with your parents' permission, Dongsaeng, I wrote to his family a few weeks ago. Reverend Cho was open to any suggestion from such an esteemed family as yours. And so, here is a photograph and a formal letter of introduction."

Father opened the envelope and withdrew a small photograph, barely glancing at it before passing it to Mother. He snapped the letter open with a crisp pop.

"He's short in stature and trim," said Hansu, watching the photograph change hands. "I'm told the eldest is a head taller than he. They were quite poor when he was young, and it's said he's short because of childhood malnutrition. There were two younger brothers as well, but tragically, both died of tuberculosis several years ago."

"How pitiable, how terribly sad!" Mother and I said. I automatically thought of medicines to relieve the symptoms of tuberculosis—ginseng tea and goldthread root powder if you could find it—but there was no cure.

Hansu talked on. "The eldest is already a minister in America, so the second son is lucky to have a brother established there. I'm told Calvin will be going to Princeton and several other seminaries. I'm not sure how he managed that."

I looked around, but it seemed I was the only one piqued by this information. His study in America was the second thing I found interesting about him.

Mother examined the photo. "Reverend Ahn said that all the American missionaries know of his father's sermons. How pleasing to think he'll follow his father's profession."

I realized that Mother had evidently queried our minister about the Cho family, and I felt further trapped. She showed me the photo. Calvin Cho had a high forehead—a sign of exceptional intelligence—and strong angles to his clean-shaven jaw. This feature of determination seemed to be softened by an almost-smile. The silvery sheen of the photograph glowed in his eyes, and I was relieved that at least he was pleasant enough in appearance. As the letter passed from Father to Mother, I noted that Calvin Cho's handwriting was firm and meticulous. I closed my eyes and heard loud drips. The rainstorm had ended. How I wanted to slide the doors wide and run across the rain-soaked slate, let the rainwater stream between my fingers as it sluiced down gutters into cisterns. I laid my hands calmly in my lap and waited.

Mother raised her eyes to Father. "Studious writing," he said.

"A proper letter," said Mother, reading quickly. "You say he'll be coming to visit you soon?"

Hansu said yes, grinning as my alarmed eyes rounded. Mother folded the letter and nudged Father's hand when she returned it to him. A look passed between them. She resumed her sewing and Father reset his pipe on its stand. Everyone waited. I slanted my eyes at Hansu as if we were still kids, daring and double-daring each other. His shoulders shook with quiet laughter, as innocent as a fox.

At last Father said, "It would please me if the young man came to visit." And it seemed that Hansu and Mother released an enormous joint sigh. For me, the walls of the sitting room shrank, the bindings of my skirt tightened and seized my breath. I caught a scent of the outside and inhaled deeply. *Be like the rain, like water,* I thought, exhaling quietly.

A FEW WEEKS later, the three of us waited in Father's sitting room for the arrival of Hansu and Mr. Calvin Cho. I hadn't yet seen Dongsaeng, who was still at school, and since it had been some years since I last saw him, I wondered how he would react to this activity at home. Based on what I'd gleaned from Mother's letters, I doubted he'd be very interested.

My father read, my mother sewed, and I sat quietly pretending I wasn't anxious. A windy day, the sound of each leaf skipping on the courtyard's slate made me quake. I thought, *I'm too old for this.*

We heard the outer gate rattle open and shut. "Don't embarrass me," said Father in a low voice. "Speak only when proper."

"Of course, Father. I'm not a child."

"See how you talk back! Will you never learn?" His tone jarred me to realize that I had unknowingly spoken, and with terrible impudence. How had that slipped from my lips? It was disturbing childhood reversion at work. "This is a pointless visit," he said. "You will grow old and alone, and forever be a burden to your dongsaeng."

I bent my neck, chagrined and obedient.

Mother whispered, "He's here." In the vestibule, the men could be heard shuffling off their shoes, then Joong led them to the sitting room.

Hansu made introductions. Being presented with my head bowed made it only possible to see Mr. Cho from the knees down. I glimpsed a pair of dark green silk socks with brilliant orange and yellow stripes on the sides. Father asked Hansu about the health of his aging parents, then directed questions to Mr. Cho about his education and family. During these structured politenesses, I surreptitiously examined Calvin Cho. He properly kept his eyes only on my parents and spoke in a soft northern accent. His voice was full, deep and round, his diction commanding, and I could easily tell that my parents were impressed. With lowered lashes, I struggled to balance my desire to be fiercely critical of him with some of my mother's equanimity. I could tell that Hansu was studying my face, and I pointedly kept it bland. I thought that Mr. Cho's features were clear and open, but yes, he was small, and noting his shiny socks and wide tie patterned with blood-red curlicues shot with yellow, he seemed quite taken with Western fashion. How silly in a man! *He does speak well,* I thought, *but his nose is too big and I am not interested!*

"This person," said Calvin with correct formality, "is fortunate to have Reverend Robert Sherwood as a sponsor for this person's further learning in America. This person will study the origins and methods of Protestant branches in America, and how they translate to the Christian practices of Korea."

"Ah, Reverend Sherwood!" said Mother. "He speaks Korean beautifully. He gave a sermon once at our church. How inspiring it was in these difficult times."

Father clasped both hands to his knees. "I understand you know something about these difficult times through the work of your father."

"We are simply patriots, sir. Who among us does not desire freedom?"

"True, true!" said Hansu.

"But what is your opinion of the Communist movement in the north?"

Remembering the Karl Marx book, I listened with interest.

Mr. Cho took time to think, then answered as carefully and formally as before. "In that its development was a reaction to the failures of an agrarian society such as ours, with its ancient and paternalistic divisions of class, it seems there could be wisdom in attempting to establish equality through an evenhanded distribution of community property."

Father's fingers twitched, and he, too, let time pass before speaking. "But what if those properties belonged to you? Suppose you were the landowner with hundreds of li of the best rice fields. And they were summarily taken from you after generations of your family members, every peasant in your home village, every brother and servant who had worked the land had benefited from it. Suppose these fields were portioned to each man in even parcels, everyone working in community as you say. Each man is also apportioned his share of human nature, wouldn't you agree? Envy. Greed. Industriousness. Foolishness. Drunkenness. Laziness. Ambition. To whom would these men turn for leadership, to arbitrate disputes? How can a legacy of thousands of years be demolished without resulting in chaos? What of ordered living? What of the lessons of our ancestors?"

Mr. Cho remained visibly thoughtful in the ensuing pause. "Excuse me, sir, for speaking thus," he said. "But I doubt that it will be possible to return to the old ways. New generations are being bred under imperialism. Modern ideas have flooded our universities. My father believes, as do I, that the model of democracy may best serve our nation—a congress of leaders freely elected by thinking men, and a president-figurehead to exemplify the dynastic traditions of leadership."

Hansu interrupted, "Perhaps someone like Kim Il-sung?"

"Yes," said Mr. Cho. "But he, like the Communists, has no God. Without Christian compassion and democratic understanding of the equality of all people, it matters little, ultimately, how strong one's arm is, who one's father is or how charismatic one's personality is."

Father cut in. "Man might be equal in the eyes of God, but heritage cannot so easily be washed away. Are you not your father's son? Was Moses not a son of Israel? How can bloodline be irrelevant?"

"Excuse me, sir. I'm not discounting heritage. I'm speaking of suffering. When people suffer, as ours do, as peasants have for hundreds of years, God has compassion, indeed, proven with the example of his own son, his own bloodline—Christ and his human suffering."

Mother said "Amen" and fidgeted with the fruit plate. I knew she worried that such a discussion might irk Father and ruin his digestion. And I thought Mr. Cho was clever to turn politics toward God, diverting rather than conceding his point. I caught Hansu searching for a reaction from me, and I flushed. With irritation? Eagerness? Embarrassment? Acknowledgment? Discomfortingly, I recognized it was all four.

Father waved the fruit aside and started to respond, but Mr. Cho bowed and said, "Honored Sir, forgive my argumentative tone. There were many such discussions at my father's house, and your hospitality has put me so at ease that I must apologize for having overstepped my manners. How can we be Korean and not respect our bloodline? Naturally and historically, it's an essential part of our national character and must always be so."

"Hm," said Father. His spine softened and he gestured that refreshment should be served. "I see we have much to speak of."

Mother relaxed beside me and Father asked Mr. Cho to pray. He prayed with authority, his intonation as careful and formal as his arguments. He prayed for the nation, the freedom of its people, gave thanks for the gathering of these three families and asked God's blessings for the bread we would break. When everyone said "Amen," Mother lifted her eyes to me, and I saw that she was pleased with his prayer. I served water and precious rice cakes, conscious of how close my sleeves came to brushing the white shirt cuffs peeking from his black suit sleeves. Then I left the room with Mother, but before reaching the kitchen, I escaped outdoors to the vegetable garden and immediately began pulling weeds to avoid her searching eyes.

Hansu and Mr. Cho stayed until midafternoon, which Mother said was a wonderful sign. "Of what?" I said, loudly pounding peas for Father's porridge. She merely smiled and talked to Cook about supper.

THREE DAYS LATER, after Mr. Cho's third visit with Father, Mother found me in the garden where I was picking lettuce leaves for supper. "Aigu!" she said, hurrying in and out again with a wide straw hat. "You mustn't get any darker."

"You wear it. I'll get another."

"No, no! Take it. I'll stand in the shade here and tell you." Beneath the eaves, Mother, incapable of being idle, searched the cucumber vines for fruit.

"Tell me what?"

"What your father said to the visitor today!"

"Oh." I tied the cord of the straw cone hat beneath my chin and bent to my task, glad my hands were busy since I didn't know what to do with my feelings.

"Those men! Always talking politics and philosophy. I go in and out, listening with one ear. Today, I hear your father say, 'I'm not a man to dilly-dally, talking from the side of my mouth.' I didn't want to disturb them with my footsteps, and I stopped and listened to everything—like you as a child behind the screen!" She laughed girlishly, and I jokingly scolded her.

"Then your father says, 'You should know the state of her dowry.'"

"Umma-nim, you already said . . ." I moved farther down the rows of lettuce.

She caught up. "Nonsense. It's very wise of your father to consider everything on your behalf. Even if Mr. Cho is lower class, it's only right as your future groom—well, if you insist, your *maybe*-future groom—that he be treated as a gentleman. Your father said, 'The girl's mother finds you acceptable, your father's letter says he's in agreement, depending on whether you and I are in agreement.' Then not another breath and he says, 'I am in agreement.'"

I wished to be anywhere other than where I was, having to experience this humiliation. A chicken in a cage being bartered!

"Also," said Mother, "he told Mr. Cho that you must be in agreement as well, so you have nothing to fear."

This concession was the result of Mother's work. I looked at her gratefully. "Did he—did the gentleman say anything?"

She smiled—smugly, I thought—and I turned my hot cheeks to the lettuce. "Well, if you mean did he speak his intention, the answer is no. Father was too busy telling him about the farm and Manchuria. Yah, Najin-ah—" Her soft tone made me look at her with concern. "His voice was very heavy, poor man. Then he became angry, thinking about it, I suppose, and he was actually quite brusque to poor Mr. Cho. What must he think of us?"

I shrugged and put Mother's cucumber crop in my lettuce basket.

"Your father said that your dowry consisted only of your personal possessions, your modern thinking and your education."

"I have to admit feeling pride in the 'modern thinking and education,'" I said, smiling.

Mother tilted my straw hat to peer at me. "I'm proud of you too." Our eyes met in a small rich instant. "You'll be pleased with the visitor's response," said Mother.

"Hm."

"'Mine is a simple family,' he said. 'We rely less on material goods than on God's goodness.' A fine answer, don't you agree?"

Any other bride would have been consumed with anxiety about how her future in-laws lived and what kind of mother-in-law she'd have, but I wanted to hear no more. Drawing water to wash the vegetables, I changed the subject. "Speaking of family, when will Dongsaeng be home again?"

"Soon. I remember when he was home last spring how he complained about the smell of boiling cocoons." Earlier, I'd admired Mother's modest silkworm farm: the healthy mulberry bushes, mesh-covered frames that protected the larvae as they ate and wove their silken shells, the paddles, reels, spools, and the outdoor cauldron used every two months to boil the cocoons, an evil-smelling process that killed the pupae and loosened the silk. Mother continued, "But it wasn't so bad that he didn't eat the silkworms by the handful later! We harvest next week—he'll be home by then."

"How much do they bring in?" I calculated how the silkworm farm could double or triple with my help. Through my own industry, I could justify my stay at home by paying Dongsaeng's tuition. "How much are his fees?"

"Not your concern."

"He's my dongsaeng. I should contribute."

"Your contribution is to seriously consider the prospect of marriage."

In my attempt to avoid thinking about exactly that, I'd forgotten that my return home meant another mouth to feed, another room to heat. "Yes, Umma-nim, I will."

"Wonderful! Mr. Cho is coming tomorrow to visit you alone."

"Tomorrow!" Water splashed from the basin onto both our skirts.

Mother ignored the stain. "Walk the gardens with him. Take lunch. Take time to think and decide."

"What's the hurry?"

"By autumn he'll be in America to study for a year or more. A betrothal could change everything for you."

I frowned. Less than a month ago, I'd been fired from my country school and had no idea what the future might hold. I had hoped to work at the Seoul Hospital with Jaeyun, but Father forbade it. Teaching was one thing for a woman of our class; nursing—a servile position—was something else altogether. I hid a sigh. Marriage was not among the goals I had cast for my future. Then again, it seemed possible to add an American medical education to my dreams. I smiled at Mother, and when she smiled back, obviously pleased, I guiltily turned to wash the vegetables. I tried to subdue this extremely selfish desire from my mind, but as I scrubbed the cucumbers in the cool water, I couldn't avoid wondering if American cucumbers were as sweet and succulent as ours.

ON THE MORNING of Calvin Cho's visit, I sat before a folding vanity case, its mirror upright, trying to measure my appearance as he might. *Wild hair, untamable.* I hastily knotted it in a braid. *No, men don't notice hair. Yah, but no one could miss this nose!* I powdered it, applied lipstick, rubbed it off. *Skin is clear, thank God,* I thought, *too tanned, droopy eyelids, a peasant's jaw—aigu!* I stood and angled the mirror for full body viewing. *Straight back, sunken belly, stooped shoulders. Skinny like a farmer . . .* I kicked the vanity case and it clattered shut.

Mother entered carrying a light breakfast of steamed barley and broth with tender wild leeks and tofu. "You give your father reason to be annoyed when you behave like that," she said calmly. "Your visitor is the kind of man, I think, who cares little about appearances, and even if he were to, there's nothing for you to be concerned about."

I remembered his fancy tie and socks and said nothing. Mother sat behind me and undid my lumpy braid, which made me feel increasingly childish. "Why can't I just get a job? Why can't I go to Seoul to work at the hospital?"

"Stop." Mother raked a comb dipped in hot water through my hair. My head bobbed with each firm yank as she folded plaits, and I felt even more petulant and childish. I handed her a green ribbon. "Forgive me. I don't know what's wrong with me today. I know we've discussed this." I took deep breaths and closed my eyes.

"Tell me truly what you think of Mr. Cho," said Mother. She swept the floor for fallen hairs with her hands.

I returned the comb to my abused vanity case and stood. Mother adjusted my slip and drew the skirt's straps over my arms. "He is very polite," I said. "He's intelligent and well spoken, serious and studious. I believe he'll make a good pastor." I paused a moment before confessing, "But I don't know if I could ever be a good pastor's wife."

"Nonsense. Think of what a privilege it would be." Mother fluffed my hem, and I suppressed further expressing my doubt. She tightened the skirt band around my bosom and tucked in the ends. "What else?"

"He's thoughtful and modern, and that's good for me." Thinking that to give voice to my new desire might reduce its intensity and conspiratorial nature, I added, "Perhaps a time will come when we can study together in America." I looked at my mother.

"Perhaps," she said neutrally.

The room seemed to lighten; it was permissible to hope. "I think he's a good man, but how can I know?"

"I, too, believe he's a good man." Mother unfolded the curved sleeves of the blouse. "He has a good heart and is a strong man of God. His even-handed character could temper your spirit. With your enthusiasm and ambition and his thoughtful ways, it's an excellent balance."

I tied the blouse closed with a single looped knot, trailing my fingers down the ends. Mother brushed my shoulders to soften the creases. "It's a good match. And Cook is right, you've grown taller."

"Have I?" I could've been six years old.

"Eat your breakfast and keep your heart open," she said, leaving the room. "I'll check that your shoes are clean."

I ate quickly and scoured my teeth. I put a dot of lipstick on each cheek and carefully blended it in. The remainder of the morning was spent straightening the already tidy women's quarters to steady my mind, which was running in circles of dread, hope, fear and excitement. Mother said to sit still or I'd wrinkle my clothes. I dusted off the Chinese-English phrasebook from its niche and scanned randomly through its pages. I began a two-page conversation titled "The Value of Fresh Water," amused to read about Willie and his father earnestly discussing the merits of drinking clean and pure water. I flipped to the back of the book and spent the remainder of the morning trying to make sense of such aphorisms as "penny-wise and pound foolish," "fine words butter no parsnips," and gave up when I chanced upon "happy is the bride that the sun shines on."

When the actual sun rose well above the bamboo, I greeted Father and sat with him to wait for Calvin Cho. He peered over his book and said sporadically, "Too much red on your cheeks . . . A decent man . . . We shall see." He cleared his throat often in his deep digestive way.

After Mr. Cho had spent a respectable ten minutes saying hello to my parents, Mother nudged us to the gardens. I carried a bundle packed with a padded jar of precious hot tea, hand towels, a stacked *bento* box carrying tiny dumplings, steamed balls of fish, rice rolled in seaweed and a single perfect persimmon with a bamboo knife. That one fruit had probably cost as much as everything else. Of course my mother knew that I would give it entirely to him. Embarrassed by the luxurious food, I wondered what had been sacrificed.

By the time the house was out of sight, we'd discussed the weather and much of the surrounding flora. He did most of the talking, which made it easy for me to conceal my anxiety. I wondered if talkativeness was his antidote to nervousness. The sky shone translucent blue, dotted with high, dry clouds, and the air was balmy and fragrant with occasional perfect breezes. His comments about the gardens were followed by a stiff silence. It seemed to be my turn to say something, but all I could think about was how tangled and knotted my tongue felt. I remembered he was going to America, and asked, "How many cities will you—" at the same time he said, "What do you think about—," and our laughter released some of our formality and discomfort.

"You first," he said, mirth in his eyes.

"How many cities in America will you see?"

"In three years of study, perhaps I'll see ten. I'm very eager to visit New York City. Perhaps someday you'd like to visit New York?"

"Oh, yes!" I immediately blushed and lowered my head to diminish my outburst.

"Why, perhaps one day you will," he said easily. "I'll write and tell you about what I see and learn. Then you can decide for yourself if you'll come. May I do that?"

"Yes, thank you." My heart jumped inexplicably against my ribs. Was it the idea of foreign travel or something else that made me feel as if I'd swallowed a bucket of air? "Three years abroad! Won't your family miss you?" I refused to guess what his appraising look sought, and gripped the picnic bundle to arrest a strange tingling in my fingers.

"I've been at school for many years, and at this point, it doesn't seem like it'll be very different. Much depends on the work I can find during my studies. But yes, I will miss them terribly. My mother's blood is as weak as my father's is strong. And," he said obliquely, "I have just met your family. What a time to be going to America!"

I understood, and felt again the thud behind my ribs. Did he walk a little closer to me? Yes. I was sure that he did.

We approached a low granite bench at the edge of our pond circled with willows. Dotted with lily pads and lotus buds, the water smelled green and earthy, the shaded grove active with dancing light and flitting insects. I untied and spread the carrying cloth on the cool stone seat, arranged the red lacquer bento box and unstoppered the tea. "Please sit and eat a little." I poured tea into the two cups nested under the padded jar, filling mine halfway.

"Thank you. How pleasant it is here!" His voice shook a tiny bit from nerves, which only made me more nervous. A silence followed. It was too soon to start serving lunch. I tried to think of something natural to say and almost asked if he'd had gardens like these to play in as a child, but remembered at the last minute that his family were commoners.

"I—I often did my schoolwork here when I was young," I said at last, uncomfortably stuck between the awkward pause and the impropriety of talking about myself.

"I can see why." He sipped tea—somewhat noisily—and seemed to come to a decision. "Well, then. It's the trees. These trees remind me of a willow we had in the schoolyard when I was a boy." He smiled. "I'm afraid I was quite a lazy boy."

Relieved, I sensed a story coming and sat receptively.

"In sixth grade, there was a difficult class where we had to recite the most complex Chinese letter writing—very hard to comprehend. The teacher insisted we memorize the readings. He said those who doubted the accuracy of their memory should bring three sticks for punishment in the event they failed to recite properly."

"Cruel," I murmured, thinking I'd never struck a single student in my charge. I opened the bento boxes and spread the linen towels, charmed to see they were from the set decorated with Seoul's gates that I had crafted with Imo. Though many years had passed since those days, sitting beside this man I felt as naive as I was that afternoon with the princess and the young Japanese guard. I fingered the golden-brown embroidered images, and unexpected sadness tightened my throat for the brief yet treasured friendship and a past that could never be revisited. The willow tendrils sighed, and I focused on listening to Mr. Cho.

"Not at all. That was the style at the time," he was saying. "Instead of memorizing the readings, I went to the schoolyard and found dead willow branches, like these, and peeled off the bark so they'd break at the slightest touch. In class, instead of reciting, I offered these branches to the teacher. As expected, he used them to whip me. But each time they broke as soon as they touched me, and I received three whippings to no ill effect!"

I laughed. "You were a clever boy."

"A clever, lazy boy, I'm afraid."

"And now?" I dared.

"I've found God."

Thinking I should have anticipated this sort of answer from a future preacher, I nodded and offered him a lunch box. After saying a simple grace, Mr. Cho ate so fast that I thought he must've been starved. "What a feast," he said between mouthfuls. "Please excuse me. I know I eat quickly, but this is superb."

I picked up my box and noticed that he'd eaten all of his whitefish. "Why, you must have more," I said, dividing my food to give him half, and in my haste I nearly thrust my box onto his lap. A miniature dumpling popped out and fell on his lap towel. I sat back as if Father had cried out, "Clumsy oaf!" but Mr. Cho said "Aha!" He picked up the dumpling with his chopsticks, tossed it in the air and swallowed it in a single chew. Both shocked that he'd play with food and amazed that he caught it between his teeth, I laughed, covering my mouth, and noticed, as he laughed too, the handsome line of his Adam's apple jumping like a fish.

"Excuse me, have some more," I said, laughing, head sideways, mouth covered.

"Miss Han, what a wonderful lunch!"

The tea released its flowery steam, the scent in harmony with the willowy setting. He sighed, finished eating and thanked me again. I was thinking that I hadn't laughed like that since being with Imo, and before the end, with the princess. Taking tiny bites of dumpling and rice, and feeling oddly protective of what remained in my lunch box, I wondered if it was his nature to always devour food so robustly. With this thought came a strong sense of his masculinity, and my body flushed from neck to knee.

"Please excuse me and let me explain myself a little," he said. "When I was young, there were years when there was no food. My mother taught me how to eat the mudworm. Do you know what it is?"

I shook my head.

"This is a small worm, just one or two centimeters long. It lives in the silt of riverbeds and streams. In such places there are no fish, not even scorpions, but the mudworm is a strong survivor."

He sounded like he was sermonizing, but I also acknowledged that he told a good story. I poured him the remainder of the tea and put my last rice roll in his box.

"At the stream my mother and I—at the time I was just a little boy, perhaps four—she showed me how to scoop bowlfuls of the mud and silt. We put five shallow scoops into one large bucket filled with clear water from the stream. It was quite hot out and I remember enjoying wading in the mud. After a while, when I looked in the bucket, there were hundreds of tiny brown mudworms in the clean top of the water, spitting mud out with each wiggle when they swam."

"*Aiu!*" I said, horrified.

"I presume you don't much like snakes and worms." He swallowed his tea as quickly as he'd eaten his—and my—lunch.

"Hundreds together? No." My back thrilled with a small terror. "Excuse me for being rude. I'm sorry, go on."

"Not rude at all. An honest reaction." He smiled and my back thrilled in a different way. I listened to his story and focused on skinning the persimmon, its orange flesh firm within my palm, the thin peels delicately curling around and tickling my fingertips, the rare bitter-flower smell scandalously tempting me to lick my juice-anointed fingers, which of course I resisted doing. I listened to Mr. Cho.

"My mother and I scooped the top mudworms and put them in another bucket of clean water, and they would again spit out their mud as they swam around. We changed the water six times until the worms were almost white, and then we strained them and spread them on a mat to dry in the sun. My mother fried them and we ate them with barley. They tasted of the stream and gave us protein. Such an insignificant creature that lives in the beds of streams, yet God gives vital purpose to each thing, no matter if it's as lowly as the mudworms who suffered for the mother and her family who survived starvation because of them."

"Amen," I said, struck by his story and the degree of poverty he'd known. Remembering the earlier cue about his religiosity, I added, "You have made it a gift from God."

"That's why I enjoy eating so much!"

I thought of the mudworms' suffering, as he put it, and it brought to mind Teacher Yee, March First, my father's torture and West Gate Prison. It seemed that people were scooped from their lives as indiscriminately as those worms. I wondered aloud, "But is all suffering to be a gift from God?"

I heard appreciation of my question in his tone. "Think of how many stories in the Bible tell how the grace of God comes as a result of suffering. Think of Christ's example."

I found this answer to be too glib and stole another glance at his expression. He seemed relaxed, and his eyes searched the far edge of the pond as if open to any answer the day might offer. I struggled a moment with the guard of proper behavior at my lips, but struck it down, weak as it was, and asked, "But why must the cost of grace be human suffering?"

I felt his appraising look and refused to accept the prick of shame that needled as a result of my boldness.

He spoke somewhat perfunctorily about evil and not judging God, then his words trailed into contemplation. I was glad he grew quiet because this response, again, seemed too easy, like the obvious answer to a math problem. I wondered if pastors and their wives had these kinds of discussions, but couldn't go further with this thought that hinted being this future pastor's wife was a wish that lay like a fold in my desires, waiting to be exposed.

Whirring insects and the lissome willows swishing in the breeze calmed me, and as I waited for him to say more, I understood, as my mother had predicted, that it was his relaxed thoughtfulness that also gave me calm.

"Perhaps *cost* isn't the right word," said Mr. Cho, referring to my original question. "Human suffering can be endured by having grace. We are lifted from suffering by God's gift of grace. Among the Protestants there are different viewpoints about man's suffering and the existence of evil, and how we find redemption from it, or the degree to which we can overcome our flawed humanity."

I was impressed with his intellectualism and seriousness, but even more, I was amazed and pleased that he would engage me in this type of conversation. "Do you mean Original Sin?"

"Yes. My namesake, John Calvin, believed our flaws were predetermined, that we are miserable beings, doomed to suffering; that we are degradations of God's gift of life, and we should be overwhelmed with shame because of our basic human failure."

I couldn't help but react. "That's so hopeless!" and I wondered why he was named after this man.

He raised a finger. "Until we find salvation."

"Of course," I said, embarrassed, sure that I'd exposed my ignorance and agnosticism.

"God gave us Christ as a human example of the divine, and intelligence to examine and accept our core of human failure, for only then can we understand that he was merciful to have let us continue to exist. In this way, we can truly appreciate God's gift of his son."

I remembered, as a child, that Mother had said the Chinese family who helped Father on March First were good Christians even if they were Buddhist. I thought of Teacher Yee, who I believed was in heaven despite the church's insistence that suicides were denied this glory. The question that had formed those many years ago still remained: was this church doctrine or true religion? Was it all just theory to be batted about in study and debate, like the classics that had been interpreted and reinterpreted for centuries upon centuries, only to now have as much meaning as ink washed from paper? It was impossible to discuss this question with Mr. Cho on our first outing. Knowing that my mother would be aghast if she were to hear our conversation, I tried to lighten the subject, "Is this why you're named Calvin? Did you choose it?"

"No!" He laughed. "My teacher and mentor Dr. Sherwood suggested it because I enjoy discourse and theory. He expected me to become a leader in theology. He has far too much confidence in me, I'm afraid."

Absorbed in our talk, I spoke spontaneously, "I doubt that."

"You flatter me, Miss Han."

Then I blushed thoroughly, remembering that he was not only a man but a marriage prospect as well. My apology died on my lips as I was made wordless by his dazzlingly warm smile. I turned to fold an already folded towel and sliced the persimmon, which Mr. Cho proceeded to devour.

I began to pack the containers, fitting them together in the clever puzzle way of the Japanese, and was shocked when he handed me the lid and gathered the cups. Never before had I seen a man help at the table this way! Its oddness made the repugnancy resurface. "Here, I can do that. You're distracting me with the cups."

"Pardon me. We were just four boys and Mother was often ill. We learned to do nearly everything." He stood to gather his side of the cloth. "I'm so relaxed after lunch that I quite forgot myself."

"Now you're teasing me," I said. Immediately regretting the familiarity with which I'd spoken to him—as if talking to Hansu!—I snatched the cloth from him and knotted its corners firmly into handles. He insisted on carrying the bundle, and we ambled slowly back. I breathed the companionable summer air and felt enveloped in the afternoon light slipping yellow through the willows, and the thoughtfulness from our conversation lingered like the languid scent of honeysuckle.

We neared the house and he said, "I'm returning to Pyeongyang tonight, but I've enjoyed my visit, today in particular." I bowed, furious to be blushing. He stopped, and when we instinctively glanced at each other, I was startled by a recognition that passed between us.

"I— I'll be passing this way in a month, for church business in Seoul for my father. I'll say goodbye to your family now, but may I visit again then?"

I nodded mutely, relieved that he'd delay any progress of this—whatever confounding thing this was—for a few weeks. He turned toward the house and I took a few steps beside him, the blood swelling in my temples as I understood that I believed he was very much a decent man and would be good for me. "Yes," I said, and wanting to show him something of my heart, I smiled and extended my hand to take the picnic bundle. I saw charmingly crooked teeth in his smile. His hand touched mine when he gave me the bundle. I was alarmed that someone might be watching us from the house, and my other hand flew up to wave goodbye. Our fingertips met again in mid-air. My neck aflame, I ran a few steps back, turned and bobbed. "Goodbye then. I'll take this—"

He bowed. "Goodbye, Miss Han. Until May." I hurried off, but not before I saw him watching me go, his own neck red, his eyes dark and shining.

I took the long way around the house and stopped to gather myself in the shady silkworm shed, my confusion acute. I believed I was loath to be married, and yet the day had opened new veins of emotion within me. I tried to drown the sensations that made my thoughts ridiculous and my body rampantly hot and cold. I smelled the dried persimmon juice on my fingers and counted the facts of his visits: four days and no proposal, one month and he'd visit again, in four months at the end of summer he'd go to America. Should a betrothal occur, I calculated that a wedding would be postponed at least three years until Mr. Cho returned. I sighed, then couldn't decide if my breath held relief or regret. The air filled with rustling sounds of creatures chewing mulberry leaves in their netting-topped shallow boxes. I thought of how the caterpillars' tiny mindless lives culminated in the miraculous prized cocoons, and remembered his mudworm story and my unvoiced thought which was laced with memories of Teacher Yee: that to regard suffering as a gift from God was an unfair measure of faith.

# By the Beach

## MAY 1934

JAEYUN INVITED ME TO VACATION AT SEONGDOWAN BEACH RESORT IN Wonsan. She sent a roundtrip train ticket and said the room was fully paid. Once Mother learned that the train to Wonsan took a mere few hours—meaning Mr. Cho could visit me there if he was so inclined—she urged me to go. I had never been to the beach, nor had I ever been on vacation. Mother insisted that I sell a beaded decorative bronze crown that had been a gift from the princess. I had forgotten about the crown, and once it was unearthed from the secret pantry, its tinkling delicacy brought a flood of memories, and melancholy. So much had changed . . .

Cook's most reliable peddler proved that such items now fetched astronomical prices from Japanese collectors. After repaying Jaeyun for my ticket and share of the hotel, I was able to give the remainder, more than two-thirds, to Mother. This helped me rationalize the trip's expense somewhat.

On the first day of vacation, I felt guilty about the leisure and carried sewing to the beach. Only after Jaeyun pointed out that the heavy woolen coat I was sewing for Dongsaeng was getting stained with sea spray and giving my legs prickly heat did I leave it in the room. The ever-present saltiness and lapping foamy cold waters, combined with Jaeyun's pleasant company, soon relaxed me. I walked hours up and down the beach, fascinated by the constancy of the breathing waves, the debris that rose from the sea floor, and bird life that called and swooped to inspect it. After two days of frigid dips, the amusing problem of finding sand in our swimming costumes and bedding, and simple meals at the hotel restaurant, Jaeyun and I hiked a pine-studded rocky promontory that jutted up from the beach.

"I almost forgot to tell you," said Jaeyun, panting. "My father says he would happily support your hiring at Gaeseong Hospital. Even though it wouldn't be obstetrics, you'd be working with him in surgery."

I climbed behind her. "If only I could. Who would've imagined that one day I could work beneath your father?" We rested in an alcove cut into the switchback trail overlooking the sea below, and admired the shimmering view. The endless sky melted into the pale edge of the water, as if sea and sky were one, spurring me to wonder where I fit in this world. With the consideration of Mr. Cho, my future seemed as distant and unclear as the horizon.

Jaeyun had bobbed her hair, and in another attempt to convince me to cut mine, said how refreshing the air felt on her bare neck. I discounted her argument by twisting my braid into a bun secured instantly with a twig. I peeled bark off another twig and idly dug in the sandy soil that filled the cracks in the rocks we sat on.

Jaeyun tucked her skirt around her knees. "Your father says no to a job?"

"I've worked outside the home before, but my father didn't like it then, and he doesn't want the women in his house to work outside now. You know how old-fashioned he is." I wouldn't insult my friend with

Father's low opinion of the nursing profession. "And besides," I added, glad to change the subject, "right now he appears to be focused on a certain husband-prospect my neighbor introduced us to."

"No! Tell me everything!"

I told her about Mr. Cho's visits, and as I finished my story, I realized I'd spoken wistfully.

"Yah, I think I can guess what you're feeling. Tell me, what's he like?"

"He's short. Strong lines in his face, though. Dresses Western style. You know how some men look idiotic in those clothes? He's very smartly turned out. I think a bit of a fop actually. But he's intelligent and obviously a good Christian. My mother likes that most about him."

"You like him!"

"Stop it!" I shoved her gently and we laughed. Sobering, I said, "I consider it fortunate if a prospect has a kind heart. He has that."

"Three years in America. Such a long time to wait." Jaeyun gazed at the glimmering water. Her chin on her knees, she said, "Do you love him?"

"Love! What an idea."

"Now it's you who's sounding old-fashioned!"

"It's not that. I'm a burden to my father." I had noticed sharpness in Jaeyun's reply. "And you? You know something of love?"

A breeze reached up from the shore and carried her sigh. "There's a doctor at the hospital."

"How wonderful for you! Now it's your turn to tell me everything."

"It's not wonderful, Najin. Well, I mean, *he's* wonderful."

"What's he like? A doctor. Why isn't it wonderful? Is he already married?"

"Not that! I'm not anybody's teahouse girl!"

"Yah, I was teasing." I suspected something amiss and decided to wait for the entire story before I said anything else that might hurt my friend. Think of others first, echoed in my mind's ear. "How did you meet?"

"At Tokyo University. Everyone was cruel to me there, except him. In assembly I'd catch him watching me from his side of the auditorium. Well, we didn't actually meet. We didn't speak the entire two years I was there, but I noticed that whenever we had rallies or assemblies, he'd sit close to the aisle separating the girls and boys, and now and then he'd smile at me."

"How embarrassing."

"It was, but I don't think anyone noticed except me. The girls would've made my life more miserable if they suspected."

"I'm sorry you had such a hard time." I touched her knee.

"Well, none of that really mattered, you see, because my Tokyo degree led me to my job at Seoul Hospital, and on my very first day there, I saw him in the hallway."

"Aigu! What coincidence!"

"He looked so excited to see me, an enormous smile, and I was so startled I don't even remember if I said anything to acknowledge him. I just continued on my first-day tour but can't recall anything else from that day except the light in his face."

"Oh Jaeyun."

"That was two years ago. He's a doctor now. We take walks together, go to restaurants and parks, but have to be careful that no one from the hospital sees us."

"They don't allow it?"

"It's not that." She turned her head.

She was too sad to be in love, and an awful idea began to form. "What's his name?"

"Ruichi Murayama."

"His Korean name?"

"He isn't—hasn't one."

"Oh, Jaeyun. How *could* you?"

"I didn't mean to! I fought it, tried to avoid him. It happened. It was meant to happen." Her eyes filled. "It's impossible! What would my parents think? Look at how you're reacting. He can't help his birth. I can't help mine."

"Poor Romeo and Juliet. Please don't let it get the better of you. It's an impossibility." Another reason to scoff at romantic love: it removed propriety and common sense. I recognized how stodgy this sounded and remembered the princess's story about her brother, Crown Prince Uimin, and his lovely Japanese wife, Princess Bangja Masako of Nashimoto. "What will you do?"

"He wants to marry me. He says he'll take me back to Japan and we can start fresh, as if I were Japanese. He thinks no one need ever know."

"But your family!"

"I know." Jaeyun covered her wet eyes. "Do you think I don't know that? Why do you think I don't come home? Every letter, every visit, it's this fine doctor here, that smart doctor there, grandsons, grandsons! I can't bear it."

I gave my friend my handkerchief and looked to the sea. Two hours by ship lay Japan, geographic sister, racial enemy, the rigid master of an enslaved nation, exiled home of the crumbling remains of Korea's royal family—and birthplace to one Dr. Murayama. I didn't know what to say. Jaeyun blew her nose, and I tucked a tear-damp lock of hair around her ear. "He must be quite something," I said. "But it doesn't take 'quite something' to see your beauty and intelligence." I tried to think of what my mother might say. Jaeyun was Buddhist, but her family did not actively practice. "If you were Christian, I'd tell you to trust God or have faith."

"Thank you. I don't know what will happen."

"I'll pray for you. I'm not much of a praying person, but for you I can easily pray."

She smiled through her reddened eyes. "It's a relief to be able to tell someone. One thing you can do is say nothing when he comes to see me tomorrow."

"Are you sure that's wise?"

"We'll go around the point to the farthest strip of beach. He'll meet me there, so we won't be seen in the hotel together. Will you be all right on your own? It's only a day. Do you mind very much? It means everything to me."

"I'll pack picnic lunches for you."

"You are a dear friend. Are you sure you don't mind?"

"There's a small library at the hotel. I'll find something to read. And there's always Dongsaeng's coat waiting for me!" I laughed, and when she hugged my arms, I squeezed back, fearful of her apparently deep involvement with Dr. Ruichi Murayama.

At the hotel when we asked for the room key, the clerk handed me a note. I thought I recognized the handwriting, although I hadn't seen his writing in Japanese before.

"You're blushing! Is it from that future minister-husband of yours?" Jaeyun tugged me upstairs to our room. "Come on! Quickly. Tell me what it says!"

"Seaside greetings, Miss Han," I read, my throat dry.

"I told you so!"

Though I wanted to read it away from the embarrassingly teasing eyes of my friend, I held the folded paper open for both our eyes.

> I send this note a day ahead, hoping you will spare a moment to receive me on Thursday. I expect to arrive midmorning and would be most pleased if you would provide me the honor of meeting in your hotel lobby an hour before noon. Perhaps we could break bread together?
>
> Respectfully, Calvin Cho

"How proper he is!" said Jaeyun.

"It seems I'll be occupied with something other than Dongsaeng's coat tomorrow."

"How did he find you?"

"My father must have told him."

"Which could only mean—"

"Don't say it! Don't!"

She danced around the room, singing, "You know as well as I know as well as you know . . ."

I sat on the floor and covered my ears, laughing, "Stop it! Stop!"

When we calmed down enough to go to dinner, I asked Jaeyun the one ridiculous thing that I couldn't believe was stuck in my mind. "What will you wear tomorrow?"

"Your dongsaeng's coat, of course. You better finish it tonight!"

"You're crazy!"

In the restaurant we ordered cold noodle soup with chopped vegetables. Refreshing slivers of ice slid between the fat noodles and soothed our tongues burning with hot pepper paste. Surrounded by a few Japanese patrons at the other tables, we spoke Japanese softly.

"I've been planning my boyfriend's visit for weeks, so I know what I'm wearing," said Jaeyun. "I just don't know which color. Wait till you see them. I bought *cheongsam* dresses, Chinese style dresses in the most lightweight silk, one dark blue and the other pale green. I think I'll wear the green, since it looks summery. Have you ever worn one?"

"Goodness, no! I can't think of where I'd ever wear one. So revealing!"

"Your wedding day."

"Shh!"

"The blue would look great on you. You must borrow it for your big day tomorrow!"

"You *are* crazy! My mother would die on the spot if she knew I was even considering it. And who says it's such a big day? I remind you that 'Perhaps we could break bread' is what his note said." And I remembered word-for-word the previous sentence: *and would be most pleased if you would provide the honor of meeting me* . . . I'd only read such flowery language in translations of English literature and guessed that he'd read the same sorts of books. One day I would have to ask him. I smiled.

"What?" said Jaeyun, slanting her eyes at me.

"I just realized that I was thinking of a future with Mr. Cho."

"First thing you'll have to do is stop calling him 'Mr. Cho.'"

"Reverend Cho is better? Cho *Moksa?*"

"Cho Moksa-*nim!* His Honorable Reverend Cho!" she said with wicked irreverence.

"And you," I said. "His Honorable Doctor Murayama!" We fell into teasing whispered silliness until even the slurp of her or my noodles, or the curious glances of the other guests, set us to giggling like children.

Later that night in bed, I stared at the ceiling and listened to Jaeyun breathe steadily with sleep. The freedom of the day with my friend unlocked my mind to introspection. Was this what I wanted or was it my duty? I wondered what his home life was like, for it might become my home life, and remembered Hansu's description of whirring sewing machines and two floors of rooms crowded with patriots. I recalled Mr. Cho's stories and his odd helpfulness in cleaning up our picnic. Although he'd described his mother as kindly and capable, I wondered what kind of mother would raise her boys to do women's work. It sounded chaotic compared to the orderliness of my father's house. Could I fit in? I'd adjusted well to many different living situations already, but I'd be the only daughter-in-law at the Cho home and far from my mother. But what was I thinking? Anything could happen in three years!

Still, he had proven his decency to my parents, and I appreciated his modern consideration of my ideas. His intelligence and knowledge were certainly appealing, but what could he possibly see in me? With my dowry, he obviously wasn't an opportunist. He seemed genuine in all things—if a little pedantic in his intellectualism. Would I be doing a disservice to God if I married a man of God? What about sex? This thought rushed through my body as if I were swimming in the sea, its salty waters wholly, coolly enveloping my limbs. I opened my eyes wide and tried to banish all thoughts of marriage from my mind by tracing Chinese characters amid the shadows and light, but I stopped when they formed the letters of his name. I chastised myself for foolishness and bluntly decided to wear my everyday summer hanbok. I forced my eyes closed and eventually fell asleep, the soft-edged characters of his name floating in and out of the edges of my consciousness.

I DECIDED NOT to break bread with Mr. Cho in the hotel restaurant where people watched and noticed things. I also wanted to be free to speak Korean, should our discussion follow a similar direction as the last time. I was certain he was fluent in Japanese, but Korean words had a richer, more fulfilling taste in my mouth. I woke early, found the village market and purchased boiled eggs, steamed buns and dried mackerel, splurging on ripe southern peaches for four picnic lunches. I ordered two kettles of water and tin cups from the restaurant. Back in the room, Jaeyun looked thoroughly modern in her Chinese dress and bobbed hair. I complimented her vigorously, noting in particular the natural shine in her cheeks, and urged her to forget about everything except enjoying the day. Who knew how many such days they'd have? She thanked me profusely for the picnic, which I helped carry until the beach rounded the point.

I walked back and sat on a wooden chaise close to the hotel, watching the waves until the sun rose halfway to noon. In the scant library, I perused the slender volumes and chose a Japanese translation of *Pilgrim's Progress*. To avoid the nosy stares of hotel staff, I sat out front in a spare little garden of scattered flowering bushes and a few old cedars, and I read, distracted by the impending visit.

He came bicycling down the sandy road wearing a broad-brimmed gray hat, his sleeves rolled outside of his black suit jacket. I stood and waved, and immediately felt idiotic about the showy hello. The bike wobbled as he slowed, braking, and dismounted. He blotted his brow with a handkerchief, rolled down his sleeves, slapped dust from his jacket and smiled. I remembered his crooked teeth, one lined in gold, and returned his smile, gesturing him to sit. There were a few people about so he spoke in Japanese. As suspected, he spoke it well. "In America, a gentleman remains standing until the lady is seated."

"Backward style." I left room on the bench for him, feeling relaxed in his easy company.

"They'd say we're backward."

"Soon you'll learn how backward they think *we* are."

"I believe what I might learn is exactly how backward *they* are. You, on the other hand," said Mr. Cho, pointing to my book, "are very forward with your language ability."

I liked his wittiness. "It's not a very good translation. I read it years ago in Chinese."

"An odd coincidence that you'd have that book. I don't want to appear as if I'm boasting, but it's my mother's favorite story. I'm sure she'll tell you one day."

My stomach lurched at the suggestion of a future with his mother. "Perhaps you'll tell me first."

Smiling faintly, he looked distantly to the sea, a view mostly obscured by the hotel. "When I was three, an aunt passed away. Many people gathered at my grandfather's house for her funeral, and my mother wanted to entertain them in some way. Not able to read Chinese herself, she'd always been overly proud that I could read at such an early age. In the bad light of a fish-oil lamp, I read a chapter from *Pilgrim's Progress* and can still hear the murmurs of surprise. My father says this is the reason I was such a lazy student—too much pride, too early. Naturally he was correct."

"The pride is justified." I thought of my own struggles with pride. "But you said finding God helped."

"It did. But that's a long story for another time."

Again a reference to the future! I quickly proposed the simple picnic rather than the stuffy restaurant on such a beautiful day. "Unless you think it's too humid."

"Not at all. If it gets hotter, perhaps you won't mind if I remove my jacket?"

I looked at him and saw only the question he'd asked. I lowered my eyes. "Excuse me for staring, but it's unusual that you'd ask me permission. Is it because of the Western learning you've had?"

"Perhaps it is. I'm sorry if I'm making you uncomfortable."

"You're not. You're very kind. Like your note yesterday." I looked directly at him, then blushed at my true forwardness and his warm smile in return. Noting his lack of luggage and the rental sticker on the bicycle, I said, "Are you at a guest house close by?"

"I took the train up for the day and will return at sundown."

I nodded, then felt at a loss. What was he doing here? What was I doing with him?

He shifted on the bench and crossed a leg. "I visited your parents for a few days before coming this way."

I didn't want to think about what might have transpired those few days. Luckily the word *visit* reminded me of my hostess responsibilities. I told him Jaeyun was visiting another friend and we were left to ourselves. He readily agreed to hike the promontory and have a picnic in the little alcove overlooking the sea. As we headed toward the rocky path, I stayed a respectful few steps behind him, but soon he stopped, removed his jacket, came back, took the picnic bundle, including the teakettle, and gave me his hat to carry. Flustered by all these activities in public, I hardly knew what was going on until I found him walking beside me up the mountain path. I covered my mouth in worried embarrassment. "Shouldn't we— shouldn't I—"

"We can talk better this way." He gestured to the few people strolling the grounds and beachfront. "Besides, most of the guests are Japanese. They won't give us a second thought." He had switched to Korean.

I didn't think I'd be able to speak any language at all and wondered if my father knew just how modern he was.

My worry about his carrying the picnic weighed heavily, making the climb seem far more difficult than yesterday's hike. He had an energetic step and a sure foot, and he paused often to comment on a rock formation or a peculiarly shaped leaf in an undergrowth plant.

"Let me take that now." I pointed to the bundle he'd set down to look closer at a fossilized shell in a rock fragment.

"See its impression in the stone? Perhaps this clam was at the bottom of the sea at one time." He picked up the bundle and went farther uphill. Shortly, I tried to claim it again. "I see that I'm making you uncomfortable," he said. "Take the kettle then, and give back the hat. I'm not sure which is making you uneasy—carrying the clothes off my back or me doing, as you say, 'women's work.'" I knew he was teasing, but the situation was too awkward for me to smile.

"Really, I'm fine." I clutched the kettle gratefully and he carried his hat by its brim. My fingers itched for the bundle, but I didn't want to call further attention to the subject. At a steep part of the path, he clambered up and turned with his hand extended. I gave him the kettle and grabbed a branch to pull myself up. He walked ahead and didn't stop or look back for some time. I flushed with confusion and shame, sure he was irritated at me because he now carried everything, and I hadn't even acknowledged the hand he had thoughtfully offered. Was I supposed to have grasped his hand rather than the branch? How improper! But is that what he wanted, and when I refused, did it anger him? Anxiety froze my tongue and his silent back nearly drove me to tears. I saw a break in the pines ahead; the alcove was around the turn.

"Eh— Excuse me, Reverend Cho, it's just around the corner."

"I see it! A beautiful spot. Fantastic view!" He set everything down and spread his jacket. I neared slowly, afraid to look at him. "But I'm not 'Reverend' quite yet, although you honor me to say so. Please sit on my coat, won't you?" He breathed heavily and turned to the sea, his hands on his hips.

"I couldn't!" I nearly shouted.

His eyes grew wide and he opened his palms. "Miss Han! What is it? Have I done something to offend you?"

"No, no!" I sat heavily on the rock beside his spread jacket, twisting my worried hands. "Please forgive me. I've offended *you*!"

"But you haven't. Not at all. I'm very sorry. What happened?"

His question unleashed a blur of tear-filled words. "I don't understand your Western ways. I don't know what you want!" Then I saw how ridiculous I was, and covered my face with my hands.

I was aware that he picked up his jacket and sat next to me. I had never felt such humiliation. He said nothing, and after a while I lowered my hands, red-faced and still. "Please excuse my outburst," I said quietly. "Forgive me. I'm really quite ashamed."

He spoke slowly. "Miss Han. Forgive *me*. I am a bumpkin. Your father said you'd spent a few years in the royal court. I can see that my manner must be coarse to you. I apologize again. I've spoken to your father and mother, and perhaps now I should make myself very clear." He rustled in his trouser pocket and brought forth a small padded silk purse, the kind used for jewelry. I refused to think it was something for me. He fumbled with its slippery string tie, and I noticed his flat elongated nails, and how clean and smooth his hands were—hands nicer than mine. I couldn't breathe when he took my left hand, his fingertips dry and trembling slightly, turned my palm up and pressed in it a fine circle of gold knotted with a fiery dot of red.

"Miss Han, will you be my wife?"

My throat caught, a small breathy gasp. I looked at the jewel. I looked at him and saw he was unsure of my response, his eyes deep, serious, open to me and yes, loving. It shocked me, the unjudging wanting I saw, and I felt my body flood with unexpected relief, gratitude and acceptance. My eyes filled and I nodded.

He cupped my hand and held the ring to show me. "I'm afraid it's another Western tradition. An engagement ring. In America they give diamonds for longevity, but I'm ashamed to say this was all I could afford." He slipped it on my finger. "You honor me if you'll wear it thus."

"I— Beautiful— Too much—"

"Does that mean yes?"

"Yes! Oh! I thought you were angry. I thought I'd displeased you somehow!"

"That *is* my fault. I was eager to reach this place. Now you can guess why."

I covered my lips and laugh-cried. "Such a beautiful place. A lovely jewel."

"A small ruby. I wish it was more."

"No. It's beautiful. Perfection." I smiled at him and saw my unexpected joy reflected in his smile, his gold-edged tooth amazingly endearing.

"Han Najin," he said.

"Mr. Cho," I responded. "I mean—Cho Calvin, Jeong—excuse me—"

"Calvin." He laughed.

"Let me pour you some water." I wished I had something to give him besides food. "Do Western women give men a token of betrothal in return?"

"They don't. I believe saying yes is enough of a token for the man."

I watched my ringed finger as I filled the tin cups and set out the buns. "Mother will be pleased, I think."

"She was very happy, and I must say she gave me plenty of assurance. I was quite nervous. Your father, too, was more than agreeable."

I appreciated this little confession about his anxiety and wanted to tell him about Father trying to marry me off earlier, but decided I'd wait a few years before telling that story, maybe after a few sons. The thought of children led to thoughts of conceiving them—with this very man!—and I was so mortified I busied myself unnecessarily with arranging our picnic.

Calvin said grace, thanking God for the blessing of our engagement. We ate looking out over the sea, gentle winds stirring the dark scrub pines above us. Everything appeared brightly saturated with color—salty, sharp and fresh—and I understood by his exclamations over the shining scene below that he felt the same.

He ate as quickly as I'd witnessed before, but this time he refused my offer of the remainder of my fish and bun.

"Miss Han," he said, and I delighted in hearing my name from his lips. "I've taken some liberties with your future." Surprised, I stopped chewing. "Your mother told me that you hope to attend medical school one day." A buzzing filled my ears and I swatted the air.

"When I returned to Pyeongyang after meeting your family, I immediately spoke to my father." He chuckled. "My father has long awaited this day. I'm afraid I've tested his patience for quite some time. He was very pleased to hear of my intentions and suggested I ask my sponsor if he knew of a school that would accept you for graduate work."

It was terribly forward, but I had to ask, "In America?" I grasped a peach and rubbed its fuzz vigorously to mask my shaking hands.

"Yes." Calvin slid off the rock and crouched before me. I concentrated on the peaches. "Dr. Sherwood said American colleges have different requirements than ours, and that you'd need to enroll in a premedical course of study: biology, chemistry, anatomy, that sort of thing. There's a women's college, called Goucher, in Baltimore on the East Coast, that's hosted émigré students from China. He knows several people there and has written to them on our behalf." Calvin spoke faster. "I—I'd like to take you to America as my wife. I know it's sudden and an unusual request of a new bride, but your mother says it's your dream and I—I couldn't imagine waiting for my return to marry."

My hands still, I looked at him at last. His features shone with excitement, his eyes round and earnest. I bowed my head, overcome.

"Please— I don't mean to give you false ideas." He leaned forward. "Dr. Sherwood encouraged me heartily in this. He said he was sure it would merely be a matter of a few letters and some minor formalities, particularly since—well, your mother told me you were second in your class, that you minored in nursing and you've been practicing midwifery. Will you consider it? We have much to accomplish by the end of the summer and I know it's sudden but can you, do you—" He stopped and bent his head a moment, as if to slow his tumbling words. "What do you think?"

I clasped the peaches in my lap and looked at him clear-eyed. "Yes, if you please." My voice, which I'd always heard inside as being low and scratchy, sounded bell-like in clarity.

He exclaimed relief and sat backward, laughing as he caught himself from tumbling off the rock.

I half stood as if to catch him, and instead caught the peaches rolling from my lap. "I never considered, I never really believed it could happen."

"God is good."

"Amen." I studied my ring, which now seemed laden with an enormity of hope I hadn't known possible. The peaches felt round and full in my hands and I offered him one.

"Wonderful." He clasped my hand around the peach. His cool palm pressed my fingers against the polished skin of the soft fruit, and I flushed to my toes.

"We have much to do. Can you send me your transcripts and list all the employment you've had? Most impressive will be the jobs you've had with missionaries. Yes, your mother told me quite a lot about you. You must ask your missionary friends for a recommendation. That's a letter they write describing your character and work. I know it's strange, but you must lose all modesty in these matters. It's important to boast about yourself if you want to be accepted into an American college. Modest pride will not serve you in this endeavor. You'll have to apply for a passport. I wish I knew someone in Gaeseong— Well, I'll ask my friend if he can help."

To answer my puzzled look he said, "I have an old classmate, a Japanese man who works in the police department in Pennamdo in Pyeongyang. He's been very helpful with my passport application. But we can address that later. Once your college admission is settled, we can set a wedding date for sometime this summer."

"You've done so much." I kept my head low not knowing where to point my eyes, directed as they were east to America! I saw in the reflection of his shined black shoes that he gripped the peach, but it seemed to spin like a top he'd set whirling with his repeated words—*our* and *we*—its wind spreading my life before me in impossibly new ways. What would Jaeyun say!

"I expect the date may change, but at this point, I'm planning to depart on my birthday—the seventeenth day of the ninth month—"

"That's mine!"

"It isn't!"

"It is! By the farmer's calendar in 1910."

"The same for me, in 1909. Yah, praise God. We were destined." His chin shook with emotion and he clasped both my hands. The simple gesture, imbued with intimacy, stirred me deep inside, suffusing heat and humiliation that crested in tears.

I pushed him away. "I'm sorry."

Confusion flickered through his eyes. "Please don't be upset."

"It's not upset. I'm overcome."

"I too." He walked to the edge of the overlook and gazed afar. Momentarily he said, "We'll be married before our birthday in September, then." His forthrightness made me laugh when he added, "Had we been more traditional, we would have known sooner about our birthday from a matchmaker."

I thought that his birth in the Year of the Rooster was a good sign, a natural-born leader, proud and forward thinking. It would be easy to follow such footsteps, especially as they would cross the ocean! I remembered the classic poem my father had quoted to welcome me home, and considering Mr. Cho's birth year, saw it now as an omen: *The way home is a thousand li; an autumn night is even longer. / Ten times already I have been home, but the cock has not yet crowed.*

Calvin said, "My father will marry us at West Gate Church. It doesn't matter that your family is Methodist and mine Presbyterian. Your parents were agreeable on that aspect. Your mother actually said that my course of study in different seminaries should eventually prove if it mattered or not. She's remarkable!" He reached for my hand. "And her daughter is just as remarkable."

His palm felt cool, dry and serene. "I don't know what to say."

"Say nothing. Say you'll be my wife! Say you'll come to America with me!"

I laughed with his exuberance, only remembering to cover my mouth at the end.

He opened his arms wide to the sea. "Nothing would make me happier than having you beside me on a steamer bound for Los Angeles."

This new sentimental language of affection he freely used felt too foreign for me, but his expressiveness brought me to my feet. The peach slipped from my lap, rolled into a crevice in the rock and dropped out of reach, smashing in a gorgeous display of orange and pink broken flesh. I said nothing, but Calvin saw and offered me his. "Too bad. Have this. What's mine is now yours."

I pushed it gently back to him. "What's mine is now yours." He smiled just the way I hoped he would. Surprised by my own boldness, I turned to the view. I could clearly see the curve of the horizon and wanted just then to be immersed in those waves whose same waters lapped on the shores of my future.

For a time, we remarked on the beauty of the water and the sky— those expansive forms in nature the only vessels large enough to contain our unspoken feelings. When the sea began to darken in the descending sun, I packed the picnic things and said we should go—he'd miss his train.

I followed him down the trail. He carried everything and I no longer minded.

# Like the Sun

## SUMMER 1934

JAEYUN GAVE ME THE DARK BLUE CHINESE DRESS AS AN ENGAGEMENT gift when we parted at the train station early Sunday morning. She looked soft and fragile. I said to her, "Don't decide anything yet, promise?" She'd told me that Dr. Murayama had urged her to break with her family, knowing he'd be drafted for military medical service when his residency ended in a year. I released my friend's hands and used my eyes to plead. My own heart, touched as it was by Calvin Cho, felt in turmoil. "Anything can happen. At least come home and see your parents before you decide."

"Maybe." Jaeyun turned away. "Back to work!" she said brightly and waved goodbye.

On the train home, I tried to find the word for how different I felt.

*Womanly* came to mind. On the sturdy wooden benches in second class, which were half filled, I jostled with the train, bouncing heavily on uneven tracks. All the windows were open and I held a handkerchief to my nose against the fumes. Through the smoke and dawn mist I saw pines clinging stubbornly to the sides of a mountain pass, and I spontaneously prayed for Jaeyun and gave thanks for Calvin and all the possibilities he'd brought. A vision of his tidy hands holding the peach made me shiver. I let my mind play back the seaside afternoon and rubbed my fingers together to feel the ring.

In Gaeseong I walked home in a reverie brought on by thoughts of my betrothal and the echo of the clacking train. Turning the corner to climb the hill toward home, I saw an unusual sight: Byungjo standing guard over a dusty black automobile outside our gate, surrounded by boys and some passersby attempting to touch it and peer into its windows. As I neared, he called, "Hello, Ahsee!" and importantly shooed the curious away from the sedan.

Inside the gate my mother greeted me hastily and said I should attend the American visitors waiting for Father, who had gone to town. "I think they want something to do with you. They actually asked if this was *your* house! I couldn't really tell—their Japanese is dreadful and their Korean is worse. Aigu! Where's Father? I'm getting them water. Too bad we have no ice. Quickly! He's a minister!"

I dropped my bundle in my room and hurried to Father's sitting room, brushing my clothes and straightening my shoulders. A bent pink-faced man with a clerical collar paced the room, and a fair woman dressed in a loose beige suit with narrow features and a distinctive nose sat squarely on Father's dinner table. When I bowed, the woman stood—a full head or more taller than me—and the minister bowed awkwardly. I said in Japanese, "I'm sorry to keep you waiting. My father should return at any moment. Please have refreshment?"

"Thank you, no. The lady already, uh, get water," said the man, bowing again.

"Please excuse me a moment." I watched the tall woman seat herself once more on Father's low table, whose spindly legs I feared would collapse. "I'll bring you something more comfortable to sit on."

"What's that? Can you speaking slow?"

I tried again using the English word for chair.

"No, no need. We can't stay greatly. Our child he waiting home."

The woman said, "You speak English?" She paled even whiter and put one hand to her collar and the other to her lips.

"No, only a nittle." I switched back to Japanese. "Excuse me. Not enough to converse."

"Same as my Japanese good." The man smiled and made his funny bow. I'd thought from his light-colored thinning hair that he was very old, but his few wrinkles and energetic pacing exposed his youth. His eyebrows were blond, almost unnoticeable. I'd never before seen such a pink man. "My name is Reverend Harold Bennett and this is my wife, Mrs. Edna Bennett. Are you the Miss Han, the fiancée of Calvin Cho, uh, of the younger Reverend Cho?"

Startled, I felt my cheeks warm. I had seen Calvin just three days ago. "Yes, but how—?"

"We know Dr. Sherwood yesterday in Pyeongyang, er, Reverend Sherwood. He give us your joyful marry news. My goodness! Blessings, my dear!" he exclaimed in English. "We stay house of Sherwood two weeks to get, um, used to living." Through an amusing mix of Japanese, Korean, English and hand signs, I learned that they had recently come from America to pastor a new Presbyterian church in Gaeseong. Calvin must have rushed home and told his mentor everything, who in turn told the Bennetts. In the sedan that belonged to the Pyeongyang Presbyterian Mission, borrowed for some extenuating circumstance I couldn't grasp, they'd driven down this morning, and after stopping at the manse, had spent an hour trying to locate our house. They had a small son waiting at home with a nanny and were eager to leave. Mother brought water, apologizing for the lack of ice, and a bowl of plums from our tree, which I knew would be as hard as wood.

Everyone bowed again. Reverend Bennett asked in his funny language if this was my mother, and I understood that he originally thought she was a servant. For the first time in my life I faced the impossible situation of introducing my mother. Clearly these foreigners, esteemed as they were, knew little of our customs. In addition, I acutely felt the impropriety of receiving guests, not only in lieu of Father but in his very sitting room!

Fortunately, Mother bowed and said, "Yes, Reverend, this person is Najin's mother," easing the discomfort.

"I'll get something for Mrs. Bennett to sit on," I said to Mother in Korean.

"No! You stay!" Mother almost ran off.

"Miss Han," said Mrs. Bennett, coming forward to take my hand. "Reverend Sherwood talk you teach Korean and Japanese. We also job, uh, new house."

My face showed nothing other than my lit eyes. "I'll have to speak to my father, but I'm overcome by your thoughtfulness. Thank you!" I was anxious enough wondering how Father had reacted to Calvin's proposal and our future plans, and had no idea what he'd say to this added development.

"Dr. Sherwood talks, uh, good wages and help papers to American college. My goodness! You come highly recommended, my dear, highly recommended," he ended in English.

I bowed again, surprised and pleased. Mother brought a stool with a cushion on top and gestured that Mrs. Bennett should sit. When Mrs. Bennett did so, she glanced at where she had previously sat and realized her gaffe. "Oh! I'm so sorry!" she said in English. "Please forgive me, I have—" She turned and whispered something to me. When I smiled politely, uncomprehending, she tried in Japanese, "Baby sick morning. Automobile is bad, large bad."

I waved my hands in understanding and gestured a swollen belly. When both the guests said, "My goodness, yes!" I said I had something that could help and hurried to the kitchen.

"But wait— We really going now. Sick not, really—"

I heard Mother saying how honored we were to receive an American minister and his wife, how sorry she was that the man of the house was out, how pleased he'd be to meet them, wouldn't they like a plum, and naturally they must stay for supper. I returned soon with a chamomile and ginger infusion. The Bennetts and my mother were smiling awkwardly at each other. "Please sip this. It's completely safe for the baby."

The Bennetts exchanged a few hurried words and Mother interrupted, gesturing a calm stomach. "Please excuse me, Reverend sir, my daughter graduated with excellence from Ewha in nursing as well as education, and also is a skilled midwife. Try just a little. See how it tastes." My eyes opened wide at my mother's proud and enthusiastic description of me.

"Go ahead, my dear. It's some kind of herb tea," said Reverend Bennett. "They're trying to help. I'm sure it's completely safe. A little odd tasting? No? Good." Mrs. Bennett shifted on the stool and patted her hair. I found myself staring at her complicated mass of curls and knots, all accented with a variety of brown and orange hues, and her petite yet sharply pointed nose remained a wonder from every angle. She sipped the tea and indicated it was fine.

Reverend Bennett asked me how soon I could start working for them. Mother looked at me, and I summarized the conversation. To Reverend Bennett I said, "Excuse me, but I must speak to my father before I—"

"She can start tomorrow!" said Mother. My eyes opened wider.

Trying to get directions to their manse proved impossible. I retrieved paper and pencil from my room and drew a map to the market square. Reverend Bennett then marked the church's location and the nearby manse and the matter was settled. "How very wonderful," said Mrs. Bennett. "I feel good absolutely fine now. Thank you very much. You cherub! How do you say *angel*?"

"Please, Madam, it's nothing. Thank you for coming, Reverend sir, for the job and the assistance with my education. I am indebted to you and Reverend Sherwood."

More thanks and the Bennetts stood to leave. Reverend Bennett grabbed both our hands and pumped them, causing a small commotion. Mother insisted on tying Mrs. Bennett's shoes for her while I wrapped chamomile leaves and ginger powder in a square of paper. "For the morning, Madam, with hot water. I'll bring more tomorrow." We walked them to the gate and waved at the departing automobile. The little crowd coughed in its exhaust. I caught Byungjo peeking to see that Mother and I were well inside the yard, then he showed a toothy grin to the roadside gathering and remarked that the black beast was impressive but had smelly farts. The crowd laughed, as did Mother and I, knowing we wouldn't be seen enjoying his joke.

Entering the house, I said, "Umma-nim—"

"If you're going to American college, you'll need money." She went to the sitting room, gathered the cups and told me to wipe and polish Father's table. She described Calvin's visit prior to his coming to see me, and explained they'd agreed to a September wedding to accommodate my traveling overseas with him. "After Mr. Cho left—yes, he was quite nervous but also quite charming—your father was convinced you'd need a job for steamer passage and moving, and this one is a godsend. The Bennetts can help you practice English." She gave me a conspiratorial and merry smile. "Truly you are blessed!"

"Yes, Mother, I am. God is good," I said, copying Calvin's simplicity that first time together beneath the willows, and I thanked my mother for convincing Father about my need for work.

In the garden we picked ripe summer vegetables. As I described the beach days—avoiding Jaeyun's dilemma—I confirmed that each element of Calvin's proposal had received approval from Father. "He's very pleased with Mr. Cho," said Mother, tugging scallions easily from the earth. "And more agreeable than I've seen him in some time. Naturally we'll miss you. Is anything harder for a woman than to see her daughter depart in marriage? Yah," she sighed. "Now I clearly understand why my own mother wept every night for a week before my wedding day. But we're too blessed for crying!" I checked my mother's eyes: wet but bright with satisfaction.

"Where is Father?" I asked, suddenly aware that he'd been absent for longer than a walk to town.

Mother straightened from searching the squash vines and her expression darkened. "He's out with Dongsaeng."

"He's home again? Is it another term break?" I had seen my younger brother the weekend before I left for vacation. At fifteen years old, he was a few inches taller than me, his cheeks fully rounded, his waist slim and his shoulders broad. He'd been cranky when I measured him for the winter coat that I'd foolishly attempted to sew at the beach. He remained sullen and silent and the air around him was murky and jumbled. He seemed to be having particular difficulty adjusting to his young-man years, and I wondered if he believed that somehow I had influenced Father's decision to bring him home after I had graduated from Ewha. He wouldn't know that I hadn't told anyone about his falling grades and unsavory friends in Seoul, and he didn't seem to notice or care how events

reported in the newspapers affected his life. When he was home last weekend, I'd asked about his boarding school and teased him about girls, but
he only mumbled, "I have to study, Nuna. Leave me alone, won't you?"
Later that day when I brought him a snack, I used all my big-sister skills to
draw him out, but he said nothing and refused to meet my eyes.

I had obviously lost track of his school schedule with the excitement
of the beach and my betrothal. "Is he home for the weekend? I can't wait
to see him." I thought my news might inspire him to believe in untold
possibilities for his own future. I knew that in many ways Father was
stricter with Dongsaeng than he'd been with me.

"The term isn't finished until July," said Mother, "but you'll have
plenty of time to see him now." She turned to comb the vines. "Your
brother flunked out of school. He was asked to leave last Monday, the day
after you left for the beach." She smiled weakly. "It's been a busy week!"

I took the squash she'd found and held her hand. "What happened?"

"His grades and they said his attitude. Aigu, why doesn't he work
harder? He's so intelligent! If he did the work he'd show them how brilliant he is. And what do they mean by *attitude*? They must not be feeding
him enough. No one can concentrate on an empty stomach."

I wondered if I should have told about his school troubles in Seoul.
I saw that my attempt to protect him by withholding information about
his problems might have contributed to his downfall. "Umma-nim, I—"

"Yah, never mind," said Mother, firmly clasping my hand. "You have a
new job to worry about. He's home now where Father can watch him. We'll
find another school, and I'm sure he'll be happier at home and do better.
Certainly we'll feed him better!" Mother placed another squash in the basket and we headed toward the kitchen. I asked what Dongsaeng and Father
were doing in town, and Mother frowned. "You know that tax man who—"

From the vestibule came Father's voice. "I'll hear no more on this. My
mind is made up." Mother's face closed somewhat. She told me to help
Cook make lunch and to say nothing about the Bennetts. "I'll tell him
myself after he's eaten and not so . . ." She waved me to the kitchen.

Later when I unpacked, a large and perfect scallop shell from the
beach, bleached by nature, fell from Dongsaeng's unfinished winter coat.
I tucked the shell in my waistband and went to his study, keenly feeling

my sisterly obligation toward him, particularly since I'd overheard those few terse words of Father's. Remembering Father's eagerness to have me married at age fourteen, I wondered if a wife would soon be found for Dongsaeng, which would force him to accept responsibilities as master of the household. He was still a boy! How could he feed a family and take care of our parents?

In the breezeless sultry afternoon Dongsaeng sat at his desk in an old shirt and school trousers, swirling an inkstick in jerky uneven circles on his inkstone. He didn't acknowledge my scratch at the door. "I'm going to the graves," I said. "Come with me?"

"Too hot."

"Later?"

"Maybe."

I gave him the shell. "From the beach. See its symmetry?"

He barely looked when I set it at his elbow.

I sat beside his desk and said, "I have something to tell you."

"I heard already from Abbuh-nim." He rudely splashed water on the inkstone, and I resisted the urge to caution him against spilling.

"Dongsaeng, I worry—"

"Everybody's worried about me! Why can't you leave me alone!" He threw the inkstick, spattering black on his desktop.

Quickly blotting the mess, I used my gentlest schoolteacher voice to say, "Yah, what is it?"

"At least you're escaping from this prison!" He rose and thumped his hands.

"I know it's hard to live up to Father's expectations, but you must try."

"It's impossible!" His narrowed eyes pooled and reddened.

"Did something happen?"

"I sold a scroll! You'd think he'd be proud, but he was furious. At least I'm trying to keep my pockets filled!"

"Art for money makes tainted art."

"Yes, yes, I know—loss of creative purity, innocence of expression— all that crap!"

"You know he thinks it belittles your talent to work for profit."

"What else is it for then? To sit in my study and read newspapers and study classics for the rest of my life? That's what it's for? I don't want his life!" His voice scraped and broke.

I stood to allow him to compose himself. "Let's go to the graves before they hear you."

"Who cares who hears? My life was ruined before I was born."

"Fresh air is better than sitting around making a mess in your studio."

He shrugged, rubbed his face and followed me to get his shoes. Going through the garden, I grabbed a straw hat, a hand scythe and an empty bucket. Ilsun plucked a cucumber and munched it noisily. He scuffled his sandals on the courtyard flagstones, and though irritated with his unruliness, I said nothing.

Tall waving branches shaded the steep path that circled the bamboo woods, and I walked faster in its coolness, eager to be out of sight of the house. "Slow down. I don't want to sweat," he said behind me.

By the time we reached the stone steps, we were both climbing slowly. We paused at a break in the trees to look down at Gaeseong. To the far west on a hill, I could just make out the steeple of the Methodist church. I looked south to see if I could find Reverend Bennett's new church, but a haze obscured it. I wondered how American cities looked from above, doubting that any valley could be as enchanting as the one below. Dongsaeng pointed out the plain low buildings of his school and said he could make out his favorite restaurant farther off. "They told you, didn't they?" he said.

"What?" I wanted him to talk, knowing how talking often helped to understand things differently.

"That I flunked all my classes."

"Yes." I knew it was pointless to scold him. "Umma-nim says they weren't feeding you well."

He laughed. "They didn't. But that's not really it. Everyone was mean! Hitting and hollering, making us march around for nothing, shouting slogans and waving flags, and nobody cared about my calligraphy. After all that work with the classics and all those damned hours painting, none of it matters. What's the point? I can't earn anything if I can't sell my work. Why bother?"

Poor Dongsaeng! Caught between two worlds, like Jaeyun and her doctor. But his obvious lack of respect for Father wasn't acceptable. "You know it's Abbuh-nim's way, and one that's been correct for hundreds of years. You can't expect him to change. Instead, you have to find a way to live two lives." As soon as I said this, I realized, disturbed, that I was advising my brother to live a duplicitous life, an idea that had obviously come from my own life. "I don't mean that. I mean you have to find a way to adapt to how things are."

"But things are impossible, and now he wants to find me a wife!"

"You still like going out to eat, don't you? And cinemas? Is that why you never have enough money?"

He didn't answer, and I guessed that he still visited teahouses. "Perhaps if you obey and study hard, Abbuh-nim will allow you to have some say in your marriage. There are some things he can't stop from changing." I heard my insolence and felt ashamed, but I wanted to encourage my brother. "I never thought he'd acquiesce for me, but you see that he did. You never really know what might happen."

He spat. "I doubt it. He told me today that he's been looking for *years* for a suitable wife, and also that tired story about how his brother refused to obey him."

"See how deeply he's concerned about your welfare?"

"Not *my* welfare! The family name!" He kicked a loose piece of shale down the steps.

"It's both, Dongsaeng. You're his favorite—his heir. Of course you know that." I ignored his pout and sing-songed a familiar refrain from our childhood years, "Remember the story of when you were born?"

He didn't answer, but he seemed to soften.

"I hid outside Mother's room and saw him carrying you for the first time. In the lamplight his face glowed when he looked at you. I've never seen it so lit up."

"Like a candle?" he said faintly, caught up in the recitation despite himself.

"No."

"Like an oil lamp?"

"No."

"An electric light?"

"No."

"Like fire!"

"No. Like the sun." Our eyes met and connected in an old and comforting closeness.

I turned up the path and whacked the scythe at overgrowth blocking our way. "Let's go see the fathers of that family name, then. Perhaps they'll have some wisdom for us."

"Let me do that." He took the scythe. I beamed at this small consideration, and when he hacked away wildly, I ignored the unsightly gashes he cut in the weeds.

Nearing the cemetery, as the daylight danced among the stones and pebbles and made the spongy moss look cool and inviting, I thought of how many hundreds of ancestors had trod the rocky path. And when the mounds appeared before us, speckled with shade and light, I felt the same quiet reverence of family history and longevity that I imagined all those who had walked the path before must have felt. Dongsaeng, too, seemed becalmed, his cheeks relaxed into their fullness, his eyes at rest.

"Cut those and I'll fetch water." I pointed at gangly grasses clumped around the tall stone markers. On the far side of the burial ground, I filled the bucket from a trickling stream and stood a moment. I heard wood thrushes whistle and chitter, and my brother's thwacking scythe. Dipping my hand in the bucket, I drank the fresh water and wet my face. My neck felt sticky, my forehead cool, and I smelled a pleasantly sharp pine tar. In the cemetery I gathered armfuls of grass cuttings and tossed them in the woods. When Dongsaeng finished, red and sweating, I offered the bucket for him to drink and splash himself, after which he retreated to the shade. As I washed the grave markers, I pictured the ancient bones lying within the mounds and silently spoke to the souls once housed in the earthbound remains below. *I'm going away, Grandfathers and Grandmothers.* I traced my finger on the weatherworn ink of their names. Father would come in autumn with a feast and would repaint the letterforms. I wondered, as I had every autumn, spring and New Year's Day, if during those holidays Father kept one eye on the gate for his brother. I felt the gratifying weight of family and also understood how its heavy pull could bring unhappiness to Dongsaeng, upon whom, according to the old way, so much depended.

*Watch over the ones I leave behind: Mother, Father and Dongsaeng. Imo and Jaeyun. Younger Uncle and Grand Uncle, wherever they may be. Yee Sunsaeng-nim. Kira and Joong, Cook, Byungjo. If your spirit can cross the oceans, help me to honor your names as I journey far from this place.* I felt an unexpected swell of tears and gazed at the sky—pale blue stretched high and striated white with cirrus, the heavens seeming to blow an eastbound pattern.

Dongsaeng reclined on a bed of pine needles at the edge of the glen and chewed a grass stem. I sat beside him in the shade. "I'll miss you, Dongsaeng, more than I can express."

"Me too, Nuna." He smiled. "Maybe I'll see you in Los Angeles one day."

I doubted Father would allow him to leave Gaeseong. "When I get a job, I'll send you money."

He threw his grass stalk into the woods. "You wouldn't have to if I could've kept what I made today. I sold a scroll for twenty won!"

Twenty won could buy several weeks of food. Few Koreans had that kind of money readily available. "He's probably saving it for your new school."

"No. He embarrassed me terribly! I had to return the money *and* let that bastard keep the scroll!"

"Who?"

"Watanabe. That pig-faced stewpot bastard!"

Watanabe was the tax officer assigned to our neighborhood. So this was what Mother had started to tell me when the men came home. How foolish of Dongsaeng to approach this man. "Tell me what happened. How did Abbuh-nim find out?"

"That pig bastard told him! Summoned him to the office and told him everything."

"Oh Dongsaeng, what a mistake." I spread my arm wide toward the graves. "Do you think they would have done what you did?"

"They were once young men with fathers—so, yes."

"But now Watanabe-san knows you want money—enough to disobey your father. This gives him more power over us, especially your future. He can have you drafted."

"But he's been paid for that!"

"You would trust a money-hungry tax collector over your own father? I'm sure he was only too happy to buy your scroll."

"I'm not that stupid! I didn't accept his loan and I could have—just by grabbing the bigger stack of bills."

"Don't you see? That's exactly the power he wants over you. You mustn't seek him out again, ever."

"Yah, now you sound like Father!" He scrambled up and shook his trousers free of needles.

"You know I'm going overseas. How can I leave knowing you'll be reckless? You know better than I how hard it's been at home. Why do you think there's no pocket money? Father needs medicine! Kira does too. Cook starves herself so you can eat. Mother has sold all her jewelry and silver to send you to school. She boils cocoons and feeds worms—like a farmer—to feed you!" I stood and clenched hands that wanted to slap the selfishness out of him.

"They're parents! It's their duty."

"It's *your* duty to take care of *them*. You're grown now. A man!"

His lip curled. "Man enough to do whatever I want."

"No, Dongsaeng. Man enough to understand your obligation to the family, especially to your parents."

"He'll never relinquish his authority. Even if he finds a wife for me, he'll hold the purse strings always!" He walked toward the graves, his shoulders tight.

I wanted to shake him, shout at him, even knowing that yelling was fruitless. I walked among the stone posts painted with the solidity of my father's considerable talent, the talent he had passed on to a son who could find no moral virtue in having it. To my ancestors, I said quietly, "How can I leave?" And as I walked in the old silence surrounding their mounds, the tart smell of cut grass scenting the air heavily imbued with the stilled breath of Han souls, I knew that I shouldn't. *I* was the selfish one, wanting to pursue a career abroad, wanting the attention of someone interested in helping me fulfill my own narrow needs. Love! I saw how unreasonable it was, how foolish it had made me. My brother was too volatile, too restless and disrespectful to govern the household. I couldn't leave. *I can't leave, can I?* No wind answered me, no sigh of a single blade of grass. My eyes burned and I let their fire drop on the graves. My duty was here.

I pressed my handkerchief to my eyes and said clearly, "I've been a bad example for you. Father was right. If I'd been more attentive and willingly followed his wishes rather than being stubborn and selfish, you would've done the same. I apologize to you for that." I turned to him. "I'm going to stay here. I'll wait to get married."

He whirled. "You're crazy!"

"No. It's best for all of us. Mother can't do it all by herself. I'll work for the Bennetts and help out at home."

Dongsaeng approached, his eyes wide with surprised happiness, then plain and loving as he touched my damp cheeks. "Nuna, you would give up your freedom."

"It wouldn't be freedom if our family was in disarray." I took his hand. "It's my duty to watch over you. Mr. Cho will return in three years. I can wait until then."

He stared at me and squeezed my hand. "You would wait?"

"I will. Gladly." But a sob broke my words.

Dongsaeng dropped my fingers and walked to Grandfather's grave. He laid his hand against the stone. "One day I will join you, *Harabeoji*, Grandfather," he said. "My life planned for all this before I could hold up my own head."

He turned to me. "No, Nuna. Go. You can help me more by finding a college that will accept me. Los Angeles has summer year-round, they say."

"Father will never let you leave." There was no reason to give him false hopes.

"Like you said, times change. If I marry—anyway, it doesn't matter. Of course you must go now. Three years is too long to wait. I'll work harder. Things do change." His smile was guileless, as sweet as when in his childhood he'd finally admit to losing a game of checkers after denying it for several days.

I looked carefully at my brother, very nearly the master of the household, and nodded. My breath cleared. I had needed his permission to go to America more than I realized—no, not his permission, but his understanding that every action of his affected all the family, and that our individualism was meaningless without accepting our bonds of blood.

"Let's go back," he said. "I'm hungry."

I touched his cheek lovingly and he grasped my hand. We stood a moment, then he tucked the scythe in the back of his trousers while I took the bucket, and we slowly climbed down the mountain path toward home.

# There's Time Later

## AUGUST 31, 1934

I WOKE WHEN THE MOON STILL SHONE IN THE COURTYARD ABOVE whispered hues of dawn. It was the end of August and my wedding day. I stayed in my quilts a moment to savor the disappearing vestiges of my last sleep in this room, its familiar shadow-shapes, the smell of bed and home. I heard Mother stir. She called softly, "Your wedding day, Daughter."

"I'm awake, Umma-nim." I sat up and stretched, and as I rose to the day, excitement also rose.

I had said goodbye to Kira and Joong the night before, pressing into Kira's hands precious ginseng and angelica root. "For fertility and strength," I whispered as Kira cried shamelessly and Joong bowed low.

Cook had refused to say goodbye, insisting that she would make my breakfast the next day. "How can I sleep worrying when you'll eat next?" Indeed, she was already awake and soon set a large tray of several steaming bowls in our sitting room. "Who knows when and what they'll feed you there!"

I would be married today in Manchuria. Traditionally a bride would go to the groom's house to marry, but there had been nothing traditional about our betrothal. Adding unconventionality to the wedding made little difference. The annual Far East Presbytery Conference, for which Calvin's father was the chairman this year, was also scheduled for August 31, the only possible day we could marry due to complex arrangements for our American journey, and Reverend Cho had decided to integrate our wedding into the conference, gaining the benefit of an on-site photographer and a feast for numerous guests at little personal expense. Perhaps, had I not been busy with travel plans and the dizzying activities that consume any bride, I might have seen my future father-in-law's decision as peculiar. But I was getting married and going to America!

Mother and I shared the enormous breakfast, and when I returned the dishes to the kitchen I started to thank Cook for all her artistry. She kept her back to me and I knew she was crying. I stacked the bowls and said quietly, "Every time I touch food I will think of you. You have given me so much more than training in the kitchen." She turned and we held each other's hands. We did not speak of such things in a Confucian household, but this moment was thick with love. To ease the pain of our parting, Cook and I did what we did best together, and prepared packets of food for the long day ahead.

My mother and Dongsaeng would accompany me. Father's history with the Thought Police required a special permit to cross the border, and loath to call official attention to our family, he chose to stay home. I was afraid for Dongsaeng to travel with us as well, but Mother needed an escort for the return trip. Reverend Bennett was attending the Presbytery Conference and would escort us north, but he would remain in Manchuria for other business. We knew no one in Hsin-ching, the city of my marriage, so my mother and brother had nowhere to spend the night. Further, there was only one return train to Gaeseong which departed shortly after the church service. My mother and brother could not attend the reception. It was an enormous disappointment, but at least they could attend the ceremony.

Father had risen early for my departure and I greeted him in his sitting room, its tranquil lines gradually growing solid in the slow daybreak. After lighting a lamp and serving him water, I faced him and bowed low to the floor. "Honorable Father, forgive this disobedient child all the heartache she has brought to this family. This person wishes only that she might have served this family better. She is grateful beyond human measure for your guidance, patience and direction." I bowed twice more saying, "Thank you."

Father stroked his beard and sat in contemplation for a time. A moth flitted just beyond the lamp's flame and cast flickering patterns on the walls. "Obey your husband in all things." He spoke slowly, his voice as quiet as the rising dawn. "Be dutiful and serve your new family with decorum and propriety as you've been taught. I'm pleased with this union, and trust that you will honor your ancestors with diligence, honest work and many sons, no matter where you land. Go with God." The depth of feeling behind his words moved me to tears, and I bowed my head to hide them, and having so rarely seen such emotion from him, to hold on to the moment for as long as was polite.

Going to the station, Mother and I walked side by side, following Dongsaeng. Behind us Byungjo pulled a cart with my luggage: a footlocker from the Bennetts and Imo's well-worn suitcase. Our steps fell soundlessly in the soft humid morning, while the cart creaked noisily.

"You have all your papers?"

"Yes, Umma-nim." This simple utterance filled me with pain and I stopped talking to contain my feelings. I had earned enough from the Bennetts for train and steamer travel and a gift sum, a dowry of sorts, for my in-laws. The Bennetts were my gracious sponsors for a full scholarship at Goucher College in Baltimore, where I was expected for delayed fall enrollment in a premedical course of study.

All our original wedding and travel plans had been disrupted when we learned I was ineligible for international travel as an unmarried woman. I was required, after marriage, to apply for a passport in my husband's city of residence, Pyeongyang. In addition, the policeman friend who'd helped procure Calvin's passport in Pennamdo had been reassigned to the southern city of Busan, our departure port. Before this friend left

Pyeongyang, he alerted Calvin to rumors about a coming freeze on foreign travel and recommended that we leave the country at the earliest opportunity. He assured us that any problems that might arise could usually be solved with a bribe to the passport clerk.

The day after our wedding, Calvin would leave for Busan to meet his policeman friend, who would help secure our visas. Meanwhile, Calvin's father would escort me to Pyeongyang to apply for my passport. If my papers were issued that day, I'd have time to catch the train and reach Busan to travel with Calvin, who had a nonrefundable ticket for a steamer departing September 2. The unlikelihood of an immediate issue of my passport prompted contingency plans, so I delayed in purchasing a steamer ticket. If my documents weren't ready in time to cross the Pacific with my husband, I would stay with my in-laws and take the following week's ship, or travel later if necessary. We would rendezvous in San Pedro, spend a few weeks in Los Angeles at Calvin's brother's house, acclimating and practicing English, then we'd cross the United States together by train. A complicated arrangement, but the best that circumstances would allow, and one we trusted to God.

The sun emerged over the distant hills and I felt a sheen of warmth. "Rain coming," I said. "Kira and I left the laundry out—"

"Don't worry. You know she'll take care of it this morning. Walk slower. You mustn't sweat."

"I'm not sweating from heat."

We spoke freely since the rickety cart prevented Byungjo or Dongsaeng from hearing us. As we neared town, I felt a mix of excitement, dread and sadness. My string pouch swung from my shoulder, heavy with school transcripts, identification papers, an American pocket atlas—another parting gift from the Bennetts—the worn Chinese-English phrasebook and some cash. I'd wrapped the bulk of my money in my skirt bindings and carried a bundle packed in anticipation of my wedding day: cosmetics, the dress from Jaeyun I'd wear for my passport photograph which would be taken by the conference photographer, Western-style underwear after Calvin wired to say a donated wedding dress was waiting for me, and a night dress to sleep in, the mere thought of which made me burn with embarrassment.

Mother said, "Najin-ah, don't be nervous. God will ease your mind if you pray." Startled to think that she had read my mind, I reddened further, but she said, "Yah, did you wish for a traditional wedding? Instead of walking you might be riding in an automobile sent by Reverend Cho! Think of that! In the olden days the palanquin carriers tried to disgrace the bride by making her vomit the entire way."

"All the more reason to be grateful for a Christian wedding. No humiliating games and drunkenness."

"Lucky for you, your future minister-husband will never drink."

I looked at her sideways. This would be her first train ride, her fourth journey overall and her first without traveling in a palanquin, which was how she'd traveled from Nah-jin to Gaeseong to be married. "Are *you* nervous?" I asked.

"Certainly not! Well, maybe just a little, but I have you to show me all the modern ways."

"I'm nervous about being in front of a hundred ministers." Reverend Cho had invited all the conference attendees to the wedding.

"You've stood before more than a hundred students and each one learned something from you. Be reserved and stand straight. Say a prayer if anything upsets you."

"I think I'll be fine. Honestly, I'm more excited about tomorrow than today." I saw my wedding day as a springboard for the adventure of travel and college, rather than the fearful beginnings in a new household with unknown in-laws. "Aiu! Not very bride-like. What's wrong with me!"

"Every bride is different, especially one embarking on an American journey."

I pushed my hair behind my ear to see my mother's face better in the weak slanting sunlight. My short hair tickled the back of my neck. After I had it bobbed, I wrote to Calvin with some apprehension, telling him I'd sold my braid for the passport fee. He wrote back thanking me for my thoughtfulness and enterprising spirit. I hadn't told him that my haircut was also vanity. Many young women now bobbed their hair and I didn't want to appear old-fashioned in America. I saw my mother's steady features, the outer corners of her eyes wrinkled with warmth, filling me with peacefulness and melancholy. "Umma-nim—"

"Don't talk. No need." We walked, Mother stepping stiffly with arthritic knees, humming bits of hymns.

Her quiet singing filled my throat with pain. How long would it be before I would have her beside me again? To chase away sad thoughts, I said, "They have the same hymns at the Presbyterian church." In deference to the Bennetts, I'd attended their church and had come to understand Calvin's curiosity about the different Protestant denominations, since the order of worship was virtually identical. I remembered my first walk in the garden with Calvin and our conversation about suffering and the origins of his name. And at that moment I sincerely thanked God for Calvin and the probability that if all went well with my papers, such subjects would be thoroughly discussed on the long passage east.

"A Presbyterian wedding!" said Mother. "I hope someone will show you where to get ready and what to do. Write as soon as you can to tell me about your mother-in-law." I would not meet Calvin's mother until the next day, after my papers were secured. I was told she was too frail for the journey, and I wondered about her ailment, which seemed continuous since Calvin's youth. When we passed the hospital, Mother said, "That baby will miss you." Mrs. Bennett had delivered a blond, three-and-a-half-kilo boy the previous month, and I had helped with his care. When I first visited Mrs. Bennett at the hospital, I was astonished by the baby's pure whiteness. I visited every day, once dragging my mother along to see his porcelain skin. I'd nicknamed him "Little Turnip."

"Perhaps, but I'll miss him more. And home—" My voice broke and we couldn't look at each other.

At the station, we found Reverend Bennett waiting for us. He was now nearly fluent in Japanese and his Korean was also quite good. He still bowed in his funny bobbing way, his skin as pink as ever. I said a sad goodbye to Byungjo and watched him leaning forlornly against his empty cart while the train pulled out, until he was only a dot on the platform, lost among the other dots of people left behind in Gaeseong.

My MOTHER AND I held hands on the train ride like girlfriends. In Hsinching, Dongsaeng stored my luggage while Mr. Bennett hurriedly walked with Mother and me toward town and church, where we were met by four American ladies whose loud congratulations and fussing hands took over. My mother sat patiently in a large room with maroon velvet furniture they called the parlor, while I changed into the dark blue cheongsam and had my passport picture taken. I longed to ask for a portrait of my mother and me, but propriety prevented this. The church ladies kept saying, "Everyone is waiting," and were so eager to dress me that there wasn't a moment to say another word to Mother. Reverend Bennett knocked and said that Dongsaeng had successfully found the church from the train station and was sitting in the front pew. He escorted my mother to the sanctuary. The complicated Western undergarments were donned, snapped and secured, the donated ivory dress hooked to the neck, the veil attached, and then, with mincing steps in tightly tied and too-big white shoes, I followed the ladies to the sanctuary, my head spinning like a fallen bowl.

In the narthex someone gave me an awkwardly shaped bouquet of white gladioli and chrysanthemums, and my free hand was firmly taken by Calvin's mentor, Dr. Sherwood. With the veil on, I could only see his large outline, but when he bent to murmur, "Miss Han, it's an honor to deliver the charming bride to my most promising graduate," I saw white sideburns and full lips stretched over big and perfect teeth in a magnificent smile. I managed to compliment him on his fluent Korean. He firmly tucked my hand into his elbow and held tight, and I was too startled and unsure to do anything but hang on.

An insistent organ note followed by crashing chords came from the sanctuary, and the music swelled when ushers opened the doors. I reflexively clutched Dr. Sherwood's arm and he patted my hand. "I'm going to walk you up the aisle to the altar where your husband-to-be is waiting. Reverend Cho will tell you what to do. Just follow his instructions and you'll be fine. It's your wedding day, Miss Han, and I want you to think of nothing else. We'll go slowly, I promise, and there's nothing to fear. See if you can fall in step with me and we'll march to the music, shall we?"

I nodded, grateful that he knew I was terrified. He took a step, I took a step, and we walked in together. With back erect and neck slightly bowed, I kept my veiled eyes exactly one meter ahead on the white-draped aisle. I heard people standing and felt hundreds of strange eyes on us. As we neared the altar, it calmed me to catch glimpses of my mother and Dongsaeng standing in the front pew, though I didn't dare look at their faces.

I took three steps up, negotiating lifting my hem while holding the bouquet. Dr. Sherwood placed my hand in Calvin's. A fresh-soap smell greeted me, and he ceremoniously held my hand on his, his touch warm, firm and exquisite.

During the service, I thought Reverend Cho's delivery was similar to Calvin's careful vocal tempo. All I saw of my father-in-law were his worn but polished shoes, the hem of his minister robes and the fringed ends of his shawl. I concentrated on the instructions given, prayed when I was supposed to pray and repeated what I was told to repeat, until I realized I was hearing Calvin pledge his life to me, and then I was saying my own marriage vows, bonding in word with this man, whose face I had not yet seen on this day. My heart flooded for a moment, but anxious about what might be next, it was only a moment. I remembered that Calvin, in a letter, had apologized to me about not exchanging traditional Western wedding rings after speaking our vows. He hoped that I would forgive him for the assumption that our steamer fare took precedent over the expense of wedding rings, and that I would accept our verbal promise to each other as solid and as true—in God's eyes and in our own—as gold. Naturally I agreed, and I was also touched by his earnestness and found his practicality appealing. I wrote back that one gold ring in this woman's lifetime was more than she had ever expected.

Another prayer, then someone came and lifted my veil. The air, open and refreshing on my face, also left me feeling exposed. I raised my eyes to see Mr. Cho—Calvin, my husband—nearing, his features serious yet shining, his skin gleaming in afternoon light colored and subdued by stained-glass windows, his eyes rich with love. He pressed his lips lightly on my cheek, people broke out in applause, the organ exploded in music, and he clasped my hand in his arm and walked me back up the aisle. To be the center of attention and see all the strange faces smiling and clapping at us made my cheeks flush red, except one little cool spot where his lips had touched.

We reached the outer lobby followed by crowds of people shaking our hands and saying congratulations. I was soon separated from my new husband, until Dr. Sherwood formed a receiving line where well-wishers wrung my hand into a bruised mitt. My poor mother and Dongsaeng were forced into awkward introductions and greetings with hundreds of ministers, their wives, missionaries and church dignitaries. My mouth ached from smiling; my fingers throbbed with pain. I finally met my father-in-law, a dark-skinned balding man with glasses and a quiet but powerful demeanor. He bowed, patted my shoulder and said we'd have a real chance to talk later. As people left for the conference hotel, the photographer took over and in relative calm, gave instructions for formal poses. I was relieved that the solemnity of the day required a sober face, allowing my smile muscles to rest.

My mother and Dongsaeng had to catch their train right after the photography session. Too soon, we were saying goodbye in the church lobby. Just outside the doors at the top of steep stone stairs, Calvin and Reverend Cho were surrounded by friends and colleagues who were waiting to walk with us to the hotel banquet. "Before he comes," began Mother, referring to Reverend Bennett, who would walk them to the train station, but she said nothing more. Instead she fixed her eyes on mine and took my hand. I gave her the flowers and pressed her hand against my tear-stained cheek.

My brother grasped my shoulders. "I'll miss you, Nuna." His tired smile showed love. Then he remembered his family position and his voice grew adult and serious. "Study hard with your husband and see as much as you can of America. Write to us."

Reverend Bennett called from the doorway, and Mother said quietly, "You are always a part of me, my daughter." I squeezed her hand and she slipped her damp handkerchief into mine. Before I could think another thought I was looking between the gaps of many black-suited bodies as Dongsaeng and my mother descended the steps. She appeared so small, her receding back sedately moving farther and farther down the sidewalk, her head held gracefully high, her shoulders a little stooped with sadness, and I wanted to reach through the crowd and clasp her to my breast. Reverend Cho said it was time to go and our group turned in the other direction. The image I held in my heart during the long walk from the church to the hotel was Mother's serene back and the silver shining in her hair, gleaming with sunlight that had broken through the clouds.

IN THE BANQUET room of Hsin-ching's most modern hotel, I sat poised beside my new husband. I clutched my mother's handkerchief in my lap, trying to hold her presence within me and trying not to feel the pain of knowing that half the world and many years would separate us. My sadness, the intensity of the day's events and my anxiety about what would happen next left me dazed. The instructions for my "big day," as the church ladies called it, had ended with the reception. Punch and fancy sandwiches were served and conference speeches made. I couldn't eat and time passed in a blur.

Eventually everyone stood and Reverend Cho gave the benediction. As the ministers began to depart, Reverend Bennett made his way through the crowd toward us. "Well, Mr. Cho, Miss Han, er, Mrs. Han—pardon me, Mrs. Cho!" He took my sore hand. "Blessings, my dear! This is where we part. A lovely wedding it was. I'll be sure to tell Edna all about your special day."

I wanted to thank him, but words wouldn't come. Calvin said, "You've been most generous, Reverend sir, and kindly considerate of my fiancée, now my wife—" I breathed easier, glad that my husband spoke for me, as was proper.

"Now, now. My goodness! We're the ones who benefited from your wife's excellent tutelage. She's a fine teacher." He shook Calvin's hand. "A fine teacher and a wonderful friend. We'll miss her! Good luck to both of you on your travels and studies. Keep us apprised of your progress, Mrs. Cho." And with a practiced bow, Reverend Bennett took his leave. I watched his bent shoulders blend into the other black-clad shoulders, sad that my last contact from home was gone.

"Ready?" Calvin smiled nervously.

"Yuhbo," I said, shyly using the term of familiarity between husband and wife. "My bundle—" I worried about my documents and money as well as my clothes.

He steered me through a door to the hotel lobby. "Reverend Sherwood's wife and his secretary took care of it after the service. It should be in our room. I'm sorry," he said at my surprised expression. "No one told you? A gift from my father. The hotel gave him a complimentary room as coordinator of the conference, but he's going back to Pyeongyang tonight. I thought we should go with him because I wanted to introduce you to my mother, but he insisted that we meet in Pyeongyang in the morning. Wait here." He pointed to an ottoman. "I'll explain everything after I get the key."

Conspicuous in my wedding dress, I was certain that every one of the few scattered people in the lobby were smirking at the thought of my wedding night. My stomach churned. I recognized Calvin's shoes approaching and saw a large manila envelope by his knee.

"The photographer's assistant developed our pictures during the reception as a special favor for the newlyweds." Calvin smiled at that last word. "We can inspect them upstairs." I followed him up a grand curved staircase, then another more modest stairwell, and down a plushly carpeted hallway to a double shutter that opened to a dark wooden door, into which he inserted the key.

"Yuhbo," he said when the key in his shaking fingers refused to unlock the bolt. "It's a beautiful night. Change clothes and let's walk a while."

I nodded and heard relief in his breath. His next attempt with the key opened the door to a plain room with a huge Western bed, an armoire, side table and armchair. My bundle drooped shabbily over a shiny portmanteau that had the gold initials *CJC* embossed by the latch. He pointed to a half-open door across the hall, and I clutched my clothes and escaped into the gleaming bathroom that had an enormous porcelain tub. I bolted the door, struggled to unclasp the complicated veil, dress and garters, and marveled at the wondrous bathtub. What an incredible waste of water to fill this tub for one person! I carefully folded the gown and donned the navy blue Chinese dress, buttoning the frog closures high to the neck.

When I finally reappeared, it was wonderful to see Calvin sitting in the armchair, looking completely relaxed and strikingly handsome. "Comfortable?" he said. My tongue had apparently died in the suddenly intimate and still room, and I nodded, self-consciously smoothing my hair. "It flatters you," he said of my bob, which made me happy and abashed. "Come and see." He had arranged the photos on the table.

Unable to look at him further, I gladly studied the pictures. I was surprised to see his hand resting on my shoulder in the portrait where I sat and he stood behind me, not remembering his touch then. He looked as appropriately solemn as I, and I loved seeing the sharp clean lines of his face, polished with the glow of the photographer's flash. My solo portrait for the passport seemed foreign to me, the dress making me seem more Chinese than Korean. I frowned at an unruly dent in my bob, and at my nose which appeared even larger in the two-dimensional image. Calvin named the half-dozen men and women who had posed with us at the altar, describing their relationship to him or his father. I gazed longingly at the image of Dongsaeng and my mother in this group shot. He divided the pictures and slipped a copy of my passport picture in his pocket, a tiny gesture that encouraged a blossoming sense of closeness to him. "I'll give these to my father to show my mother tomorrow. You keep the rest until we can frame them." I thanked my husband, glad to have in my possession the photograph with my mother and Dongsaeng in it, and hoped I'd have a chance the next day to send one of the images home.

To become accustomed to walking in raised heels, I decided to wear the leather shoes handed down from Mrs. Bennett, tying them tightly. We went out. Lit with electric lights, the streets were quiet, a few automobiles and a tram passing now and then as we strolled the paved sidewalks. The stars loomed high above the cluster of tall buildings, the night breeze cool and gentle on my arms.

"A full day," Calvin said presently.

"Yes." I thought hard to say something else but was feeling stupidly shy. We passed the stone and brick church where I'd been joined to this man. "A big church. Beautiful," I offered.

"I'm very pleased." He touched my bare forearm.

Instinctively I withdrew and crossed my arms, then regretted my reaction. I disengaged my arms and smiled at him. "A good day." His eyes reflected streetlight and calm, and I relaxed. "Thank you," I added. His smile warmed me to my toes, and I wondered if this was what love was.

We approached a large stately building fronted with pilasters, surrounded by tall iron railings and draped with a huge imperial flag. "Perhaps this is the Manchu palace," said Calvin, pausing as if to take in the enormity of change that fact elicited. If it was indeed where the last Chinese emperor resided, we were witnessing the home of the end of the Qing Dynasty, as ignoble an end as our nation had suffered.

We walked on and passed other buildings newly built in European styles, their austere profiles brightly lit. I looked to the heavens and noted how few stars were visible from beneath the streetlights, and I thought that maybe the price of progress was too high. "It's as modern here as downtown Seoul."

He smiled. "The government office in Pyeongyang is not as prominent as any of these. Yuhbo, here's the plan. Tomorrow early, we'll take the train and I'll pick up the trunk I stored at the Pyeongyang station. My father will meet us, then he'll take you to the passport office while I travel on to Busan. After you get your papers, he'll help retrieve your luggage from the stationmaster and you'll follow me to Busan. I hope you'll have time to visit my mother. I'll give you the cable address of the Presbyterian mission, and you can wire when I should meet your train."

"Thank you for thinking of everything."

"We'll see. I'm afraid it might take more than a day to secure your papers. You'll have to wire in any case. There's a telegraph near the passport office; my father will show you."

"Yes, thank you." Our footsteps fell quietly side by side.

"If you're delayed, at least you'll have a few days with my mother. I do want her to meet you."

"It would be an honor to serve your parents."

"I'm afraid the house is small, not at all what you're accustomed to, but it would only be for a short time."

I wondered what happened to the two-story house busy with patriots and serving as a sock factory. "Please don't worry. I already regret that I'm not entering your household properly." We turned a corner where the buildings stood short and squat and the streets narrowed, and instinctively we turned back toward the hotel.

"We should practice English," he said. "Where can I send a cable?" He repeated the phrase in English, as did I, savoring the consonants in my throat. He corrected my pronunciation with new phrases pertaining to travel, and I recorded them in my mind in phonetic Korean. By the time we entered the lobby, we were laughing lightly from the lessons, and I didn't flinch at all when he took my elbow to climb the stairs.

He excused himself to the bathroom, and I busily packed the photographs and turned down the bed. He appeared in shirtsleeves, his tie unknotted and draped like a minister's shawl. I lowered my eyes and slipped past him carrying my nightgown. "Dear God," I said silently disrobing. "Help me to not be afraid." Trying to banish anatomy textbook images of reproductive organs that floated behind my eyes, I tied my nightgown over breasts swelling helplessly to quickened heartbeats, and scrubbed my feet, face and hands. Noiselessly, I hurried across the empty hallway and was grateful to see the room darkened and him beneath the covers.

The silhouette of blankets lifted to welcome me. I placed my dress over the chair, my fingers shaking, and lay beside him, flat and scared and as far away as possible. Shifting near, he drew a finger from my ear to my chin as my eyes adjusted to the dark. I saw his full lips smiling, his lopsided front teeth, and focused on his night-deepened eyes. His hand traveled to my neck, over the knobs of my collarbone, sending coolness through my body. Putting his lips to my ear, he fumbled with the ties of my nightgown and whispered, "My wife." His hands slid to caress me.

Surprised that my body warmed, I wasn't sure if I wanted to push him away or embrace him, but I lay still, conscious of my duty to my new husband. He tugged the gown aside and caressed me, his hands fumbling across my hips. On their own, my legs parted and bent. I gasped when his fingers pressed against me, opening. He lifted the blankets and moved on top, while my unwitting hands gathered him close and my legs received him. I cried out with fullness, then pain that made me grimace. He pushed once, twice, more, and in the confusion of sheets and sensation, I opened my eyes, flushed with unexpected pleasure as he moved.

"Najin," he said. I felt a pulse on my thigh, then wetness. I loosened my body and he breathed against my neck, his lips soft. He turned on his side with a contented sigh that pleased me. He touched my face, then threw his arm across my chest and fell asleep. Worried about the mess below, I gently raised my hips and tucked my nightgown beneath. When he breathed deeply with sleep, I crept out of bed, donned a slip and tiptoed across the hall. I washed the nightgown and myself, then by the pale streetlight filtering through the curtain in our room, spread a hotel towel over the wet bedsheet. Lying wide-awake, I smiled at his throaty snores. My thigh tingled as if remembering him there, and I was grateful he hadn't released himself inside me—pregnancy would be impossible for a college student!—although I wasn't sure if it was intentional or not. The ceiling fixture seemed to form the characters for woman. I closed my eyes to unweave the feelings trapped in my body. A small ache below caused me to clench my pelvic muscles, and the wave of deepness recalled my solitary nights in Changdeok Palace down the hall from the princess. Now a married woman, I gave myself permission to continue until my hips tensed, then lightened, and a small sound sprang from deep in my body. After checking that Calvin's breathing remained unchanged, I lay flat and straight on the too-soft mattress, and slept.

I woke in complete darkness as Calvin pressed against me. His legs guided mine apart and he hovered above. His lips brushed my lips and his rough chin scratched my ear and neck. I hoisted my pelvis to straighten the towel, and he grasped my hips. I willed my body to comply with his and hid involuntary cries in his shoulder. He moved faster, and as I felt his tension mounting, I pushed him out with my legs. He splashed on my belly and I reached down to contain it. My fingers raked across his sex. Frightened by his sharp intake of breath, I said, "Are you all right?"

"Yes, thank you," he murmured and rolled to his side. I lay still, my hand cupped on my sticky belly and waited for him to fall asleep, but he tossed a while, tugging the sheets. Eventually he said sleepily, "And you, Yuhbo. Are you all right?"

Struck by his consideration, I thanked him and said that I was. I felt grateful to him for asking, and so blessed and undeserving all at once that tears filled my eyes. I waited until he slept then sneaked out of bed again, this time wearing his jacket to cross the hall. I put a luxurious two inches of warm water in the bottom of the tub, deathly afraid that the splashing faucet would wake him or another hotel guest. I'd paid scant attention to my womanly nakedness before this night—too unchaste an act—and I studied my body as if seeing it for the first time. The hot water burned between my legs and my body shuddered with the memory of him. *So, this is marriage,* I thought. It made me feel full and warm, and I believed this most certainly was love.

Returning to the bed, I slept fitfully, afraid I'd oversleep. When he reached for me once more, I saw the room outlined in dawn and pulled away. "Nearly time to rise. Sleep a little longer, Yuhbo." I washed and dressed in a plain hanbok, glad I'd thought to bring the rags needed for bleeding. I woke him cheerily and he leaned against me, groggy with sleep. We laughed as he crossed the room tripping over his falling pajama trousers. That simple, spontaneous laughter, a mere few seconds, was a moment I would come to cherish.

As I stripped the bed and listened for the toilet flushing and the faucets running, I thought of Kira that day throwing salt on my father's bloodied shirt, and sudden homesickness burned my eyes. Gathering the sheets, I brushed aside my tears and barged into the bathroom. In the tub, Calvin raised his knees in surprise, and before averting my eyes I glimpsed his shoulder's sylvan curves, his smooth wet skin.

He angled his body just so in the tub. "You don't have to do that. They have maids."

"I couldn't! It's too embarrassing—" I quickly ran water on the linens.

He laughed. "More embarrassing than walking in on a man taking a bath?"

"I'm not looking at my husband!" I left the sheets to soak and ran out.

A bit later I thought I heard him rinsing the linens. I hurried across. "Let me do that. That's my work. You shouldn't!" I didn't want him to see my blood.

"If you insist on sharing the bathroom with me, bring my shaving kit from the suitcase."

"Yuhbo," I called after a few minutes. "I can't open it."

Dressed in his trousers and undershirt he brought the wrung linens, which we spread over the end of the bed. We bumped as he leaned to show me how to release the suitcase latch, and he held me then, my head naturally drawn to his shoulder. A sigh passed through me as quickly as his touch had awakened the ache from below, but I slapped at his hands and said lightly, "There's time later." Then I reddened thoroughly, for I'd meant to say there wasn't time.

"A lifetime!" Calvin pressed his lips to my palm. He swept up his shaving gear and retired to the bathroom, and I brought my hand to my nose to see if I could smell his touch.

# The Linen Closet

## SEPTEMBER 1934

In the crowded second-class coach to Pyeongyang, Calvin spoke little and smiled often. We'd eaten the rice balls from Cook earlier in the privacy of our hotel room, with coffee and iced water he had somehow ordered to be delivered. The train stopped at the border town of Anteong on the Yalu River, and passengers quickly filled every available space. For the remainder of the uneventful trip to the city of my married residency, with food from home in my belly and his companionable jostling against my hip and shoulder, I was content.

Reverend Cho was waiting for us at the depot, and Calvin, before boarding his train, reviewed the plan once again. Conscious that my father-in-law was present, I said goodbye to my husband with a simple bow. I needn't have worried, for Reverend Cho grasped Calvin by the shoulders, pressed lips to his son's forehead and they embraced fully, both their eyes wet. Stunned by the public display, I turned aside. Calvin's train pulled out from the station and I waved once, whereas Reverend Cho held his arm high, waving long after the smoke had cleared. I remembered that on the promontory overlooking the beach Calvin had said, "I am a bumpkin," and also, "Your father told me what a refined upbringing you've had." I felt both shamed and proud and understood I'd have to work on humbleness in my marriage. But it was not an immediate concern; in America I'd be mostly separate from my husband, busy with English language studies and coursework.

The Pyeongyang station, three times the size of Gaeseong's, bustled with vendors, porters, passengers and police. Streetfront trams rattled below their electric wires, men with carts jostled by, a few rickshaw drivers boasted speed and beggars cried for alms. I clutched my bundle to my chest and dutifully followed my father-in-law into the city. He stopped at corners to offer me a ready smile and a few words of chitchat.

"Heavy clouds coming. Perhaps just a shower this time. Maybe thunderstorms, eh? We go down this street and turn left. See that high wall? That's the west side of our mission compound." He pointed out a few churches and named landmark buildings, each time waiting for me to respond.

Thus far I'd merely nodded, but his persistent remarks seemed to require something more. "So big!" I tried.

He smiled as if discovering that indeed I could speak. I took note of his large narrow teeth, all the uppers edged in gold. It appeared the Cho line suffered with soft teeth. "The manse is behind the church. See that steeple? This restaurant is patronized by Westerners and that one across the way, Japanese." He waited until we passed a checkpoint and said, "That's their means of surveillance on the American missionaries. Not terribly enlightened tactics, I must say." I looked around to see if anyone else was listening to his carefree talk.

A plain building of whitewashed mortar housed the government offices. Cultivated rows of marigolds and begonias edged a graveled yard and paved driveways, all surrounded by iron fencing. Showing my papers, Reverend Cho explained our business to the men in the guardhouse.

They refused his request to accompany me and gave brisk directions to the proper office. My father-in-law encouraged me on and pointed across the street to a restaurant next door to the telegraph office where he'd wait for me.

I passed beneath the imperial flag and through glass doors. My papers were checked again and my bundle was inspected. The poured stone floor held my echoing footsteps and those of a few others in need of official business. Signs above two entrances to the passport office divided nationals and Japanese citizens, and from a queue that spilled from the Korean side, young men filled out forms or shifted their feet. The small drab room was quiet except for the occasional whisper of one assisting another with paperwork, and a murmur coming from a grated window behind which a single official asked questions of the applicant before him.

"Excuse me," I whispered to the young man at the end of the line who wore a student's uniform. "Where is the application?" He sent a request up the line and a form was passed back.

"Elder Sister, do you need brush and ink?" He looked from my bobbed hair to my traditional hanbok to Mrs. Bennett's shoes with curiosity. When I nodded, he whispered up the line again and room was made for me at a counter where I could stand and complete the form. I filled it out carefully, firmly writing *education* in the reason-for-travel box. Back in line, I drew out my other documents: crisp marriage certificate and declaration of Pyeongyang residency, identification, work and tax permit, graduation certificates and transcripts, my photograph in Jaeyun's dress, a letter of support and sponsorship from the Bennetts on official Presbytery stationery, and the embossed letter of acceptance to Goucher College. I waited patiently for more than an hour, refraining from searching each departing applicant's face for disappointment or victory. Their stooped shoulders and bowed heads were obvious enough, but I was convinced they weren't as thoroughly prepared as I was.

At last the passport official nodded for me to approach, his round glasses reflecting glare from an overhead light. He asked perfunctory questions about my birthplace, education and work. I presented my papers and he raised an eyebrow. "Your Japanese is accomplished." I hoped this was a good sign. "Married yesterday, I see."

"Yes sir."

"Did you marry in order to leave the country?"

I hadn't expected this sort of questioning. "No sir. I was betrothed in May." I knew that made no sense and remembered what the Bennetts had coached me to say. "I—I am traveling to further my education in medicine, since the women's professional school in Seoul has limited opportunities in that field."

"Where is your husband?"

"Traveling to Busan at the moment."

"And from there you both plan to travel overseas?"

"Yes sir."

"Same university?"

"No sir. I am enrolled at a women's college in a nearby town." I pointed to the Goucher letter.

He scanned the American letters and their translations, the papers mirrored in his spectacles, little miniature documents of hope. He tossed them back under the grate. "Foolish to accept enrollment without official sanction."

A stone fell, hollowing my body. I kept my tone even and my face impassive. "Forgive me sir. The Presbyterian mission arranged for the college. I was told the matter had been taken care of. These letters show—"

"Denied."

"What? But sir, the letters—"

"The letters are in order. If you want to further your education, a student visa to Tokyo is granted."

The fear that pulled inside drained to cold panic. I shoved a prepared wad of bills under the grille. "Please sir. Here is the fee. Tokyo offers nursing only— I'm not accepted into Tokyo—"

The money disappeared. "Our Korean sisters are welcome in our universities. With your education, fluency and high marks, you'll be admitted with ease."

"Sir, my husband waits—"

His lips thinned. "He can go to Tokyo with you. It is among the finest universities in the world." He frowned when I leaned heavily against the counter. "Madam, it is not a difficult matter to rescind his visa." He wrote something across my application, placed it on a stack beside his elbow, collected my documents, stamped my identification—a red seal with a line across it—and slid my papers back to me.

"I beg you, sir!" The whispers from the queue of applicants behind me were meaningless winds passing through my body.

"Denied. Do not attempt to reapply unless for a student visa to Tokyo."

"I beg you, sir. I plead for your understanding— My husband—" I grasped the bars and the whispering behind me grew louder.

"Denied! Shall I call the guard?"

I took my documents with wooden hands. My eyes were dry, yet I couldn't see my way out of the passport office and bumped into someone. I dropped my pouch and left my bundle. "You forgot your things, Elder Sister," said a young man. "Let me walk with you outside." I followed him numbly, the sound of our footsteps vacant and pounding. At the entrance he said, "Here we are. Are you alone? Do you want me to escort you home?" The concern on this stranger's earnest face gave me strength and my manners surfaced.

"No, thank you. My father-in-law waits for me. I'm sorry to have troubled you. You're very kind."

"If you're sure—"

I tried to smile without success. I turned to cross the street and was cursed by a man running with a cart, into which I nearly collided. Reverend Cho must have been watching, for he was beside me in an instant. He thanked the young man, grasped my shoulders and led me to the safety of the telegraph office's sidewalk. He studied my pale expression. "How bad?" he said.

I knew that the word *denied* wouldn't pass my lips without a flood of vitriol or tears. I unfolded my identification and gave it to him.

He examined the red stamp and uttered a sympathetic "Hmm." He returned my document and steered me inside the café. "We'll have something to drink before we send a cable." The proprietress smiled at his rapid return and teased him about having a crush on her. He ordered two roasted barley teas and moved to a back table. I sat stiffly.

He sipped and sat silent across from me for some time. "Please drink something. I don't want you to faint." I complied, forcing the tea past my throat that was tight with disbelief, my stomach leaden with so much lost in an instant. "That's good," he said. I bowed my head to hide my eyes, for at that moment I hated him, his condescension, his patronizing warmth. I hated the clerk behind the grille, the cart man who had cursed at me, the Japanese police who were always everywhere. I hated them all. I remembered from my youth the red-eyed palace guard's iron stare, the pockmarked soldier who had exposed himself to Kira and me, and they justified my hatred. And yes, I hated my husband. He had taken my future and dreams in his hands and had instead led me here. I had given my body to him, the ultimate act of trust, and he had brought me to this empty table. It would have been better if I had never hoped for America, than to have hoped and have it denied. And I had wondered if my feelings for him were love! Reverend Cho cleared his throat, and I struggled to keep the tea from coming up as bile. Then I felt shame for my weakness in succumbing to such emotion, yet what is shame but hatred turned inward? I closed my eyes and told myself to be still, act properly, dutifully, close the door to the storm inside.

Reverend Cho spoke gently and softly in Korean, as if only our native tongue could give solace. "The stamp on your identification restricts you from leaving the imperium. I have the same as a result of March First, as do many other patriots who were arrested that day and the many days since. You should consider yours an equally honorable badge." I said nothing and he continued. "Of course you're greatly disappointed, but you're young. Another chance will come. They are not to be our false masters forever. I know the most difficult part for you at this moment must be the separation from your husband at the dawn of your marriage, and that indeed is a great misfortune. However, God has his reasons for both the lightness of joy and the burden of disappointment in our lives. Have faith in his wisdom and his greater plan, and trust that all will come to good once more, that all will be shown in time. Let's pray together and perhaps your faith will grow to contain this kind of bad news, and much more besides."

I kept my head bowed, vexed that he'd seen something of my feelings and accurately attributed it to wavering faith. Let him see then! I had nothing left—why hold on to propriety?

He clasped his hands and prayed, "Father in Heaven, my daughter and

I come before you in bleakness and anger. She is burdened by the loss of her plan of international travel and American schooling, the separation of her new husband—my second son—married in your house only yesterday . . ."

I chafed under his prayer. It took all my training to suppress the urge to kick my chair across the room and run from the table. I thought then of my mother, her tear-soaked handkerchief tucked into my skirtband, and I breathed hard to feel it pressed against my heart. It quelled the wrathful buzz in my ears, enough to sit and hear Reverend Cho's impassioned prayer, which seemed to go on forever. But it was a kind prayer, and after the *amen* I found myself somewhat chastened by his sensitivity. I glanced at my father-in-law's eyes, which were wet. I lowered mine, dry, and said, "I will pray on this."

"That's all I ask."

I caught a glimpse of his smile and thought derisively that it was the practiced minister in him that made such obvious kindness shine in his eyes. No, this was impossible, hateful thinking. I pushed it down, found comfort and even pride in my ability to do so.

"Now then." He patted my hand and pulled a fountain pen and small pad from inside his jacket. "We'll need to send a cable to your husband." His rough palm on my hand recalled the demonstrative goodbyes shared by father and son. I cringed to think what more I would see of the Cho family's ill-mannered sense of physical propriety.

"After that," said the minister, "I'll take you home. Your mother-in-law waits eagerly to meet you, especially since she's heard your charms extolled for several months now. Naturally, you'll come home with us. As to what the days ahead might bring, we'll leave that to God with, perhaps, a little help from common sense and the American Post Office." He opened the pen and handed it to me.

I wrote more crookedly than I thought possible, and flushed with longing for home and Gaeseong, ended my message to Calvin with my father's parting sentiment from yesterday morning, eons ago. I pushed the paper across the table.

"Fine. See if you can finish your tea while I send it."

During his short absence, I wove an invisible wall around my emotions, strong enough to carry me through the next few unknown days, resilient enough to permit access to my feelings when I felt more able to wrestle with them.

INSIDE THE CHOS' brushwood gate, a small weedy yard led to tall dusty shrubs that hid most of the house. Mrs. Cho welcomed me warmly at the door. She grasped my arms and came quite close, peering into my face. I stiffened until I saw her cloudy eyes. I thought of poppy root and gingko extract with gentian to improve her obviously failing vision. This automatic educated medical response made me bitter, it being largely the cause of my present disillusionment. God had punished me for ambition, for failing the test presented in the guise of my husband—a man of God—who had brought with him the dream of an American education. Had I sincerely cared for him, or was it what he offered that had attracted me? It was hard to believe that God, any god, would be so vindictive, so petty as to bother with my tiny worthless soul. And yet here I was, abandoned by my husband, stuck with my in-laws, everything lost. I drowned these spinning thoughts in the darkness covering my heart.

Small and brown-skinned, Mrs. Cho demonstrated that her numerous wrinkles were earned from frequent smiles. Reverend Cho explained the situation. Still holding my arms, she said, "*Omana!* Such a shame!" I shook my head to discount the disappointment. I did not want their sympathy. Reverend Cho retrieved a raincoat and hat from inside the house, told us to watch for my luggage, which he would arrange to be delivered from the station, and left. My mother-in-law led me into the grass-roofed house just as it started to rain. "We live simply," she said, "but I pray you'll find comfort here."

When my eyes adjusted to the dim interior, I was glad that I knew well how to hide my feelings. Not larger than my mother's kitchen, the one-room hovel—for that was my first impression—had a coarse floor of loose boards barely covered by a worn and stained hemp mat, two haphazard chests, a small bookshelf and table, a closet crammed with bedding and a narrow earthen stove built into the back wall. The room reeked of smoke, old food smells and damp earth. Mrs. Cho kicked off her shoes and hurried to the kitchen area. She grabbed a gourd and two tin pots off wall hooks and placed them strategically on the floor. They soon splashed with raindrops leaking through the thatch. I bent to unlace my shoes and to hide any indication of my utter dismay.

"Luckily, we still have my son's bed," said Mrs. Cho, "which, of course, is yours now. Put your things here until your trunk arrives." She pointed to a corner beside the bookshelf. "Those are all the books he had no room to pack," she said proudly.

I felt as if I were hearing her through layers of fog and veils, and struggled to speak normally. "May I look?"

She crouched beside the books, her arthritic fingers fluttering along their spines. "Of course! They're yours now too."

I heard those words with dread. How could I live here? Knowing I had no choice, I relied on my training and bowed to the floor. "Thank you, Umma-nim, Mother, for welcoming me home. It's— It's unexpected to have the burden of this daughter unexpectedly on your hands, yet you've shown me only kindness."

She smiled warmly. "Well then, Daughter, what is a Christian family for but to welcome their son's bride? I consider the unexpectedness of it a special blessing!" She fingered the books again. "Before he left for college, Second Son used to read to me from the Bible and some of these others. Perhaps you'll humor me by reading to me occasionally? Your father-in-law has no time for a foolish old wife with no education."

"I'd be honored to." I hadn't known Calvin's mother was illiterate. Once again anger flashed through me at the careless thoughtlessness of men. With a houseful of intellectuals and men doing women's work, why had no one taught her? I was doomed if I continued to nurse such emotions. I bowed again and spoke as politely as I could, praying the formalities would even out my tone. "I apologize for coming empty-handed, but my gifts are in my luggage." How easily my manners brought this lie to my lips.

"Don't worry about that. All the gifts we need come straight from God." She leaned closer to examine my features. "Clearly you've had quite a sophisticated upbringing. I worry— Perhaps you— Well, I hope you'll find comfort here."

"Your consideration is most kind, Ssi-umma-nim."

We sat awkwardly as the rain blew against the shutters and dripped into the gourd and pots. Presently she said, "I'll show you where everything is and you can help me prepare supper. I used to feed all the students, but I'm afraid that was too much for me and the church took that over."

"Students?"

"Oh yes. Next door." She opened a window and pointed to the two-story brick building between the church and the house. "We lived there for a time. All those rooms to clean! So many visitors staying for months. Too much! Especially when my eyesight worsened. Your father-in-law grew weary of hearing me complain, and we moved back here. The church houses seminarians there now, a much better use of the place. Besides, I worried all the time that those bricks would cave in on me as I slept. All that worry made me old and wrinkled before my time." She laughed and I forced a smile.

She showed me how the stove extended through to the back of the house where the roof overhung an outdoor cooking and working area sided with floppy walls of woven matting. A path through a tangled vegetable garden beyond the outdoor kitchen led to the outhouse. We prepared a plain lunch of clear soup, millet, gimchi, steamed beansprouts and dried fish in pepper sauce. When Reverend Cho returned, we ate together around the one small table. They conversed throughout the meal, which took me aback. I couldn't help but cover my mouth, though neither of my in-laws did, to answer questions about my parents and education. I knew I hadn't eaten much that day but had no appetite, and with my mouth too full of talking, I ate very little.

After the minister went out again, Mrs. Cho said, "You're a very lucky newlywed. Your father-in-law won't often be home. His duties call him at all hours and he regularly eats at the mission." *Lucky indeed*, I thought bitterly. And then I remembered Imo telling me her tragic story after I'd asked about Queen Min. Imo had married in 1900, considered an auspiciously lucky year. The terrible losses and personal dangers she had weathered in her loyal decades devoted to the royal family made the intensity of my disappointment and dismay seem petulant and deplorable.

When my footlocker and suitcase arrived, I paid the porter and thought about my money and possessions, all of which had been packed with an opposite destination in mind. I knew what my duty was, but couldn't yet part with my hard-earned steamer fare. I decided to do nothing for the time being. My unopened trunk dominated the small room like a misplaced palanquin until I shoved it on its end into the bookshelf corner and leaned the suitcase against it.

Rain fell steadily. I asked about the ways of their house. I was to draw water at one of the mission compound's pumps on the other side of the dormitory, and every morning visit the market just outside the compound walls. Laundry was done with pans and buckets in the outside kitchen, and the garden tended as needed. I readily accepted these duties, causing Mrs. Cho to deliver a prayer of thanks. She would now have time to visit church members at the hospital and mend the seminarian's clothes. I was too polite, too anxious and too dazed to ask about sleeping arrangements.

That evening after the dinner dishes were cleared and washed, in the pungent smoke of a fish-oil lamp, I presented my in-laws with prized Gaeseong ginseng, sacks of rice and beans, lengths of silk, decorative fans and several embroidered towels. I remembered the original intention of each item I gave—the ginseng for Calvin's elder brother, the rice and beans to cook on the overseas journey, the silk, fans and towels for my American patrons and teachers—and I felt that a part of me disappeared as each item left my fingers. Mrs. Cho delighted in all the gifts, commenting on their richness and the fine quality of my handiwork, and Reverend Cho suggested the ginseng and rice be given to certain church members who had greater need, the fans and silk be sold for food. I nodded and said nothing more, feeling guilty about the numerous possessions still hoarded in my trunk.

Reverend Cho handed me a folded yellow paper, the copy of my telegram. "I forgot to give you this."

I absently tucked it in my skirtband. "Thank you. I should tell my parents about—that I— May I write a letter tomorrow?" I felt I should ask to use the one table to write on.

"Of course. Give them our blessings and best regards. You may tell them, despite the unfortunate turn of the day, how pleased we are to have you here," said Reverend Cho. My mother-in-law reiterated the sentiment by clasping my hand, a gesture that only added to my deepening sense of dread. The minister said an evening prayer and announced it was bedtime.

I followed Mrs. Cho's instructions to empty the linen closet and spread the heavy quilts—my bedding next to the bookshelf, and beside mine, theirs. With the blankets spread, there was no space left on the wooden part of the floor. Even when she indicated she'd sleep beside me, it remained a layout of considerable discomfort. She brought her husband a basin of warm water. Without further ado, Reverend Cho undressed and, completely naked, wiped himself all over with a washrag. Thoroughly shocked, I turned to the wall and buried my eyes in my hands, too appalled to be polite, and mortified that I'd seen more of him than I had my own husband. Mrs. Cho added water to the basin and I heard her splashing. "There's hot water on the stove still for you too, Daughter." She snuffed the lamp, crawled into bed and settled on her side facing away from me. "Goodnight."

I waited until they breathed evenly with sleep, and still I couldn't move. It was impossible to remove my clothes in this setting. Impossible to bathe, to sleep! I huddled in the corner with my face to the wall, tugged Calvin's stained blanket around my legs and agonized. After a few hours of uncomfortable dozing, I tiptoed out of bed and filled the basin with now-cold water. Holding the blanket around my shoulders, I stepped into the linen closet and gingerly undressed. I washed quickly and silently, donned a nightdress and added a jacket for extra coverage. I rearranged the blanket on the rough floor as far away from them as possible—a few centimeters' gap. Although exhausted, I slept hardly at all and woke at the first hint of dawn to dress, scrub my face and use the outhouse before my in-laws stirred. I folded my bedding quietly and packed it in the closet. The yellow telegram fell from its folds. I went to the back porch to catch the sun's first rays to read what I'd written—a lifetime ago!

TO MR. CALVIN CHONGSO CHO C/O PUSAN PRESBYTERIAN MISSION STOP PASSPORT DENIED STOP I STAY IN PYEONGYANG STOP STUDY TWICE HARD STOP GO WITH GOD STOP WRITE YOUR WIFE

The words blurred as the wall around my emotions burst. I ran through the garden and beyond the outhouse until I tripped in my socks and fell in the wet brush, sobbing. I wept with grief and fury, and railed against God for teasing me so cruelly—giving me a summer filled with boundless hope, only to erase it in an instant with a single word delivered in hated Japanese. Even though I'd told Calvin to continue on, I cried out in my heart to call him home. I knew that he must go on, and that he would, but I wanted him to not leave me, to not abandon me to this deprivation and hopelessness. I felt shame for my jealousy, knowing his foot might at that moment be leaving this land to board the steamer, and failure for not being beside him. I grieved not only for the missed journey and loss of my dream but because I longed to be near him, to see his slow smile, hear his thoughtful questions, feel his warm and dry hands again on my neck. At least that much was true, that I did love him, although it now meant less than nothing, only yearning and pain.

When my tears were done, I remembered my father-in-law's prayer and knew I was undeserving of Calvin, of America, of anything good. The demeaning peasant's life I faced was punishment for pride, willfulness and Christian doubt. I refused to aspire to martyrdom, to accept suffering as the way to salvation. Still, I tried to pray for forgiveness for my arrogance and selfish wanting, for relief from the hurt I felt, but my bitterness was too acute to receive any sense of grace. I had seen the crude life that lay ahead and knew I had to accept it. My rage would not make the days pass any easier. I sat up at last, feeling empty and resigned. For that, I gave grim thanks.

I wiped my nose with leaves and returned to the house, resolved because of my love for my husband and my pious sense of duty to do right as his wife, to be my mother's daughter, to do right by God; subdued because I had no choice. In the outside kitchen, Mrs. Cho stuffed kindling in the stove. "Let me do that, Umma-nim," I said.

I didn't care that my mother-in-law knew I'd been crying. She ran her fingers through my blunt hair, handed me a pair of dry socks and held my hand. "Sad face, daughter-in-law. Jesus will see you through."

I thought, *If only it were that easy,* but I said, "Thank you. I'm grateful, Ssi-umma-nim." I lightly disengaged my mother-in-law's hand and added what I knew she'd want to hear. "I'll pray for guidance."

Mrs. Cho's face curled in all its wrinkles. We fixed breakfast. Before setting the table, I dug through my suitcase and brought out my brass rice bowl, which I filled with porridge along with my in-laws' bowls. I greeted Reverend Cho, who was dressed and jotting notes at the table as dawn's light filtered through the shutters, and I announced the meal. I wanted to erect invisible walls of discretion and form in this household. After I served them both, I bowed and gave him all of my money.

He handled it, gave one of his sympathetic grunts and returned a few bills. "You keep this until you decide how you'll occupy your days."

I thought for a moment. "Am I to decide?"

"There's little work for you in this house. Your mother-in-law has time on her hands even with her duties here. You could offer your services to the church. You could work at the mission or teach. Watch what goes on around you the next few days and see what work you might do. I'll introduce you to the mission director's wife on Sunday. I understand you play the organ. We do need an organist."

I spoke directly. "You're very kind. I'll do that, thank you."

His smile was friendly and inviting, and I felt even more ashamed about my earlier suspicion of his ministerial sincerity and revulsion at their home life.

"Come," said my father-in-law, "let's eat."

Watching them eat this time, I discovered they both devoured their food as quickly as Calvin had. I'd have to increase my pace or go starving, for I couldn't continue eating when they were done.

I FOUND AN excellent herbalist in the market and began to treat my mother-in-law's eyes. After learning that Mrs. Cho was slightly diabetic, I regulated her diet based on my own knowledge, enhanced by the advice of the pharmacist and what I could glean from copies of the ancient *Compendia of Korean Pharmacopeia* in the mission library.

I washed and relined Calvin's tattered quilt with a deconstructed night-colored skirt and meters of cotton I had in my trunk. Every evening after I arranged my in-laws' blankets and their washbasin, I went outdoors to dampen the stove until they were in bed. I undressed in the linen closet wrapped in my quilt, and laid as close to the wall as I could, but still heard every sound their bodies made. I was relieved that I never heard them being man and wife at night.

I chose to teach kindergarten in the mission compound partly because the innocent, earnest children made me forget my unhappiness, and it gave me a private physical space. It also left adequate hours to clean house and repair the thatch, tote water, visit the market, cook, wash clothes, tend the garden and keep the fuel stores filled. I couldn't refuse Reverend Cho's urging to play the organ, though it meant half a day at church every Sunday, and on Wednesday evenings hurrying to cook and leave without eating to rehearse with the chorus until the moon rose. Fortunately the choral director was a funny and energetic man who made rehearsals enjoyable.

One morning several weeks after my arrival, Reverend Cho opened his jacket and delivered a letter from Calvin. My heart leapt, and I thought I'd wait to read it during the half hour of quiet in my classroom before kindergarten began. I noticed the torn envelope at the same time that Reverend Cho said, "I was hoping he'd write more about the progress of his elder brother's church in Los Angeles, but he only talks about how charitable he's been. Well, you'll see what he says."

I stared at my father-in-law as I tucked the letter into my classroom notebook, incredulous at this invasion of privacy. He and Mrs. Cho ate speedily as usual, which meant that reading my mail would be routine. Then Reverend Cho met my eyes, smiled in that practiced ministerial way and said he'd forgotten to mention something about the house. One of the incoming seminarians, a rising star of a student, had a wife and an infant child. Since the dormitory was men-only, it had been promised that the new mother would live at the manse. "It'll be a little crowded, but you've been managing the house well and I'm sure you'll find a way to accommodate her and the baby. There's really no other place for her. Originally, I thought she might be helpful to Mother, but that was before you came. He's considered a prize for our seminary. His wife is yangban like you, and it's likely you'll become friends. Your mother-in-law is certainly experienced with babies, and it will bring her some joy to have an infant around."

I studied my porridge, hiding anger and the sense of violation over my opened letter, and also the horrible prospect of one more—one and a half more—bodies living in this room. We would have to share a bed. I prayed that the woman was at least well groomed.

Midday when I came home from teaching, my thoughts lingered on the faint hopes Calvin's letter had brought, and my resolve to try harder to make peace with the situation. I found my mother-in-law with an infant boy in her lap and the baby's mother sitting nearby. Lim Yonghee looked puffy with postpregnancy and decidedly unhappy. We were introduced, and I said, "Welcome, Dongsaeng, Little Sister. I hope that *Ssi-umma-nim* has familiarized you with our humble home."

"Humble indeed!" she said. "Unnee, Elder Sister, where do I put my son's diapers to be washed? I can't find room for my bed and Auntie said I should wait for you to fix me something to eat." Yonghee's perfectly shaped lips pouted and the faint vertical line between her eyes sank into a well-worn frown. When she saw my expression, she looked wounded. "Well, I would do it myself, but I'm still recuperating from the baby, you see, and such a long journey for my husband to come here. Naturally, I insisted we go to Pyeongyang because of the superior education he would receive, even though it would be a hardship on me, but I had no idea there'd be no other servants than—that there'd be no servants."

Mrs. Cho said, "We live very simply, but you'll see how helpful Daughter-in-law can be. It's an honor for your husband to be here. Don't wrinkle your pretty forehead, dear. You mustn't sour your milk."

I attempted friendliness and pointed to the linen closet. "That's where your bedding goes, but come to the stove and I'll show you how to heat water to wash diapers. I heard you were nursing, so I bought seaweed for soup. Why don't you come and make soup?"

"I'm tired from travel, Unnee, and I need to rest. It's only been a month since the baby, you see. Set out my bed and bring me the soup, won't you? It sounds delicious." Yonghee waved at a soiled diaper on the floor and displayed a sweet smile that rounded her cheeks beneath eyes glittering with ice. Aware that my next move would set a precedent, I refused to budge while my head spun to find a polite way to make this lazy girl take care of herself. I wished I were as practiced as she obviously was with the acerbic sarcasm of a spoiled brat.

Unfortunately, Mrs. Cho intervened. "Unnee will make a nice place for you to rest and I'll watch the baby. Such a handsome boy! Come, Grandma will rock you and sing you a song." I wanted to slap Yonghee's smirk away; instead I efficiently unstrapped her bedroll and spread it on the floor, swept up the dirty diaper and primly went outside to make soup.

I washed diapers, gardened and prepared food while the two women fussed over the baby. When he slept, Yonghee lay beside him in bed, flipping through a cheap Japanese magazine. When my mother-in-law asked her to read the Bible aloud, Yonghee complied in a drone that I likened to a wasp ready to sting. At sundown Mrs. Cho said Reverend Cho would come home soon, and Yonghee visited the latrine and lingered in the garden so long that I had to fold her bedding to make room for the table. She sat with Mrs. Cho and the baby until Reverend Cho's footstep was heard in the entryway. Yonghee dashed to the kitchen and brought bowls to the table. She greeted him warmly. "Auntie has kindly watched the baby all day so I could make dinner." My eyes widened in disbelief at this trivial maneuvering. I looked at my mother-in-law, who gestured that it didn't matter.

Yonghee had no problem with the bedtime routine and freely exposed her ample figure when she readied herself to lie in the blankets I'd repositioned next to Mrs. Cho. Once again, I stayed busy in the kitchen, waiting to hear rhythmic sleeping breaths before I undressed. With no more room for my bedding, I remained wrapped in my quilt and made myself as comfortable as I could on the linen closet floor, where I continued to sleep for all the miserable days I lived with my in-laws, days that slowly lapsed into months, then years.

Each time I gave my earnings to my father-in-law, he accepted them without comment and gave me a small amount back for food. At first I saved fifty jeon to visit the public bathhouse down the street, but saving became impossible when I saw that cash flowed through the house like smoke. Because of our dependency on the market for food and fuel, we were vulnerable to its rapidly rising prices and decreasingly available goods. Yonghee ate large portions and always asked for more, and I sometimes pretended I'd eaten at school so my in-laws would have a balanced meal. Within six months, I had sold all of the supplies I'd packed for American college. By the end of the first year, I had sold most of my books, more than half my clothes including the wedding dress, Western underwear and shoes, and then I sold the locker, and finally, Imo's suitcase. Even as I handed it to the peddler, I wondered that I felt little emotion about parting with my beloved aunt's thoughtful and cherished gift. I was tired, and empty.

My hands and feet became calloused and cracked as I washed diapers in all seasons, chopped wood, wove mats, mended the stove, walls and shutters. Without a proper entryway, mud, dirt and dust tracked through the house, and I was forever cleaning the floor.

Because I had asked Calvin and my family to write to me in care of the school, my father-in-law began to treat me with a coolness that grew into unfounded suspicions. He accused me of having an affair with the choral director and then, laughably, of trying to seduce Yonghee's husband. I couldn't fathom how such ideas entered his consciousness, but suspected that he had recognized my distaste for their way of living, and, perhaps, my despair, and had thus found fault with me. This sort of petty and calculated thinking exhausted me.

My cheeks sunk, my skin dulled and my lips were always held tight to hold resentment in and to mask my outright hatred of Yonghee. I enjoyed the kindergarten children and the choral rehearsals, which I defiantly continued attending, and even found time to study for my license to practice obstetrics. But when I came home, the spark faded from my eyes and my spirit darkened. Sometimes the baby cried at night and Yonghee breastfed him. I listened to the soft nestling of mother and child. My body ached for my husband then, for the future I'd counted on and lost, for Gaeseong, for anything different from this peasant life, this slavery. I wondered if the despicable living conditions and my despair would ever end, but I did not pray.

# Saved Letters

September 16, 1934
Los Angeles, California

My Dear Wife,

I regret that a letter cannot express my emotion, my deep sorrow, after I received your telegram. For all the days of travel, I could not look forward to the journey ahead, so burdened was I with sadness. I blame myself that you suffered alone at the passport office. While it is a relief to know you are safe and in the welcoming arms of my parents, that fact is scant compensation for the hopes you had harbored, hopes I had fostered, which were taken from you. It was indeed unexpected news, and without reasonable explanation.

Despite my friend's warning about certain rumors (which apparently are true), it seemed that improvement was coming. I have heard the Depression has ended. From fellow passengers, I heard many tales of new factories and industrial advances—which makes your experience even less understandable. From Busan to Shimonoseki, then by train to Tokyo, I was surprised by the stringent review my documents received. In fact, in Hawaii I had to rely on an American pastor from first class to intervene on my behalf and verify my itinerary before I was allowed to debark. I can only pray and ask that you do the same. It is certain that God's plan for you—for us—will soon be revealed.

Tomorrow is our birthday, and a sad one it will be. I had hoped to have you beside me on that day, our first together as husband and wife.

I am writing to you in haste from my brother's home, wishing to send you encouragement and to urge you to not give up. As quickly as the policy changed to create this situation, it may change again. I will press my father to assist you as he can. I know you will be loath to request further support from Rev. Bennett or to approach Dr. Sherwood, but they may have some recourse or information regarding this matter, and it may be to your benefit to swallow pride for the time being and write to them, at the least for guidance.

I am astonished with the multitude of strange plant life and the mild temperature at this time of year in Los Angeles, as well as my brother's consuming hospitality. It seems he desires that I meet and dine with every one of his parishioners. Perhaps because my stomach did not fare well on the ocean journey, these parties seem excessive, but my weakness in that department is not the problem that concerns me in the slightest. My concern is that the Pacific ships that dock in San Pedro are empty of my wife and all the possibilities she had placed in my hands. Therefore I take your words to study twice hard as my promise, and pray that we will soon be reunited.

Yours in Christ

September 23, 1934

My Dear Wife,

I trust this letter finds you and the family well. I wonder how you occupy your days and if you are finding your way around Pyeongyang. Naturally, I miss home, but it is the unfolding of our marriage that I am missing more. I have hardly had time to breathe, but every spare moment I have is spent in prayer for your good health, safety, and your forgiveness for my inability to have you beside me today.

I am astounded by the vastness and beauty of this country. My brother has put me on the train to Richmond, Virginia, where I will meet with those who will help me begin my studies. I am presently in the dining car of this modern train, which has tables covered in white linen and small electric lamps attached to the wall. Nevertheless, the rails are bumpy, although not as bad as at home, so please forgive my crooked penmanship. From a marvelous galley kitchen in the next coach, you can order hot coffee, hot dogs—a soft ground-up meat cake (pork) in a wheat bun—vegetables hot and cold, pastries and many other kinds of sweets, and even beef and mashed potatoes with a meat sauce called "gravy." My brother's wife packed several days' meals for me, so I am fortunate to be able to save my few coins. I was surprised to learn the small value of the money I brought, and was quite dependent on my brother. I have faith that one day you will meet him. His church, Yungnak Presbyterian, is impressive with a congregation of nearly three hundred Koreans, an inspiration to me. But God knows my path, and I leave thoughts of my future in His hands, praying only that it will soon include our reunion. I have entrusted my father to assist you in any way he can.

The Americans I have met are cautious with me until they learn about my country. Then they ask all manner of questions, which I am glad to instruct them on as best I can. It is sobering to realize that not a single person I have met on this train knows anything about us. Most have never heard of us. The church people I will meet in Richmond have set up evening meetings to teach others about the mission and to raise funds, and although my accent concerns me, I look forward to speaking about home. Your family is in my prayers, as are you.

With blessings and the love of Christ,

Calvin

November 29, 1934

Richmond, Virginia

My Dearest Wife,

Just this morning your letter of September 13 arrived, forwarded to me by my brother, and how glad I was to receive news of you and my parents. I am pleased to hear you are well and that your constitution is strong. I praise God that you have taken this turn of events as an opportunity to examine His presence in your heart. I commend your industrious teaching position and hope that your work in the mission is rewarding. I cannot thank you enough for the care you deliver to my mother, and give thanks that you have adjusted to their plain life, and with generosity.

This is the American holiday of Thanks Giving and the campus is closed. I am staying with the dean of student affairs' family during the break, learning how to cook and clean American style. I know you will find this amusing, but Dean Howe believes I can become what is known as a Houseboy, since I am in sore need of employment. As it is, I must shamefully rely on the seminary for pocket money. Luckily the cafeteria has an abundance of good food and I have a ticket that allows me three hearty meals a day. A single trip down the steam table line, where cafeteria workers serve you all manner of hot food, is enough to grasp the wealth of this country. My fellow students take it all for granted, and I am beginning now to become less tongue-tied about choosing country ham or fried chicken. It is still warm here. They say it snows hardly at all.

A curious thing occurred earlier this week when we had a class picnic out in a field. Excuse me for mentioning it, but when I found the latrines, I saw signs posted for "Colored" and "White." I headed toward the door marked "Colored," but my classmates pulled me from that entrance, saying, "Cal, you are not supposed to go in there. That is only for Negroes." I protested that I was colored and that no one would accept me as White. They said, "Yes, you are. You're very well accepted as White among us." And so, though I'd read about such things, this was the first time I understood the special connotation of "Colored." There are no Negroes at the seminary and scant few to be seen in town. I am told they live in their own section of the city. One day soon, I will visit that area. They tell me that Negroes are mostly Baptists, and of a particular variety called Southern Baptist. I must learn why.

I have much to catch up on in my studies. I may be sufficiently versed in the classics, but that means nothing here. I have tended to the schoolwork as never before, and when I grow weary of thumbing through my dictionary and am discouraged by the number of books before me, I remember my wife's situation and then can easily apply myself with diligence.

While I am saddened that it is not possible at present for you to journey overseas because ███████████████████ ███████████████████ I trust that God will see us reunited, and that soon you will complete your education despite ███████████████████████████████.

You are always in my thoughts and in my prayers.

Yours in Christ

Sunday, January 13, 1935
Gaeseong

Daughter,

It is odd to write to you at your school, but since you insist, I continue to do so. I hope you do not keep secrets from your in-laws. We received the New Year's money for Dongsaeng, and while he is grateful for it, you must give all your earnings to your in-laws. It is not proper otherwise. His school is not expensive, so do not worry about him. You say your father-in-law returns an allowance to you, but instead of sending it to Dongsaeng, give it to his church if you have no need for it. Do not worry, we manage fine. Sadly, there is no news to report from Kira. She is thankful that you ask after her.

Your father's health has greatly improved. It may well be because our diet is more balanced with a wider variety of food available lately, even after the winter. But his wellness is partially due to this other news: he has found an excellent prospect for Dongsaeng, a lovely young woman from Seoul recommended by Imo. Min Unsook is her name, and yes, a descendant of the royal family—one of the ███████████████████████ ███████████████████████████████ majored in secondary education at Ewha. Best of all, she is a devout Christian. Her photograph shows her as being quite pale and thin. I worried that she appears frail, but Imo says she is a woman of great inner strength and elegance. Your brother complains, as you did, that he is far too young to be thinking of marriage, but otherwise he seems content. They will be married when he graduates in two years. She is just a little older and has another year at Ewha herself, and then she plans to work with the church, probably teaching. You should take comfort in the fact that your independence eventually had a positive effect on your father, enough that he approves of this plan. Once they are married, she will stay home.

Here is something else that will surprise you. Your father is carving many decorative doors and shutters, a hobby that he discounts as mindless and meaningless, but the pieces are exquisite with vines, flowers and birds. Naturally we never speak of it, but I think this also contributes to your father's improved health.

As to your living situation, I hope that my daughter would find a way to adjust. Ask yourself, where is Jesus's example in your life? Of course it is an enormous disappointment that your husband is not at home to guide you in his household's ways, but it is small of you to call it "exile," and it is rude, as well as pointless, to complain. Is it so bad that you have completely forgotten your upbringing? The student's wife is your guest, is she not? You say it is not easy to live with her, but remember how Imo took such good care of you? You should return that hospitality to this woman. Some new mothers need more help than others. Try to be more generous in spirit. As for your father-in-law, he is a famous minister, ██████████████ ███████████████████████████████████████████

certainly a great man of God. What else matters? You should be honored to be in service to him and his church. In James it says, "Humble yourselves in the sight of the Lord, and He shall lift you up." Pray for guidance and patience. Think of your in-laws first.

Mother

April 16, 1935
Richmond, Virginia

My Dearest Wife,

During our long Easter vacation, I am glad to have a letter from home to mull over. First let me say how heartened I am to hear from you on the matter of your struggles, and that contrary to your fears, I welcome your confession and admire your frankness in searching for a way to Jesus. There is no shame in admitting weakness in faith. In fact, it is often a necessary step to open one's eyes to God. The Holy Spirit cannot easily enter an ignorant soul. Nor do I believe that our separation is punishment for lack of faith. That occurrence is not God's doing but others'. You know of what I speak. However, the opening of your eyes is, I believe, God's doing.

I laughed at your description of how your neighbor described my youthful days back in the big house. I can see it left quite an impression, and yes, you are wise to have extrapolated that I was searching for the meaning of God at that time. So I will tell you what changed for me, although I believe that faith does not always grow in such a dramatic way. Some people, like your mother, come naturally to grace. I would remind you of her Christian example as one most sincere and inspiring.

What happened is this. In early 1926 I accepted a job as principal of the ChoongKang Christian Elementary School, high in the north, not far from the Yellow River. Now please excuse this long description, but it is an important detail. From Pyeongyang it took almost three full days to reach the school, it was that remote: a half day by train to Gaecheong, a dirt road by bus to Gangweo, then a very treacherous mountain road several hours by bus to Jasang. From that point, there was scant regular transportation, but now and then a few nine-passenger cars went up the mountain, each taking about four hours to reach the destination.

I taught twenty pupils in the third and fourth grades, and supervised another teacher who had thirty-five children in the first and second grades. Another part of my job was to assist the minister of the church in that community who served seventeen different parishes. He seldom stayed in one parish but traveled around to take care of many scattered churches. When the minister was not in town, the elders and I alternated on the pulpit, and I preached once a month. Fortunately, there were no funerals during the absence of the minister! After one of my sermons, an elderly woman said, "Principal Cho, your sermon was good, but how come you did not mention Jesus Christ?" I told her I would keep it in mind, and the next time she was apparently satisfied. So you see, at one time I practiced my faith without full sincerity.

For the summer vacation I thought to venture home by the river route, which would save me a day's travel. At that time of year, loads of timber are floated down the rapids. A group of farmers and timbermen allowed me to ride in one of seven boats carrying soybeans down to Manpo where the rapids end. None of us realized that recent rains had made the water unusually wild. For a time we were lined up with the logs rushing in the same direction as the current, but at a narrow section of the river the logs went every which way and rammed the boats. The men jumped onto the logs, and with their lifetime of experience balancing on spinning timbers, all of them managed to reach the shore. I knew I could not walk on the logs and clung to the boat, which nearly capsized several times. Surprising everyone, for I'd been given up for lost, my boat was pulled to shore in Manpo. The other six boats had been crushed.

At the end of that summer I returned to open the fall session. At Jasang there was a car but no driver available for the last leg of the journey. I waited many hours, and finally when a group of five other passengers arrived, one of them claimed to be the driver, although we learned later that he was not. We gladly climbed aboard and began the ascent. At one of the sharp turns, the inexperienced driver hit a bank and the car stalled, slipped back and fell over the edge. It rolled and I was tossed from the window. It rolled again and crashed farther down. I received only a bruised elbow and knee, some big bumps and a torn jacket. The driver and two men were killed. The women who sat near the front suffered serious injuries, and I learned later that they both had died.

You will recall that my two younger brothers perished from TB. My life had been spared twice. Furthermore, each of these accidents occurred exactly on the one-year anniversary of my brothers' deaths. There had to be a very particular reason for this, and as I began to investigate, all the answers were larger than what I could fathom. So I came to believe in God's plan: first, because there was no other answer; now, because of His love. I decided to devote my life to the cause of the church. When I resumed my post as principal, I began reading the Bible, which I'd neglected for many years. I wrote to ask my father his advice on how best to understand this book and its intent, which led me to my study today. I pass his wisdom along to you, praying that you will take it to heart and find your own way. The best way to understand the Bible is simply to read it, and not rely on someone else's interpretation, but to read interlocking interpretations and discover them by yourself. He suggested starting with Psalms, Isaac and Matthew.

As I mentioned earlier, the way to God is as unique as our human individuality. I'm afraid God had to knock rather hard before I let Him enter. Read as you will, knowing the words themselves and then the numerous translations over the centuries sometimes had political origins and motivations. I hope my story did not bore you. I share it with you so you will know that I understand something of one's struggle with faith. Please write me with your questions and discoveries, as I am eager to know your thoughts.

It is very late. I will close now. My boss will frown at the electric light burning this long. I am houseboy for the Wilcox family three blocks from campus. For a few dollars, a room and two meals a day during school breaks, I clean, cook weekend suppers and otherwise help Mrs. Wilcox as I can. She is quite patient with me, and it will amuse you to know that I have become like a bride at her in-laws, learning all their odd ways. I have new understanding of your position, dear wife, and am glad that my family is not as particular as my employer.

Yours in Christ

23 November 1935

Gaeseong

Najin, dearest friend,

Congratulations on your certification! If only my father were still alive, you know how surprised and pleased he would be to hear about your obstetrics license. Mother is well, thank you. When I told her to whom I was writing, she said to say hello to "that freethinking friend of yours." Since father died, his sense of humor has been reborn in her! So take what she says as a compliment, for she thinks highly of you, especially since she attributes my decision to marry Dr. Song to you.

No, I have no regrets. He is kind and good to Mother, and he is quite modern. He is actually proud to have a wife in medicine, even if it is not his field of dentistry. I do not think of the past. No point. Besides, he makes me laugh sometimes, saying he is lucky to be the youngest in his family and therefore accustomed to following orders. He teases me that I am the big boss, not him. I suppose it is true. Have you heard from your husband yet? I would not worry that it is anything other than ███████████████████████ ████████████████████████████████████████

these days. It took a month for your last letter to reach me.

Congratulations on your first official delivery. And a fat healthy boy! I am glad that the mother showed you something of her fine character, especially since she is ██████████████████. I certainly cannot imagine giving birth to four kilos and not letting go a single cry. One thing I have definitely learned in medicine is that our bodily needs are equal to those of ████████████████████████ heart, the kidneys, liver and lungs all function in one body like the next. In that part of our humanity, we are all the same. This and, of course, the other thing of the past probably makes it easier for me than it has been for you. Besides, my father was never quite as busy as yours was in that way, perhaps because he too dealt with the flesh and organs of all kinds of men and women every day. You are lucky to have a father-in-law and your own father still alive, especially since your father-in-law is esteemed. Lucky that he allowed you to take those classes and the examination, and that he lets you go out to deliver babies. You make me laugh when you say you wish you had a bicycle to get to mothers faster!

I am glad you have found a friend in the choral master. What is so improper about having a friend, especially someone who works in the church with you? Surely, your father-in-law is jesting when he accuses you of falling in love with this man! I cannot quite interpret the hidden meaning in your words sometimes, and look forward to the day when we might be together again, laughing over one silly thing or another.

It was great to hear from you, dearest friend. I promise to write sooner than the last time you heard from me!

Jaeyun

Sunday, February 16, 1936

Daughter,

It disturbs me to address my letters to your school. As you wish, then. I have posted at the same time a separate note to your father-in-law with an appeal to allow you to return home to tend to your very ill mother who is increasingly in need of care since the winter is severe. I pray God will forgive me for the lie, but I do it for you. Under no condition are you to accept any money from him. This is to be completely at your own expense and on your own conscience. While I am eager to have you home, I am also disappointed that you found the situation impossible. You must learn that there are all kinds of people in the world and there is something of God in each of them, even if they do not show it on the surface. I blame myself that I did not prepare you for a different kind of life, instead always encouraging you to think independently and to set your goals higher than traditional expectations. But I have learned something from this lesson, disappointing as it is, and see that I must pray hard to overcome the uncharitable thinking that I have passed on to you.

I will say no more, other than to say we have met Min Unsook, who is indeed as lovely as reported. Even your stubborn brother is taken with her. Think little of the fact that letters from your husband ███████████████████████████████████.
Take heart. I doubt it is anything other than ███████████ ███████████████████████████████ which your father ███████████████████████████████████████.

Come home then.
   Mother

                                                    August 31, 1936
                                                    Wilmington, Delaware
My Dearest Wife,

   This afternoon I was relieved to receive the one letter dated "fourth month" from you, the only letter from home this year so far, and it ████████████████████████████████ ████████████████████████████ for I have written steadily every week. That the ███████████████████████████ ████████████████████████████████, and is what I surmised since your letters simply ceased to arrive. I was quite worried, so my relief that you are well is enormous, especially on this, the second anniversary of our marriage. By my absence I have not been a good husband to you and I beg your forgiveness. A classmate from New York tells me that the talk at the ████████████ ████████████████████████████████ as well as the rising temperatures toward ██████████████████████. I hear also that the controversy about ████████████████████, and that the division is along class lines as it has historically always been. We are starved for accurate information. Know that I continue to keep you in my prayers and my mind as the distance between us, with unpredictable correspondence, seems to grow.

   I hope your mother's health is benefiting from your wise hands as well as my own mother's health benefited. I also have not heard from my parents for some time now, but I know from what you have written to me that my mother will never forget the caring and gentle soul of her second son's wife. And you needn't feel sorry that now she has no one to help her. The seminarian's wife is there for another year and will undoubtedly be of assistance. How frightening it must have been to see a glimpse of your mother's mortality! I pray for her and for your continued strength in providing for her wellness. As for what you say is your failure as a wife, that is nonsense. It is I who have failed you, for no new wife should have had to suffer the transition from one household to another without her husband. I assure you that my parents will get along fine. They have the strong presence of their church and the mission community surrounding them. ███████████████████████████████ and I am more than grateful for all that you've done for them and their church. It is difficult to express my emotion realizing that two years have passed without having you beside me. I pray every day for your forgiveness, and that soon we will be reunited.

You need not apologize nor suppose that I would have anything other than feelings of pride for your profession in obstetrics. Our situation as husband and wife is extraordinary, and you have adapted to it with both grace and strength. I applaud your enterprising spirit in pursuing at least some version of the plans we had laid, and hope the work gives you satisfaction. The only shame there is comes from my not having been able to properly provide for you. You need not ask my permission nor fear any judgment I may have over your decisions or actions. I am the one indebted, to you. Nor do you need to apologize for selling your engagement ring. I can ███████████████████████████ for you to have sold it. If the ticket home and the medicine it bought helped to relieve one hour of your mother's illness, the choice to sell it was well made.

███████████████████████████████ I feel it necessary to let you know of my plans, as far as they can be known at this time. I can only pray ██████████████████████████. You will note my new address, as I now study at Faith Theological Seminary trying to make inroads into the question of the separation of the Presbyterians. This seminary is the more extreme fundamentalist group. I see few theological differences, but there is definitely a difference in attitude. I am somewhat ostracized here because I attend many different churches, including Episcopalian and apostolic churches, to which the student body is strongly opposed. However, I shall be moving next month to Princeton Theological Seminary. With all my credits from various colleges, I expect to graduate in less than a year and become ordained. Here is the English address: c/o Dean of Students, Princeton Theological Seminary, Princeton, New Jersey. He will have some idea of my whereabouts.

Thereafter, I will need to earn passage home, and will keep you apprised. The New York Presbytery is receptive to my inquiries, and it is likely that I will pursue work there. I can always rely on being a houseboy, though the payment is only a few pennies along with room and board. I hope for an assistant pastorship, but being a foreigner decreases that likelihood. Since my English has greatly improved, I can also translate. While long-term plans are difficult to make, I wanted to give you some idea of my possible whereabouts. And, as our distance grows ███████████████ at home, I can only pray that God will provide as He has so far. I pray that His mercy and goodness keep you and your family safe and well.

Your husband in Christ

# The Moon's Portent

THE SCHOLAR HAN'S BREAKFAST LAY COLD AND UNEATEN ON A TRAY beside him. A note listing several classic poems and an open Bible were centered on his writing table in preparation for the words he'd speak at his son's wedding. Beside his elbow were the household accounts he'd soon relinquish to Ilsun as master of the family. And at his feet two Seoul newspapers, *Dongah Ilbo* and *Kidok Shinmun*, bore headlines of another student protest in Seoul, this one spurred by the imprisonment of each newspaper's editors for superimposing an image of the Korean flag over the Rising Sun in the victory photograph of the winning Olympic marathoner, a Korean national. Rumors that the papers would soon be shut down concerned him as much as reports of the foreboding policies of the new governor-general, Minami Jiro. Among them was the required recitation of the Imperial Oath and Pledge at any public gathering and in the schools. *Endless brainwashing!* thought Han. It was the subtlety of the smallest-seeming acts that proved to be the most coercive. On one of his recent walks, he'd heard a gaggle of young schoolchildren speaking Japanese, and when he addressed them in Korean, they looked at him uncomprehending. He rationalized that they were peasant children or Japanized orphans, but it needled him.

"Abbuh-nim, would you like your soup reheated?" There was his daughter, two months home from her failed marriage. He waved her away, not wanting to deal with the unanswered question of her procuring a job. *A bad example for the new wife*, he thought as he scanned the list of poems. He was trying to remember a sijo about marriage written by a poet, a former military commander, who had famously commemorated the end of the Japanese invasions at the close of the sixteenth century. It was bad enough that he couldn't recite the poem, and now, was it possible that he'd forgotten the poet?

His stomach growled and he called for Najin. "You can reheat."

"Yes, Abbuh-nim."

He sensed her lean form as she bent for the tray and regretted that her husband had gone to America before providing a real chance for a grandson. He would remember to ask for that blessing during his son's wedding. Preparing his message, he culled from the Confucian theologian Zhu Xi, early Joseon Dynasty poets and the Bible. His wife had once accused him of being so old-fashioned as to be unable to see beyond the woods of his ancestors' cemetery. He could now concede to this, feeling reassured that Ilsun's classical training had prepared his son to have a foot in both yesterday and today. This made Han frown, knowing that more often than he liked to admit, Ilsun had both feet planted firmly in the present without regard for the past whatsoever.

*Well*, he thought, *marriage will cure that.* When one's seed sprouts beneath one's roof, what was, and what will be, take on new meaning.

Najin returned quietly, startling him. "Here is chamomile tea with peppermint," she said, pouring. "Please drink this first."

He smelled its restful steam and nodded, pleased with her herbalist skills.

Najin's eyelids flickered with a faint smile, and he suppressed his pleasure at finding a rare moment when they understood each other. She bowed and left.

He sipped the tea and soup and his stomach calmed. Then he remembered Pak Il-lo as the poet and knew that the words he sought referred to the primacy of the spousal relationship. He also remembered that Pak's sijo and his "Song of Peace" were in a bundle buried beneath the floor of the hidden pantry. Too much trouble to dig it up, and he didn't want to hear Joong's grumbling if put to the task. He thought that the bookseller, Mr. Pahk, would have recalled the poem word for word, and regretted that the bookstore had gone under during the Depression. Father wondered if his old friend had survived the long journey to Nanking where he had relatives. Tension between Japan and China was as taut as a hangman's rope, and unfortunately, Han believed the prevailing news of an imminent and full-blown Sino-Japanese war. Already the Mongols had aligned with the Russians—what was it they now called themselves? yes, the Soviets—against further Japanese aggression. China was preoccupied with its own conflicts between the Kuomintang and Mao's Red Army. Mao's policies of violent revolution were also erupting in skirmishes in northeast Korea, and while Han believed any resistance against the Japanese was a good thing, the poorly armed and disorderly "justice fighters"—peasants led by peasants—seemed doomed to failure. Things were stewing with Western nations too. There was civil war in Spain, and the Showa Emperor had pulled out of naval treaty talks in London with the British and the Americans. It seemed the world was rife with controversy and foment. Han knew he wasn't so old yet as to be forgetful, but he was feeling overwhelmed by the many things he heard and read in the papers that he knew little about: Rhineland, Tunisia, Mussolini, the Nazis, and the Showa Emperor's talks with Hitler.

His eyes swept over his desk. What had he been looking for just then? *The sijo, of course*, he thought, relieved to be in the familiar if momentarily forgotten territory of Korean literature. Perhaps Reverend Ahn, a classically educated man, would know the poem. Han also wanted to ask the minister about Bible passages used in traditional Christian weddings. He decided to visit the church and called Joong for his coat.

The street smelled crisply of leaves and fall debris. Han clasped his hands behind him and walked slowly, the sun warm on his neck. Some families had pasted banners written with harvest thanks and blessings outside their walls. Han wondered that thanks could be offered at all these days. Yes, the Depression was over and food was more plentiful, but the change was a by-product of the industry of war. He felt that preservation of the Korean way had become an afterthought. Instead, the northern insurgents and the youth, who had grown more vocal, were calling for a new paradigm that had little to do with the proven traditions, little to do with Korea's long history. How had Russia managed to spread its Bolshevik ideals? He felt a disquieting inner conflict, because the Japanese agreed with his distaste for communism.

A woman wearing anklets, high heels and a yellow cloth coat brushed by him. "Excuse me, Harabeoji." She ducked her head and hurried on. It wasn't the first time he'd been called Grandfather rather than Uncle. Naturally he didn't mind the misnomer. He attributed it to his appearance, as few men wore Korean clothes anymore. Frowning at the woman's bare calves and the visible sway of her hips, Han thought that his daughter might be forward thinking, but thank God she dressed with propriety. He passed through the market and noted that the people wearing Korean clothes were grandparents, women, peasants and workingmen. One man, burdened by a tower of straw strapped to his back frame, wore Western trousers with his Korean shirt and vest. Han unconsciously quickened his pace.

In the narthex he heard voices coming from the sanctuary. If the minister was busy, he'd return later in the day. He decided to check and opened the heavy wooden door. A dozen of the church elders were clustered in the front pews, talking animatedly. Having recently become aware of people's attire, he noticed that all the men wore suits. He cleared his throat loudly. Deacon Hwang jumped to his feet, as did a few of the others, visibly turning red.

"W-w-we're glad you c-c-could make it," said Hwang as hastily as his speech would allow. Han chose to ignore the obvious, and content to see that the minister was not among them, asked for him.

"Please come in, sir, and have a seat," said the new assistant pastor. He was a young man from the south who had struck Han as being too strident about the need for the church's outright support of the chaotic independence movement, particularly the uneducated warmongering clansmen leaning toward communism. "The minister was called to the hospital."

"I see," said Han. He stood a moment, using his dignity to augment their discomfort at having neglected to include him in their meeting. "Good day, gentlemen." He heard their dutiful protests, their respectful goodbyes and shuffling of feet as they stood and bowed, and he suspected he wasn't imagining the relief he heard beneath their parting words.

He climbed down the broad steps of the stone church, his back bent. He noticed nothing in the market on his return trip except for an increasingly painful stitch in his side. By the time he reached the hill home, he was resolved that Ilsun, after marriage, would fight for his point of view in the church community. His dinosaur ways might be discounted in the immediate present, but time would prove that tradition and history could be relied upon as the guide to a national solution. *And it's possible,* he thought as he rattled the outside bolt to his gate, *that I'm wrong.*

HAN GRACIOUSLY PRETENDED that nothing had occurred between himself and the churchmen, who gladly joined in Ilsun's wedding celebration, which was a quiet affair followed by a meager yet costly banquet in the church hall. The bride, Min Unsook, immediately proved to be an exceptional wife: softspoken, harmonious in her manner, a capable cook and a fine example for Najin, not to mention Ilsun himself. His wife had only good things to say about their daughter-in-law's contributions to the household. The responsibility for the family's affairs shifted to Ilsun, who had graduated from upper school with respectable marks, although disappointingly not at the top of his class.

Winter draped the estate in snow and freezing sleet, and Han felt less and less inclined to take his daily walk. Reverend Ahn continued to beseech him to join in their clandestine meetings, and Han continued to send Ilsun in his place. His son reported little from these gatherings, which were held in the guise of Bible study at irregular times and locations. Ilsun merely said they were boring and that the copastor indeed had leftist leanings. Soon, the requirement that all public gatherings be police-monitored and delivered in Japanese language prevented meetings altogether. Still, the men managed to convey news and discuss politics in private social events.

Han said nothing when Ilsun permitted Najin to work at the mission school, and heard from his wife that his daughter was taking courses at the new medical college connected to the hospital. He privately hoped her training would help improve his daughter-in-law's apparent inability to conceive. Based on the nighttime sounds from Ilsun's rooms, Han didn't have to tell his son to work harder toward that goal. He continued to read the newspapers and urged Ilsun to speak for him among the churchmen. Then, by summer, darkening changes made even this simple request too risky, and he told Ilsun to avoid talk of politics altogether.

In July 1937, training exercises on the Marco Polo Bridge just south of Peking escalated into a skirmish between Japanese and Kuomintang troops. Each nation blamed the other for instigating the event, and Chiang Kai-shek refused Japan's offers to negotiate, which included demands for an apology. Within a month, Japan overcame the poorly trained northern Chinese in Peking and Tsientsin, then attacked Shanghai. By the end of the summer, just as Han had feared, Japan was at war in northern China. Winter brought newspaper stories of glorious imperial victories in Nanking, but by then the press was once again completely controlled by the Japanese. Missionaries were telling contrasting stories: massive slaughter of prisoners of war, uncountable civilians murdered and shocking atrocities. During the Battle of Nanking, an incident sparked hope that the Americans would become involved, which might soon end the war and free Korea. Japanese planes had destroyed the U.S. gunboat *Panay* in the Yangtze River during the attack. But diplomatic apologies and reparations were offered, accepted, and the Americans kept their distance. It seemed that no one wanted to confront the Japanese, whose might was largely being drawn from the Korean peninsula—Korean rice shipped to feed the Japanese military, raw material churned from Korean mines to feed hundreds of new factories, which smelted the ore into mechanical parts for the war machine. The military presence in Gaeseong multiplied again, newspapers trumpeted imperial propaganda—and occasionally included the drivel of a serial novel—and mail grew increasingly censored, if delivered at all.

Ilsun had come to him once, proposing to invest what little they had in an illegitimate-sounding deal to export ginseng, but Han lost his temper and insisted that his son continue his art and calligraphy with an eye toward the rest of his formal education, perhaps—after Unsook conceived—at Yonhi College in Seoul. He told his son to save for the tuition. But since Han no longer monitored the household accounts, he had no knowledge that within six months all ready cash had disappeared, nor was he aware of the reason for the rapid depletion. He did know that his son spent too little time with brush in hand, and that he was often not at home.

One winter night late in February 1938, Najin came to Han in his study. As she stood before him, he realized they hadn't shared this space since she was a child. He looked at the scattered shavings of maple surrounding him like termite's waste, the scraps of seasoned oak and maple limbs, rough pine boards, chisels, awls and files—a different kind of place than twenty years ago. He rubbed an oiled rag on a spindle that would become part of a shutter, and indicated that she should sit.

She brushed sawdust aside and sat on her knees. "Father, I've come to ask your advice about quitting my job."

Her words were abrupt, but her manner was pleasing enough. She had been teaching middle school for a year or more, and since he knew little about what she actually did every day, he wondered why she sought his advice. *Yah, too bad about her husband,* Han thought. Neither Najin nor the Cho family had heard from Calvin for years, and she was virtually a widow. To be sure, everyone was praying, but there was no way to know if Calvin was dead or alive, or even if he was still in America. Undoubtedly, with Japan at war, it was impossible for him to return. It wouldn't surprise Han if after all this time the man had married again. The possibility of Calvin returning to Korea had further diminished with tensions growing between Japan, America and England following another diplomatic request for information about Japan's naval capacity, which the Japanese still refused to supply. A derisive cartoon in the newspaper had appeared that very week, portraying the two Western nations as salivating dogs trying to tear off a Japanese naval officer's trousers.

He plucked a dry rag from a nearby shelf and cleaned his hands. "Have you talked to your dongsaeng? And what does he say?"

"That we need the money."

Han soaped and rinsed his hands in the basin Najin held for him, then settled onto his cushion. At these kinds of moments he wished tobacco were affordable and readily available. "And so?"

He could tell she had much to say by the way she waited a moment before speaking. "Abbuh-nim, after last fall's semester break, the students were required to come back early for ten days of Labor Service. It wasn't difficult; they swept the yards of government buildings and it was pleasant enough to be outside. But this winter we've been required to sew straps onto canvas squares for half the school day. My students don't complain even though their fingers bleed from punching needles through the rough cloth, and if the school inspectors aren't around, I use the time to teach Korean grammar. It worries me how little of their own language the girls know. Then yesterday I learned we're making military kit bags. We're contributing to their war!" She stopped until her breath quieted. "But that isn't the main reason I wish to give up teaching. They've changed the curriculum again. Korean is forbidden altogether and the Bible is disallowed; we are required to teach that the emperor is god."

He thought that they chipped away at his country, like he chiseled shaves from blocks of maple—and suddenly he felt his heart fill with hope—from which one day, one optimistic day in the future, might emerge a small work, like a lovingly carved maple panel, of plain beauty. His next thought was to pray that it might happen in his lifetime. He stroked his thinning gray beard. But perhaps not.

Najin continued, "We've been swearing the Imperial Oath every morning for some months, but that isn't the problem. Now they're saying we have to participate in all-day parades and ceremonies to show our patriotism. Not only that, but for composition the girls will be required to write comforting letters to Japanese soldiers! Two of the ten teachers were forced to quit because they say we need more Japanese instructors. Chang Hansu's wife wishes to quit her teaching post, but only if I also choose to leave. Abbuh-nim, as much as I advocate education, I cannot be the head teacher in a school that teaches lies."

He appreciated her calm voice and was amazed to learn that she was the head teacher. "No, I suppose not." He countered her surprise at his quick response with a prolonged silence. "Get a different job, if the money is truly needed." How easy it was to speak to her! Then he wondered why it had always been hard. What had changed?

She bowed and left, but not before he caught the gist of her smile. Well, it was good to have a political activist in the house! He sat awhile, thinking of the many years gone by, of old age, of youth, his youth when he was a young father, and the astonishing innocent trust of his infant daughter's newly opened eyes, which seemed as deep and dark blue as a winter's twilit sky. Yes, considering her activist attitudes now, and the practical, resourceful woman she'd become, perhaps he had done right after all by not naming her.

ANOTHER HARVEST SEASON came and still his daughter-in-law, Min Unsook, now two years married, did not conceive. Han only scanned the headlines of newspapers filled with reports of imperial victories and anti-Chinese propaganda. Within a few months, everyone's identification was recertified and ration cards were issued. Neighborhood competitions were held to see who could contribute the most rubber, wood or metal. If one's household offered nothing, soldiers were authorized to storm through the house, vandalizing as they wished. Unreported beatings, thefts and rapes were rampant. The government imposed price controls, further inflating the cost of rice. Then in October 1938, when Han read that Canton had fallen, he told Joong to stop bringing the newspapers.

He found his hands seeking chisels and rasps rather than brush or book, and prayed to both God and his ancestors for a grandson. He would rest if he had a grandson. He carved nature's forms on shutters, doors, cabinet fronts and furniture, and the house became strikingly adorned with his handiwork, the storerooms cluttered with bas-relief panels. Every now and then a shutter would be missing from a window, or he'd see Ilsun carrying a newly sculpted stool out the gate, and rice would take the place of millet, or an egg or a whole fish would accompany the garden vegetables at his meals. He said nothing and continued to carve and stack finished pieces in the storeroom.

One evening toward that winter's end, he glimpsed a stunning moon-rise from his window. So broad and brilliantly pearled was the orb that he left the warmth of his sitting room to regard it from the porch. Its brilliance drew him out to the courtyard in his stocking feet, the iciness of the clear night cutting sharply through his clothes. The moon cleared the treetops and seemed to fill half the sky, and he wondered that in all its enormous beauty it gave no warmth. He tried to capture its portent and breathed in deeply. Tiny icicles of frost broke in his nostrils as he gazed at the enigmatic features of the luminous sphere, seeking to comprehend its message.

"Yuhbo!" called his wife.

He came in sheepishly. She stirred his brazier, and he was grateful that she didn't comment on his crazy behavior. Her preoccupied manner hinted at bad news. "Chang Hansu is here. His wife is with us in our rooms. He wants to speak to you." He rubbed his hands over the coals and sat.

Alarmed by how aged and gaunt his neighbor looked, he called for his daughter-in-law to bring something hot to eat. Unsook assured him that soup and millet were coming for both Hansu and his wife. After eating and extending the usual courtesies, Hansu ran his hand through his unruly hair, suffused with gray, and said, "Uncle, I've had to sell the house. Neither my wife nor I have been working for nearly a year now. Sir, I've been drafted for labor in Nagasaki."

He heard the strain in Hansu's voice. Han sympathetically dropped his eyes. Earlier that month, Ilsun had mentioned rumors about an extensive labor conscription and local draft officials who roamed the streets with quotas to fill. Ilsun said he'd heard about truckloads of unmarried men and women scooped from rural villages, but so far the cities had seen little of this. If Hansu, who had long been married, had been drafted for labor, what would become of Ilsun? He felt guilty relief for his former ability to pay the bribes that had erased Ilsun's name from official rosters, and guilt again for his narrow and selfish concern. He looked at Hansu, his eyes full of solicitude.

Hansu, his brow deeply lined, sighed. "My parents have decided to join me. We are all promised housing and employment at the Mitsubishi truck factory there. The wages are fair, more than anything I can earn here with my red line." Following his trial and sentencing after March First, Hansu's identification papers were stamped with a red linear seal, marking him a criminal against the empire and severely limiting his ability to work. He'd been fortunate to have teaching positions with the missionaries, but since the onset of the China War, the missionaries were disfavored, and old regulations and dozens of new ones were stringently enforced. Hearing about Hansu's circumstances, Han expected that the missionaries would likely be expelled altogether.

Shoulders sloped, head bent, Hansu paused to hear his elder's response.

Witnessing the young man's unusual passivity stirred Han to anger. "You must go underground then. Your family can move in with us. We have many empty rooms here. You can arrange everything with my son."

"Thank you, but no. I've already taken too much advantage of Ilsun's connections. It was he who found the man who guaranteed a desk job for my wife and me, since we're both educated and fluent."

Han's face must have shown something of his surprise at Ilsun's involvement, for Hansu said bleakly, "I didn't expect you'd approve, but my wife is with child. My family will be persecuted if we were to run. Because my parents are following us voluntarily, they won't be required to work in the factory. It's likely some clerical work can be found for my father since he has a long record with the government."

"No, son. On the contrary, I understand completely." He quoted the second part of the primary Confucian adage, "Administer thy family well." He wanted to urge Hansu to continue on the path of resistance, but Canton had fallen and Chiang Kai-Shek had lost Hanbon. The Japanese seemed invincible. The two men sat awhile, then Han said, "Times are precarious."

Hansu stood and bowed, and the scholar also rose, saying, "Blessings for your child and family. May God be with you." The men bowed again and Hansu left to say goodbye to the women.

The brazier sputtered. Han looked to see if the moon still held its benign smile, but it had risen beyond his view. He sat feeling very worn, his old companion the stomach cramp flaring, and wondered if his countrymen would ever again have what he now saw was the luxury of being free to pursue the first Confucian directive: to cultivate the mind and body. He heard his wife and daughters giving the Changs packages of food with teary goodbyes and many promises for staying in touch, but he doubted his family would ever see them again.

Within a week after the Changs had left, a young Japanese couple moved in next door, and Han had Byungjo mortar over the gate between the properties.

# Box of Light

THE STRAIGHTFORWARD BIRTH OF A THIRD SON ON THE OTHER SIDE OF Gaeseong kept me busy through half the night. I slept there until curfew lifted at sunrise on Monday and came home in time to help my sister-in-law with breakfast. As soon as I stepped into the kitchen, Unsook handed me a steaming bowl of soybean soup. "How perfect!" I said. The days were increasingly cold, and the hot bowl in my hands felt very welcome. We fixed the men's meals, adding strips of dried fish I'd bought at the market that morning on my way home. Unsook delivered the men's breakfasts, then joined me at the table portioning our food.

Unsook had been married and living with us for two years, consistently showing selflessness in the work and service she gave to the family.

She often woke with dark circles under her eyes but never complained about Dongsaeng's demands of her night hours. Afterward, she slipped quietly into her bed in the tiny room next door to me, and even with my sensitive ears, I rarely heard her. Unsook's behavior embodied my mother's guideline for civility: think of others first. Typically she was one step ahead of anything that needed doing or might make life a tiny bit richer, such as having hot soup ready on a cold morning. Slim and delicate as a fawn lily, sometimes when her profile caught the evening light, she reminded me of Yee Sunsaeng-nim. Mother and I agreed, as did Cook and Kira, that we were especially blessed to have such an elegant and accomplished young woman in our household. With her frail beauty and gentle manner, I felt like a sticky lump of clay beside her, but we had grown sisterly and close. Mostly I felt protective toward her, motherly in a way that sometimes made me yearn for Calvin and the chance to have a child.

We brought our breakfast to the women's sitting room, and Mother gave prayer, including as always, thanks for two daughters at home taking such fine care of the house. Unsook had recently started volunteering at the local orphanage once a week. I was sure her joy at being with children was mixed with pain at not having a baby of her own. Since today was an orphanage day, Unsook described what she'd set aside for the midday meal, and that she'd dusted and cleaned the floors. "I'm sending a note to Imo-nim, and I'll stop at the post office if you have any letters to mail."

Mother nodded and reached toward her worktable. I shook my head.

"Oh! I'm sorry!" said Unsook, apparently thinking that with my missing husband, mentioning the mail would be hurtful. "How inconsiderate of me. I shouldn't have— I didn't mean—"

"Please don't worry. It's been a long time."

Unsook bowed her head. Mother and I began eating, and Unsook slowly picked up her chopsticks. Because so many emotional matters are not voiced in a Confucian household, our empathy was well developed. Unsook seemed unreasonably uncomfortable about mentioning the mail, and it made me realize that while she knew my husband was in America, we had never once talked about it. In fact, my husband had been rarely mentioned since my arrival home from Pyeongyang, except in the very beginning when I received Calvin's last letter, now two years ago.

Since then, I'd written to his parents to be courteous and dutiful, and also to check if they'd heard from him. I received one short note from his mother, transcribed by that witch Yonghee, saying there was no news from America. I wrote without reply for more than a year, but their uncommunicativeness allowed me to eventually stop writing to them without feeling too guilty. I rationalized that paper was expensive, the mail too erratic and my mother-in-law's illiteracy too much an obstacle for staying in touch. And I still fumed over Reverend Cho's accusations that I had anything less than proper relations with Yonghee's husband and the choral director.

The years in their hovel left only loathing, bitterness and shame, and it made my feelings for my absent husband all the more complex. Having lived with his family far longer than the total time I'd spent with Calvin, I wondered how well I knew my husband. And now with wartime and half a world between us, I couldn't even guess how America might have changed him, or how I might appear changed in his eyes. I could barely remember his presence at all, except on rare occasions before I fell asleep, when a glimpse from memory—the moment of recognition we shared that day by the pond, his look when my wedding veil was lifted, or his light touch on my hand unlatching his suitcase—would surprise me with the passion it roused. It was easier to put it all aside and ignore the label of abandoned wife. Obviously something was wrong with international mail delivery. Despite the brevity of our union, I firmly believed I would know somehow if Calvin were dead.

To ease Unsook's discomfort over the idea that she had caused me pain by mentioning the mail, I said, "I suppose he's forgotten me and married one of the three hundred parishioners at his brother's church."

Pause. "You're joking."

"Yes." Her face showed such relief that I felt bad for teasing her. "I'm sorry. It's been four years since he went to America and we've completely lost touch. I haven't even heard from his family. I try not to think about it. I wait, that's all. And pray. What else can I do?" Not writing to Calvin or thinking about him also allowed me to avoid dealing with unrequited love and romance and other such foolishness. Additionally, it allowed me to assume that time would prove my Christian faith. In the meantime, it seemed simpler to remain where I was, not asking, not being asked.

"I'm sorry," said Unsook.

"No, *I'm* sorry."

"I— I wish— Excuse me, I'm sorry."

"No, don't be, really. I'm happy to be home, especially now. You're the sister I've always prayed for." Surprised by the surge of feeling over this little truth, I clasped her offered hand.

"Amen," said Mother.

Later that day, after cleaning out the silkworm shed and readying it for another cycle before winter, I helped Cook fix lunch, wondering how Unsook fared at the orphanage. She would probably be more tired than if she'd spent all day at home doing chores. I gave the trays to Cook to deliver to Father and Dongsaeng, and turned to portion everyone else's.

Someone banged loudly on the gate and a man shouted in Japanese. Startled, I thought, *Not again!* then, angry, *Father's done nothing!* and I turned quickly, upsetting the kitchen table. Chopsticks and bowls clattered to the floor, spilling hot liquid. The knocks grew louder until Byungjo lifted the latch. I ran down the hall to Mother's sitting room. Heavy measured footsteps crossed the yard, then came crisp commands: "Out! Come out! Everybody out of the house—now!"

My mother stood and her hands fluttered to her pale lips. An old fear surfaced, but with it a righteous defiance. People were always being arrested, but neither my father nor brother had been involved in politics lately.

Dongsaeng appeared in the hall. "What is it?"

Soldiers stormed through the vestibule. "Outside! Now! Now!" A thunder of boots and shouts, and Mother and I hurried to the front door. Two soldiers charged into the men's sitting room and grasped Father beneath his arms. "Everyone out!" They dragged him and pushed us through the house to the courtyard. The servants were driven outside. Mother faltered and I slipped my arm around her waist.

From an open military vehicle visible on the road, a soldier and an officer came through the gate, the officer's starched uniform the same hue as the dust that swirled in our yard. We were lined up and commanded to bow to the major. The soldiers assembled in a row behind us. The major said, "Which one of you is the spy Han Najin?"

I stood tall. "I am Han Najin," I said, my breath blasts of steam. I was afraid, but also relieved that it was obviously a mistake, and they hadn't come for Father or Dongsaeng. "But I am not a spy, my lord."

"No?" He removed something from his assistant's satchel. He was clean-shaven with deep eyes, pronounced cheekbones and fair, almost delicate skin. His boots creaked as he neared. "Then what is the meaning of this?" He threw the object and it struck my cheek, then fell at my feet: a thick bundle of letters, colorful American stamps, a New York return address and Calvin's handwriting, the familiarity of which struck me deeply, far more powerfully than the blow to my face. I held my breath so as not to gasp.

"My lord, if you please," said Mother, bowing low. "They were married only one day before he went to America. That is all. We have not heard from him, nor has she written to him for several years."

Father said, "We are loyal taxpayers, my lord." The major smiled and the soldiers laughed, and my cheek burned anew at this disgraceful treatment of my father.

"I know that you are," the major said mildly. He turned to me. "You are under arrest."

I heard the words and knew what they meant, but also couldn't understand them. I looked quickly to Mother and saw the same disbelief. And pain. How easily my actions, my sorry existence, could hurt her.

"You will come with us."

*If I'm going out*, I thought simply, *I'll need shoes.* "My lord, my shoes—"
He indicated yes.

I ran to the entryway and grabbed my coat. My vision telescoped as I slipped on my shoes, each foot increasingly far away.

"My lord, where will you take her?" Mother fell to her knees and cried out in Korean, "Father in Heaven, dear Jesus, keep her safe!"

The major looked at her with curiosity. "She will be questioned at the prison."

Mother pleaded to heaven. "My daughter! Son of God, have mercy!" A soldier guided me to the back seat of the vehicle.

"My lord!" Dongsaeng stepped forward, his teeth chattering with cold, "We can pay—" The major made a quick movement to a soldier who spun my brother and butted a rifle into his gut. Dongsaeng clutched his stomach and slumped to the ground. Father reached for him and the soldier clubbed Father's shoulder. He fell to his knees.

"Abbuh-nim!" I cried. "Dongsaeng!" I heard Ilsun retching. The major's assistant started the engine and turned the car around, and the soldiers let the gate slam and marched down the hill. We drove, every turn of the wheel taking me farther from my wounded family, the trampled earth of our estate, the cold silence of its ancestors.

On the long jarring drive, the engine exhaust making me nauseous, I clung to the railing in the back of the car, and to the memory of Mother's cries for mercy. Fearful of what lay ahead, I shut my eyes to repeat my mother's prayer. Instead, I heard in my mind the childhood litany, *Like liquid, like water.*

The military prison block, massive slabs of gray concrete, seemed iced in barbed wire everywhere I looked. The old police jailhouse where my father had twice been imprisoned, was considered too small for military and Thought enforcement, and was now used for thieves, murderers and drunken conduct. Governor-General Minami had erected this prison compound two years ago, at the onset of squabbles with China.

The major said, "You will be separated from the men." He gave instructions to a guard who led me to the far side of the prison yard toward a row of vacant cells.

I was locked behind a wood and iron door in a narrow, dank cell with a high, barred window. When my eyes adjusted to the shadows, I saw a stained pallet on the rough plank floor and a beaten metal bucket. I clasped my hands, trying to pray, but all that came was *Like liquid, like water.* I leaned my back against the door, afraid to go farther into the cell, and watched a striped rectangle of light, cast through the window, travel infinitely slowly from the base of the wall, across the dirty floor to the edge of the bucket, catching a surprising gleam. Footsteps approached. The same impassive guard, who looked like he might be Korean, rattled keys in the lock. He handed me a small milking stool, a blanket and a tin of water, saying, "Major Yoshida's orders."

I sat on the stool in the far corner of the cell, wrapped in the blanket, though it gave no warmth. I watched the rectangle of light crawl along the wall. Sometimes dust visibly wafted through the light, once a pale green moth, and slowly I began to remember the Psalms. *But Thou, O Lord, art a shield about me, my glory, and the lifter of my head. I cry aloud to the Lord, and He answers me from His holy hill . . .*" The words gave me the vision of flowing green hills, the huge burial mounds of ancient kings and war-lords, around which flowed streams of pure and silvery water that soaked into the earth, encouraging the grasses to root farther, deeper, forever, until the gold-crowned skulls, bound in twisting roots, collapsed in rot. My body began to shiver and I made it stop. I closed my eyes, closed my mind to the fear that waited beside me.

Long after the box of light had swept the cell, the sky far above the window grayed with night. The crack of a hundred naked electric bulbs turning on shook me to awareness. Glassy light cast new patterns in my cell. A howl rose from the shadows. At first I thought a cat had entered the prison yard and was yowling in heat. Then I thought it was a wild preda-tor and felt almost relieved, for I knew then what to be afraid of. I heard guttural voices and realized in horror that a man was screaming. I stood. I sat. The sounds blurred. Absurdly, I thought someone was doing laundry, beating a washing stick on wet clothes against a stone. Sharp brief buzzes. Animal screams. A snap like a branch breaking.

The sounds of torture beat about me like bats and I tried to stuff my fingers into my ears. I buried my head in the rank mattress, pleading to the dread night spirits who had whisked away the sanity from men's minds and made them servants of terror.

At last, the darkness stilled, and I prayed on my knees for strength, courage and dignity to face what might befall me at dawn. Slowly, painfully, the morning rose and the weak early sun leaked into the cell. I found that my body called, and I drank the water and urinated in the bucket. Repelled by my human stink, I vomited. I looked up to a rattling of keys. A different guard handed me a wet towel and stood outside while I wiped the rough cloth over my face, neck, wrists and hands. He opened the cell and took me to the latrine to empty the bucket, then led me to a large building on the other side of the prison yard. I was shown into a small clean room with two chairs and a table with a small brown teapot and cups. The guard stood by the door and I stood by the table, breathing the delicate, glorious scent of green tea. The guard left as Major Yoshida entered. He smelled of anise and rubbing alcohol.

"Sit." He pointed to a chair and leaned against the other. He gestured that I should pour tea and drink. Nervous, but no longer afraid, I sipped, set my cup down and cast my eyes to my lap.

"Tell me about this man, Calvin Cho."

I gave his full Korean name, the location of his family home, and described how I came to know him. I hid nothing, because having seen his handwriting and the many envelopes, I was absolutely sure of him. He was studying to be a minister—perhaps he was already ordained—and he couldn't possibly be a spy. This, too, I told the major.

"Did you know that he is in regular contact with the American government?"

"I haven't heard from him in more than two years, my lord." But he had written! What was in those letters?

Major Yoshida sat across from me and nodded to the tea. I sipped, thanking the particles of tea leaves for absorbing the sun's heat on dewy terraced mountains, growing fat and lustrous, then drying in the same heat, preserving God's grace in a fragile, fragrant medium for me to drink at this table.

"Tell me about your Jesus Christ," he said. So unexpected was this turn in the interrogation that I looked directly into his eyes. I saw nothing to guide me or fool me, and so I began to recount Bible lessons. Many words, like *parable*, I knew no Japanese for, and he allowed me to use Korean as needed.

After three hours, I'd drunk all the tea. I recited the beatitudes from Jesus's Sermon on the Mount, my voice echoing in the bare room like a lingering note in the chamber of a closed piano. "Blessed are the poor in spirit, for theirs is the kingdom of heaven. Blessed are those who mourn, for they shall be comforted. Blessed are the meek, for they shall inherit the earth . . ." I paused, thinking this might have offended the major, but he remained expressionless.

When I finished, certain my chronology was wrong, I worried that I probably shouldn't have mentioned "if someone strikes you on the right cheek, turn to him the other cheek also," and fretted over what I had missed and what to say next. Why was my head so empty of the Bible? The major stood abruptly and left the room.

I felt an urgent need to urinate and was almost happy to see the guard.

He led me to the latrine, then to my cell. The tin of water had been refilled and the bucket removed. I was instructed to call the guard when I needed to use the latrine. Cold, I wrapped myself in the blanket, and in the daylight saw its filth. I tried to pray, but my thoughts were filled with the strange interrogation of the morning. I remembered the smell of anise and the expensive tea, and tried to reconstruct those scents in my nose. Sometimes I stood and paced to warm my limbs and distract myself from growing hunger. I felt my mind closing in a peculiar way, as if it were preparing for siege, then I remembered the sounds of night.

When the square of light had almost traveled beyond my cell, the guard came and wordlessly unlocked the gate to deliver a bundle that had obviously been searched. Inside the loose wrapping was a lidded bowl from home, a woolen shawl and a pair of thick socks. My heart cried out, *Mother!* and I pressed the socks to my face, trying to breathe the smell of home, the smell of the beloved hands that had held those socks. My mother was not one to say to her children, "I love you." It was an assumed truth, given freely at the gate of the womb.

I put on the socks and uncovered the bowl to find a mix of rice and millet with cabbage leaves on top and a shank of the salted fish I'd bought yesterday—forever ago. I ate with my fingers, keeping the bowl in the last square of light from the window. On the bottom of the bowl was a piece of folded rice paper, written finely with ink that bled slightly into the moist grains sticking to its surface. My fingers shaking, I kept my back to the cell door and unfolded the tiny paper.

> *Wake up!*
> *Stand in your faith*
> *with the strength of a soldier.*
> *There you'll find love.*
>
> *Cor. 13*

With tears for my mother's wisdom, steadfastness and love, I crumpled the scripture in my mouth and chewed thoroughly. I repacked the empty bowl in the cloth, knotting it just the way I knew my mother had knotted it. I felt our fingers had touched, and I was full.

MY MOTHER CAME every day for the next eighty-nine days, although I never saw her. I couldn't think how she suffered the hours walking in sleet and snow, for to do so would cause me unbearable pain. Every part of my mind and body waited for the guard to bring the bundle from home. My mother delivered food, a message and the strength of her unseen presence, a silent but desperately vital link to outside. After several days when little changed in the routine of cold, solitary days and freezing, fearsome nights, I thought less and less of life beyond the walls. I clocked the light in my cell and waited for the singular benediction of my mother's daily delivery. When I learned through the rice paper messages that bribes to Watanabe had proved fruitless and other official pleas had gone unheard, my focus narrowed even more. My breathing slowed, my eyes shrank, each sense dulled in waiting, pinpointed to the exact moment when the light would lie like a gift in my lap, the guard's boots would crack the icy dirt outside the cell door, the key would turn in the lock and he'd deliver the bundle from Mother.

Major Yoshida interrogated me weekly in much the same manner as before, once saying I could have my husband's letters when I confessed to being a spy. The letters would prove the truth of his involvement with the American government, the major said, and would also show how he had implicated me. Assured by their existence, I no longer cared about the contents of the letters. In those moments, I was oddly grateful that I'd been arrested, else I would never have known the fact of his constancy. I used my mother's rice paper scripture as the basis to tell more about Jesus toward the end of each interrogation, as was Major Yoshida's wish. He always left curtly.

The major's strange curiosity about the Bible made me wonder if my imprisonment was a call for me to declare my faith, or was a test I'd passed, as evidenced by my relatively healthy condition, though I was slowly growing weaker. I knew I should be glad for the chance to share the Gospel, but the contrast of the nights to the days confused me. Even if I could accept that it was the opportunity to speak the Word that had spared me from the other side of the prison compound, the suffering inflicted there refuted the existence of a merciful, loving God.

Because of the humiliation of having to ask the guard, I tried to hold my need for the toilet to once at dawn and at sundown. I had to overcome my embarrassment and ask for rags when I menstruated, but I only bled the first month. I felt my body shutting down as my mind closed to sensation with each passing day. I kept the wool shawl wrapped around my head and over my face when I slept. Although I shook lice from my blanket every morning, I didn't itch as much as in the beginning. I was given another blanket, but there was no protection from the frigid draft that rose from the frozen earth beneath the planks. I began to look forward to the interrogations because the room was somewhat warm and the guard would bring a washrag. When I talked about Jesus, I focused on the single brown ceramic cup of water, sometimes tea, on the table before me. I was grateful for its curve and the shimmer of light on the water's surface. It gave me something pure to focus on and made me think of life, fluidity and strength.

I counted eighteen days of snow, six days of freezing rain, thirty-four days of clouds, twenty-three days of sunlight . . .

The twelfth week, during interrogation, I talked about the book of Luke, John the Baptist and the temptation of Satan in the desert. I remembered stories out of order but told them when they came to me. I spoke of miracles: the centurion whose slave was healed, the fishes and loaves, Lazarus, walking on the Sea of Galilee, the leper cured. I related what I could of the politics in the Acts of the Apostles, and the preaching of Peter and Paul. In a long pause that followed, I prayed to be given the words to continue.

Major Yoshida stood and left, as always.

The next five nights there were no sounds of torture, an unusual—and welcome—relief.

The twelfth Sunday, I woke to the quiet world of snow. Flakes drifted through the high window to land on my cheeks and melt like morning dew. The guard unlocked my cell. He led me to the toilet as usual, but this time, afterward, he took me to the main gate. "You are released," he said without expression. I stood in disbelief for a moment and refrained from looking back, angry that I wondered if Major Yoshida watched me leave. Outside the walls, I stared at the sky, its dizzying whorls of white, and felt the free winter wind caress my face. I thanked the skies for my release and protection, and I prayed for the souls of the faceless men whose suffering I had witnessed.

Clutching my frayed coat, I tightened the shawl around my head and shoulders and walked slowly, my legs weak from inactivity. The snow slowed to a dusting about an hour later when I thought I might be close to town, and I saw ahead on the road the silhouette of my mother, her recognizable steady gait, her beloved form. I found myself running and when I reached her, I fell to her feet and embraced her ankles. We sat together on the road in the snow for some time, sobbing, searching each other's face to prove it was true, wiping each other's tears, my mother ensuring I was whole and unharmed, praising God. I was certain that in all the dampened snowy earth there was no sweeter sound than her voice, no sweeter vision than her eyes upon mine.

Mother held my arm and we turned toward home. We walked cautiously and slowly, my feet unsure and legs unsteady. With long stretches of silence in between, she talked about the goings-on at home. "Father and Dongsaeng still argue about the value of classical education. Father considered agreeing to let him teach, but decided he's too young to impart any learning. Imo writes that her nephew received top marks at university. Unsook still goes every Monday to the orphanage. The director said the children had a wonderful Christmas because of her. Unsook is a little short of breath these days and I'm praying that she'll miss this month's bleeding."

I recognized by the foreignness of what I heard that my mind had been altered, and this was her attempt to nudge it back to the life I'd known before. I tried hard to focus on the words, but it was her voice that helped normalcy seep back in.

The snow stopped fully by the time we passed the guardhouse that marked one li before entrance into the city. "We should rest. You should eat to have strength for the remainder of the walk home."

I shook my head.

"Then let's go on."

The mention of food brought the memory of the rice bowl scriptures, and I told her about the interrogations and Major Yoshida's odd study of Christianity.

"Truly you were Jesus's messenger, protected by his watchful angels," said Mother. When she delivered fervent thanks to heaven for my safe-keeping, the relief in her tone made me see that I'd forgotten others would've been concerned about my safety and chastity, and because this idea felt strange, I understood that I was changed even if my body was unharmed. I said nothing to my mother about the nights, which I knew would stay with me like the itch of prison filth, pervasive and unreachable.

As we walked in the cold, I gazed a long time at a small crack in the clouds that exposed a pale strip of sky. I thought then that her steps seemed heavy beside me and felt a terrible remorse. "Umma-nim, you came so far every day."

"You are my daughter."

I held on to these words and let them sink slowly into the fog of my heart. I knew instinctively if I heard them wholly, they would pierce with the incomprehensible truth of too much love, too quickly received, and the gratitude given could never be enough.

We passed the snowcapped walls of other family estates on the narrow walkway next to gutters blanketed with clean whiteness, under which I knew was rank trash and frozen sewage. I listened steadily to the freedom of our cold footsteps shuffling in the snow.

We walked up the hill together in silence. The familiar columns of our home gate and the pleasing curve of the tile-roofed archway I'd passed beneath so many times gave me stabs of joy. Dongsaeng, Unsook and all the servants cried out to see me. I heard something splinter in Father's study. Joong rushed in and out to say that Father, hearing us, had accidentally shattered a carpentry project. Byungjo let his tears fall shamelessly while Cook squatted and sobbed into her apron. Kira and Unsook reached out to me, but I warned them not to touch my infested clothes. I noticed the furnace chimneys smoking, the shuttered windows, the house sealed like a package. I had missed much of the winter season. How tiny everything looked, and how beautiful and precise. I was overcome with this blessing—to have all this familiar to me, to know it as home, to feel the mortar of blood and ancestry holding firm its walls. And it had been returned to me. I praised God then and thanked him for this in my life, this joy of belonging, this ability to recognize it.

Mother helped peel my clothes off in our rooms while Cook, Kira and

Unsook stoked both stoves to boil vats of water for an immersion bath and to make a medicinal soup: dried antler to strengthen the blood, simmered with ginseng to restore strength. Once again I became her child as Mother helped me bathe, spent hours on my hair and scalp, dressed me, urged me to eat and coddled me in blankets until, at last, I felt warm. Along with warmth came the weight of an exhaustion I hadn't known I had, and I slept.

Evening approached, bleak and still. Mother lit a lamp, stoked the brazier and prayed quietly, steadily. Her voice rose and fell in and out of my consciousness. I heard fragments of modulating scripture and prayer, but my mother's breaths between verses and her passionate tone restored me far more than if I'd been fully awake and able to comprehend the words.

Unsook brought steaming bowls, but I couldn't eat and returned to the silent womb of dreamless sleep. When I next awoke, Mother still sat nearby, her table spread for letter writing, her tranquil profile outlined in lamplight. "You're awake," she said. "It's evening. You should sleep until morning."

I sat up and rubbed my head, appreciating her earlier thorough combing that had at last rid my scalp of nits. "I'm rested, Umma-nim. I'm grateful—" My voice broke and I wept while Mother held my hand and murmured, "Praise God, praise God."

When my tears were finished I sat silently for some time staring at the coals in the brazier, feeling its heat on my face. I folded the bedding and said, "I'll go and see Father."

"Daughter, you should know— Najin-ah, there is bad news."

I saw my father being struck by the rifle and waited to hear more. I remembered on nights of torture the visions I'd had of my father being hung by his thumbs, his lax body bloodied and broken, and when he finally came home, his deadened eyes. A cold gust rattled the windows. I shivered.

"We will move to Seoul in twenty days."

I didn't understand and looked at her.

"They came last night, waved papers at Dongsaeng. The government is taking this land, this house for officers' quarters—Major Yoshida and his cadre."

I saw the pain in my mother's eyes and slowly understood that all I'd known of my childhood, my family's entire world, was obliterated with this news. "Umma-nim," I gasped.

"Yes, it's true." She spoke with a firmness I'd never heard before. "Father went to see Watanabe-san. He asked him how this could happen, after years of generous and regular gratuities. That man said he never claimed influence with the Japanese military. They give us twenty days to vacate. Father has yet to finalize his decision, but it's likely that we'll go to Seoul to live with Imo. Dongsaeng suggested trying to locate Father's brother in Manchuria, but your father, rightly so I believe, refuses to leave the country. Besides, there isn't enough time to learn where he might be, or even if he is alive. There is war now. We must trust God."

I was overcome with the news, and through my exhaustion felt a hard kernel of unbearable remorse beginning to form.

"There is much to do. Your father is beginning to fall ill from the upset. We have to sell what we can and let the servants go." My mother stopped to let me grasp this. "Your father is growing ill," she repeated.

I looked blindly at the fire. "It's my fault."

"Najin-ah, there is no blame. Blaming is pointless. God's will is not comprehensible at times. We are given the greater gift of faith."

The words passed through me like a splinter, a meaningless prick in the heart of a terrible wound. I was responsible. Father would cast blame and he would be justified. I had escaped torture and my husband's letters had doomed my family. Somehow I had failed the test of prison. I had never once considered taking my life, but perhaps I should have.

Mother touched my hand. "We have much to do."

"Yes," I said. This was my true punishment. I would suffer more from a lifetime of guilt than I had suffered the ninety days in my cell.

She talked about what we'd move and where the servants would go. With the exception of a handful of history books, Father had decided to keep his library buried, and would seal the secret pantry. "Who knows?" said Mother. "Perhaps one day . . ."

"I should see him now," I said, and Mother nodded.

I combed and knotted my hair, put on a quilted top and went to his study. My father was packing books and scrolls, hand tools and art materials in a shipping crate. I saw a brushstroke of relief wash over his face when our eyes met. He deliberately picked up a planer and wrapped it in a cloth. "Are you well?" His voice trembled, and I couldn't tell if he was relieved or enraged.

"Yes, thank you, Abbuh-nim. This person is home." I bowed fully. There was a long silence. I listened to the cloth being rubbed against the planer.

"Your mother," he began, then silence. I remained low in my bow and smelled sawdust and pine tar in the old floor mat. He cleared his throat. "You're whole and home." His tone said I should rise. I saw his hands shake as he set the planer down.

"I'm grateful, Abbuh-nim, and ashamed. Forgive your worthless daughter."

"You do realize what has happened." He spoke slowly, intensity belying his softened tone. "Your father, your brother, your ancestors—all—can see only loss." He laid his hands carefully on his knees. He continued, his voice husky. "The dust in this room is the same dust breathed by my father, my father's father and his father. By all your ancestors. Numberless generations . . ."

In the silence that followed I could only breathe with him.

"Almost five and a half centuries of men buried in the Han mountain graves," he said. "And now, a single daughter . . ."

In the ensuing silence, I thought about the two things my father had done over which I had often harbored resentment: he hadn't named me and had wanted me married at fourteen. Yet he had come to accept my desire to learn and work, and had even allowed the thwarted dream of America. I had brought into his household contrariness, unwanted change, and now, immeasurable loss. "I am to blame, Abbuh-nim."

He seemed to want to say something but instead turned aside, his face lined with pain. "Go. Your mother needs you."

I bowed and left. It seemed too easy to get up and walk away, down the familiar hallway with its gleaming dark wood, and past the screen, now folded and tied, the winter air seeping through the walls. The screams of the tortured men surfaced in my ears and I shivered with the cold of the blackest nights in prison. I thought about how I had looked forward to seeing Major Yoshida, though I'd couched it in terms of being grateful for the warmth of the interrogation room. His clean orderliness and cool demeanor were reassuringly civilized and seemed admirable in such a place. I had felt pride in describing Bible stories to him, in God's choice of me to deliver his Word, and in God's watchfulness that had kept me whole. It was because of me that Major Yoshida had noticed our estate. Because of me, Major Yoshida would take from my father, from all of my family, the markers of our ancestry, tradition and history that creaked in the ancient beams, lived in the mortar, the stones and soil, and sang in the trees and stream. And then I thought that man was small, so easily overcome by demons of pride and hatred, but I was less than small, and should have been among those who screamed in the night.

PART III

Seoul

# Empty Pockets

## END OF FEBRUARY 1940

IN AN ICY DOWNPOUR, ILSUN PACED BENEATH A STREETLIGHT ON THE far edge of Poncheong, Seoul's black market district. With hands shoved deep in his pockets, he watched his shadow grow and shrink in the bleak circle of electric light, aware that curfew approached. He had already walked half an hour in snow that had turned to sleet, and his leather shoes were soaked. Across the road, movement in the pink slits of the teahouse's shuttered windows caught his eye. Earlier when he'd called for entry, the proprietor smiled at his familiar face and opened the door wide until he'd failed to slip the customary wad of won into her ready hand. Stung by the slammed door, he'd cried out, "How dare you! I am a Han!" Having welcomed him dozens of times before, she could have shown a hint of courtesy!

He knew it was pointless to trade on his father's name. Nowadays, few knew and even fewer cared who his father was. Ilsun shivered and sighed. He'd have to start working soon. His father had finally acquiesced to the necessity of Ilsun selling his artwork to the Japanese and their collaborators, for they were the only ones who could afford such luxuries. They weren't all heathen. Some were learned enough in art history to know that his father's style would have lasting significance, and others saw that Ilsun's work expanded and modernized his father's breakthroughs. Ilsun enjoyed the attention he received for his work, and had discovered two interesting and ironic facts about his ability for art. The less he cared about the work he was painting, the more it was judged worthy. He was best when he wasn't trying, and for that he knew to thank his ancestors who had cultivated the talent that had culminated in him. The other irony was how long it took to reach the point of not caring, of being free of worry about how the work appeared and to just be doing it. It was the buildup that was the hard work. He suspected that if he worked more at it, the easy part would come sooner, but the hard part was enough of a hurdle to discourage him.

He enjoyed the accolades and he certainly enjoyed the money his art garnered. It wasn't about food—the women mostly took care of that somehow. The responsibility of providing for the household made him feel tired and less apt to work. It was about a man's need for pocket money. The last time he'd seen Meeja behind those shutters had been thanks to Najin. This morning, though, when he'd asked his nuna if she had anything else to sell, the only thing she gave him was a hard look.

Weeks ago, Najin had given him a smoky topaz to buy medicine for his wife. The stone had been a gift from a delighted Japanese jeweler whose wife, assisted by Najin, had successfully delivered a healthy baby boy. Ilsun had accused his sister of hoarding from the family, demanding to know what else she had squirreled away. She ignored his queries and instead listed the medicines, herbs and rich foods needed for Unsook. Nuna told him to use anything left over to buy the manure-and-mud briquettes they used to stretch the coal. On this very street, he had quickly found his most lucrative contact and bartered the topaz for much more than his original estimate of its worth. When he handed his sister the ginseng and goldthread root, cardamom pods, packets of other herbs and a handful of change, he reported that the pharmacist's prices had doubled since medicinal trade from China had all but ceased. Najin said nothing, but Ilsun had never seen such coldness in her eyes. "It's enough for several weeks!" he'd said, raising his voice to assert his authority over such matters. The cash he had put aside to visit the teahouse was none of her business. He did not voice his other thought: that one had to be realistic about Unsook's illness.

It wasn't as if he didn't care. In Gaeseong, she'd been the ideal bride and a perfect wife. Father had complimented him on her tasteful and balanced cooking more than once. She was delicate and bony, and compliant in bed. He could easily admit that he loved her, truly, but a man has needs! And now, since there was still no heir, and none likely because of Unsook's consumption, he knew he was completely justified to go elsewhere. Nuna, an excessive worrier and righteous in her big-sister way, had merely overreacted.

No matter. The criticism Nuna had tried to cast on him withered to nothing during those evenings at the teahouse. The warmth of the memories trembled in his thighs, and he looked again at the shuttered windows from which he faintly heard laughter and singing. This was his favorite teahouse. These ladies boasted lineage to famous courtesans—a status that fit a man of his distinction and talent. He thought it shouldn't matter that his family's wealth had dwindled. Life was worse for everyone, yet Koreans still knew what was important, particularly if it was prohibited, such as their given names. The teahouse ladies had certainly fussed and cooed when he explained how he'd come up with the name Kiyamoto. He'd drawn the Chinese ideographs on a scrap of paper with the proprietress's fountain pen, to show those ignorant girls how *Kiyamoto* meant "deep well" or "deep source," a fair iteration of *Han*, which meant "ancient dynastic place in time."

When the edict came that all nationals must choose a Japanese name, Father had accepted Ilsun's choice of the Japanese surname Kiyamoto, but refused to officially register at the precinct, saying that task was Ilsun's responsibility as master of the house. It seemed to Ilsun he was master only when it came to dealing with outside affairs. Lately, however, Father kept his door shut more often than not, carving panels out of cheap pine or reading the same tired books from what little was left of his musty old library.

The name-change ruling outraged many. Spontaneous demonstrations by students ended with spilled blood, more arrests, more prison terms. But it warmed Ilsun to think of the name change, for that was how Meeja had caught his eye. Wine had spilled on the scrap of paper and wine-diluted ink dripped on his lap. A woman he hadn't noticed before crouched beside him in an instant with a cloth and a cup of water. She grasped his leg and dabbed at it, saying, "We can't have your prestigious name running down your leg. It will want to go back to the well!" Her wit made him laugh and her touch made him interested. She had coarse hands, the knuckles large and the skin loose, but her fingers were bold yet discreet in exploring where the ink might have fallen. Although her features were unexceptional—eyes too narrow to be alluring and lips too thin to convey ripeness—she had charming ears and a gracefully curved chin. The confidence in her back and neck appealed to him. When she kneeled at his feet, he could smell the perfumed oil in her hair. She wrung the cloth, looking directly at him, and her inviting smile made her eyes darken sensually.

By the lamppost, a chill crept down Ilsun's collar and made his testicles itch. His woolen suit was useless in the sleet, but it corrected an unflattering line in his shoulders, and Meeja had admired it. He hoped for a glimpse of her. One glance and he swore he'd be satisfied. He willed the door to open, or perhaps a shutter would blow wide and her silhouette would be haloed in yellow light as she searched the road for him. He was convinced that she felt his presence nearby, just as he still felt her firm palms pressing him into her. He pictured her closed-eye little frown, the wink of her tongue as her mouth parted, the soft warmth of her energetic hips rising to meet him. Aroused, he stopped pacing. He had spent hundreds on food, dancing and wine for three days before she had allowed him to lie with her. And she had moaned and thrashed, her breathlessness tantalizing, goading him unlike any woman he'd known. He'd been with her twice and felt bewitched. She was all he could deliciously, painfully think about.

The teahouse rang with laughter. "Damn her!" he said, certain she was coyly teasing someone else, "She's just a *gisaeng*—a peasant or bastard's daughter—nothing!" Yet he could see her beguiling chin turned charmingly toward some other man. He kicked the light-pole and scuffed his ruined shoe. *Shiang!* Tapping ice from his hat brim, he turned from the beckoning windows and trudged home, thinking about Meeja, sex, the burden of secrecy and the boring necessity of work.

# The Price of Jesus

STUBBORN ODORS OF GARLIC AND PEPPER CLUNG TO THE WALLS LONG after the dinner hour had passed. I closed the sliding door to the sickroom and removed my facemask. Mother neared in the darkening hallway, hands tucked into jacket sleeves, socks swishing on the floor. "Do you know where your brother is?" she asked.

I carefully phrased my answer to avoid lying. "He said Father told him that Elder Kim was interested in a scroll to commemorate his grandson's naming ceremony. He said he would visit Elder Kim to ask what he might want."

Mother's eyes crinkled in approval and I turned quickly. Who could tell what Dongsaeng did on his evenings out? I knew he'd squandered the money from the topaz, but there were no new silk socks or factory-made shirts. I had my suspicions. I'd been doing his laundry ever since my sister-in-law had taken ill, and took precautions to protect Unsook and Mother from learning about his behavior. His clothes reeked with tobacco and drink, and I scrubbed face powder and lipstick stains with fury.

Mother raised an eyebrow toward the sickroom and I held my fingers to my lips. In the kitchen and out of earshot of the sickroom, I said, "She feels cold so I'll stoke the fire. I'm making herb tea and soup." We didn't know when or where Unsook had contracted tuberculosis, but it flowered after she'd caught a cold that Mother said had all the children at the Gae-seong orphanage sniffling during the Christmas play. After that, Unsook's little cough receded and we were preoccupied with moving. Almost three seasons later, two months after autumn equinox, Dongsaeng told us that Unsook was pregnant at last. But this jubilant news was quickly dashed when the doctor reported that she was also chronically ill. Our first dole-ful Christmas and New Year's in Seoul were further shadowed by Unsook's steady decline.

"Not much coughing today," said Mother.

"Not much blood in her phlegm, either. The new medicine seems to be helping. A better day."

"Thank God. I'll wait up for your brother. He'll be hungry when he gets home. Father's annoyed he had to eat alone again." Her phrasing made me smile. Both of us had eaten supper with Father, but we maintained the pretense of certain traditions. The women's partition had been dispensed with after we moved. The house, a right angle, lined two sides of a large courtyard and a grassy yard, which we turned into a vegetable garden. The sole sitting room took the corner and part of the north-south wing. Then came a tiny anteroom studio followed by Ilsun's room, Unsook's sickroom and an indoor toilet that drained to a side alley sewer. The east-west wing started with the kitchen, then my room, Mother's room, a storage room and Father's rooms, followed by the entryway beside the sitting room. Some of the rooms, like Unsook's, were only big enough for one pallet, while the sitting room could sleep three, and all were close with low, exposed roof beams, traditional *ondol* floors with built-in flues for heating, and paper walls.

Initially, it was difficult for everyone to eat together—Mother could barely part her lips for fear my father would glimpse the inside of her mouth—but it was both practical and economical, and after ensuring that the men had plenty and started before us, we were able to eat with them without too much embarrassment. However, it would be impolite to speak of it.

Mother took a pillowslip and went to join Father. She looked shrunken, but her back was still straight, narrow and graceful, and her silvery hair framed only the tiniest of wrinkles on her oval face. I pictured Father reading, the lines of his long face stern. He would be cross-legged on the mat and stroking his white goatee, his sharp angles still clothed in his old-fashioned vests. He was thin, as we all were, but his health was now stable, recovered from a dangerous and painful ulcer he'd suffered during the first several months in Seoul. I had found a good pharmacist two tram rides downtown, and while discussing treatment options, discovered he had classical training and a wealth of traditional remedies. But one night not long ago, probably because of his relationships with Chinese herbalists, the pharmacist disappeared. His shop was taken over by a cranky suspicious man who asked too many questions. I felt safer buying the rare plants and powders I needed from Dongsaeng's clandestine and expensive contacts.

I heated broth and tea for Unsook, then went to the outbuilding to fill the scuttle. The Seoul house and a stable full of coal had been gifts from Imo. By the time of my release from prison, it was clear that all of Korea's and Manchuria's resources were being siphoned to feed Japan's war with China. Another new law mobilized hundreds of young Korean men and women to fill a void in manpower caused by the war. They called it voluntary, but I'd heard of missing sons and daughters, and few youths dared to loiter on city streets. Being married and having been recently arrested made me ineligible for "government service." Though I would never forget my imprisonment, I understood it was merely a kink in a tightening noose of government wariness and suspicion. I wasn't sure if I was trying to make myself feel less guilty, but once we'd moved outside of our Gaeseong walls, I saw how fortunate we were to have kept our estate for as long as we did. As we packed and sold furniture, we learned that many other landowners had suffered a similar fate. Downtown, Gaesong's main thoroughfare had become a noisy stream of trucks shuttling troops to

China, pushcarts jammed with contents of homes, and foot traffic as thousands of people migrated either forcibly or for safety. We tended the graves a last time and bid painful goodbyes to Kira, Joong, Byungjo and Cook, who would venture north to Nah-jin or farther, if necessary. We prayed we'd meet again, but by now, a year later, I realized there was little hope of that. On our day of departure the Japanese soldiers came, immediately knocked down the gate to widen the entrance for vehicles and razed the front gardens for parking. We left quickly and no one looked back.

In Seoul we fought our way through a train depot filled with people and confusion, blasts of steam and the clamor of trains coming and going, the squalor of refugees and beggars of all ages in pitiful condition. My mother, taking the fifth journey of her life, was admirably fearless and mainly concerned with Father, who could barely walk for the pain of his ulcer. After hiring carts for our possessions, we found Imo's house occupied by a few pieces of heavy furniture, gourds, some crockery and kettles, and an old man from Imo's church who guarded the vacated property. He delivered a letter from Imo, in which she explained her decision to finally leave the capital, fearing that her adopted son, who had recently graduated from college, was vulnerable to the labor draft. She had moved to Busan and purchased a house on the outskirts of the city, away from hubbub and scrutiny. "And so," she wrote, "what a blessing that you have decided to come to Seoul, eliminating for me the headache of trying to sell this house, which is much too large for just us."

It was when she read this letter that I saw Mother cry for the first time since the Gaeseong house was lost. I understood that her tears were for the shame of having to accept Imo's thoughtful generosity, and I felt so undeserving of my own tears of remorse that they remained deeply buried.

I bent to scoop from the diminishing pile of coal and thought about Unsook. The costly orchid infusion had worked well, opening her breathing passages. I didn't dwell on Dongsaeng's folly with the topaz, knowing that my last length of silk would bring a good price. The skirt with embroidered chrysanthemums was one of the few things I hadn't sold when living with Calvin's parents. I had once hoped to wear it crossing the Pacific, but it was pointless to even allow those old memories to surface. The deep green silk would've flattered Unsook's fair complexion, and I had set it aside as a future gift for her, but I had to recognize that Unsook was only getting worse. If Dongsaeng sold the silk, I could also buy powdered milk, kelp and rice for a new mother whose twin boys I had delivered. I wanted to see them thrive. There were rumors about hundreds of male Korean infants being taken from their mothers to be adopted and raised as Japanese. With the mother's grateful permission, I had registered the twins' birth certificates, reporting them as girls.

It was a shame that Unsook couldn't tolerate milk, which might help to strengthen her. I hurried to replenish the firepit that heated the sickroom. At the doorstep I looked to the sky and saw through departing snow clouds the far night blackness speckled with stars. I said to the darkness, to the wonderment of stars, "Thank you for this coal, and please help her gain strength." I lamented that my obstetrics training had done little to prepare me for the slow devastation of consumption. When I first learned about Unsook's baby, something forgotten within me had stirred, and I felt Calvin's absence in a vivid physical way I hadn't ever before. But it quickly dissipated in the crisis of Unsook's illness and the fear of what could only become a tragic pregnancy. I had put thoughts of my husband far behind me, as far away as Gaeseong. I never spoke of him and thought less and less about our reunion. And now the war had spread. There seemed to be no end to Japan's oppressive power and growing strength.

Thoughts of Calvin, of Unsook's baby, of any future at all, were always accompanied by the echoes of my mother's and Calvin's faithful declaration to trust God. In prison, I thought simplistically that God's wisdom would feel unquestionable to me, that my faith would grow resolute. But the refrain that now persisted was the reductive question: how could all of my family's loss be the price for one Japanese major's spotty education about Jesus? And I couldn't reconcile martyrdom and human suffering as models for redemption. Here was Unsook, so lovely that her every movement said beauty. Her body had once held great promise—still held promise—and her faith was so sincere that she accepted illness without complaint, yet she faced a slow and painful death. The price for her was high, too high, and unfair.

# The Calligrapher's Design

## END OF FEBRUARY 1940

AMONG THE SCORES OF LOSSES THAT HAD MADE HIM ILL FOR A YEAR, Han felt the privation of partitioning most frequently. The sole compensation was his wife sitting by him more frequently, always with some task in hand like the needlework she now held. He nodded to welcome her and saw a modest smile reshape her features with beauty. True, when she had an opinion she could be persistent, but that was a minor complaint. He still acted coolly toward her, as was proper, but he knew she understood his approval, for even through the worst of it, she had been consistently soft-spoken and deferential.

It surprised him how adaptable she'd been in the transition, their lives so suddenly grafted to subservience and—with the house, inadequate as it was—obligation to his wife's cousin. He took her resilience to be a measure of her faith. He stretched his legs and took in the now-familiar smells of this room: sawdust, scratched lacquer flooring, the steam of soup and boiled cabbage sealed in its beams. A recurring thought irked him. Was it not a mark of personal failure that so much had been lost during his generation? He wasn't prone to sin, though pride was a struggle, and he had acted rightly and responsibly all his life. Still, the stain was there and he prayed it was contained in him alone. Others had suffered much more than he. He readily blamed politics and subjugation, but doubt had damaged this assertion and he wondered if his ancestors, or God, measured his accountability.

His wife sewed quietly by the lantern, her frequent glances toward him meaning she had something to say, probably about their lazy son. A sputter of flame, then smoke fouled the air as his mind darkened with thoughts of Ilsun. He maintained an outer appearance of calm reading, his thoughts beginning to burn.

Damn that boy! Ilsun had more talent than he knew. What waste! In his father's day, Ilsun could have been a renowned calligrapher, perhaps not the greatest of scholars, but a respected artist who might have become as famous as Han's own teacher. The revered Chang Seungop had been a follower of the venerable Kim Cheonghui, who had founded the Southern School of painting, famous for diverting from Chinese tradition and originating an intense and original style. Scholar Chang was the last man to be designated a Korean Royal Treasure before the Yi Dynasty fell. How his work was lauded! Even China and Japan had recognized his genius. Who knew how many of Chang Seungop's scrolls now hung in the "sacred" halls of the imperial palace?

As it was, Ilsun would never even reach Han's level of scholarship. No one cared any more and his son had little awareness of his natural ability. Ilsun's careless personality, irritating as it was, added spontaneity to his brushwork. Han's work had tended toward restraint, a quality that had once given him great satisfaction, and that he later came to regard as academic and stodgy compared to the controlled yet vivid expressiveness of Scholar Chang's brush—living strokes with a vitality also evident in Ilsun's work.

Where had his son gone off to again? Ready to hear what the boy's mother had to say, Han exhaled and looked at her.

"Yuhbo." She kept her eyes on her sewing. "Dongsaeng told Nuna he was going to see Elder Kim about the scroll for his grandson." The lines in the corners of her eyes bunched when she smiled, as if pointing out her pride for Ilsun.

He said nothing, glad that his hands were in his sleeves, for they twitched with fury. He turned to his book to hide his rage.

After a silence, she said carefully, "That was very enterprising, don't you agree? He knows it's distasteful to sell his art, but you yourself said he should apply himself to his work, and it seems he's showing initiative."

His anger had nothing to do with the mercantile aspect of his son's work. Times required that such purism be sacrificed for the sake of food and medicine. Elder Kim, Han knew, was not in town. He had gone to his home village and his mother's deathbed. A few days ago, Han had chanced upon him outside a photographer's studio, where Elder Kim had picked up a portrait of his grandson to show his dying mother.

Han cleared his throat to release tightness in his neck. His wife glanced at him, expecting the conversation to continue. In a growing silence, he blindly read while she sewed tiny green knots on the hem of the pillowslip. They waited for Ilsun.

Najin appeared in the doorway with hands clasped, and he nodded to indicate she could enter. No matter how much he prayed, disappointment and anger still grated when he saw her. It made him tired. He knew that the reasons for the loss of the Gaeseong land were far more complicated than her husband's letters and her imprisonment, but the old reaction of placing blame still flared. It's not that he blamed her exactly, but rather what she represented in his family, in his country, whose continued existence depended upon the strength of its youth to uphold its history and traditions. Yes, even its women. Yet it was those very traditions that had rendered them unprepared and powerless. They had allowed for—perhaps even bred—corruption and weakness. He wanted only calm in these after-sixty years—years he had once anticipated being rich with poetry, philosophy and art, and in the background of his contemplative hours, a smoothly run house full of grandchildren. He felt the black pull of the enormity of his loss and failure. But here she was, his daughter, virtually a widow—and admittedly a woman of competence with a medical education that was helpful for Ilsun's sickly wife.

She slipped to her knees to bow goodnight. The practiced movement soothed him and he remembered that the anger he held at this moment was not with her. He relaxed his shoulders to make his voice even. "What did Dongsaeng say?"

His wife beamed as Najin spoke. "He said that Father said Elder Kim was interested in a calligraphic scroll to commemorate his grandson's one hundredth day. He said he was going to visit the elder to ask what he wanted."

*Clever, cautious girl*, thought Han. She had kept her eyes lowered and moved not a muscle, betraying nothing of her feelings about her brother's unacceptable absence on this winter's night. He dismissed the women with a gesture. His anger revived, he easily ignored the gentling sound of their conversation fading toward their rooms.

Soon he heard Ilsun stamp snow off his shoes and the boy's mother hurrying to the door. "Your hands are so cold! Come greet your father. I'll heat soup."

Han stood as his son entered, trailing wet sock prints. Ilsun bowed and shifted his feet, his eyes quickly scanning the room. "Good evening, Abbuh-nim."

Satisfied that Ilsun was taken aback to find him standing, Han knew his son would remain awkwardly on his feet until he himself sat down. The collar of Ilsun's Western suit was turned up around his earlobes, and he rubbed and blew on his hands. *If he insists on wearing Western clothes,* thought Han, *he ought to keep up with his haircuts.* And when had the hunch of his son's shoulders become so intensely irritating?

He stepped closer, his back erect and sore with old wounds. "You mean 'goodnight,' don't you? Nothing else to say?"

"Forgive me, Abbuh-nim," he said in the exact intonation of his earlier greeting, infuriating Han. He clenched and unclenched his hands. The silence grew. Ilsun glanced at him nervously.

"Well then. What did Elder Kim say?"

Ilsun's frightened blink was obvious. Would he have the audacity to keep up with the lie? "He— They said he was too busy to see me this evening."

"Liar!" He struck Ilsun with the back of his hand. Ilsun staggered, his hand to his cheek, eyes bursting with tears.

"You bring lies into this house! Where have you been these nights? You shame this family with your laziness! Your mother is relying on you as the man of the house, but you're useless to her! Useless! Do you hear?"

Ilsun fell to the floor, prostrate. A sob escaped him.

"Yah! Are you crying like a woman? What kind of son are you? No *yang*! Are you even my son? A disgrace. A waste!" Han paced, too disgusted to touch him further.

"I'm sorry, Abbuh-nim. You're right. Please, please forgive me."

"Like a woman! Lies and laziness! You ask my forgiveness? *You're* supposed to be the man of the house."

"Yes, you're right. I'm worthless to you." Ilsun shuddered and huddled on his knees, a wet ball of sour wool.

Han sat and breathed deliberately to slow the beating in his chest. The house was unnaturally still—not even the flame of the lamp flickered. This had to be woman trouble. Ilsun had shown this weakness before at boarding school. His son never knew that the principal had sent more than one humiliating letter to collect overdue fees—money Ilsun had spent in those fancy brothels. With his son's marriage, Han thought he'd put an end to this problem for good, but it seemed a wife had solved nothing and, in fact, may have made it worse. Yah, how could Unsook be so ill? A crushing realization struck him and he sat heavily. His own will, his hopes, his expectations alone could do nothing to correct Ilsun's weak character. He had wanted all his life for this son to be something other than what he had actually become, what he had always been destined to be. With sudden despair, Han saw that he had no control over his own blood. And if not his own blood, then what was his to govern?

"Sit."

Ilsun kneeled and wiped his face with a handkerchief.

Han saw that his son recognized the depth of his disappointment, and it calmed him to see Ilsun's features drawn with contrition. "Such places are beneath us," he said.

Ilsun opened his mouth, his lips defensive, then he lowered his head. "I swear, Abbuh-nim, I tried. For years, there was nothing, I swear to you, but you might understand how difficult it's been."

Yes, Han had expected too much of the man before him. He had done what he believed was right, what had been left available to him, to make him the man of character he had once prided himself as being. Here was the embodiment of his failure. Like his mother nation, he had failed stupendously. Before him was the proof of his inability to shape the future of his family—and by extension his country—in the right way, the Confucian way, the way that had always guided his life, the only way he knew. Without self-discipline, how could his son master his own household? Without the strength of his family behind him, how could he lead his countrymen? Instead, here was a careless, confused man, born a decade after the annexation, who thought little about the meaning of the world except what it might offer him. It seemed that the Japanese had succeeded in conquering this most basic principle of a father handing tradition to his son.

"It's impossible that you frequent those places. Who sees you enter and leave? Who else visits there? Not only do you put yourself and your family at risk, you've sullied your character. It cannot be."

"But there's Meeja. She's—" His voice was ugly with desperation.

"Have I finished speaking?" So the worst had happened: Ilsun had actually become attached to a whore. Han realized he should have paid more attention to the missed meals, late hours and moping about. A petulant curl spoiled the defined curves of Ilsun's full lips and strong chin—two of the recognizable features that had reappeared over generations of his family line. But he was still his firstborn son, his only son, and a man with the potential to be among the finest calligraphers in Korea. And was it not his own generation—and he, himself—who had lost stewardship of the world they had been charged to tend for Ilsun and all the world's sons?

Han settled further into his cushion, his spine sagging. As to the problem at hand, there was no help for it except that Ilsun must finish the thing or be ruined by it. That his son frequently walked the dark streets of unsavory neighborhoods put him at enormous risk for conscription or any number of police troubles. An arrangement must be made, and it would be costly. Ilsun would have to work as never before. Once the arrangement was discovered, Han knew he would suffer the household's silent uproar, but more was at stake than the sensitivities of women.

"You can have her," Han said. Ilsun showed his surprise by staring directly at him, his reddened eyes incredulous.

Han then understood that acquiescence and his acceptance of Ilsun's whore had two other wholly selfish motivations, but with a slow blink he managed to rationalize them as having Confucian virtue. First was the possibility of an heir. The law had changed to allow sons of concubines to inherit, and besides, should a son be born, he could be officially adopted. It wasn't possible for the woman to be accepted into the household as in the olden days. Her lowly profession forbade it, not to mention Ilsun's Christian vows. Han blinked again, and the sad and delicate face of Ilsun's sickly wife faded from his mind. As for his second motivation for allowing Ilsun his teahouse lover: his sanction of the expensive affair would stimulate his son to work, to develop his artistry despite his persistent laziness. He reached for his pipe, though it had been years since it held tobacco, and the customary motion sealed his resolve. "You're not to go to her again. She must come to you and only in secret. The neighborhood association is full of busybodies and traitors. No one must see her. No one. Do you understand?"

Han saw Ilsun's fingers shake as he bowed and pressed his hands to the floor. The house shivered in the winter wind and a shutter slapped open and closed. Cold fresh air cleared Han's head, but an old man's weariness blanketed his spirit. Trying to remember the writer who coined the phrase—was it, ironically, the Chinese concubine poet Yang Guifei?—Han said, "When it comes to illicit love there are two kinds of gentlemen: one has restraint, and the other has discretion." He replaced his empty pipe on its rack, and when Ilsun sat up, he saw how his son's eagerness for the gisaeng beat at the pulse in his neck. "Clearly you have little restraint, so I insist that you practice discretion. You are forbidden to visit the teahouses again. You understand how risky it is."

Ilsun nodded.

"You can have her as often as you want, but it's been obvious by the thinness of the soup that you've been neglecting household expenses. You've been neglecting your family. It pains me that you must be reminded to fulfill your primary responsibilities. You may do as you please once your first duty is met. She'll be a costly night-bride. You'll have to work very hard."

Ilsun bowed deeply to the floor, tapping his forehead on the mat. "Thank you, Abbuh-nim. I'll prove to you how hard I can work. I'm indebted to your wisdom and understanding."

"Go."

With his head down, Ilsun stood and backed out the door, bobbing. Han turned his eyes, but not before he was sickened by the giddy joy that he himself had caused to appear on his son's flushed cheeks.

# Night Demons

A WARM BREEZE SHOOK THE TENDER LEAVES OF THE ROSE-OF-SHARON bushes bordering the kitchen garden. I wrapped my skirt in a sand-colored apron and squatted, tilling with a bamboo hand-hoe. When the home inspectors began collecting metal goods, garden tools were among the first items to go. I was grateful for the childhood years spent outside with Byungjo, watching his able hands fashion tools from bamboo, sticks and hemp rope. Mother and I planted cabbage, cucumber and squash. The warm wind smelled green and soft, but the earth was still frozen in places where the winter clouds had lingered. I broke up those clumps as if beating them into submitting to spring.

From the porch, Dongsaeng called a cheerful goodbye and sauntered off, a wrapped scroll strapped to his back. I waved and smiled at his exuberance. Everyone seemed pleased with him lately. Whatever had happened on that cold evening when Father shouted at Dongsaeng must have been the seed for this welcome change. He was home all the time now, studying, writing and painting. He visited Unsook regularly and showed her his scrolls. His work had grown extraordinary, infused with a rawness that gave energetic power to the strokes. Among those who could afford it—mostly Japanese art aficionados—his reputation as a talent of note was growing. If in the old days calligraphy had been regarded as a lesser art form, now any art created at all seemed a wonder.

"Aigu!" Mother sighed with satisfaction, poking seeds into the soil. "We'll have squash blossom soup in six weeks' time."

I remembered early last autumn when Mother, Unsook and I searched the vines for young fruit, planning delectable salads of cucumber gimchi and squash pickled in chilies. Unsook had gathered squash blossoms and twirled them in her slender fingers. White moths fluttered in the light that bathed my sister-in-law, a basket of aromatic vegetable flowers on her arm. In her high clear voice, Unsook sang, "Butterfly, butterfly, come fly this way." She laughed. "Hyung-nim, Sister-in-law, I forget the words! Sing with me." We sang the children's song together, Unsook's breath vital and clear until the second verse brought coughs. She blamed the flower pollen, but I had noticed the stained handkerchief she'd pulled from her skirtband.

I tilled the cold earth and worried. Unsook, whom I called *Olgae,* Younger Sister-in-law, had grown increasingly weak ever since being quarantined in mid-November. She never complained, but I noticed circles beneath her eyes, and sallow cheeks. Lately her coughing had been typical, the fevers had abated and she seemed otherwise stable, but there was listlessness and malaise. Was it melancholy? Sometimes when I entered the sickroom, she appeared as if she'd been weeping. I didn't want to ask what was wrong unless she showed her tears. The invalid had such little physical privacy that I wanted to respect her other privacy as much as possible.

When I returned the hoe to the outbuilding, a spray of striped yellow crocus caught my eye. I unearthed the sprouted bulbs whole and potted them in a crock for Unsook. It might encourage her to see a token of the earth's miracle of rebirth.

Wearing a facemask and carrying the crocus and a gourd of hot water for a sponge bath, I slid the door to the sickroom open. She was asleep. I set everything down quietly and straightened her blanket over her feet. A small choking noise made me turn. Unsook stared at the crocus, tears spilling. She coughed, then gasped for air, and I leaped to help her sit. Unsook's shoulders heaved as her body worked to claim breath. Her fit subsided, leaving her wheezing and feverish. The sputum in the bowl I'd held to her mouth was yellow and gray. I felt awful. "I'm so sorry!" I folded pillows and blankets and propped her upright. "I thought the flowers would cheer you, but I've only brought misery! Say nothing— you'll have another fit." I rubbed her back until her shaking subsided.

"Beautiful— I didn't mean—" she whispered.

"Quiet. Not a word. Stay sitting up. I'll get fresh water." I flew out the door and returned as quickly as it took to wash and fill the bowl with heated water. Gently, I massaged Unsook's neck and shoulders and bathed her. I smoothed the bedding, changed her bedclothes and sat behind her, holding her in my arms like a child, humming, until she breathed evenly. "Can you say what's wrong?"

Unsook's next breath was a sob, which she controlled. She steadied her intake with effort, her breaths shallow. Newly combed into a long braid, her hair fell from her back to her lap. She twisted the braid into a bun, arms gaunt and tinged blue, and covered her eyes. "I think I must be going mad."

Alarmed by her dead tone, I said, "Hush. Jesus is with us, you've got to trust him," and was dismayed to hear how empty those words sounded.

"It's nightmares or demons. No—the Devil himself! Or my imagination. Oh, Hyung-nim!" She fell against me and I held and rubbed her cold arms.

"Quiet now. We can pray. We can ask Mother."

Unsook turned and grasped my hands. "No! Say nothing to Mother. It will kill her. Tonight—it will happen tonight! I know you shouldn't— you'll get sick—but won't you, can you stay with me tonight, say that I'm not imagining it, I beg you—"

"Shh, let me feel your forehead." Her irrationality made me worry if fever had done its damage. Unsook's pupils were huge and black, imploring, and I said, "Of course I'll stay. Don't worry, nurses never get sick."

"Tonight again. He was here today, so tonight— It was as if, as if—the demon!"

"No more talking. You're getting excited over— Don't fret, I'll stay with you for as long as you want. Tonight, tomorrow, it doesn't matter. We'll pray. It's nightmares or fever. Hush now."

"You won't say anything to Mother?"

"No." Gently massaging, I simultaneously pressed her furrowed brow and the top of her spine to release tension. "But if I'm to spend the night I'll have to tell her something." I wondered fleetingly about hiring a shaman to exorcise the nightmares, but there was no money for a *mudang* and her entourage, and besides, who knew what such a woman would do to my poor patient? "We wanted to try the other steam treatment overnight. We can tell her that I must tend to it, and also that you're feeling lonely and cooped up in the springtime."

She slumped in gratitude and whispered, "I thought I would go mad."

"No tears! You mustn't cry! Think of the baby!" The forbidden word slipped out like an easy delivery, and I felt Unsook stiffen. Her unborn baby had been much on my mind. Surrounded by the obvious parallel of a profusion of greens sprouting from the inanimate earth, I couldn't avoid harboring hope. We were told the fetus would not survive her illness, that her disease would become too advanced to expect a healthy outcome. As if a pact had been made, no one ever mentioned the doomed baby. But seven months had passed and my sister-in-law was still alive. Bedridden, sick, but very much alive. The child *moved* in her womb. If, every spring, God could bring such renewal of life, why couldn't this baby have a chance to come to term? I hadn't meant to put words to this. As a family, we had all resolved long ago that planning for the baby would be as hopeless an endeavor as the deadly progress of Unsook's disease.

Unsook and I looked at each other and held hands, afraid that to say more would curse the faint hopes we both held for the baby. She wept, and I sang hymns to soothe her.

THAT NIGHT I tied a thickened face mask over my nose and mouth and stretched out next to Unsook's pallet. The small room allowed me to spread only half a quilt. I kept my eyes wide open, determined to stay alert to watch and wake Unsook from the dreams that troubled her. We held hands in the dark and waited. *For what?* I wondered.

I must have dozed, for I was disoriented when I felt my hand tightly squeezed. Unsook was crushing my hand, and then her fingers went icily limp. I was only aware of this peripherally because the sickroom swelled with strange noises. It was startling more than frightening—night spirits could only mean her time was near—but I was being foolishly superstitious. I listened carefully and discerned whispering, and then a woman's voice. Two spirits were talking. I could barely make out word sounds. Was it Korean? Japanese? Laughter. Moans! The ice from Unsook's fingers clutched at my heart. I recognized my brother's voice.

The unintelligible whispers became sighs, breaths, muffled groans, and I realized in horror and humiliation that I was listening to a couple fornicating. My brother with a woman in the room next to his own wife's sickroom! I sat up, outraged, and toppled the crocus.

The sound of flesh against flesh stopped and the woman whispered, "There's that noise again next door."

Dongsaeng must have looked at the adjoining wall because I heard him say distinctly. "It's nothing."

Unsook's fingers tugged at me. Too paralyzed with rage, I couldn't respond.

"Someone is watching us!" hissed the woman.

"No, I told you before. There's a sick aunt. Don't worry—she's deaf. Only be a little quiet. There are others in the house."

"You mean quiet like this?" There were kissing, smacking noises and stifled laughter.

In a panic to do something, anything to stop what we were hearing, I tried to cover Unsook's ears. I felt wet cheeks and pressure mounting in her neck and shoulders. She erupted in coughing.

"Who, who—?" the woman said in rhythm to their slapping bodies.

Unsook coughed mucus and saliva. Helplessly I held her head, supporting her while still trying to cover her ears.

"Shh!" Dongsaeng said, huffing as their tempo heightened and he grunted—

A terrible riff of coughs—

Then sudden quiet across the two rooms. Dongsaeng exhaled, "Ya-ah—shh," and the woman sighed.

Unsook's coughs deepened and were productive, each spasm releasing another clot of crumbling tissue from her heaving lungs.

# Master of the House

## July 1940

Ilsun sat near the open window of a restaurant. The day's heat, thick with humidity, made him sweat as he sat waiting for the black market fellow. An occasional faint breeze did little to dissipate the stench from the street. The heat had cooked the gutter filth to emit even worse odors than usual. A wad of notes bulged in his pocket, and he wished he had worn loose hanbok instead of Western trousers. The street was quiet—too hot for work or even loitering outdoors—and he lazily regarded the occasional passerby for his go-between man. Perhaps it was too soon for such a purchase, but what was the point of waiting?

Najin was wrong. He had told her it was Father's idea, but she still wanted to blame him for everything, including his wife's illness. She almost went as far as to blame him for Unsook's death. He admitted there was a time when he ignored his wife, but he was good to her toward the end. He had provided for whatever medicine she needed and had sat with her frequently.

He remembered one spring day how she'd smiled when he showed her some of his calligraphy. "It's work to be proud of," she said quietly. She appeared increasingly drawn and pale as the days passed. When she looked at the scroll, he noticed she had trouble focusing.

"How are you feeling? You look tired," he said.

"Me? I haven't been sleeping— It's nothing. Here, look." She grasped his hand and placed it on her belly. Before he could draw away he felt movement beneath the skin.

"You mustn't think everything will be okay. They said it probably wouldn't live, and even if it did, it would be an idiot." He gently disengaged his wrist and saw her skin was waxy, translucent. "I don't mean to be cruel, but it's not good for you to hope."

She turned to the wall and he tied the scroll and stood to leave. "Yuhbo." She sat halfway up. "I must ask something of you." Her eyes were bright and Ilsun could guess what she wanted.

He moved a step backward. "It's impossible. It's not up to me."

"But if the baby is born? Will you?"

"I can't promise you something that isn't going to happen. You're only making yourself unhappy."

"I ask nothing for me. Please? Just keep the child. Raise her. Educate her. Teach her about God."

"Her?"

"I think so. Will you promise?" She closed her eyes and was as still as death.

He wanted to say it was pointless to swear to something that wasn't in the realm of possibility, but she was his wife, and dying, and he promised her he'd do as she wished.

And he did. It's true that a mother knows, because the baby was a girl. Small, early, but miraculously whole. He named her Sunok, pearl of Korea. Nuna said she'd raise the baby in the way Unsook would have wanted. Even Father seemed pleased to be Harabeoji, Grandfather, to this firstborn girl.

Meeja wasn't happy about all the fuss he made over his baby girl, but she was complaining about everything these days: the gifts he gave her, the hours they were separated, the crowd of teahouse girls where she lived, and in particular, having to visit him in secret.

The waitress brought a cup of wine with a quickly melting sliver of ice in it. The black market fellow was late. Ilsun hoped the man had found what he wanted.

Najin was wrong. It had all worked out well, and what other people said really didn't concern him. He repeated those words in his mind to mask the remorse that had taken shape inside him. He pressed his lips in a frown and justified his having tears as grief. Finally, Unsook was at rest, free of suffering. He felt proud of the funeral he'd given her, especially since times were so hard. Certainly she was in heaven. And by the grace of God, he had a wonderful baby—a girl, true, but a healthy child.

Najin, who months ago swore she'd never speak to him again, talked to him frequently about the child. He was selling his art at good prices, and Father was satisfied with his work. He put enough food on the table and had extra on hand. Mother had praised his generosity with Unsook's funeral and had complimented his responsible handling of the family.

Yes, it had all worked out well. As for Meeja, he knew she'd be happy with the wedding ring he meant to give her when she came to him that night.

# Korean Royal Treasure

SEPTEMBER 3, 1940–JANUARY 2, 1944

MORNING LIGHT STREAMED THROUGH THE PAPER SCREENS AND LIT the baby's cheeks with soft rose pink. I hummed and cooed to welcome her from the dreams of her clean, pure world. The baby's bones felt as delicate as her mother's, her skin as pliant, her scent a whisper of summer. One hundred days ago, her mother's suffering had ended, and I had lifted the baby from her wasted body. Being a Han daughter, nothing had been planned for her one hundredth day. I doubted that Dongsaeng had any idea how many days old his firstborn was. I saw him rarely and spoke to him even less, ever since that woman, my brother's concubine, had moved in. I was glad that it was proper enough to call her Dongsaeng's Wife, so

I'd never have to feel her name on my tongue, nor would I have to sully Unsook's memory by calling her Sister-in-law.

At the end of last winter, with war spilling from one continent to another, Korea had become fully incorporated into Japan and we were now considered Japanese citizens. Ration stamps and new Japanese identifications were distributed. They had erected Shinto shrines inside the churches and, last month, had deported all the missionaries. So on this Sunday, no one prepared for church. It was just as well. Father didn't have to face the emperor's portrait at the altar, and Mother didn't have to face the gossips.

Because the police monitored the church services, we had never grown friendly with our fellow parishioners in Seoul beyond acquaintances with a few men like Elder Kim, whom my father knew from the resistance. It was likely that my family's old-fashioned manners made the others uneasy, or the mere fact that we were newcomers made them look at us askance, and after Unsook's funeral—and the sudden appearance of Dongsaeng's new wife without the benefit of a Christian wedding—even fewer churchfolk took the trouble to greet us. And now, since Shinto worship was required on the numerous Japanese festival days and for all public gatherings, we abandoned going to church altogether, choosing instead to attend the required neighborhood ceremonies, which were shorter and where our attendance could be noted.

I fed baby Sunok millet and soybean broth mixed with precious drops of honey. Like her mother, Sunok couldn't tolerate milk, and even if she could have, milk wasn't to be found, neither fresh, nor canned nor powdered. I quickly dressed, changed Sunok's diaper and took the baby to Mother's room, eager to take advantage of the spare morning minutes before the men woke looking for breakfast.

My mother—who was now called *Halmeonim*, Grandmother— looked tiny beside the window as she combed her hair, her legs tucked beneath her skirt. I explained my idea and she readily agreed. We unsealed the false bottom of Mother's linen chest and dressed Sunok in clothes she'd saved there for thirty years: the blue-peaked cap edged with a gold geometric pattern and the finely woven shirt with striped colorful sleeves. Seeing those sleeves made me remember Dongsaeng at his One Hundredth Day naming ceremony, and how his pudgy fist had grabbed the sorghum ball that fell into his lap. I recalled Mother's worried look and my unvoiced question about the symbolism of that first item—did it foretell a pattern of self-gratification? And then he chose the king's signet, and the men at the party had lauded my father's legacy. It seemed both predictions had come true. Sighing, I cleared my mother's tabletop and arranged the objects gathered the day before. In a semicircle, I placed an abacus, a twist of thread, the king's bronze signet, an old inkbrush I'd found on a dusty shelf in Dongsaeng's studio, and a pencil stub. I added my mother's wooden crucifix and a sliver of wormwood for nurse or doctor, and covered the table with muslin.

My mother said a prayer with Sunok on her lap. The baby touched her waxen finger to my mother's murmuring lips, and the air grew sweet with the child's movement, the scent of her perfect skin and the muted hues of dawn. I lifted the cloth with a flourish. "What will it be, little one?"

Without hesitation Sunok grasped the old inkbrush and swept it across the table, strewing everything else to the floor. Her laughter was so delightful, we laughed too.

"A scholar-artist, then," said my mother. "Just like your father and grandfather." She cuddled Sunok and stroked her temple. The baby waved the inkbrush close to her eyes, and my mother took it from her. She exhaled with wonder. "Najin-ah, where did you find this?"

"In Dongsaeng's room when I cleaned yesterday, on his top shelf."

She handed me the baby and held the brush to the sunlight. "Your father thought he lost this many years ago, long before the move. He has its case still—but how wonderful that you found it! See on the handle that it's engraved?"

"It looks like an old brush. What does it say?" I was absorbed in Sunok's musical giggles from our game of tickling.

"This was a gift to your father from his teacher."

It took me a moment to understand what my mother was saying. "Scholar Chang's brush?"

My mother nodded and we smiled at each other knowingly. "Korea's Royal Treasure," I said, and kissed the baby's wiggling, agile fingers.

During the next several years our lives seemed to shrink in a tightening spiral focused on food, money and fuel. Thankfully, contrary to

Sunok's delicate appearance, she had Dongsaeng's sturdy constitution, and while not robust she managed to avoid illness. My mother sold some of our garden yield at market, and over time, having gradually cut down three of our trees for fuel, my father sold his woodcarving tools. I had gained a reputation as a competent midwife, but no one had a gourd of grain to spare or even a yard of muslin for my services. Instead, I received vegetable seeds folded in a scrap of newspaper, a cool drink of water or words of gratitude and blessing. Even if I had wanted to teach, schools for Korean children—who could barely speak their native tongue—were closed. With my arrest record, I couldn't work for a Japanese employer, and nearly all enterprise was Japanese-owned.

After the attack on Pearl Harbor, Japan heightened already-stringent controls on rationing and patriotic duty, which usually meant donating more things to the cause and showing up for endless rallies. Americans soon rimmed the Pacific with warships, and it seemed the entire world was at war. All forms of Korean and Chinese culture and expression were banned. Occasionally one of Dongsaeng's former buyers would remember him, and he'd receive a referral to paint a sign or a banner in Japanese, but as the war escalated it became too dangerous for Dongsaeng to leave the house. We eventually sold all his art materials save a few brushes and sticks of ink.

I overheard Dongsaeng's wife complain about his inability to feed his own daughter, with whom she'd grown attached—a relationship I mistrusted until I happened to see Meeja giving Sunok half of her porridge when she thought I wasn't looking. Meeja, who had not yet conceived, proved to be a dreadful cook and a lazy housekeeper, but she sang all manner of songs to Sunok and found countless ways to amuse her, and anything that could distract the child from her hunger was a blessing.

Then came the worrisome realization that we had nothing left to sell. The false bottom of my mother's linen chest had long been empty of the precious ceremonial clothes that two infants had worn to be named, and the chest itself had been sold. The neighborhood association had even collected Sunok's rubber ball for the war.

Since I was truly the most able-bodied person in the household who could work a steady paying job, I finally found a position—thanks to Elder Kim—at a Methodist-built orphanage run by Korean nationals in rural Suwon, a day's journey from Seoul. I hated to leave Sunok as well as my mother, who would have to rely on Meeja to help manage the household, but with hunger clawing at our doorstep, my responsibility to my family was clear.

Tending to the needs of more than one hundred children made my years at the orphanage pass quickly, and I was thankful that the money I sent home every month helped sustain my family and allowed Sunok to grow and thrive. I rarely thought about my husband, except in the summers when the children searched the streams for crayfish, an endeavor which mimicked how Calvin's mudworms forestalled starvation. Then, the day after Sollal in 1944, in the middle of a bright snowy day, all the orphans over the age of twelve—about forty youngsters—were taken away by truck. It was the first time I'd seen a truck powered by coal-fire rigging, and because it hinted that Japan's resources were nearing depletion, it was the first time I dared to imagine that the war might finally end. We were told the boys would become soldiers, and the girls, comfort nurses. The orphanage would receive no further government funding, and my job ended that afternoon.

On the journey home, the train nearly empty and the roadsides crowded with beggars, I thought that my father's presentiment of a bleak future had come to pass a thousand times over, and I wept for those children I'd taught, fed and slept beside, who now had a future of hardship and misery, if they had one at all.

I reached home safely, was lovingly welcomed, and felt gladdened to see our dear Korean Royal Treasure—almost four years old—proudly and beautifully writing her name on a slate with a brush dipped in water. And when I examined Sunok closely for signs of malnutrition, I was gratified to see she had healthy pink gums and displayed plenty of energy when she gave me a shy but solid hug.

# A. P. O.

THE MAGICAL LEAFLETS DROPPED BY B-29S THAT HAD ANNOUNCED Japan's unconditional surrender could still be found scattered throughout the city—caught in a treetop, composting in a gutter, happily displayed in a store window next to the flyer from the first drop, which transcribed Hirohito's unprecedented radio capitulation. I went outside often to eagerly scan the heavens for those sweet silver birds whose high mechanical roars had heralded freedom. Rumors about the terrible bombs were confirmed. We feared the worst for Hansu and his family in Nagasaki, not because of the bombs but for being Korean in a defeated Japan. We had no idea about the vast fields of death and annihilation those single bombs sowed.

In Seoul, food was as scarce as before liberation, although American rations, cigarettes and amazing foreign sweets at exorbitant prices began to appear in the black market. What had been criminal was now patriotic, and the red linear stamps on identification papers became marks of pride. Collaborators who hadn't joined the Japanese exodus were rooted out, tried and imprisoned, or murdered, and squatters quickly moved into homes hastily abandoned by Japanese nationals. Hunger was everywhere, but there was talk of free food coming soon from the Russians and Americans.

I walked downtown to pick up newspapers for Dongsaeng and my father, whom we now called Harabeoji, Grandfather, and who, after liberation, was most eager to read the news again. And though we had no money, I wanted to see if rice had become available and at what price. The sun burned as hot as midsummer, and I walked slowly to stay cool and to preserve the crumbling grass sandals Grandfather had crafted last year.

Since this day was our birthday, I wondered about my husband. Thoughts of Calvin had grown along with the optimism that everyone was feeling as vividly as the fresh colors painted on impromptu flags hanging everywhere. After the monsoons, when I first saw those silver planes soaring high against dramatic receding storm clouds, I wasn't afraid like others were. They called my soul to open and to believe again in possibility—possibilities that were once as remote as Japan's defeat, as war ending, as the rebirth of our independence, as being reunited with my husband.

Calvin would know nothing of our move to Seoul or even if we were alive. Years had passed since I'd communicated with his parents, so they wouldn't know we'd left Gaeseong, and then as the war intensified, mail delivery declined to near nonexistence. The few thoughts I had about the Cho family came from a wifely sense of obligation that diminished over the decade of our separation, and were mostly worries about Mrs. Cho's health. I considered that the remote chance of Calvin returning in the near future and finding me might mean I'd have to live with him and his family. But too much had changed and everything remained unstable. He probably wouldn't come back for a long while, and his parents might not have survived the past few years of hardship. *I* certainly had changed and could refuse to live with them. In any case, as my mother used to say, it was pointless to worry about problems I didn't yet have.

I could only assume that Calvin was still in America. Thinking of the packet of letters that Major Yoshida had taunted me with years ago, I felt sure my husband would attempt to find me. His earlier letters I had saved were long gone—they'd been stuffed into holes in the rafters or wadded as shoe lining—but I could still visualize that packet of unread letters at my feet, the New York return address in his strong handwriting, and inside all those envelopes, sheaves of words that said a thousand things I would never know.

I had resumed studying English when those planes flew triumphantly over the city dropping food packages and the leaflets, as well as handkerchiefs with a similar message printed in Chinese, Korean, Japanese and languages I'd never heard of or seen before. Walking to town, I reviewed the morning's English lesson, mumbling, "I should like to call on you someday. Come whenever you like. I shall be delighted to see you. Are you free this evening? Yes, I shall be quite free this evening."

Nearing a checkpoint that American soldiers now occupied, I noticed a G.I. leaning against the stone archway, smoking a cigarette, his eyes closed to the sun. He had similar coloring to the Gaeseong missionary Christine Gordon, with freckles and sand-hued hair. He'd stripped to his undershirt and I modestly looked away, but something he wore glinted in the sunlight. A gold cross, just like Cook's cross—except surely without the teeth marks—dangled on top of his dog tags. Curious about a G.I. wearing a cross, I stopped and overcame my shyness in favor of practicing English. Perhaps he'd know when the missionaries would return. I blurted, "Esscoos me, herro," laughing and frowning simultaneously at what was certainly frightful pronunciation.

"Hello there," he said with a surprised smile.

I tried again, "Hello," and pointed to his cross. "I am also Christian!"

"You speak English!"

"A nittle."

"You're a Christian?"

"*Neh*, yes. I am Methodist."

"Hey, no kidding! I'm Protestant too. Presbyterian. That's terrific! I didn't know there were any Korean Christians. Where'd you learn English?"

"Missionary teaches, ah, teaching lessons long time past."

"Well, whaddya know, and you're the first Korean lady I've met. Don't worry! I'm a happily married man. Ha ha. Hey, excuse my manners. How do you do?" He extinguished his cigarette underfoot and stuck out his hand. "I'm Neil Forbes." He was tall and skinny, with eyes of an indeterminate hue: gray then blue then brown all at once. His narrow nose cascaded into a slight bump and his transformative smile exposed beautiful teeth that made his face as cute and happy as a squirrel eating acorns.

Attempting to sort through his fast speech, to remember Americanisms I'd learned from the missionaries and my *Guide to English Conversation,* and trying to introduce myself, I bowed and shook his hand awkwardly. "My name is Han Na—, ah, Najin Han." He wouldn't understand that Korean women kept their family name, so I said, "I am Najin Cho. Mrs. Calvin Cho. It is a pleasure to meet you."

"The pleasure's all mine! Your English is great."

"No, it is, uh, very young, like baby. My husband, he is same like you. Presbyterian. He is minister. He is living America." Then it struck me. "I think New York City. Do you know how is New York City?"

"Sure, it's right across the river. I'm from Fort Lee, New Jersey. You ever heard of Fort Lee?"

I shook my head. "I know Princeton, New Jersey . . ."

"Of course you wouldn't know Fort Lee or the Hudson, but Princeton? Ya don't say! Your husband's in New York? It's a small world! He went to Princeton? Must be a smart fella. What's he doing there? I didn't know there were any Koreans stateside."

"Can you talk softer, uh, slower, please?"

"I'm sorry, Mrs. Cho. Right? Mrs. Najin Cho. Sure thing." He retrieved his shirt from where it hung over a rail and put his long arms through the sleeves, waving me closer to the stone archway and ignoring the odd whistles his fellow soldiers delivered from their posts. "Come on over to the shade. It's awful hot out."

I spent twenty minutes by the roadside with Private Neil Forbes, who was greatly impressed that my husband was a Korean pastor, and more, that I hadn't seen him for eleven years after just one day of marriage. I complimented the beauty of his wife in the photo he pulled from his wallet and sympathized with missing his newborn daughter—a pale blob of blankets in the picture—he'd left ten months ago. He suggested I write to my husband in care of the New York Presbytery and promised he'd post it through the military mail. He said he was completely charmed to have made my acquaintance, wondered if I'd coach him a tiny bit in the Korean language, and said I should bring the letter tomorrow at the same hour and place. We agreed that our meeting was a blessing, and when we parted, I said, "I shall be delighted to see you tomorrow."

He shook my hand energetically, saying, "Me too!" I was glad my English was understandable even if it was apparently funny enough to make him laugh so heartily.

That evening, after a plain supper of fishbone soup and millet, I told my family about Pfc. Forbes and the possibility of writing to Calvin. Necessity had erased the habit of separate living quarters, especially on the coldest nights in winter when there was only enough fuel for a single brazier. To preserve fuel, we had also used the braziers to cook in the sitting room. Venting the awful fumes sometimes made it as cold as if there were no embers, but then the wind would die and warmth would glow on our faces. On warm summer and fall days such as this, we reclaimed the kitchen and gathered as usual in the sitting room for meals, all of us by now completely accustomed to eating together. Grandfather sat with Sunok happily ensconced on his lap, her favorite place of late, and his favorite place for her as well. The child had done more for my father's health than any combination of herbs. Next to Grandfather sat Ilsun, with Meeja a little behind him, and on the other side I sat with Grandmother. We three women picked the few flakes of fish from our bowls and popped them in Sunok's mouth.

I asked Dongsaeng if he could spare two sheets of paper for me to write a letter and craft an envelope.

He shook his head. "I've nothing left."

"In my study," said Grandfather, "there's a history book on the middle shelf. Its end papers would do."

I looked at him appreciatively. These five years in Seoul, either something in my viewpoint or something in his had changed. I worried at first that he'd given up completely, that time had defeated his personal battle for the righteous old way. But when I learned that the cause of his refusal to leave the house was to avoid speaking Japanese, I felt reassured. I also guessed that some of his reticence to go out resulted from the catcalls and stares directed at him as he walked the streets wearing yangban hanbok, as threadbare as mine but always clean and pressed.

After my father had turned sixty, without fanfare much to everyone's regret, I'd noted his steady withdrawal into woodcarving until his tools were sold or "donated" to the cause. I had also assumed that his retirement age and status as grandfather were the roots of his inner calm and steady good health, rather than a submission to Japanese rule. Or perhaps scarcity in material life had accented for us both the richness we shared in family. I also attributed it to Sunok's blissful presence among us, and how a simple origami frog or a crumpled ball of paper tied to a string could give her joy. This was the cause of Ilsun's lack of available paper for letter writing and therefore Grandfather's willingness to deface a precious book of history.

I saved a few grains of millet to use as paste, and after the sun had set and the house was quiet, I composed my letter, writing tightly with a narrow brush, filling every centimeter of the thin paper.

> September 17, 1945, Seoul. Husband, if this letter finds you we must give thanks to an American G.I., Neil Forbes, a Christian angel, who kindly offered to post it through U.S. Army mail. Forgive the funny paper. You will see from the return address that we moved. We came here at winter's end in 1939. I could not let you know this because of the China War, then the big war. Although I received no letters from you for many years, I learned later that you had written frequently. That knowledge gives me the courage to try contacting you. They said you were a spy for the Americans. I do not know if you can come back any time soon, but at least you can know we are all well and in Seoul. I cannot remember when I stopped writing to you, but remember clearly your last two letters. The story of your twice-over survival is one that I cherished through the many years separating us. It gave me hope that God does indeed have a plan that will vindicate the inhumanity of war, the suffering of its victims. The second letter I remember because you said you would

be ordained and go to New York. This is why I write to you in care of N.Y. Presbytery, a suggestion made by G.I. Forbes. Another reason to bless this kind soldier. Dongsaeng's wife, Min Unsook (did you know he married?) died of T.B. on May 27, 1940. At the end, we were able to save her baby, a wonderful girl named Sunok. Your niece has brought us much joy in hard times. Dongsaeng's second wife is Chae Meeja. No babies yet, but we pray when things get better, then maybe. There is no post here and I have not heard from your family for many years. When everything turned Shinto, I worried that your father suffered persecution because of his high church position. Please let me know what you have heard. I pray for them daily and beg your forgiveness for not fulfilling my duty to your parents. Hundreds of refugees fill the streets. My father has lost hope of finding his brother in Manchuria, and my mother prays she can contact her family once the mail is working. When things improve, we hope to return to Gaeseong. Dongsaeng says many homes and buildings there that were used by the J. are now housing Russians. He thinks town records will help us prove ownership. We heard about the bombs. The world is changed. More soon. Write back c/o Forbes's A.P.O. Blssngs in C, yr wife.

# A Korean Dressed Like a G.I.

## OCTOBER 1945

THE DAMP AUTUMN WIND PREDICTED RAIN. IT SEEPED STIFFNESS INTO my hips and knees, hinting at loss of youth and making me worry about my mother's painful joints. I wrapped an old blanket around my shoulders and slid my feet into Dongsaeng's torn and battered leather shoes, glad that he sported a decent pair, courtesy of G.I. Forbes, who had visited us several times since that day by the roadside. Everyone in my family adored him, and not just because of his generosity; he was comical and made us all laugh with his antics trying to communicate with horrible Korean, gangly gestures and animated features.

Dongsaeng had gone downtown to meet someone about designing

a logo. He'd gained notoriety when he redesigned into Hangeul the masthead of *Dongah Ilbo,* and was featured in its first Korean-language issue: "Seoul Artist Restores Traditional Korean Calligraphy." Soon, he was called upon by editors feeding the explosion of new newspapers and magazines in the city, people who fervently expressed their politics and opinions in a wondrously free and open press. Dongsaeng's earnings went first to rice, then art supplies and a little treat for Sunok, and with outrageously inflated prices, the money evaporated like hot breath on a cold day. Luckily, our diet was supplemented by the generosity of Pfc. Forbes, who brought gifts of military kit rations.

I went to reap the last vegetables from the garden, an empty crock in hand, fretting over the impossibility of repaying Neil Forbes's kindness. A vehicle passed the house and honked. I thought it odd that a car would drive through this remote neighborhood, but my main concern was if the cabbages had yielded a few more leaves. I slid the door open, the broken soles of Dongsaeng's ruined shoes flapping on the threshold.

A man said, "Yuhbo."

The sound of his voice alone made me scream. My hands flew to my face and the crock smashed on the step. It was an apparition, I was sure, grown out of hunger from the depths of my memory. He touched my elbow. I turned and met eyes as serious and calming as I remembered. But how strange! Here was the face of a ghost, a thought, a glimpse in a mirror, and yet here he was—my husband, real, smiling, crying like a child, and handsomely dressed in an olive drab military coat and hat.

"How—?"

He clasped my hands and said, so softly I wasn't sure if I heard correctly, "Forgive me. Never again. Never."

Dongsaeng ran from the Jeep parked on the road. "Look who I found! Harabeoji! Halmeonim! Yuhbo! Make coffee! Hyung-nim, Brother-in-law, come in. Nuna, don't just stand there. Make him welcome!"

I was aware of my faded dress, the tattered shoes, gnarls on my palms and deepened lines on my face. The broken bowl forgotten, I drew him indoors, my heart beating as if for the first time.

Calvin greeted my parents with a bow to the floor. "My deepest respects, *Jangin-eurun, Jangmo-nim,* Father- and Mother-in-law. Profound regret for the hardships you have suffered."

"Yes, yes. Look at the prodigal son, come back as an American soldier!" Grandfather reached for Calvin's hand and held it a moment in both of his. "Come in, come in. Daughters, something to eat and drink!"

"I found him at the Bando Hotel! Can you imagine?" Dongsaeng crowed. "We came right home." Amid the confusion of introductions to Meeja and baby Sunok, the surprise of his monochromatic army uniform beneath his coat and the repeated cries of wonder, I dashed to the kitchen, patted down my sleeves and skirt and hastily wiped water on my face and hair. I slapped my cheeks, as much to ensure I wasn't asleep as to put color in them. In the sitting room, as I served drinking water and a tin of cookies—another gift from Pfc. Forbes—I saw that Calvin kept his eyes on my every move, and I felt him smile when I smiled as Grandfather took three cookies for Sunok in his lap.

"I'm sorry that I come unprepared," said Calvin. "My hands are empty today, but my heart is full."

If I hadn't been completely stunned by his presence, I might have been embarrassed by the tears that wet my husband's cheeks once more. When I sat across from him, Grandmother nudged me to sit next to him. Preferring to see his features, to watch him sitting in this room talking, drinking, breathing, I didn't move. Grandfather asked him to pray.

"Father in Heaven," said Calvin. "We give thanks for this joyful reunion and are humbled to witness thy mystery and grace, which has gathered us here together in the most extreme coincidence. We pray in thanksgiving for this reunion . . ." He paused a moment to collect himself, and I peeked at his face. His cheeks seemed rounder, his jaw softer, his mouth fuller. His eyebrows were a little wild, but his skin shone with the same polished gleam that I remembered from when I first saw his photograph. He prayed, his voice sounding deep and as solemn as what I'd heard in my head when I read his letters years ago. A thousand questions flooded my mind, and I wished he'd finish praying so I could learn how he'd found us, how he managed to get here, was he a minister now, did he really know how to drive a Jeep, and what was the meaning of those colorful patches and bright insignia on his clothing? I closed my eyes, nearly laughing out loud at the sheer joy and shock of him, and at my mounting impatience for him to quit praying so we could talk!

He mentioned Unsook and the Gaeseong house, and I was glad that Dongsaeng had briefed him on all our major life events, which allowed me to sidestep speaking to him about hardship. I kept sneaking looks as he prayed with his head bowed, hair parted as before, still thick on top and cut short around the ears and neck, his eyes shut, frowning, tears coming now and then. Finally, I sensed he was winding down, and I closed my eyes as he prayed for our liberated country. "That its leaders find the strength, compassion and wisdom they need to undertake the tasks of rebuilding and uniting us as a democratic, self-determined free nation. We ask this in the name of thy son, Jesus Christ, who taught us to pray, saying . . ."

During our recitation of the Lord's Prayer, I remembered our years-ago conversation about the Protestants and self-determinism, and excitement sparked when I thought that discussions barely begun could be continued. Then I quaked, for he was not some fellow student to bandy intellectual ideas about, but my husband—now obviously a man of God—and I, his wife, a Christian hypocrite! Shame and anxiety surfaced for a moment but were easily lost in the excitement of his being here. The ritual of prayer gave me time to gather my spinning feelings.

"Amen," said Grandfather. "Thank you, Calvin, you've completed your minister education, I see!"

Warmed by the gentility Calvin's formal intonation had restored in rooms that had long missed such civility, my blood soon became a tranquil current calming my pulse and thawing my heart. "Yuhbo," I said, the familiar address feeling as foreign on my tongue as his sitting across from me. "How is it that you came here in this American military uniform?"

"It's impossible to think it mere coincidence." Calvin looked directly into my eyes.

"It was amazing!" said Dongsaeng. Grandfather cautioned him to silence with a glance.

"I flew into Gimpo this morning and had just checked in with Army

Headquarters at the Bando Hotel. I requisitioned a Jeep right away and set out to find this house." He reached into his breast pocket. "Yuhbo, I received your letter two days before I left New York."

"Thanks to the American!" said Dongsaeng.

"*Ajeosi* Neil?" said Sunok boldly to this new elder. "Is Uncle Neil your soldier-friend too?"

"Hush, child. You mustn't interrupt the long-lost husband," said Grandmother.

"Go on," said Grandfather, giving Sunok another cookie to ease Grandmother's mild rebuke.

"Ajeosi Neil is indeed a kind soldier-friend, child." His inclusion of Sunok in the conversation impressed me. He was much the same yet completely different somehow. Even the way he sat on the floor seemed foreign. I wondered what changes he saw in me and lamented my gaunt cheeks and farmer's hands—hands that had cracked and bled during the years at his father's house in Pyeongyang, which now, with him sitting there almost a stranger, didn't seem to matter in the slightest.

"How wise to write me in care of the Presbytery! Your handwriting alone . . . I cannot express to you the joy . . . your letter . . ." He paused again to collect himself. "Thanks to you, I had your address, but I can barely remember the roads in Seoul, much less recognize the city at all . . ." He would never be able to tell his story if every suggestion of his absence choked him to silence. We waited quietly—Dongsaeng with eagerness, like a child being good in anticipation of a treat, my parents with compassion, Meeja with inquisitiveness, and me with the patience born of eleven years. I listened to Sunok's crunching of cookies and neglected sounds from outdoors: leaves blowing in the wind and acorns falling from our last oak tree. Their hollow plops in the courtyard reminded me of the bitter acorn porridge we ate last winter and how our fingers blistered from shelling the dry and frozen meat.

Calvin mopped his eyes, cleared his throat, looked straight at me and said, "My apologies."

I mouthed, "None needed," and we smiled at this small exchange between us.

He continued with a restored strong voice, "My next wish was to find someone who could give me directions. Since getting off the plane, I couldn't help but search every Korean face, not necessarily to see if I could recognize anyone, but because I was among my countrymen and welcomed seeing so many Korean faces. It was as if I was home and not-home at the same time, a very strange sensation. Upon leaving the hotel, I tried to spot a local person of whom I could ask directions. That's when I noticed a man staring at me. He looked familiar, and I thought he might be a former schoolmate. As we neared," Calvin said, smiling at Dongsaeng, "he raised his arms and cried out. I wondered if he thought I was going to arrest him, he was that excited."

"That was me!" said Dongsaeng, unable to contain himself. "I could hardly believe my eyes. I'm walking home and see this strange sight: a man who has a Korean-looking face dressed like an American G.I. Such a curious thing, and I stare like a peasant! And when he comes closer, I think I recognize him, I see *Cho* on his coat—see it, there!— and all the hairs on my head jump up and down, and I can't help but cry out. There's your picture, always with us." He pointed to our wedding portrait hanging on the wall. Dongsaeng's enthusiasm was infectious, but it was the chance meeting downtown that made all our eyes widen.

Dongsaeng continued, "I said to him, 'I am Han Ilsun. Could it be you, Brother-in-law?' and he said, 'Dear God!' and then I knew it was him!" Everyone laughed and Sunok clapped her hands.

"To say I was surprised is an understatement," said Calvin. "It's God's work that you would be there at that very moment. It was meant to be." He addressed the family, "Once he identified himself, I got the Jeep and he showed me the way. He's told me something of your years of difficulties, and I was very sorry to hear these things, very sorry. I must ask, again, your forgiveness—" He stopped.

As he gathered himself, Grandmother said, "There is only God's will, and we are among the truly blessed to be reunited."

"There is no blame, and so no need for forgiveness," said Grandfather. His eyes met mine for a flick of a moment, less than a glance, but I understood with the convincing truth of tears that my father had spoken to both my husband and me. Combined with Calvin's presence, my father's words released a weight that had crowded my soul since leaving Gaeseong. This physical sensation and my enormous gratitude untethered me to an emotion so rich I felt that if I were to lift my eyes to see my husband and family in this room all around me, I'd fly into the heavens, soaring with light.

Grandmother echoed Grandfather's statement with a firm "Amen."

My eyes met Calvin's and I saw that his showed an unnamed determination. My features relaxed, and I hoped he could read from my expression the limitless measure of acceptance that poured from my heart.

Sunok said, "Harabeoji, how can he be a G.I.? Only Americans are G.I.s, aren't they?"

"Yes, child," said Grandfather. "It's a good question."

"The letter took more than a month to find you," I said. "So yes, how did you become an American soldier?" while others chimed in, "Tell us about your studies. Is your family well? What's New York like?"

"Start at the beginning," I said. Meeja refreshed the water and I passed the cookies. We settled in beside the sputtering brazier to hear Calvin's story, while outside, the sun seeped through the clouds and slowly arched across the sky.

"Four years ago, I finished a course of study at New York Biblical Seminary. Before then, I'd attended three other seminaries and wasn't sure what I should next pursue. My studies thus far were seen as unusual, and I was advised to pursue a bachelor's degree in sociology, then a master's in philosophy of education, which I did. At that point, I had studied theology and Western culture to such a degree that I believed it would be best if I returned to the Bible; hence, the Biblical Seminary. But after Pearl Harbor, I knew I had to contribute somehow, and found a clerking job in the New York Office of Censorship. From there I was hired by the OSS—that was the American intelligence organization during the war—to translate various Japanese and Chinese communications, until the OSS was disbanded early last spring."

This startling news made me quickly calculate and compare the years, and with irony and relief, I concluded that Major Yoshida's accusation was wrong by three or four years prior.

"I briefly worked at the *Herald Tribune* newspaper in the classifieds department, a simple job that barely managed to pay for a room and a bowl of soup. A friend found work for me on the weekends cleaning houses, cooking and serving at parties. I know, odd work for a man, but I was grateful for the wages and learned a great deal about the American way of life."

I recalled from an early letter that he had been a houseboy at times, but I hardly knew what to do with this additional information about his domestic jobs. Had I been with him, I gladly would have worked those jobs in his place.

"Shortly after Pearl Harbor, the New York Presbytery ordained me as a postwar missionary. I hadn't yet been ordained because I needed to be sponsored by a local church. Naturally I attended church, but as part of my studies it was one church or another, which left me without a church to support me as copastor or even assistant pastor. The Presbytery chose to ordain me as a missionary, thinking ahead to when the war would end and the potential need for an indigenous missionary. But after V-J Day," he defined the Americanism and went on, "I appealed to the Presbytery to send me home, and was told that an American missionary had just returned from Korea and had reported that the people were not yet prepared to receive an indigenous Korean as an American missionary. I was greatly disappointed.

"Several years ago, a group of friends and I had formed a society to publish a journal called the *Korea Economic Digest*. Since very few Americans know about Korea, our aim was to educate and publicize the political situation. Then two years ago, when we learned that the Cairo Declarations said Korea would eventually have independence, we wanted to propagate discussion on what Korea was like and what it should become after the war. Somehow, we managed to raise enough money to distribute the journal, not only to subscribers but also to libraries, government offices and influential people in Washington. On August 15, I was with this group of friends in our makeshift office at a boardinghouse, and we all stayed up through the night listening to the radio, until finally we heard Hirohito's surrender. One of my fellow editors was so overcome he fell to the floor and burst into tears. Soon we were all crying with him."

"I hope to hear that radio broadcast one day," said Dongsaeng.

"I'm certain you will," said Calvin, "since it's the first time a Japanese emperor, their god figure, spoke publicly in this way." The men talked more about the radio broadcast and Japanese ethos, then he returned to his story.

"Our journal had become a contact point between Koreans and Americans, and the society received word that the army needed interpreters. That very day I had also received a phone call asking me to become an interpreter for the military. They particularly needed men who were fluent in Korean, Japanese and English, and the government knew about me from the OSS. That I could also read Chinese made them quite pleased, and I was immediately hired as a civilian employee and given the rank of field officer. I was trained briefly in army protocol and what to expect of the U.S. military government installed here. I flew on army transport and arrived this morning."

Everyone exclaimed, and Sunok smiled with the happiness that filled the room. Calvin's experiences were far different from anything I could have ever imagined, and I marveled at both his accomplishments and perseverance.

Calvin looked at me and said, "It is eleven years since I left this land. During that time I heard only sporadically from my father. Not long after you saw them last, my parents moved to Manchuria in self-exile. My father believed religious persecution would only increase as the China War escalated, and he was correct. I have not heard from him since then but believe they'll return to Pyeongyang if they haven't already. I worry that my mother is in fragile health and hope to gain permission to visit my parents. I know that wherever they are, they're living the word of God and are at peace. Too many families have suffered."

We murmured agreement, and some time passed in spontaneous silence, prayer and remembrance for the countless lost.

"What news of your families?" asked Calvin. Relatives and politics were discussed, and a sad lunch of rice and cabbage prepared, served and eaten. The afternoon waned. Rain came and left, as Calvin, Ilsun and Grandfather each tried to compress the decade into words. Grandmother took Meeja and Sunok to the kitchen to prepare as much of a supper as they could muster, insisting that I stay with my husband. As the sun set and cold seeped into the sitting room, I lit lamps and kept the brazier blazing using a three-day supply of fuel. Meeja set the table and my mother said, "I'm afraid we have only poor food to offer."

"To break bread with my wife and her family is a meal that is richness itself," said Calvin, which both pleased and embarrassed me. During our simple dinner he exclaimed how wonderful it was to eat perfectly cooked rice and told amusing stories about American rice. Then, after inspecting the house and yard, he promised to return the next evening. I walked outside with him, and when we reached the far side of the covered Jeep, hidden from the house, he took both my hands and gazed at me, his face tight with feeling. "Najin," he said. Overcome, he embraced me fully.

I stiffened, then realized that naturally he'd become even more Westernized. Being outside, I couldn't relax into his embrace, but he held me long enough for his rough wool coat to itch my cheek, and for me to feel his warmth radiating through his many garments. He released me, his eyes wet once more. After composing himself, he folded my hand around won and American bills that totaled the largest sum of cash I'd touched in years. "Take this," he said, with such solemnity that I imagined this was how he would administer communion. Unnerved by this sacrilegious image, I kept my eyes to the ground, distressed that everything between us seemed to emphasize differences that would be impossible to overcome. "I'll bring food tomorrow, some things . . ." He held my hands again, then climbed into the Jeep.

I watched him drive away until his taillights faded like the eyes of a cat one couldn't be certain had really been there, slipping into the comforting shadows of night.

THE NEXT EVENING, the Jeep rattled to a stop in front of the house, packed with all manner of goods: tins of foodstuff, cooking pots, winter coats and rubber shoes for each of us, sacks of briquette fuel, soap, salt, toothbrushes, razors for the men, paper, pens, candy, a bottle of aspirin and—an item of wonder that everyone had to try—a coloring book and crayons for Sunok. Since no army accommodations were available for married men, Calvin was given permission to live with us, but he stayed in the barracks for its convenience to his job working meetings of marathon length and translating speeches and piles of documents. He said he expected to move in when things were less urgent at his job, and he added, "Yuhbo, the house is for one family: Dongsaeng's family. It isn't proper for us to raise our own family in these rooms. I'll talk to your brother and see if he'll agree to an addition."

Left speechless by his mention of raising a family, I was barely aware of concerns about the cost, inconvenience and propriety of his proposal. I understood, however, that he truly was here to stay, and as I began to see farther ahead than the day's meals, I also understood how narrow our lives had become during the war. His decision making felt like a respite, and I was pleasantly compliant to anything he proposed, but I was also conscious that my acquiescence came from the novelty of having my husband home, and also that it was my duty as a wife.

During the next few weeks, our lives improved dramatically. Dongsaeng's advertising and printing connections and Calvin's military sources produced a lucrative job. Dongsaeng and my father simplified and translated into modern Hangeul the history books written in Chinese and old-style vernacular that my father had carried from Gaeseong. This work would then be printed as textbooks and distributed to schools. Grandfather thanked Calvin for his influence in delivering the true history to the nation's people, and Grandmother thanked God that Grandfather had the foresight to have chosen to bring with him those texts over all the other classics in his library.

My husband, busy translating for his general, visited one or two evenings a week and on Sunday. I said those two words, *my husband*, frequently, to get used to their sound and shape in my mouth. Fortunately, the winter was unseasonably mild, and he spent time with the men working on the large addition he had contracted to be built behind the original house, along with the installation of running water, flush toilets, electricity and telephone service. In the shifting, fluid postwar economy, Calvin's biweekly paycheck in American dollars managed to cover the materials as well as the earnest, plentiful labor.

He met and profusely thanked Neil Forbes. Calvin mentioned that he had once visited a congregation in Fort Lee called Eden Presbyterian, which turned out to be the church of Private Forbes's youth and marriage. They spoke rapidly in English with some excitement upon this discovery. Forbes revealed that his trade prior to joining the army had been carpentry, and the two men became close friends as they drew building plans, stretched level strings between stakes, pounded nails and supervised workmen. I watched them talking and working together, awed at Calvin's ease in English conversation, and how quickly and sincerely he bonded with the American soldier. It reminded me that I knew essential aspects of my husband's character and could speak unhesitatingly about his true nature, yet I knew very little about him in daily life.

Calvin was careful to discuss the second house with a consideration that allowed my brother no loss of face, and so, with the exception of a few bumps inevitable on such a rapid road to change, harmony and comfortable living came to our family. In a rare moment of camaraderie with Meeja, she said with a teasing smile, "You're a lucky woman to be lavishly courted by your own husband!" I returned her smile and hid my own thoughts about his generosity. While I was exceptionally grateful for the improvements he brought to our lives, especially the comforts for my parents, the excess of it embarrassed me, though I was also aware that his abundant giving helped to alleviate his profound remorse.

I fed the workmen, found places to store the goods that Calvin and Neil Forbes continued to bring, swept the pervasive sawdust, practiced English and kept a hot meal always ready for my husband, should he show up. My transition to being a wife was made easier by his scruple for separate living quarters. I'd be peeling turnips or washing the floor, and then I'd hear the Jeep and suddenly have a different purpose, one that aimed to serve and please my husband. It gave me a sensation I'd never known. I tried to name it—complacency, obedience? No. Contentment, wholeness, belonging—love? When I dressed in the morning, I dressed for him. I brushed my teeth and wondered if he was shaving at the barracks or showering in hot water, the idea of which, even with the difficult years behind us, seemed immensely wasteful.

He was an active if not everyday presence, and I grew conscious of the pleasure this gave me. At the same time, I held back, as if it were a simulation of happiness that couldn't be sustained and would end as abruptly as it had before. This irrationality gave me moments of relief. If he were gone, I'd be released from having to confess my paucity of faith.

He watched me when we were together, and sometimes I was glad for his attention, but other times it made me painfully self-conscious. I was frequently unsure of what he wanted. If he stood to pour himself a cup of water, was it his way of demonstrating how I'd failed to provide for him? Was he deliberately trying to embarrass me in front of my family, or—more likely, but still very strange—was he trying to be helpful? When he insisted that I stay for the men's talks, was it because he saw how woefully uninformed I was and wanted to educate me? Or did he want me to contribute to these conversations and further embarrass me in front of my family? Did he simply want to have me in his sight? I wished we were writing letters again, for then I could cautiously ask these things and he could explain his manner toward me. I liked it best when he gave me tasks with the new house and when he complimented my cooking, saying how much he had missed Korean food. I knew how to be that kind of wife. I also liked it when I walked him to his Jeep in snow, rain or sunshine and he would turn to me and say, "Yuhbo," in such a way that both warmed me and made me shiver, and these feelings in turn would ease my discomfort when he touched my fingers, took my hand or stroked my cheek.

Then he'd be gone again, and I would miss him with a fierceness that I hadn't known for all the years of our separation. I missed his eyes following me when I crossed the room. I missed hearing his voice as he solved a problem with the workmen, his gentle and diplomatic persuasion when they disagreed on how to approach a task. I missed the flat way he wielded his chopsticks, the questions he asked about the years apart, the foreign stiffness when he sat or stood, the stories he told about colleges and America, the woolly smell of his army sweater, his breath mixing with mine in the same house.

At night I crawled into bed in the room that Grandmother, Sunok and I shared in the winter. I awaited sleep, exhausted, and the image of my husband behind my closed eyes gradually changed as the days since his homecoming grew in number. I envisioned his charming smile, how his shoulders rolled and his hands moved, the smart way his cap accented his chin, the handsome cut of his coat when he belted it, the interesting line of his three-quarter profile. But the last two thoughts I had were always the same. First was the mortifying anticipation of sharing his bed, and any nervous or pleasurable thrill I felt was always quashed by my second thought: that I must tell my husband the truth about having lost my battle of faith. It brought a frown to my brow that stayed until morning.

# The New House

## December 1945

A week before Christmas, inches of powdery snow covered the entire city, and the workmen left until spring thaw. The front of the new house needed carpentry—trim, doors and windows installed—but the back was ready to live in. Calvin said he'd move in Friday evening. I laid planks to bypass the unfinished front rooms and tested the floor heating and the rear chimney's draw. Although the house was wired, electricity had yet to reach our street. Similarly, the bathroom had a working toilet but lacked running water. I thought the house waited for an uncertain future, much like myself, and fretted over the effort and expense it was taking to build. I filled kerosene lanterns Calvin had provided, swept sawdust and arranged a cistern and washbasin in the bathroom.

Three rooms were livable in the new wing—bedroom, sitting room and bathroom—and knowing I would have privacy with my husband for the first time since the hotel in Manchuria, I gladly cleaned them to counter my nervousness. Wiping the porcelain surfaces, I recalled being that young newlywed. It wasn't the memory of my innocent bride's optimism that struck me now, but the realization that I'd been consumed with scraping meals together for so long that I had truly banished all the dreams of those days. I refused to consider them now because too much was in flux, both with the return of my husband and the return of independence to our country. I also believed I was undeserving, and I had yet to confess the dismal condition of my soul. I couldn't think a moment beyond that.

With a wet rag and soap from the PX, I scrubbed the walls and yellow ondol floors of the new house, hoping the perfumed lather would lessen the noxious new flooring and lacquer smells. It brought to mind how I'd washed all the surfaces of my in-laws' house as a way to accept responsibility for the leaky hut, but I had been a slave there and not a family member. I would never tell my husband about the misery of those years.

Friday morning brought a steady light snow, but not enough to prevent the Jeep from reaching the house. I immediately expunged this disgraceful thought and focused instead on the preparations for my husband's formal return and our move into the new house. After a tepid and bland breakfast prepared by Meeja, I sat for a time with Grandmother during her morning ritual. In the odd gray light of muffling snowfall, I bent my head, and as sometimes happened when praying with my mother, I felt my will release itself into the stillness that I thought was all that remained of God in my spirit.

I donned a navy blue wool coat and a headscarf of white magnolia blossoms on a dark green background, both gifts from Calvin. Wearing two pairs of socks for warmth and the rubber shoes he'd bought, I walked to the market, stopping now and then to appreciate the tiny sprockets of fat snowflakes on my dark sleeves. I bought pork bones with rib meat, an impressive fresh flounder, flattened dried squid, precious dried mushrooms and lotus root, and onions, potatoes, carrots and rice wine. There were no greens, not even winter kale, but Calvin had given us cans of green beans, peas and peaches—the latter a concoction so sweet it gave me a headache. I shooed Meeja from the kitchen and spent the remainder of the day cooking a welcome-home feast.

The snow stopped and low clouds opened to a blazing gold and purple sunset. Calvin arrived in the Jeep with a footlocker containing his belongings and two boxes of books and papers. These items were moved into the new house. Everyone joined Grandfather in his sitting room for the lavish dinner. The talk centered on the delicacy and variety of dishes, and it was easy for everyone to pretend that Calvin's presence was as natural as if he'd been living with us for months. After the meal, however, Grandfather cleared his throat several times and said, "Rice wine?" which Calvin steadily refused.

Grandmother asked for a prayer from Calvin, signaled Sunok and Meeja to join her, and said goodnight a little earlier than she might have on a typical evening. Her nonchalant departure gave me the courage to also say goodnight. It was understood that my husband would come later. The men had the usual news and politics to discuss, especially Calvin's inside information about the resurging civil war in China, tensions with the Russians about the temporary border dividing north and south, a disturbing rehiring of Japanese collaborators in many government jobs, sweeping reforms in education, and the guidance of the American military government toward democratic elections.

I added fuel bricks to the banked firepit of the new house and fanned its embers until they blossomed into flame, taking pleasure in the cold on my cheeks contrasting with heat on my hands. In the vestibule, I tucked my shoes on a plank step by the unfinished doorway, which I had draped with an old blanket. Inside, I fired a brazier to heat water for the washbasin, rolled out our bedding and lit kerosene lanterns, turning them low. Regretting that I'd left my sewing in Grandmother's room, I opened my husband's footlocker and proceeded to unfold and refold all of his clothes, marveling when I discovered the elastic waistbands of his undershorts. The brazier flared and the room grew hot, making the floor coating emit a fusty resinous smell. I opened the window fully and dampened the fire. Still warm, I removed my jacket and sat with chin on knees, waiting with—for the first time in as long as I could remember—idle hands.

The waning moon rose, a not-quite circular disk of mother-of-pearl, small and shining. Through the open window, I caught its mystical smile above the trees. It seemed to invite me to say nothing to Calvin. Since the mask I wore was almost fully integrated into my being, it would be little different than what the days before had been. Nights were for secrets, an easy hour for things best hidden. I thought of the royalty murdered at night, Unsook's demons, the tortured men, the selfish desires I'd stowed in the night shadows of the rafters that had all turned to dust. No, there was no hiding. Instead, recalling the dream I shared with my mother when Ilsun was born, I would be like water and pour forth my shameful truth around the feet of my husband.

All these years I had been waiting for this moment. I knew he would be disappointed in me—how could he not be?—but I remembered our first walk by the pond and his letters. He had welcomed my questions and my confessions, unjudging, and had even asked for more.

In the dimly lit room, the flickering lamplight danced smokily against the walls. The winter moon gleamed and cast a faint square of light on the floor. It brought the memory of prison and how I had clung to hope because of my mother's visits, her loving encouragement delivered in a folded paper at the bottom of my rice bowl. As I waited for Calvin in this silent sitting room, I saw that I had also kept faith in a certain reunion with my husband, this man who might hear me, understand me, know me. I had believed that being with him again would one day bring to light some larger reason, some just cause, that would explain the suffering we had witnessed and lived through.

It seemed I had waited long enough, for there he was, not forty steps away, talking about the reformation of our nation with my father and younger brother. Korea, too, had waited long for the liberation that had ended many hardships and had also brought new questions and challenges. I thought of how quickly the people had struck down the Shinto torii and opened wide the doors of churches and temples, the men I'd seen being released from Seodaemun Prison, who fell sobbing to kiss the dirt road, the jubilation that met the first American soldiers parading through the streets, the pride of the old shopkeepers to speak freely in Korean, the spontaneous fires in the squares fueled by the hated identification papers with our required Japanese names. In shared oppression, the people of this beloved land had grown strongly united in their hope for freedom and, like my father's books buried in the unreachable secret pantry of the lost Gaeseong house, had harbored their Korean identity through all those years of waiting.

I thought of my own identity, and now saw that my father, by not naming me, had unwittingly accorded me enormous freedom. In the cemetery with Dongsaeng when I was newly betrothed, I remembered how he'd despaired, saying, "My life planned for all this before I was born." Unlike my brother, my identity had been less encumbered. Without having to confine my dreams to the destiny outlined in one's name and the expectations bestowed during one's naming, I was left free to embrace the natural turns of my character and to determine my own future, drawing from the deepest well of unnamed possibilities. Yes, I was the calligrapher's daughter, the daughter of the woman from Nah-jin, and I had grown to embody the singularity of my name, Najin.

I remembered Emperor Sunjong, Empress Yun and Princess Deokhye, and how they had to the extent possible maintained their responsibilities of royal blood amid compounding difficulties and death, until the gates of the last palace had clanged shut behind them. I thought of Imo's generosity and devotion to duty, the constancy of my mother's great faith in Jesus and the intensity of my father's insistence on tradition. Along with their never-spoken love of family and country, these were the ways they had held on to hope. As for me, I realized it wasn't the answers I was seeking all those years that mattered as much as the act of seeking itself. It was incredible, this human capacity for learning, for hope, for love, that persisted like the box of light in my cell, the waters that flowed in my dream. It was beyond my understanding. Tears came as I surrendered to this wonderment of being.

During our first private time together by the willows near the pond, Calvin had said, "And what do you think is the answer to your question?" It wasn't for him to forgive or reject my struggle of faith, but for me to accept it, to embrace it rather than deny or pretend. There were discussions we'd have about God's plan and the price of salvation through Jesus, but I was here at this moment, asking, and that was what was true. Who better than a minister-husband to explore this with? "Keep your mind open," Teacher Yee had said. "Keep your heart open," my mother had said.

I heard my husband remove his coat and shoes at the makeshift door. I stood to close the window and to look at him fully when he entered. It strengthened me to see his solid form fill the doorway, to see his gently receding hairline that made his handsome forehead even higher, to have been gifted the beauty of his patience and loyalty over so many years. His eyes glowed in the lamplight and I saw my calm features reflected in his. "Yuhbo," we said almost simultaneously, and he gestured with the smile I recognized from our first days together that I should speak first.

I accepted his outstretched hand and we sat not quite facing each other. "Yuhbo," I said, "Since you've been home, there's much I've wanted to tell you."

The moon swelled as the evening advanced. Its silvery light shone through the clear glass windows and diffused the shadows between us.

# Historical Note

WHILE *THE CALLIGRAPHER'S DAUGHTER* IS A WORK OF FICTION, IT TAKES place in a country whose antiquity, often alluded to in the novel, might be unfamiliar to some readers. Korea is one of the oldest unified nation-states in history and is also one of the most homogeneous societies in the world. Two of Korea's dynasties, including the most recent Joseon Dynasty* (1392–1910), are among the longest sustained monarchies in world history. Graced with peace, reformation and enlightenment, these monarchies also suffered strife: royal filicide, internecine coups, attempted rebellions, factionalism, invasions and oppression. It is the

* Yi Dynasty of the Joseon (or Choson) Kingdom, the latter meaning "Land of the Morning Calm."

extraordinary longevity of Korean political, ethnic and cultural continu-
ity that remains a wellspring of the nation's proud identity.

Korea's legendary origin is remarkably pinpointed to a specific day
more than 4,300 years ago, October 3, 2333 BCE, and is a mythic saga of
a heavenly visitation to a she-bear on a mountain who ultimately gives
birth to Korea's first king, Dangun. In the years leading to the Japanese
occupation, the Dangun legend rose to importance as newspapers pitted
Korea's ancient heavenly heritage against the Japanese emperor's relatively recent divine pedigree in a contest of primacy. But until the modern
age, neither country disputed the supremacy and longevity of China.

In all of East Asia, China was regarded as the center of the civilized
world. Those who were friends were like little brothers who, in exchange
for loyalty, symbolic tributes and trade, benefited from Chinese military
protection and advances in culture and civilization. Those who were enemies, like the Mongols and the Manchus, were considered barbarians.

Clearly China had a profound influence on the Korean peninsula, but
over the centuries Korea transformed those influences into its own distinct advances in literature, art, ceramics, printing, philosophy, astron-
omy, medicine and scholarship. Korea invented movable metal type
(c. 1230) more than two hundred years before Gutenberg. The world's
first self-striking water clock was constructed in 1434 at the dawn of the
Joseon Dynasty, followed by the invention of new sundials, the precision
rain gauge and several other astronomical and horological devices in
Korea's golden age of science (King Sejong's reign, 1412–50). The most
significant invention under King Sejong was the Korean phonetic alphabet, simple enough to be learned by all classes, yet so comprehensive it is
still used today. In terms of philosophy, the establishment of Confucianism in the Joseon Dynasty as state policy, religion and social norm was so
transformative it has been distinguished as *Neo*-Confucianism by histori-
ans. Also, Korea is the only nation in the world where Christianity first
took root without the presence of priests or missionaries, but exclusively
as a result of the written word—Bibles, translated into Chinese by Jesuits,
that a Korean scholar-official brought home from a diplomatic trip to
Beijing in 1631.

In contrast to Korea's brotherly friendship with China, Korea and
Japan shared a long-standing acrimony, exacerbated over the centuries by

repeated Japanese pirate raids and the brutal Hideyoshi Invasions in 1592–98. China came to Korea's defense, and that conflict ended in stalemate, but not before Korean Admiral Yi Sun-sin invented the world's first ironclad ship, the famous turtle ship, and used inventive explosive shells and mobile rocket launchers to repel the Japanese fleet.

The Hideyoshi Invasions initiated an era of wholesale change in the old East Asian order. Japan's samurai tradition gave way to the Tokugawa shogunate and the beginning of the Edo or modern period of stability (1603–1867) in that country. China's great Ming Empire fell to the Manchus, a tribal people from Manchuria, who founded the Qing Dynasty, China's last empire. These key changes fostered Korea's isolationist policies, and being geographically outside of major trade routes, it became one of the most insulated countries in the world. When the turbulent political climate ebbed in East Asia in the seventeenth century, friendly relations were reestablished, but the animosity between Korea and Japan, and China and Japan was never forgotten.

The 1800s brought wave after wave of Westerners pounding Asia's shores—Prussians, French, Russians, the British and Americans—an influx that signaled the fall of the Joseon Dynasty. All but Prussia gained footholds in East Asian territory or trade. In particular, a U.S.-forced trade agreement with Japan yielded a new Meiji government (1868) so eager to adopt Western ways that when Japan made its next annual trade tour to Korea, the Korean ministers were shocked to see the Japanese diplomats' radical change in dress and attitude.

This international influx led to four wars, China's Boxer Rebellion, and numerous treaties in the latter half of the nineteenth century. In this climate, King Gojong acceded to the throne in 1864 at age twelve. Power devolved to his father, known as the Daewongun, a staunch isolationist. Two years later, Gojong married a fifteen-year-old from the powerful Min clan, which favored modernization and relations with Japan. Bitter power struggles between Queen Min and the Daewongun resulted in waffling policy extremes of isolationism versus Western enlightenment, plus land reform, hefty taxes, growing ideological foment, a major peasant uprising (the Donghak Rebellion) and, overall, a vulnerable Korea. Using gunboat diplomacy, Japan forced Korea's doors open in 1875 to exclusive trade, and Japanese advisers and military flooded into the Korean court.

Four nations decided the fate of Korea in 1905 without once giving the Yi monarchy or the Korean people an opportunity to voice a single plea for independence. Russia had invaded Manchuria in 1900 and mustered for China, spurring the Russo-Japan War. To protect its interests in China, Great Britain allied with Japan and in turn acknowledged Japan's interests in Korea. Both England and America believed Japanese control over Korea was an effective preventative against Russian expansion. President Theodore Roosevelt also saw Japan's domination of Korea as quid pro quo for U.S. control of the Philippines. And finally, in the American-engineered 1905 Treaty of Portsmouth that ended the Russo-Japan War, Russia pledged not to intercede with Japan's interests in Korea.

Japan moved quickly. In November 1905 a Japanese statesman, backed by troops, commanded the Korean prime minister to sign the Protectorate Treaty (also called the Treaty of 1905), giving Japan "protective" control over all government offices excluding the new Korean emperorship. The prime minister refused and was dragged from the palace. Someone was dispatched to find the official seal, which was then affixed to the treaty by Japanese hands and considered accepted.

As Japan's interests began to spread beyond Korea's borders, dealing with Emperor Gojong's diplomatic attempts to regain Korea's independence and quelching the frequent student protests and popular insurgencies grew burdensome. In 1907 Japan coerced Gojong to abdicate to his son, Sunjong. Then on August 22, 1910, Sunjong was forced to sign the Treaty of Annexation, which made Korea a colony of Japan and ended the long autonomy of the Korean nation. Less than a month later, at the dawn of the thirty-five-year era of the Japanese occupation of Korea, Najin was born.

# Glossary

With the exception of personal and family names, most Korean words in this book are spelled using the Revised Romanization of Korean system. Because the vowel combinations used in this system might be unfamiliar to readers, nonstandard spelling has been applied to the following words: *abbuh-nim, ahsee, oppa, umma-nim, unnee* and *yuhbo*.

**abbuh-nim** (ah-buh-NEEM). Father, with the honorific suffix *-nim*. Revised romanization: *abeonim*.

**ahsee** (ah-SEE). Higher level female address, used by servants. Revised romanization: *asi*.

**aigu** (EYE-goo) or **aiu** (EYE-yoo). An expression whose meaning—surprise, alarm, fear, delight, concern, pity, etc.—is derived from tone.

**ajeosi** (AH-juh-see). Uncle. Also how a person would address an older, unrelated male who is otherwise without a professional title, such as a shopkeeper. The counterpart for an older female is *ajeomeoni* (AH-juh-muh-nee), though there are specific terms for maternal aunt and paternal aunt (see *imo* and *gomo*).

**chinsa** (CHIN-sah). Certified scholar of Korean Confucian classics, similar to a doctor.

**cheongsam** (chong-SAHM). Chinese word for the traditional women's silk dress with Mandarin collar and frog closures.

**Daewongun** (TEH-won-gun). Literally, "prince of the great court," the father of the monarch who acts as regent.

**Donghak Revolution** (TOHNG-hahk revolution). A major peasant uprising against tyranny, foreign influence, government corruption and the yangban class. The revolution climaxed in 1894 and threatened the Joseon Dynasty to such an extent that Chinese and later Japanese troops were required to quash the peasant army. The Donghak (Eastern Learning) Revolution was a significant factor in Korea's instability at the turn of the century.

**dongsaeng** (TOHNG-sayng). Younger sibling. How a sibling addresses a younger sister or younger brother.

**gayageum** (KAH-yah-gum). Elongated zither- or harp-like stringed instrument, usually with twelve strings.

**geulsae** (KUL-seh). Expression of agreement or wonder, similar to "really."

**gisaeng** (KEE-sayng). Courtesan, akin to the Japanese geisha.

**gomo** (KOH-moh). Paternal aunt, versus *imo*, maternal aunt. Both are often paired with the honorific suffix -*nim*.

**gosari** (KOH-sah-rree). The edible young fiddlehead shoots of the ostrich fern, *Matteuccia struthiopteris*.

**halmeoni** (HAHL-muh-nee). Grandmother. With the honorific suffix, *halmeonim*.

**hanbok** (HAHN-bok). Korean traditional clothing for men or women.

**Hangeul** (HAHN-gul). Korean vernacular language and writing. Until the invention of the Hangeul alphabet in 1446 by King Sejong, Chinese characters were used phonetically to transcribe Korean, which limited literacy to the educated upper class.

**harabeoji** (HAH-rah-buh-jee). Grandfather.

**hyung, hyung-nim** (hyung-NEEM). Older brother, older sister-in-law, or older friend. How a male sibling addresses his older brother; a female addresses her older sister-in-law; and a friend addresses an older, close friend. Typically with the honorific suffix, as shown.

**imo** (EE-moh). Maternal aunt, versus *gomo*, paternal aunt. Both are typically paired with the honorific suffix -*nim*.

**jajangmyeon** (CHA-JAHNG-myun). A noodle dish with sweet black bean sauce (jajang), typically purchased from a street vendor.

**jangin-eorun** (CHAHNG-een-uh-run). Father-in-law, as used by a man. A woman would refer to her father-in-law as *Ssi-abbuh-nim*.

**jangmo-nim** (CHAHNG-moh-neem). Mother-in-law, as used by a male. Includes the honorific suffix -*nim*. A woman would refer to her mother-in-law as *Ssi-umma-nim*.

**jeon** (CHON). Korean monetary unit, both coin and currency, used during the occupation. One *won* equaled 100 jeon. One Japanese *sen* was equivalent to one Korean jeon. *Sen* and *jeon* are different pronunciations of the same Chinese character.

**Kabo Reforms** (KAH-bo reforms). Six hundred reform laws passed by King Gojong in 1894–95. Also called the 1895 Reforms.

**li** (LEE). Chinese measure of distance equal to five hundred meters.

**man-se** (mahn-SEH). Literally, "ten thousand" in Chinese. The Korean language uses Chinese for days/dates and counting money. It is the slogan cry for "Long Live Korea!" originating from the March 1, 1919 national demonstration for independence.

**Meiji** (MAY-EE-jee). Reign/era name of the period when the 122nd emperor of Japan, Mutsuhito, was in power, 1868–1912.

**moksa** (MOHK-sah). Minister, reverend. With the honorific suffix, *Moksa-nim* (mohk-sah-NEEM).

**mudang** (MOO-dahng). Female shaman who acts as intercessor between humans and the spirit world.

**nuna** (NOO-nah). Sister. How a male sibling addresses his older sister (versus *unnee*, used by female siblings).

**olgae** (OHL-geh). Sister-in-law. How a female addresses her younger sister-in-law; versus *hyung-nim*, how a female addresses her older sister-in-law.

**omana** (OH-mah-nah). Exclamation of surprise or alarm.

**ondol** (OHN-dohl). Literally, "warm stone." A type of granite and concrete flooring interlaced with flues for heating.

**oppa** (OHP-bah). Brother. How a female sibling addresses her older brother (versus *hyung*, how a male addresses his older brother). With the honorific, *oppa-nim*. Revised romanization: *obba*.

**Sam-il** (SAHM-eel). March First, a Korean holiday commemorating the national independence movement's demonstration on that day in 1919.

**Showa** (SHOW-ah). Reign/era name of the period when the 124th emperor of Japan, Hirohito, was in power, 1926–89.

**sijo** (SEE-joh). Classic Korean form of poetry consisting of three lines, each with fourteen to sixteen syllables, with the middle line the longest. The first line presents the theme or idea, the second line develops, challenges or counters it, and the third line resolves the poem, sometimes with a surprise ending.

**Sollal** (SOH-lahl). New Year's Day.

**ssi-abbuh-nim** (SHEE-ah-buh-neem). Father-in-law, as used by a female, with the honorific suffix -*nim*. (A man would call his father-in-law *Jangin-eorun.*) Revised romanization: *ssi-abeonim.*

**ssi-umma-nim** (SHEE-uh-muh-neem). Mother-in-law, as used by a woman, with the honorific suffix -*nim*. (A man would call his mother-in-law *Jangmo-nim.*) Revised romanization: *ssi-eomeonim.*

**sunsaeng-nim** (sun-sayng-NEEM). Teacher, with the honorific suffix -*nim*.

**Taegeukgi** (TEH-guk-EE). Korean flag. Designed by Bak Yeong-hyo, the Korean ambassador to Japan, and proclaimed by King Gojong to be the official flag of Korea on March 6, 1883. *Taegeuk* refers to the red and blue symbol in the center, which represents the origin of all things in the universe.

**Taisho** (Tah-EE-show). Reign/era name of the period when the 123rd Emperor of Japan, Yoshihito, was in power, 1912–26.

**umma-nim** (uh-muh-NEEM). Mother, with the honorific suffix -*nim*. Revised romanization: *eomeonim.*

**unnee** (UN-nee). Sister. How a female sibling addresses her older sister (versus *nuna,* used by males). Revised romanization: *eonni.*

**won** (WON). Unit of Korean currency issued by the Bank of Joseon during the occupation. Its value was equal to the Japanese yen. *Won* and *yen* are different pronunciations of the same Chinese character.

**yah** (YAH). Familiar and casual form of address similar to "hey." Also an expressive sound like "ah" or "oh."

**yangban** (YAHNG-bahn). Aristocratic class, or an aristocrat, through heredity.

**yuhbo** (yuh-boh). Familiar way of saying "hey you." Also a term of endearment when used between spouses. Revised romanization: *yeobo.*

# Acknowledgments

In addition to my parents' papers, numerous resources helped inform this novel. Among them are works by JaHyun Kim Haboush, *A New History of Korea* by Ki-baik Lee, and *Sources of Korean Tradition* edited by Yongho Ch'oe, Peter H. Lee and Wm. Theodore de Bary. Three books were instrumental in shaping the Historical Note: *A Concise History of Korea* by Michael J. Seth, *Everlasting Flower: A History of Korea* by Keith Pratt and *Korea Between Empires: 1895–1919* by Andre Schmid.

The four illustrations displayed on the title and part title pages were painted by my mother, Alice Hahn Hyegyung Kim. Unlike her father and brother who studied painting in their youths, my mother deferred pursuing her love of art until widowhood in her eighties. She soon proved that her brush flowed with as much talent and authority as that of a king's calligrapher.

My gratitude to Nat Sobel and Judith Weber and their staff, and Helen Atsma and her colleagues, for expertise and enthusiasm.

I am grateful to my sisters, friends and my family for their unceasing support of this writing that took many forms, including reading, story-telling, travel, translation, great meals, greater conversations, generous loans of beach houses and the all-important cheerleading. Thank you.

## About the Author

EUGENIA SUNHEE KIM is the daughter of Korean immigrant parents who came to America shortly after the Pacific War. She has published short stories and essays in journals and anthologies, including *Echoes Upon Echoes: New Korean American Writings*, and is an MFA graduate of Bennington College. She lives in Washington, D.C., with her husband and son. *The Calligrapher's Daughter* is her first novel.